The Pearl Singer

by

Hannah Allen Abbott

Dedicated to my children,
Natalie Schuyler Moss and
Casandra Montgomery Moss.

Silvering Owl Press

Table of Contents

Map

Map

Chapter 1: Ayr

When I was little—no wait. I still am. I'll always be little.

When I was a child, my Mati used to tell me how she came to be my mother.

Mati's father was the village tailor. He had four daughters. Tirsa, my Mati, was the youngest. In proper time, all her sisters married and moved away from Ayr. The eldest sister married the son of a net maker, who went to sea and became a sailor, so she moved to a port on the south coast of Pini. The second married the son of the tax collector, who went to Coffer to work in a spice shop owned by a cousin. The third married a traveling weaver who took her away to see the world and never came back. Tirsa looked around Ayr and wondered who was left to marry her.

Then her father died and Tirsa's mother became the tailor of Ayr.

Being the tailor of Ayr wasn't too demanding. Ayr was one of the twenty pearling villages of Pini, which made it important but didn't make it large or rich. The villagers grew their own chickens and vegetables, bought rice and oil, hunted and fished, and bought cotton cloth which they brought to the tailor to make into clothes. They wore simple, traditional garments. Britches and shirt, or a gown and chemise, girdled with rope or leather. A better set for festivals. In winter, a quilted jacket and cap. All made from cotton, boldly patterned in cheerful colors or rich earthen hues. An adult might need a new garment once in five years. Children's clothes were passed around until they wore out, and only the eldest got new. But it was enough to make a living.

Tirsa helped. She had learned to stitch a seam at five. At ten she could make an undergown with an even hem. At fifteen she could quilt a jacket and build a cap. She sat by the window and sewed with her mother. When she wasn't sewing, she did the cooking, gathered the eggs, and tended the garden.

By the time her mother died, Tirsa was used to living there at the end of the village, to being a tailor, to sitting beside the window to sew. She was lonely after her mother died, but she no longer thought about having a husband. What she wanted was a child.

So one day Tirsa went into the forest to visit Zenaida. Zenaida served as the village healer, with a garden of herbs, and the wild plants all around her. And if someone had a problem they didn't want to take to the priest, they took it Zenaida. With a gift. She'd give them woodruff tea or a cup of plum wine and entertain their requests.

"I took eggs," Mati liked to tell me.

I had been in Zenaida's cottage. I could imagine it. Mati ducking respectfully through the door with a square-sided box, woven of thin strips of bamboo from the mountains, containing four clean brown eggs. They had spoken politely about events in the village. The recent good fishing. A marriage contract. A new baby.

"A child is such a blessing," Tirsa commented, absently searching her tea.

Zenaida nodded and folded her rugged hands in her lap.

"And a comfort," she added solemnly.

I could hear their silence as they contemplated how Sia, the goddess of fertility, could ever bless Tirsa with a child.

Zenaida stood up, found a tiny box of cedar wood, sat back down, and placed the box on the table between them.

"Some find comfort in Nazha's gaze."

I could see my Mati sipping her tea without looking at the cedar box. How could Nazha, goddess of night, whose eye was the moon, grant a child to a woman who had no man? Her voice was tentative.

"Perhaps a woman could make an offering and pray to Nazha for comfort?"

Zenaida poured more tea.

"A woman could plant a seed under Nazha's gaze, with an offering of a bowl of moonlight."

Tirsa finished her tea and set down the empty pottery cup. She cradled the delicate box in her palms. I had seen that box. It sat on a shelf in a corner of our cottage. I knew every miniature leaf and flower carved on its surface. I could feel her tremble as she tipped up the lid. Inside was a single white moonflower seed. I could hear the hope in her voice.

"Such a comforted woman would be grateful forever."

A few nights later, at the first full moon of spring, Tirsa planted the moonflower seed. She held a black glazed bowl in her hands, a bowl of water from a clear forest pool, with the face of Nazha reflected in it. She

2

poured the moonlight onto the seed. Then she went inside and watched the silver garden shift and rustle in the midnight breeze.

When she woke in the morning, a beautiful moonflower had appeared. She rushed outside, and there in its heart was a baby girl, small and brown as a hazelnut, who sang as sweetly as the nightingale. So small and precious was the child that Tirsa named her Amalisa, Beloved Little Girl, and thus became my Mati.

That is the story my Mati told.

Our neighbors, however, had not been schooled in Mati's version of the tale, and in a village the size of Ayr, you can't hide much from anyone, so I learned a very different version as I grew up. It wasn't as pretty.

But neither was I.

*　　*　　*

"The old witch told her to water it with honey and fresh goat's milk!" confided the rice merchant's wife to a customer.

Not that Mati had a goat. She hadn't bought the goat until after my arrival. But my passage down any path in Ayr could excite such comments, whispered or murmured or blurted out loud behind my back.

"So that very night, didn't she plant that seed in her back garden," cackled the carpenter's mother, "right there in the carrots and cabbages."

Not all at once, mind you. Not the whole story. Just bits and pieces scattered randomly through my early childhood. It took me years to piece them together in any kind of coherent order.

"Well," confided the potter's wife, "don't you know she poured honey and goat's milk on that scrap of dirt and took herself on in to bed, just like that moon-mad witch told her to."

The potter lived next door to us. His wife had probably watched out the window while Mati planted the precious seed.

"And she had to shutter her windows as tight as a miser's till," mocked the sail maker's daughter dramatically, "so she wouldn't see the *amazing* flower sprout from the soil, put forth a single *enormous* bloom, then wither and die back into the soil *all* in the *same* night."

I never told Mati the things they said. She probably knew. I just didn't want her to know that I knew.

"And in the morning," sighed the dyer wistfully, "there was a fine, fat baby girl."

The dyer was Mati's dearest friend. She lived on the other side of us, in the only cottage nearer the forest than ours. I didn't mind her version so much. She told it kindly.

"A bit on the small side," Sitta resumed in her high, flighty voice, "but certainly healthy. Maybe not pretty, but with a good, lusty voice. True, half of her face was red as Tirsa's beets, but what beautiful deep brown eyes she had, when Tirsa had a chance to glimpse them through all that caterwauling."

Sitta had been there. My bawling had drawn her out of her cottage to hover over Mati's shoulder and coo at the baby dropped from the sky as if from the hand of Nazha herself.

A bit on the small side. That was mild. I wasn't even Pinian. I was Curran. Through and through. Only on Curra, an island beyond the Gulf of Yar, beyond the entire Erien Ocean, were the people of such small stature as I. Even now, I'm little more than half the height of a tall man. Distinctively Curran. Mati never tried to tell me otherwise.

But no one in Ayr really knew where I came from.

Most of the neighbors held that I had been left in Mati's garden by some girl who fell afoul of a Curran sailor, but this merely led to speculation as to which local girl could have ventured as far as Darcy, or Coffer, or any other port, to encounter a Curran sailor. Never mind that Currans and Pinians rarely if ever bred together.

Some with more logical minds argued that I clearly wasn't just half Curran. Not at my size. These folks preferred the notion that some Curran girl with an accidental child had fled her own village to escape dishonor and dropped her brat wherever the unfortunate child was born, then made her way home with tales of her lovely holiday.

If anyone cast their eye on the only other Curran in Ayr, it didn't linger long. Old Kes was seventy when I was born, his wife long dead, all his children grown and gone. He was grave, reserved, and blind with age. Revered by the village, he tended to his sacred duties with reverent punctuality. Morning and evening, he sang to the pearls, and seldom spoke to anyone else. He would no more have touched a Pinian girl than a Pinian girl would have ventured near him.

Sitta suggested Zenaida had put me there herself, but where Zenaida got a baby just came back around to the same speculations.

As for me, I invented a version in which one of the Pinian princes had fallen in love with the daughter of the Curran ambassador, and they had a passionate if brief affair before having to marry the carefully chosen mates they were each betrothed to since childhood. After all, what girl wouldn't want to imagine that one of the Pinian princes might be her true father? The pious princes who danced beneath the equinox moon to worship Suna, the goddess of wisdom. They were reputedly all so beautiful, it didn't even matter which one. And that, of course, was the problem with my fantasy, since beautiful was something I most decidedly wasn't.

*   *   *

My looks didn't matter to Mati. I knew Mati loved me. Completely. In Mati's eyes, I was perfect. She didn't care about the blotch on the side of my face. It started in my infancy as a raised red lump beside my left eye, and by the time I was two years old, it extended in a pebbly mass from my temple to halfway down my cheek.

There were no mirrors in our cottage. Not many in Ayr had such finery. And few had glass in their windows to cast my reflection back at me, even if I had been tall enough to see them. But there were puddles after rain, and ponds in the forest.

I knew I was different from everyone else. I knew I was Curran. I knew I would never see eye to eye with any Pinian past the age of eight. I knew my skin was a darker hue, the color of a hazelnut shell, rather than the olive brown of most Pinians. But none of that mattered. The Curran singers were too important in Pini for any of that to matter. No, it wasn't my Curran parentage that set me apart. It was the birthmark.

I was six the first time I asked about it. I had just finished cleaning the breakfast bowls and scrubbing the rice starch out of the pot. The winter rain hissed softly into the thick thatched roof. I poured boiling water over a spoonful of spearmint leaves and lemon grass and carried the little cup to the window where Mati was working.

"What is it, Mati?" I asked, reaching to set the tea on the sill. My Mati was neither short nor tall, but I could barely rest my chin on the arm of her chair.

She answered absently, not looking up.

"What's what, my love?"

I turned the left side of my face to her and waited until she raised her eyes. They were brown and gentle as oxen eyes.

"Oh, that," she smiled. She set down her sewing, a fine stiff jacket for the rice merchant's daughter, who was to be married later that winter. He was wealthier than most in Ayr, and had brought a length of yellow silk for the wide cuffs and upright collar. "That's Nazha's kiss. That's how I know when you were born. In the dark moon. Six weeks before you came to me." Unafraid, she laid her palm against my cheek, stroking the mark with a loving thumb. "The goddess loved you, and so do I."

I watched her return to the jacket, making straight, tidy stitches, attaching one of the bright golden cuffs to a scarlet sleeve with leafy designs of green and black. She snipped the thread with miniature shears.

"Liise, my love." Her thick, graying braid fell over her shoulder as she sorted through the little skeins, and she absently pushed it back behind her. "Would you go ask Sitta for more of this thread?"

She placed the wisp in my tiny hand.

There was no one outside in the chilly morning. I pulled on my jacket, slipped my stockinged feet into my winter clogs, and took the scrap next door to Sitta.

Sitta's cottage was full of steam and the earthy smell of madder root, edged with the sweet acid scent of the alum she used to set the crimson dye. She was dying a bolt of cotton. Big enough to swallow me whole, the kettle bubbled on the great raised hearth in the middle of the room. I left my clogs on the mat by the door. They were half the size of Sitta's clogs.

"May Suna's wisdom come into your house," I greeted her as I had been taught. Everyone in Ayr invoked Suna, the goddess of wisdom, at so much as a sneeze. It was Suna who had given the knowledge of pearls to the Pinian priest-princes centuries ago, and everyone in Ayr depended ultimately on the pearls.

"May Suna's wisdom be on your head, my child," answered Sitta, setting the stirring pole aside. She wiped her hands on a cloth as spotty in hue as an ancient tree with a coat of many colored lichens. "Will you have some tea?"

"Thank you," I replied politely and climbed onto one of the chairs at her table. Even the wood was stained by the dyes, reds, yellows, browns, and greens.

Sitta brought two cups, a box of herbs, and a small horn spoon. Sitta's husband and sons were fisherman. Since the water was too rough for fishing today, they were down at the fishing beach mending their nets.

"I'm not sure Suna has given me much wisdom," I sighed as she measured dried olive leaf into the cups.

She glanced at me before fetching the water from the stove. The crockery cups whispered faintly as she poured. Sweetness rose in the steam. She sat and offered the crock of honey.

"What wisdom are you lacking, child?"

My spoon made a quiet scraping sound that rose in pitch as I stirred in the honey.

"I have Nazha's kiss, but no understanding of Nazha's kiss."

"Ah," sighed Sitta. She held her cup between hands that were calloused by mending nets, gutting fish, digging herbs, and stirring the sodden cloth in the kettle. "Sometimes in the dark of the moon, the goddess slides down from her perch in the sky and roams the land. And sometimes an infant born at the previous dark of the moon will catch her

6

eye and her fickle heart, and she'll kiss that child, staining its face with her scarlet kiss."

We sipped our tea. My whisper was almost lost in the whisper of rain outside.

"Why me?"

Her eyes were gentle, dark as walnuts.

"A mother with a dark-moon child protects it with a yellow forest poppy blossom, or a golden pheasant feather. Something sacred to Tol. Tucked under the baby while it sleeps."

I understood. The protection of Tol, the god of the sun, the god of light, would have warded off the touch of his sister, the goddess of the moon. Sitta sadly shook her head.

"But Tirsa didn't have you then. At your first moon. She would have protected you if she had."

I felt a chill crawl over my skin. If Nazha loved me, what if she came back again? What if she kissed my other cheek? I placed the snip of thread on the table.

"Mati needs more thread. This color."

Sitta rose and fetched a skein. She placed it on the table between us.

"It will be different when you're a woman."

I didn't know what she meant by that. I was six. I would never be a woman. Not like Sitta. Not like Mati. I would never be their size. Sitta's words made so many questions in my mind I didn't even know what they were.

I picked up the thread, exactly the color Mati was using.

"Thank you," I said.

As I slipped on my clogs and opened the door, her voice came behind me, high and soft, like the comforting chirps of a mother bird.

"There is no shame in Nazha's kiss."

I went home and put the thread in Mati's lap. I wanted to put myself in her lap. Her lap was comfortable. Soft and safe. I wanted to be safe from Nazha's kiss. I wanted to be safe from the villagers who muttered protective prayers when I passed and made signs against evil, as if the kiss of Nazha were some kind of spell I could cast on them instead of a curse the goddess had bestowed on me.

That spring, before my seventh birthday, I searched the woods. I gathered handfuls of forest poppies and carefully laid them under my pallet lest Nazha decide to come again. The blossoms went moldy overnight and I had to throw them out, but later I found the feather of a golden pheasant in the woods and stitched it into my pillow. It wasn't permitted to harm such a bird, which was sacred to Tol, but finding a feather was good luck for anyone. It must have been good luck for me. Nazha never kissed me again. But just in case, I never took the feather out.

*   *   *

In my childhood, I avoided people.

Our house was at the end of the village, near the woods. This meant few passed our way unless they were visiting Sitta or Zenaida. Of course, it also meant I had to pass more houses to go to the merchant for rice or oil, or to go to the temple on days of prayer, but I only went with Mati or Sitta.

Most of the time, I worked at home. Like Mati, I started sewing young. My fingers were small, so my work was delicate and neat. At six, I could stitch a fine straight seam. At eight I could make a flat rolled hem for the sleeve of a chemise or shirt. By the age of ten, I could make beautiful button loops, cut and sew a pair of britches, and quilt the layers of cloth for a jacket. I sat at the window for the light, in a smaller version of Mati's chair that she had the carpenter build for me.

Even when people came to the house, I could evade them. While Mati designed and draped, measured and marked, I could weed the garden, gather eggs, or milk the goat. And if the weather kept me inside, I simply hid behind my hair. Most girls my age were already plaiting theirs down their backs, but I still wore mine loose like a child who has not seen seven springs. If visitors came, I could bend my attention to stitching a cap or a baby shirt and let my hair fall over my face. The thick black curtain shielded me on either side, and I could avoid being seen from the front just by looking down. Since I was so short, a person would have to bend nearly double to get a good look at me. And curious though they might have been, no adult in Ayr would have been so rude.

Children, of course, were another matter. They sometimes crept along the fence at the back of the garden where the moonflowers grew, and pelted me with stones or sticks. I never told Mati. She would have had them skinned if she knew. But of course, she found out anyway.

I was ten. It had rained that afternoon, so I went out later than usual to pick the vegetables for our supper. Sitta straightened from picking spinach to greet me over the fence. I cheerfully waved a handful of green onion tops, when a burst of pain hit the side of my head and the sun blinked out.

Usually, I heard them coming. They'd giggle and hiss behind the fence, but this time there was only one. He had taken advantage of Sitta's distraction to chuck a stone the size of a plum.

When I woke, I wished I hadn't. The world was bouncing painfully past me as Mati marched into the village with me in her arms and Sitta

8

dragging the boy behind her. He howled like a cat with its tail in the door. Through the hammering in my head, I caught blurs of faces, alarmed, eager, jolting out of their houses, trailing aromas of spicy soups, chicken and oranges, cardamom tea. I wanted to hide. I lifted a hand to my throbbing temple and found hot, sticky blood. My pulse jumped with fear. Mati's arms tightened around me and pressed me closer to her breast.

The temple stood at the heart of Ayr. Facing east, it overlooked the wide white beach, the turquoise water, the wooded islands that sheltered the bay from the open sea. From either side, at front and back, clusters of cottages strung themselves out on the wooded slopes, down to the beach or up toward the forest. Flanked by the village's low thatched rooftops, the temple complex seemed palatial as Mati strode through the open gate in the high slatted fence of smooth golden cedar, eight feet high, topped by a cap of lacquered blue.

Behind us, the crowd swelled in like the tide. Their feet crunched loudly on the white gravel of the courtyard, and their voices fell silent as Mati stopped. She faced the temple, undaunted by the cedar walls, the lacquered azure window frames, the imposing roof of cerulean tiles. It was large enough for four hundred people to kneel in prayer without being able to touch each other. This was where the village prayed. This was where women brought daily food offerings to serve the gods and feed the priests. This was where people could sacrifice in supplication or thanksgiving. This was where they came for comfort, advice, or support. This was where they came for justice.

I pushed myself up against Mati's shoulder, completely forgetting the pain in my head.

Tallis stepped out through the open doors to stand on the porch in a girdled robe in swirling tones of ocean blue. His long straight hair was still thick and dark. He had come to Ayr as a youth of twenty, just two or three years before I was born. From the shadows inside the pillared temple, Kes emerged in his pearl-white robes, patterned with threads of milk-white and gold, with its wide round yoke of creamy pearls. His step was deliberate, his hazelnut skin patched with age, and his silvery hair hung loose to his waist in an airy cloud. Though he barely came up to Tallis's waist, his frame was slight and still quite straight. His white eyes scowled under silver brows.

Tall and slender, Tallis looked down with calm dark eyes. He squinted slightly, but not from age. Tallis could read.

It was Sitta who spoke, holding up the boy's arm and shaking it as if she were selling him like a plucked chicken. The browns and yellows of his clothes had faded to an indistinct beige and the shirt flapped loosely. He was clearly not the first child to wear it. He swallowed a yelp.

"Abuna," she said, addressing the priest by his honored title. "This boy struck the child with a stone."

Kes's nostril's flared. His wispy white hair seemed to tremble.

Tallis only looked at the boy. His voice carried clearly through the courtyard and echoed faintly off the priest's and singer's houses, off the cottage for the temple attendant, off the royal guest house that stood empty except for a week each year, off the storage buildings for village provisions against invasion or famine.

"Xander." He spoke the name flatly, with just a hint of the nasal tone I had heard in his chanting. Tallis knew every name in Ayr. "You hit Amalisa?"

Xander tried to shrink from their scrutiny. He wiped his nose on his sleeve.

"Dint hit her," he whined. "Just tossed some pebble by the fence."

Sitta turned on him with such a glare I thought she would strike him. She yanked his arm.

"I saw what he did," she insisted with passion. "He threw that stone. This stone!" I hadn't seen the stone before. It looked like an egg as she thrust it aloft. "Straight and true. Struck her down cold. Cut her face open."

Mati swept back my hair from the bleeding birthmark and murmurs rose throughout the crowd. More people had pushed into the yard. I wondered if it were the blood or the blight that made them mutter. I wanted to duck out of sight but didn't. Tallis was looking at my face. Kes seemed to be feeling it with his mind. Again Tallis spoke directly to Xander.

"You threw a stone at a child."

Xander squirmed, but faced the priest with brash resentment.

"She'n't no child. She's older 'n me."

I considered the boy. His hair was no longer loose like a child's but pulled back into a messy plait. He couldn't have been more than eight or nine, but I wouldn't have stood as high as his shoulder. His behavior was so bad I wondered if he had a mother. Or a father. Or if either were there in the temple yard. Tallis waved Xander's words aside.

"She is Curran," he stated crisply.

Xander squirmed harder.

"She's marked!" he cried out.

I heard the gasp as if the people breathed as one. It was one thing to whisper snide remarks around the village, and another to blurt out the insult in front of the priest. Not to mention the singer. I saw Kes stiffen. Tallis's brows descended over his narrow nose. His voice went deep and the nasal overtone disappeared.

"She is Curran," he repeated.

The sound bounced around above our heads. People turned to look, as if the words were butterflies they wanted to catch but didn't know how. Then their eyes returned to the priest.

Tallis bent his head and closed his eyes. He seemed to be praying. Then he turned to face the Curran singer. He did not speak, but Kes raised his head and seemed to hear.

It was Kes who pronounced Xander's sentence. For one so small, his voice was surprisingly deep and rich.

"Flog him."

I heard one gasp above the others. The mother was there, hiding herself, shamed by her son, shamed by her failure to teach him respect.

Two men stepped forward. One of them was Sitta's husband. Like most men in Ayr, he wore a single braid down his back. The other was the raft inspector, who ensured that the oyster rafts were kept in good repair. His four braids showed his respectable rank within the pearling hierarchy. His frown was stern as they approached the whimpering boy.

Xander plunged and howled as Sitta released him into their hands. They pulled him to the temple porch, unbound the cord that girdled his waist, and bound his wrists to the lacquered railing. The priest's attendant, a stringy, serious stork of a man by the name of Onald, stepped out of the shadows and passed the flail to the raft inspector.

No one in the courtyard spoke. Only Xander's bawling clawed at the air as the raft inspector raised the flail.

I flung my face into Mati's shoulder just before the flail snapped across Xander's skinny back. But I heard the scream, high and piercing, a child's scream of pain. If I had already eaten supper, I would have been sick. But Mati watched, stiff and silent, full of anger. I could feel Sitta and Sitta's husband standing beside us, rigid and righteous.

I was confused. It didn't seem right to beat a boy for hitting a misfit with a stone. Scold him, surely. Dishonor him in the eyes of the village. But no one I knew would have beaten an ox as they beat that boy. They only struck him three times, but it was enough. Xander's sobbing filled my ears. When I was certain they had stopped, I shifted enough to peek out with one eye. The raft inspector was returning the lash to the temple attendant, and people were starting to drain from the yard, buzzing with delicious horror. A woman pushed against the flow, weeping silently, shoulders bowed. She untied her son. His shirt had torn and three thin traces of blood crossed his back. He collapsed in her arms and they sagged to the ground, holding each other in rocking pain.

The village voices were fading behind us as Tallis raised his eyes to Mati. She nodded stiffly. Sitta snorted and turned away. Her husband took my Mati's arm and steered her toward the temple gate.

I raised my head to look back over Mati's shoulder. Tallis turned and went into the temple. Xander's mother helped him struggle to his feet and they staggered toward the gate together with heads bent low.

On the porch, Kes still stood, as motionless as a statue of Ri, blind goddess of music, his white eyes staring straight at me.

*   *   *

If the flogging earned me a new level of respect in Ayr, I was too intent on avoiding people to notice. When I wasn't working, I wandered the woods, though I never strayed farther than I felt safe. There was only one real road into Ayr, a hard-packed highway that came from Darcy through the pearling villages north of us and wandered the coastline to those beyond. But there were plenty of paths in the forest. Mostly the village hunters used them, but anyone might gather firewood, berries, mushrooms, or roots. I quickly learned the ones least used.

In the forest, I could be myself. I wasn't shy. I wasn't small. I wasn't marked.

And it was the forest that taught me to sing.

All my life I had listened to Mati singing lullabies over my tiny cradle, rhyming songs as I learned to walk, sewing songs in time with her needle, and tuneless hums at the garden or hearth. I could sing all of those songs with her, even the random tuneless hums. This wasn't the music the forest taught me.

All my life, I had gone to the temple to celebrate festivals with the village, to give thanks for recovering from a fever, to ask Skira, the temperamental goddess of the sea, for the safe return of Sitta's husband when he was lost for three days in a winter storm. I had listened to Tallis's nasal chant and sung the responses with Mati or Sitta or all of Ayr. This wasn't the music the forest taught me.

All my life, I had heard the singer standing on the wide white beach, chanting over the peaceful bay, over the thirty floating rafts with the oyster cages hung beneath them. Every day he chanted into the flaming dawn, and again in the darkening shadows of sunset. Although I was seldom there to see him, the thrumming music filled the village, telling us when to rise from bed and when to sit down to our suppers. His resonant drone came from deep in his chest, with a flutelike whistle from high in his head, and the words in the middle, clear and carrying. I never understood the songs and sometimes wondered if the wind-like sounds were words at all. As a Curran, I knew I might have his gift and someday learn the pearling songs, but this wasn't the music the forest taught me.

The forest taught me the sounds of Ayr. I learned the sound of the wind in the trees, teasing and elusive in the languid heat of summer, cheerful and refreshed as it rattled the fiery leaves of autumn, fretful and comfortless under the chilling rains of winter, whispering mischievous secrets as it stirred the soft bright leaves of spring. I mimicked the countless songs of birds staking out their territories, courting mates, protecting young. The chirps and croaks, the peeps and trills of frogs in the plants and the placid ponds. This was the music the forest taught me.

When I was alone in the woods I loved, the sounds bubbled out of me, wordless and happy. I could rumble with the distant thunder and croon like a soothing mother bird. My belly could thrum with the growl of a bear while the winter wind whistled through my head. By the time I was twelve, I thought nothing of it.

Mati, however, thought plenty.

I was planting a row of spicy peppers behind the house. The springtime soil was moist and cool as I poked my finger to make the holes, while the sun shone warmly on my back. A pair of cranes flew overhead and their honking call caught in my chest. Beyond the fence, I heard a thrush and echoed his haunting flutelike note through the top of my nose. The songs flowed smoothly in my blood, matching the beat of the flat round seeds disappearing beneath the dirt.

A crashing sound of breaking crockery shattered the music and jerked me, panting, to my feet. Mati stood in the open door at the back of the house. The water jug was scattered in pieces at her feet, and her hands were poised in front of her as if they still held it, ready to moisten the new-planted seeds. She stared as if her heart had stopped. The seeds spilled forgotten as I stumbled toward her in alarm.

"Mati! What is it?"

Her dark eyes blinked as I approached. She kept her voice calm with visible effort.

"Liise?" She eased my name out as if she weren't sure it was really mine. "How did you—? How long have you—?"

I reached for her hand and guided her carefully down to the sill.

"Are you sick, Mati? Do you want some tea? Should I go for Sitta?"

She waved one hand as if swatting mosquitoes and pressed the other to her breast.

"You have the gift," she choked out in amazement.

I stood up quickly.

"No, I don't," I contradicted. "I just sing. It's not the same."

Her eyes plumbed mine.

"It is," she whispered. "Liise, it is."

I had to sit down beside her to think. The sill was high, for the house was raised above the ground. Only my toes reached the dirt.

I couldn't think. My mind was a muddle. So I just listened. A pheasant called with a strident croak. Wind played in the pines and ruffled the bright new leaves of the feathery maples. Our tethered goat pulled at a patch of dock with a ripping jerk, and the chickens muttered about the scarcity of bugs. Everything sang to me. All I did was sing it back.

"What Kes does is different," I insisted. "He sings in Curran. The pearling songs. The pearling voices. I don't know any of that."

Mati gazed across the garden, over the fence, into the forest where I had been learning to sing.

"You're singing in voices."

I stared at my hands. My tiny hands, darker than Mati's, brown as a hazelnut. Curran hands. I knew she was right. When I spoke, my voice was as small as my hands.

"Please don't tell Kes."

She covered my hands with one of hers.

"He ought to be told."

I saw Kes's eyes, blind and perceptive, staring at me. Why did he have Xander flogged? Was it just because Xander had hurt someone smaller and weaker than him? Or was it because *I* was someone of value? Not to be treated with disrespect. Someone who could become a singer.

I edged closer to Mati and leaned my disfigured face against her arm. If I became a singer, I would have to live like Kes. I would have to go out on the beach every day, at dawn and dusk, to sing to the pearls. I would live in a temple, in one of the twenty pearling villages, possibly far away from Mati. People would see me. I'd never be able to hide again.

"Please don't tell him," I begged.

She pulled me into her lap as if I were only four years old. Her breath was warm against my hair.

"All right," she yielded. "I won't. Not yet. I'll wait until you're ready."

I buried my face in the softness of her shoulder. I didn't believe I would ever be ready. I didn't want to be someone of value. I didn't want to change my life, to leave my home, to move into the eye of the world. I didn't want to be visible. I didn't want to be a singer.

Not until I met Aedon.

Chapter 2: Aedon

That summer, I added the beach to my frequent wanderings. Not the beach in front of the village, where Kes walked down to the sapphire water to chant his songs. Not that beach, where the fishermen pushed their boats out into the burning bay at dawn and the women later gutted the catch and spread the fish on racks to dry. Not that beach, where the boys too old for the crib and too young for the boat pitched rocks at the gulls and chased the scavenging village cats. No, not that beach, but a separate beach, a quiet beach, an empty beach.

The pearling coast of eastern Pini was squiggled with bays and fingered with spits of flat, jutting land, all shielded from the open sea by scattered ranks of lumpy islands. The pearling villages were strung a day or two apart by land, with stretches of uninhabited beaches between. The land approaches were guarded from bandits by mounted patrols, and the coastline was protected from pirates by royal ships, for the pearls were the property of the crown, the pride of the princes, the wealth of Pini.

My private beach was north of the village. I found it one summer afternoon when even the forest felt too hot and I trudged further and further in search of some innermost pocket of cool amongst the slopes of pine and spruce. Instead, I emerged on a little bluff overlooking a bay much like Ayr's, but quite deserted. Alone, I swam, refreshed by the water and savoring the solitude. Returning to Ayr, I discovered a straighter path that took me home in half an hour.

I went to my beach once or twice a week, whenever people came to the house or I finished my work with daylight to spare. At first I went silently, digging for clams or gathering mussels to take home for supper. But the wind whispered secrets through the trees, the water murmured restlessly against the sand, the seals barked their love songs on their private islands. How could I not sing back to them?

I wasn't afraid of discovery. The woodsmen kept their donkeys close to the village edge, the hunters went high into the hills, and few other citizens of Ayr had reason to roam. Even the bothersome boys would be thrashed if they dared to venture so far astray. No one I knew was likely to find me in that haven. The last thing I expected to find there was a stranger.

It was the spring I turned fourteen, and I had been working outside all morning. While I washed, Mati ducked out to gather eggs.

"Liise, my love," she teased when she returned. "There isn't a single weed in the garden. What have you done with them?"

I was setting out bowls for our noonday meal. "Silly Mati. I gave them to Nanny.

"We'll have to grow more," she continued in jest, setting the eggs aside for supper. "Else what will we feed that goat tomorrow?"

"I guess I'll have to work on that," I grinned as we sat to ask Suna's blessing over the food.

"Well, not today," Mati smiled while she served. "You've earned a rest. At least until supper."

"Why?" I squinted suspiciously. "Is someone coming?"

"Yes," she confessed, lifting a forkful of fresh green sorrel.

I picked apart the flakes of whiting brightened with turmeric. Whiting was one of my favorite fish.

"Who?"

"Just someone who might want a garment made."

It wasn't like Mati to be enigmatic.

"Will they be here long?"

She savored the fish with a bite of rice.

"I'm sure they'll be gone by suppertime."

The spring afternoon was clear and splendid. I made directly for my beach.

He was there when I reached the top of the bluff. I dropped to a crouch, amazed and alarmed at the sight of a boy tracking footprints across my sand, his plain white britches wet to the knee from wading in my water. Even from twenty feet above him, I could see how small he was and judged him no more than five or six. His hair was long and black, like mine, but not yet braided. I couldn't imagine where he lived.

From high in the shade of the spreading pines, I watched him stop and study the bay. His afternoon shadow fell motionless over the rippled sand. I held my breath and wondered what he was listening to.

Then I heard his voice. He was singing. Not a rhyming song or temple hymn, but a pearling song in wind-voiced Curran. Only one voice, clean and pure, a voice not yet changed by beards and braids. A beautiful

16

voice. My throat ached to echo it back to him, but I hid in the grass like a cautious hare, afraid to startle him and more afraid to be seen by him.

The singing stumbled. He repeated a phrase, then sang it again. He shook his head and started again. I felt a rush. He was practicing.

My belly leaped like a fish after flies. He wasn't a child. He was Curran like me.

The song flowed clearly over the water. Flat on my belly, I jammed my chin onto my hands to listen and to keep my own voice from bursting out. He finished the verse and began the chorus. I saw him dip his chin and lift his chest and out swelled a throaty humming drone so much like Kes's I nearly jumped up to look for the singer. But except for the boy, the beach was empty, and the drone was at least an octave higher than Kes's bellowing resonance. The soughing syllables floated out above the drone, only faltering once near the final words.

He finished the chorus and raised his head. I found myself panting on my knees and could see his ribs heaving just like mine. I wished I had paid more attention to Kes's songs all these years so I could tell if the boy were doing well. I almost wished he would turn around so I could see if his face held exultation or frustration.

Instead, he raised his arms to the bay and began again. When he reached the chorus and added the drone, it was oddly doubled, as if the bluff itself were singing.

He choked on the sound and whirled in a flash of hazelnut skin and white cotton shirt. Just for an instant, the second drone hung over the bluff, and I clapped my hands to my mouth in shock. The second drone was coming from me.

His quick black eyes scanned the beach and bluff and pinned me sharply. Caught like a mouse in the glare of a hawk, I felt my blood freeze. Then I leaped up and ran.

"Wait!" I heard him call from the beach below, but I didn't wait. I fled along my path to Ayr, my bare feet light on the leafy track. By the time he could even scale the bluff, I'd be safe at home.

If I hadn't tripped.

"Uuufff!"

I crashed to the ground where my toe had caught on a hidden root, my breath knocked out, too stunned to move.

"Wait!" I heard his voice from the distance, bounding through the woods behind me.

I tried to stand, but my knees were shaking, my elbows bloody. I could hardly walk, much less run. I stumbled off the trail to a tree, a tall straight pine with the stubs of old branches laddering up the shaggy trunk. I could hear his feet, his searching call.

"Wait!"

I climbed. Hand over hand, I pulled myself up, laboring where I could have flown if I hadn't jarred all the air from my lungs. Halfway up to the canopy, I had to stop, but it was enough. I edged around to hide myself behind the trunk and saw him coming, glancing right and left as he ran. But he didn't look up.

Nor did he trip. He pelted past me and disappeared down the village path. I clung to the tree and closed my eyes as his calling voice faded and lost itself in the whispering leaves. When I got my wind, I climbed further up and roosted among the peeping frogs and protesting birds, afraid he'd return the way he had gone. An hour later, as the angle of light slanted over my shoulder, I dared to climb down. Just to be safe, I took a roundabout way back home, barely reaching the house before Mati put supper on the table. My heart was still racing as I sat down.

"Gracious, Liise," she said when she looked. "What happened to you? Your hair is a fright!"

My shaking fingers found bits of bark and pine needles. Alarm came into Mati's voice.

"And look at your elbows!"

I lowered my arms and quickly pulled my sleeves back down.

"Go wash at once!" she scolded.

I retreated obediently into the end of the room where we slept and dipped water for washing into the basin. I could feel Mati watching me strip off my short sleeveless robe and cotton shift while she set out our blue ceramic bowls and translucent horn spoons.

"It's time you had new clothes," she muttered, scooping cabbage out of the pot. "You've worn the elbows out of that gown, and it doesn't quite fit you any more."

At fourteen, I was still just beginning to bud and hadn't thought about how that affected the hang of my clothes. Abruptly self-conscious, I washed to the waist.

"I'm sure it can wait," I suggested. I opened my cedar dressing cabinet to pull out my other shift. I didn't really want new clothes. I liked the short hems of a child of five, which only came halfway down my shins. I couldn't have climbed a tree so nimbly in the longer hems befitting my age. Maybe I could distract her by luring her into telling me about her mysterious visitor. "You must have other work to do."

"Hmmph," she sniffed, pouring water to make our tea. "I can make you a proper shift before starting on that."

I joined her at the table and we made our prayers, thanking Suna for wisdom, Tol for life, and Skira for the bounty of the sea.

"How can I help?" I asked, now genuinely curious.

She squinted at me cannily, but gave in with a little smile. Deliberately, she filled her mouth with a spoonful of cabbage and chewed as if it were princely venison. I had to wait until she swallowed and took a leisurely sip of tea. Her brows rose loftily.

"It was Kes who came this afternoon."

Kes! The singer hadn't been to our house in my memory. All his robes and Tallis's were provided by the princes.

"Perhaps he has something in need of repair?" I speculated.

"Not at all," she informed me after more tea. "He has a new apprentice. The boy comes from the next village up the coast and has no proper robes yet. Kes will bring him in a few days for measuring."

My brain snagged on this information. Kes had an apprentice. An apprentice singer. The boy I had seen was the new apprentice.

"Kes must be teaching him to sing."

Mati shrugged.

"Kes says he has the gift. But he's still young, just about your age. There's much he'll be taught before learning the songs."

My eyebrows rose and my spoon hung suspended halfway to my mouth.

"Is it forbidden? For someone my age to sing the songs?"

Mati squinted a little, assessing my interest. I carefully kept my expression open, feigning a taste for delicious gossip.

"It's sacred," she reminded me. "A singer must learn the prayers and rituals first. A child with promise would train for a year or two before beginning to learn the songs."

My eyes went wide. I lowered them hastily to my bowl. The boy had been practicing not in Ayr but on a lonely, empty beach. Afraid he'd get caught.

Mati chewed her cabbage. Her tone was casual.

"Maybe you'd like to start training, too. Now that there's another child, you wouldn't be the only one. It would nice for you to have a friend. Someone your age."

I finished my cabbage and lifted my cup between my hands. It *would* be nice to have a friend. Someone my age. Someone like me.

But the boy on the beach was not like me. Like me, he was small, with hazelnut skin and thick black hair that hung to his waist. Like me, he had the singer's gift. But unlike me, he was beautiful.

I tried to sound nonchalant like Mati. Instead, my voice came out hoarse and frightened.

"Not yet," I whispered.

She touched my wrist. Her eyes were comforting, reassuring.

"Not until you're ready," she smiled.

I gave her a wavering smile in return. She wouldn't tell Kes. Not yet. But I did want a friend. I wanted the boy to be my friend. I would just have to find my own way to befriend him.

*   *   *

Three days later, Mati told me they were coming.

I decided to stay.

I was already wearing my new set of clothes. To make the shift, we had cut down a robe the merchant's daughter had left behind when she got married. It was bright with oranges, yellows, golds, and very soft from previous wear. The gown was calmer in ivories, browns, and dark maroons. The potter's wife had given it to us when her child outgrew it. We shortened the sleeves, turned up the hem, and took it in across the back. The front didn't actually need much adjusting.

I sat by my window at the back of the house where the morning breeze played in our blossoming plum and bent assiduously over a quilted vest I was mending for the shipwright, who had torn it on the teeth of a saw. I jumped to my feet when they arrived.

Kes bowed to Mati as he entered, with his mottled hand on the boy's shoulder, bringing the fragrance of saffron and incense. He wore his everyday shift and robe of white and cream, not the grand ceremonial robe with its collar of pearls. Close up, however, I saw that the cloth was most intricately made, with swirling waves patterned into the weave. I also saw that his left ear was pierced, not once but many times along the outer edge, from the round brown lobe to the frontmost curve where it curled into the inner hollow. The whole rim of his ear was lined with pearls the size of peppercorns, glowing with creamy radiance. There must have been a score of them.

He tipped his head as if sensing the space and his voice filled the room like the sea, deep and fluid.

"May Suna's wisdom reside in this house."

Mati bowed.

"May Suna's compassion be on you," she welcomed him.

Beside him, the boy bowed nervously. He smelled like the sea, sharp and salty. His arms were filled with a soft, flat bundle wrapped in unbleached muslin and tied with a cord.

"May Suna see your kindness," he faltered, holding the bundle out toward Mati.

Mati blinked. So did I. It was like hearing my own voice at the door. Mati regained her composure more quickly than I and took the bundle.

"May Suna grant you her favor," she smiled as she bowed in response.

Kes left his sandals on the mat. The boy was already barefoot.

"You know my daughter Amalisa," Mati presented me with a lift of her hand.

I bowed my greeting, averting my face to hide the mark. Kes couldn't see, but the boy certainly could.

"May Suna guide your steps," I offered a little uncertainly, although Mati had told me it was an appropriate greeting for the singer. I stole a glance lest he disapprove.

This time it was Kes who blinked, inclining his head to listen sharply. I don't think he had ever heard me speak before. I must have sounded as much like the boy to Kes's ear as the boy did to mine. But the boy and I were both Curran, and of an age. I wondered with a fleeting smile if Kes had sounded the same as a child, but I didn't dare look up at the boy. His eyes were still too new for me.

"And this is Aedon," Kes said of the boy.

We bowed to each other. I daresay he was as glad as I that we weren't required to say any more.

"Will you have some tea?" Mati ushered them in, simultaneously dismissing me and setting the bundle of cloth on her chair.

I resumed my work as they sat at the table where three cups waited. The visit was business, and none of mine. Kes crossed the room with his hand on Aedon's shoulder and seemed easily to raise himself to the seat that was clearly too high for him. Aedon pushed himself onto another as gracefully as he could manage, which wasn't, I fear, an entirely successful effort. I could see him stiffen with embarrassment.

I had never really noticed before how badly our table fit Curran proportions. Aedon looked like a child, but that was alright since he *was* a child. It was Kes who looked odd. The singer's chin was barely higher than the board, and his hems hung several inches above the floor. For me it was natural, just the way it had always been, but it was different to see an adult sitting there, looking almost like an eight-year-old child. Not quite, however. Somehow, with his hands folded calmly in his lap, Kes maintained his dignity.

"Suna has done all you've wished for us," he spoke as Mati poured. "Her compassion has shone in bringing me this gifted child." He waved off the honey that Mati offered with a quiet word. "She has truly favored the boy," he continued. "His voice is clear and strong." I tipped my head enough to glimpse the subtle reddening of Aedon's smooth, unblemished cheeks. "And," Kes concluded, "she has guided us here to provide a suitable robe for him."

Mati's hands stroked the table as if she were smoothing invisible fabric.

"We will look at the cloth and discuss your requirements. Also, I will take his measure."

If anything, Aedon turned redder at this. He stared at his hands. They were clasped in his lap. He was too nervous to drink his tea. Mati smiled at him gently.

"I've lived in this house all my life," she remarked. "My heart would ache if I had to leave it and go where I knew no one and no one knew me. But maybe I would find a friend, and in time I would feel less alone."

To hide my blush, I ducked my head as if in diligence over my stitches. I could hear Aedon breathing while Kes and Mati finished their tea. His breath was irregular and slightly rapid. It occurred to me that he wasn't shy—he was afraid. Afraid I would tell what he had been doing at the beach. Afraid of me. I wished I could somehow reassure him, but all I could offer was silence.

"Such things take time," observed Kes at last.

Mati cleared the table, fetched the bundle, and untied the cord. The pearl-white fabric opened like clouds.

"Good," she appraised it with knowing hands. "A good strong weave, but not too stiff. It will make a sturdy robe, but comfortable, too." She pulled out a garment, already made, from under the cloth. It was a robe for a temple attendant, of Pinian proportions, of course, but it would serve for the style and shape. Mati pulled out her measuring string.

I really didn't watch while Aedon was measured. I didn't even listen. Instead, I was filled by an odd sensation. I had never been in the same room before with other Currans. I had only been with Pinians, had only seen Kes among Pinians. In the village, it was I who was the odd one. Even Kes, revered though he was, didn't match. But this was different. Now it was Mati who didn't match. There were three of us and one of her. Three of us. Three of *us*. I tried to focus on my stitches, but all I could think was *I'm not alone. I'm not alone.*

Only half an hour later, Mati folded her string, now knotted with various lengths and girths, and set it aside with the pearly cloth.

"It shouldn't take long," I heard her tell Kes. "A fortnight at most."

"No need for haste," he reassured her. "The boy won't need it until the seeding."

The seeding wasn't until midsummer, six or seven weeks away. We could make three or four robes by then.

"In three days we'll have it ready for marking," she said nonetheless. "Would that be convenient?"

His white eyes crinkled at the corners.

22

"The boy is free in the afternoons. I'm sure he can find his way without me."

"The boy is welcome to come alone," Mati smiled at Aedon.

As was expected, I stood as Kes slipped on his sandals at the door, and we all exchanged the proper blessings. Except for our greetings and farewells, neither Aedon nor I had spoken a word. But as I watched them walk away between the too-large cottages, with Kes's hand on Aedon's shoulder, my mind was filled with a dozen questions I could hardly wait to ask.

*   *   *

That afternoon, Mati and I picked apart the old robe, carefully laying the pieces flat. The following morning, she showed me how to compare them to Aedon's measurements and plot out proportional marks on the cloth with a wedge of chalk. By noon, every part of Aedon's new robe was ready to cut.

"We'll cut it tomorrow," Mati told me while setting our dinner on the table, "and still have it ready in plenty of time."

When I reached the bluff an hour later, he was already there. From the shifting shadows of spruce and maple, I saw him stalking up and down the trampled beach. Dozens of lines of little footprints showed how long he had been waiting. He scanned the heights repeatedly. His whole face lit up when he spotted me.

"There you are!" he shouted. "I was afraid you weren't coming!"

He ran toward the bluff. In an instant my questions flew out of my brain and a wave of fright washed through my blood.

"Stop!" I cried, startling myself as much as him. "Don't come up!"

He slowed and halted. "All right," he agreed, and watched for me to begin my descent. When I didn't move, he shaded his eyes in irritation. "Aren't you coming down?" he yelled.

A squirrel scolded shrilly as I shrank back into the sheltering shadows. "No."

He spread his bare feet and crossed his arms impatiently.

"Look," he called. "It's not like I don't know."

"Know what?" I challenged stupidly.

"About the mark."

My cheeks went hot.

"Is that why you're here, then? To see the mark?"

He waved one hand and stuck the other on his hip.

"Of course not. I've already seen it. I just want to talk."

I pressed my back against a tree and slid down weakly to hug my knees.

"Go away!" As petulant as a three-year-old, I buried my face in my arms. "No one just wants to talk to me!"

I heard a burst of exasperation, somewhere between a huff and a roar.

"Liise!" he cried. "Please!" The word grew long with desperation. "You can't believe how lonely it is!" I heard his voice swing back and forth. He was pacing again. "I've been in Ayr for two whole weeks and there's no one to talk to!"

I hiked my new skirts and crawled to the edge of the bluff.

"How can you say that? You live in the temple! There are plenty of people to talk to!"

He found me with indignant eyes.

"No," he insisted. "There's *no one* to talk to."

There was a path down the face of the bluff. He met me at the bottom as if I were bringing him sweet water after an unplanned week at sea. When I ducked to hide behind my hair, he gave a snort.

"It isn't all that bad, you know."

Purely out of shock, I raised my head to meet his eyes. They were exactly level with mine. Close up, they didn't look black at all, but a warm umber brown with golden lights.

"That's better," he smiled. "It's ever so much easier to talk this way."

I searched his gaze. It was clear and open, framed by broad, high cheeks and wind-tangled hair. He really, truly didn't mind.

"Don't you talk to Kes?"

He sniffed a laugh and casually started down the beach. I walked beside him.

"Kes doesn't talk. He sings to the pearls. And prays." He linked his hands behind his back. "And teaches," he added, as if to be fair.

"He's teaching you the pearling songs," I observed, even though Mati had said he wasn't.

He rounded on me, walking sideways, eyes enlarged in contradiction.

"No, he isn't. I'm learning the prayers but not the songs. I don't get to learn them until Kes says so."

"But—" I frowned, thinking back just a few days ago. "You were singing the—"

"You won't tell him?" He leaped in front of me, stopping abruptly. I thought he was going to grab my hands. "Please don't tell him. Yesterday I was so afraid you were going to tell him. I'm not supposed to be singing them. Not until I'm properly taught."

I pursed my mouth as if in thought, but really more to hide a grin.

"If you won't tell him I can sing."

24

"You mean—" I saw his mind flick back to the moment he heard his drone being doubled by mine. "You mean he doesn't know?"

I shook my head.

"I don't want him to. I don't want to live in the temple. Learn the rituals." I dropped my gaze to his sandy toes. "Leave my mother."

He rolled his eyes in agreement and started to walk again.

"It's awful," he groaned, swaying emphatically. "I hate being so far away from my family." He hung his head and I heard a tightening in his throat. "I really miss them."

I shivered with horror. I couldn't imagine being taken away from Mati. My voice went husky with compassion.

"Where are they?" I asked.

He kicked at the sand. It hissed into the water.

"At home, of course. I come from Cant. The pearling village north of Ayr."

I listened to the soft crunch of sand beneath our feet and tried to imagine Aedon's family.

"Are your parents…Curran?"

His glance flitted sideways, saw my Mati in my eyes, and darted away again.

"Yes," he said with a hint of apology, but then his expression brightened. "My first mother was the singer in Cant. That's why they knew I might have the gift. But she died when I was born, and my Tadde took another wife when I was still a baby. She's my Mati. And I have three little sisters." His head bent low and his sigh was laden with homesickness. "I miss them awfully."

A whole family of Currans. I could barely picture it.

"Are there other Currans in your village?"

He swung his hair back over his shoulder. The laughing breeze promptly blew it back into his face.

"Just the singer. Some time after my first mother died, my father went to Darcy to find a new wife. There are Currans in Darcy."

"Have you been there?" I asked in astonishment.

"To Darcy?" he laughed. "No. This is the first time I've ever left Cant."

We turned and absently wandered back the other way. I looked down where our footprints paced precisely side by side down the strand. Our strides matched perfectly.

"Why aren't you learning from the singer in Cant?"

"I did for a while, when they realized I could sing in voices. But after a few months, they brought me here to be trained by Kes. He's actually pretty famous, you know. I'm told he's trained half of the singers in Pini.

He has a pearl in his ear for each of them. Of course, he wouldn't train you."

"Why not?" I retorted on reflex, though I didn't want to be trained at all.

"You can hardly be trained in your own village, right there where your family is."

I didn't understand this at all.

"For Suna's sake, why not?"

He shrugged. It clearly made perfect sense to him.

"Well, your family's a distraction. If you go to another village, you can focus on the singer who's teaching you and on what you're learning."

I made an incredulous face at him. He certainly wasn't focused on any of that at the moment.

"It doesn't seem to be working for you."

He laughed a little, wistfully.

"No, well, I'm still pretty new at it. I suppose I'll get used to it. And Kes isn't really so bad. He's kind and patient and doesn't beat me when I make mistakes. Of course," he added with a distant sigh, "as soon as Kes says I'm ready, they'll send me off to Darcy."

"To Darcy? Why?"

"To study with the Master Singer. To be consecrated as a singer."

I suddenly felt very cold despite the warm sun on my back.

"You have to go to Darcy to become a singer?"

"Officially. Sure. That's where the Master Singer is. That's where they ordain you."

I stopped walking. I stopped hearing the shush of the water, the rising and falling breath of the wind, the whispers of the trees on the bluff. I didn't even hear the gulls searching and crying overhead, or the little sandpipers fretting at the edge of the strand. This was worse than I had realized.

"So if they find out I can sing in voices, they'll make me live in the temple in Ayr, then send me to some other village for a year or so, then make me go live in Darcy?"

He stopped and looked at me openly, but when he saw my obvious terror, his arched black brows peaked with alarm.

"Oh, Liise." His hand rose toward me in compassion, but I backed away.

"I won't leave my Mati. I won't go live in some other village. And I won't go to Darcy. Ayr's bad enough. You don't know what it's like for me."

He dropped his gaze.

"I know a little. I heard about the lashing."

26

I lifted my hands in appeal.

"Please," I begged, "don't tell Kes I can sing in voices. Mati said she wouldn't tell, and she's the only one who knows. Except for you."

He took my hands and gazed at me with his gold-flecked eyes.

"I won't tell. I promise."

He held my hands a moment longer. His were the same size as mine. It was strange, but wonderful, as if it were something I'd always missed but didn't know it. My breathing slowly settled and the sounds of the bay crept back into my ears.

"All right," I agreed. "And I won't tell anyone you've been practicing the songs." I let my hands slip out of his and fall back to my sides. Then I looked at him with sudden mischief. "So," I suggested. "Can you teach them to me?"

He burst out in laughter that echoed faintly from the bluff.

"Sure," he grinned. "Come on."

He grabbed my hand and we ran to the water, and he taught me my first pearling song.

*   *   *

He started me with the Morning Song that Kes sang to the pearls every dawn. I barely made it through the chorus.

"It's long," laughed Aedon with sympathy. "It must have twenty verses."

Having grown up speaking Curran at home, he explained the Curran words to me. The chorus sang in the soughing sighs of waves and wind, in the deep rich bellow of courting seals, in the shrill high cry of mournful gulls. "O Pearls," it rejoiced, "who possess the pristine perfection of Nazha, grow bountiful in the beauty of Eia and bear to us abundantly the enlightenment of Suna." There was more, but that was as much as I could remember.

"I can teach you some exercises, too. It's one of the things we do in the mornings. The singing. Prayers in the temple. Breakfast. Lessons."

The sun hadn't set, but our shadows were stretching along the strand and the air off the bay was beginning to cool. We walked to the base of the bluff.

"I can come almost any afternoon. Kes sleeps after dinner, sometimes clear to suppertime. When can you come again?"

I stopped at the bottom of the path. Aedon was going back by the beach, the way he had come.

"Not tomorrow. I have to help Mati with your robe."

"Right," he remembered, brightening. "I'll be trying it on the day after that. I'll ask your Mati when we can meet."

"No, don't do that!" I panicked.

He picked up a stone and tossed it idly in his hand.

"Why not?" he asked, more amused than I wanted him to be. "Don't you think she knows we're together?"

I thought about that. Of course she did.

"I guess you're right," I had to admit.

In a boy's display of enthusiasm, he pulled back his arm and threw the rock all the way to the water.

"Then I'll see you in a couple of days," he stated with satisfaction. "I'd better go. Kes will be waiting."

By now the sun had set. He walked away backward with a wave. I waved back and called after him, teasing.

"You'll be late!"

"So will you!" he chortled back and ran off down the beach.

I grinned to myself as I climbed the path. We'd both be late. I don't think either of us cared.

*   *   *

"May Suna's wisdom come into this house," said Aedon when Mati opened the door.

"May Suna hold you in her heart. Would you like some tea?"

Three cups were already on the table. Since I was helping with the robe, it was proper for me to join them.

This time when Aedon hoisted himself onto the seat, he didn't turn red.

"I'm still not used to Pinian furniture," he explained without embarrassment. "At home, everything's my size."

Mati poured without taking offense.

"Your family is Curran, then?"

"Yes," nodded Aedon, explaining his family as before.

"You must miss them very much," said Mati kindly.

"I do," he agreed, though without the same homesick tone. "But Suna was kind to send me here. It is an honor to learn from Kes. Only—"

I passed him the honey. Our fingers touched. Mati noticed.

"Only?" she prompted.

He dropped his gaze and spooned out honey into his cup.

"It would be ungrateful of me to wish for more than I have, or to wish that I might learn more quickly than Kes is teaching me." Curious, I watched him stir. His words were modest, but his tone was not. "But even

28

a simple apprentice could yearn for another voice to practice with. Another ear to listen with."

Mati sipped, taking her time, but as if she already had an answer. I wondered if she had been talking to Kes.

"I have little of Suna's wisdom, but it seems that a teacher would wish his apprentice to practice in ways that would further his learning. Within the bounds of propriety."

I watched Aedon tip his head in thought, completely unintimidated. How could he dare to be so bold?

"An apprentice could practice with a friend. A friend with similar gifts. Within the bounds of propriety."

Mati nodded in apparent agreement.

"Such a friend would be of great value. I have long hoped my Liise could find such a friend."

He lifted his head and met Mati's eye as if he were her equal, asking not her guidance but her opinion.

"But would it be within the bounds of propriety for her to spend the occasional afternoon alone with a singer's apprentice?"

Mati considered the depths of her tea.

"She is young. But she is sensible. And a singer's apprentice is bound by the honor of his master."

Aedon nodded in contemplation.

"Such a friendship would be comfort."

"Yes," agreed Mati, who understood the longing for comfort. "A blessing to both."

Then both of them smiled contentedly and Mati stood up to clear the cups. Astounded, I stared.

"Have you no respect?" I whispered.

His forehead puckered in bemusement.

"Of course I do. I spoke correctly."

"But not like a child," I murmured low, afraid Mati would hear. "You're just a child, Aedon."

His smiled tightened ever so slightly.

"I'm not just a child. I'm a Curran child. Just like you."

The subtle challenge startled me and sparked indignation in my tone.

"Not just like me. My Mati has taught me humility."

"Ah. Humility." His eyes narrowed with some realization that was still eluding me. "So you've been raised with humility."

"Yes," I bristled. I could hear Mati humming while she washed the cups, carefully not overhearing our words. Aedon placed his hands on the table, the table that was too high for him but which felt exactly right to me because I had sat at it all my life.

"Perhaps you're right," he conceded stiffly. "I'm not like you. I'm the son of a Curran singer. And you have the blood of a singer, too. But you've been raised like a Pinian."

I sat back, stung. He only leaned toward me more earnestly.

"Listen, Liise. Didn't Kes have a boy flogged because of you?"

I recoiled from the memory.

"Because he threw a stone at me."

"And would they have flogged the boy if he had thrown a stone at any other child?"

"I wouldn't know," I scowled.

"I doubt it," he insisted. "It was because you're Curran."

That was true and I knew it. I remembered Tallis's words at the flogging.

"But—"

"You have a gift. An important gift. That means you're important, too. You don't have to live as if you're not."

I crossed my arms and stared at the table. I didn't want to be important. Aedon didn't understand. In my brooding silence, Mati brought out the basted robe.

"Here," she said cheerfully. "You can slip it on right over your clothes."

I sat on the floor to mark the hems while Mati adjusted the fit through the sleeves and across the chest. Aedon chattered airily about his family and his life in Cant. Mati laughed as he recounted how one of his little sisters had dropped a pot of red pepper paste on the floor and the entire mass of its sticky contents had shot straight up and hit the ceiling, clinging there like a threat from the gods as the whole family stared in utter shock. I, however, was still too shocked by Aedon's behavior to laugh or smile or even speak.

At last Mati stood to lift the garment from Aedon's shoulders. I helped her spread it on the table.

"Liise, my love," she spoke as she folded. "You may see our guest to the door."

Aedon bowed.

"May Suna grant you a peaceful evening."

She bowed in return from across the table.

"May you ever grow in Suna's wisdom."

I held the door, my eyes downcast. He stood on the threshold, halfway in and halfway out. He hung his head.

"I'm sorry, Liise. My words were unkind. I didn't speak from Suna's heart."

I didn't look up, but kept my face hidden behind my hair.

30

"But you were right," I told him flatly. "I'm not like you. The boy was flogged because I'm Curran, but he threw the stone because I'm marked. I'm different, Aedon. I'll never be a singer like you."

I felt him look away, felt his gaze sweep down the hard-packed path, between the houses, toward the temple.

"Maybe so," he allowed. "But I still need a friend to sing with."

I raised my eyes and followed his gaze. We were so different, yet so alike. He gave me a hopeful little smile.

"Will you come to the beach tomorrow?"

I let my hair fall back over my face.

"I don't know. I have work to do."

I could hear him breathing, watching me. Then he straightened and stepped completely outside.

"Then may Suna guide your steps, Liise."

"And may Suna abide in your heart."

He walked away. I didn't watch, but closed the door and went to help Mati start supper.

Chapter 3: The Seeding

I went, of course. But I hid in a tree on top of the bluff and didn't let him know I was there. He waited an hour. I watched him pace, hunt for mussels, and skim flat stones in fidgety boredom before trudging back to the village, scuffing and kicking at the sand until he was out of sight.

The second day was exactly the same.

The third day he didn't come at all.

By the fourth day he had stopped expecting me. He lifted his hands to the water and sang. He didn't sing the pearling songs, but practiced the voices used in the songs. I perched on a branch and listened.

His voices were good. Round and solid. His drone was steady, from low in his throat, pitched like mine since his voice hadn't changed. The high piercing whistle fluted clearly through his nose, bright as a jay's voice. And his middle tones were open and clean, with flowing vowels and whispering consonants. He didn't sing words, but exercises of patterned sounds. He made them well, but they were lifeless and had no feeling. After an hour, he chucked a rock at the water and left. I sat in my tree for a long time, listening to the whispering leaves, the mixed chorus of birds, and rustle of life in the woods all around me, but hearing the echoes of Aedon's singing in my mind.

The following day I was there before him. I watched him coming up the strand, picking up stones and skimming them carelessly while he walked. His dejected posture vanished when he saw me standing at the base of the bluff.

"Liise!" he cried, leaping toward me. He grabbed my shoulders, nearly shoving me into the wall of dirt and stone behind me.

"Suna's tears!" I exclaimed, seizing his arms. "If you're going to knock me down, maybe I shouldn't have come!"

The gold lights sparkled in his eyes. He flattened his hands against the crumbly wall.

"By Suna, I'm glad you're here. I was afraid— But never mind. Shall I teach you the exercises now?"

I ducked under his arm and shook my head.

"No. Just close your eyes and listen."

He screwed up his eyes as if he thought I'd hit him if he closed them. I couldn't help laughing.

"Relax! Just listen."

He was silent for several minutes. One eye squeezed open.

"I don't hear anything."

I made a face and shook his shoulders in mock frustration.

"Then you're not really listening."

He gave himself a little shake, like a dog shedding water after a swim, and stood up straight. His eyes closed smoothly.

"All right," I said softly. "What do you hear?"

"Birds."

"Good. What do they sound like?"

"Chirps." More listening. "Whistles. Trills. Someone's warbling, running scales, twice up, once down." He tipped his head. "A hawk. Or an eagle. Over the water. Very high."

I nodded, pleased, and pulled his sleeve to lead him away from the bluff.

"What else besides birds?"

"Wind." I watched his senses reach out as he spoke. "In the trees. Playing in the leaves. Over the water. On the sand."

"Excellent. Now sing that."

His eyes tried to open. I very gently pressed them shut.

"Just try to sing it."

He opened his mouth. I heard a playful breathy sound like the breeze in the trees. He added a warble through his nose, a rising scale. One eye peeked open and I grinned.

"Lovely," I commented as he stopped. "I could feel it when you sang it."

"Really?" He looked delighted. "Is that how you sing?"

I nodded. Then I closed my eyes and sang for him.

I sang the sunrise over the bay, with the mist on the water and seals guarding their pups on an island beach. I sang the forest in early spring, with birds squabbling over breeding ranges, new leaves unfurling in the breeze, and a bull seal grunting his contentment in the sun. I sang a storm blowing through the village, moaning at the windows, raining down the chimneys to hiss into the hearths, with Mati's comfortable humming reassuring me of safety.

When I stopped and looked, he was staring at me as if Suna had laid her hand on me and my head was glowing. It made me laugh.

"Teach me that," he breathed in awe. "Please?"

I took his hand.

"Let's walk," I suggested. "And listen."

*   *   *

For several weeks, we met as often as we could. Aedon learned to sing the forest, the wind, and the sea. He learned the moods of the sun and the clouds, the moon and the mists, the flowers and forest. In turn, I let him teach me the drills and exercises Kes was teaching him, expanding my range of voices and sounds, of depth and control, and tone and attack. I even went down to the water sometimes at dawn, when the mist was thick and I wouldn't be seen, to listen to the Morning Song. I could only pick out the words Aedon had taught me, the first few lines of the chorus, but little by little, I started to feel its rhythm and mood. When we sang it together, our voices blended perfectly. And soon, so did our hearts.

I couldn't get away every day. At home, I helped Mati. As the seeding festival approached, there was plenty to do. There were two great annual festivals in every pearling village. One was the winter harvest and the other was the summer seeding. People liked to look their best for both. Accordingly, we were sewing a whole new gown for the rope maker's wife, who had grown too stout for her old one. I was doing a good deal of mending for the youngest village woodcutter, who had taken a tumble out of a tree and torn everything he had on at the time. And the elderly sandler's aging wife had to ask us to replace the sleeve on her summer gown because she had burned it while banking the hearth one night.

Mostly I worked on Aedon's robe. I was slow and careful because Mati was letting me do it entirely on my own. She had never let me touch Tallis's or Kes's robes when one of them required repair, but Aedon was only an apprentice. It took me weeks. I stitched the seams with special care, made the hems exactly even, and sewed the borders meticulously. It would bind the labor of my hands to the labor of his soul.

When the robe was finished, Kes came to approve it. The breeze that came in with him when he entered was sweet with summer, soft and mild in the cooling evening. His small gnarled fingers adjusted the robe on Aedon's shoulders, smoothed the front, and examined every stitch and hem.

"Amalisa's hand is very fine," Mati remarked. I turned behind my curtain of hair, not to hide the mark but to hide the blush.

Kes's hands swept once more lightly over the robe. Aedon stood very straight.

"It is well done," Kes approved with the hint of a smile. "Most lovingly made."

I resisted looking up at Aedon. Kes couldn't see me, but Mati could. Mati bowed.

"It has been an honor to serve the singer."

Kes inclined his head.

"The work is more than worthy of a singer's apprentice."

He waved a hand and Aedon obediently removed the robe. Together, Mati and I folded it neatly and wrapped it in a hemmed square of the extra cotton. The original garment that had served as a model was already bundled in its muslin.

"I regret that it wasn't finished sooner," apologized Mati, placing the parcel in Aedon's arms. Kes walked to the door without assistance.

"Not at all," he reassured her. "It is perfectly timed for the midsummer seeding."

"Yes, of course," remembered Mati. "The boy will assist you."

Aedon modestly bowed his head and said nothing. In his master's presence, he remained silent unless invited to speak. Kes, however, nodded with obvious satisfaction.

"I value his assistance every day."

Mati smiled significantly at Aedon.

"Suna has blessed us all with his presence."

Kes turned his eyes in my direction, opaque yet somehow uncomfortably knowing.

"May her bountiful wisdom continue to bless us," he offered in parting, "in the seeding of the pearls."

* * *

Aedon wasn't so modest the next time I saw him. He lay on his back at the top of our bluff on a carpet of pine needles, staring up through the branches that were utterly still in the hot afternoon. His elbows stuck out as he tucked his hands behind his head.

"It's the first time I've assisted in the seeding," he warbled happily. "You'll get to hear me chant the prayers."

Sprawled beside him on the ground, I grimaced. I only attended as much of the seeding as I had to, and that wasn't much. At my silence, he rolled over and lurched up onto his elbows. There were pine needles stuck all over his shirt.

"You'll be there, won't you?"

The sharp, heavy scent of the pines filled my lungs. Their shade offered little comfort from the heat, nor from the prospect of a public appearance.

"Well," I hedged. "We come for the festival."

He frowned. This was clearly insufficient.

"But that's only the day of the consecration. What about putting the buildings up? And the seeding itself?"

I squirmed.

"I think I might have seen that once...."

"But, Liise," he protested. "It's what I've been training for all this time. I want you to be there."

I knew I had to go. To hear him chant the prayers. To see him in the robe I had made.

"I'll come," I bargained, "but only if you promise to teach me the Evening Song."

He threw a pinecone at me.

"I'm not supposed to do the songs!"

I threw it back, striking his chin.

"That hasn't stopped you so far."

"Suna's ears." He flopped down and cradled his chin on his hands to stare out over the glittering water. "It's too hot to sing."

"It's never too hot to sing," I objected. "It just sounds different." I sat up, crossed my legs, lifted my palms as if in prayer, and raised my face toward the sweltering sun that lurked behind the pines. A froglike croak came out of my throat and a whine like cicadas thrummed out through my nose. Aedon jumped up to his knees and crowed.

"I dare you to do that at the seeding!"

"Ha!" I sniffed. "I'll come to the seeding, but you won't see me."

His sun-flecked eyes turned quizzical.

"Why not?"

I shoved back my damp hair and screwed up my face with the left side toward him.

"Oh, that." He waved it away with a careless hand. "Forget that. If you want me to teach you the Evening Song, I want to see you right out front. At least at the festival."

"Suna's pearly teeth," I snorted, crossing my arms in mock indignation. "If that's what it takes, I'll just have to show up."

He flopped back into his original posture, with hands tucked contentedly under his head.

"That's right," he concluded and closed his eyes with a satisfied smile. "You will."

*　　*　　*

That very evening, fifty slaves and a dozen guards arrived with twenty ox-drawn wagonloads of posts and planks and panels, and construction of the pearling buildings began the following dawn. Mati didn't question me when I asked her permission to go and watch.

"You might want these," she said and handed me a packet wrapped in a cabbage leaf and a leather bottle full of water. I grinned and hugged her before running off.

Beneath the daybreak chatter of birds, I could hear Kes singing the Morning Song as I went a long way through the woods to hide in a patch of spotted laurels where I could look out without being seen.

As usual at that early hour, Kes and Aedon stood on the strand with the sun rising over the islands beyond them. Not as usual, Kes was wearing his pearl-white ceremonial robe with the broad yoke of pearls. His arms were raised, his blind face lifted to the dawn, his white hair fluffed in a shining cloud around his shoulders. His voice floated out like the bellow of whales, like the call of the wind, like the piercing whistle of frolicking dolphins, over the glittering, glassy water, out through the shadows of the oyster rafts, to thrum down through the bamboo frames to the cages of oysters hanging below. Beside him, Aedon stood still and silent, a delicate statue of white and brown, in the beautiful robe I had made for him, with his long dark hair hanging straight down his back.

Beyond them, on the fishing beach, the fishermen were raising their sails and starting out on the tide to join the boats from other villages, north and south, to fish in the open Gulf of Yar. The sails of Ayr were solid green with a huge white pearl in the uppermost corner and family signs on the lower edge. They huffed with impatience, then crisply snapped as they caught the breeze, and the boats plowed out with a *shuush* and the voices of men calling out to each other in the exuberance of a new day.

But nearer to hand was the noisier bustle, the vigorous action, the heft and swing of posts and planks being hoisted and pegged into raised wooden floors for the sleeping hall. The slaves were men of various colors, walnut, copper, almond, and bronze, even olive-skinned Pinians, all of them strapping, strong, and quick. Their broad bare backs already shone with sweat in the early heat, and their brightly patterned cotton britches were already limp with moisture. The guards, in their blue-and-white leather armor, supervised the entire scene, from the ox-drawn wagons that lined the road to the foundation that was taking shape on the hard-packed sand.

Kes finished his song and came back with Aedon up the beach. Tallis was waiting in his sea-blue robes, with Onald, the temple attendant, who carried the brazier and spices for purification. Together, the four of them moved from corner to corner of the platform, chanting the blessings in wonderful harmony. Kes's voice was deep as the ocean, rich and low. Tallis's chant buzzed straight through the middle, nasal and sonorous as bees. And Aedon's tones, pure and clear, rose up to the gods in crystalline notes. My heart expanded with the sound.

So it went throughout the morning. Walk and stand, chant and pray, all in the midst of the back and forth, the lift and peg, the grunt of voice and thud of mallet. I marveled at the dance of it all, the grace and precision of every movement, the vast coordination of work. Hour by hour, I watched them erect carved cedar posts, framing a huge building unlike any house in the village, with one great room for the pearling party that would follow later. Drinking water came in buckets and went in dippers; a midday meal of spicy rice and fish was delivered by the village women, my Mati among them, and almost instantly disappeared. Hidden in my laurel patch, I unwrapped my dinner, discovering a rice-flour bun and cold slices of chicken spiced with cumin.

All afternoon, they fitted the cedar panels, carved and polished, into the vertical slots of the posts. Walls appeared, enclosing the room in airy screens with shuttered windows. They raised notched beams and great long rafters, all roofed with lengths of split bamboo from the mountains of southwestern Pini. The stifling air whined with the squeal of wood on wood and pulsed with the pounding of mallets on the panel frames. In the humming heat, the slaves hissed and panted, too hot to talk. Tallis and Kes persisted in praying over every joint, each door and lintel, every section of bamboo.

Then suddenly the day was done. Women brought another meal, and the weary men slumped down on the sand to eat in silence. I could smell the sweet rice and the scent of cedar as Tallis climbed back to the temple. The boats returned, riding low on the tide with their catch. Wives and children pulled in the haul, set to cleaning the fish, pitched their singsong voices across the waves in greeting and gossip. And Kes went down to the water to sing.

In the Evening Song, the tones were more somber than those of the Morning Song, more introspective. The high notes were sweeter, the low notes softer, the chorus syllables more sustained, and the verses fewer. In the shadow of the building that had not been there at dawn, Kes held out his arms to the darkening bay, where the islands looked unnaturally bright in the gilding light of the setting sun and the haze beyond was diffused with lavenders, yellows, and pinks.

Birds squabbled and chattered in the trees. The fishermen dragged their boats up the sand and women gossiped amiably while they spread the nets and collected their men. Children's voices shrilled up the beach as mothers called them in to supper. The women who had brought the workers' midday meal reappeared with rice and greens. The slaves sat on the sand to eat, then washed in buckets brought down by boys from the village well. Then they took up the mats they had slept on under the wagons the previous night, and the guards shepherded them into the dormitory to sleep. The village grew quiet.

Kes finished his song and turned from the water. His hand rested lightly on Aedon's shoulder as he trod back up the slope. Aedon didn't see me. He didn't even know where to look.

"I thought I might find you here."

I jumped at the sound, and whirled to find Mati smiling behind me, holding out a bowl of rice. I laughed and took it gratefully. She sat down beside me among the laurels, looking decidedly pleased with herself.

"I used to bring you here to watch when you weren't even old enough to walk."

"You did?" I mumbled around a bite of rice and salty fish.

"I did," Mati nodded, looking around my hideaway. "Of course, the laurels were smaller then." She regarded the golden, improbable structure on the beach. "I'm always amazed. All those people, all that work, all so perfect. Every year, always the same. The buildings go up, the seeders come through, and the buildings come down. In twenty days, you won't even see their tracks in the sand."

I chewed more slowly, thinking about the dance of the day, seeing it happen again and again, year after year, as set and reliable as the seasons, as laurels blooming in early summer. Mati folded her arms across her knees and laid down her head to look sideways at me.

"It's part of your life," she noted gently. "Not just because of where you live, but because of who you are."

I concentrated on scraping up the last few grains of gummy rice.

"Someday," she continued, "you might want to be a part of that instead of hiding in the bushes."

My belly tightened at the thought. How could I ever be part of the pearling? I could barely walk down the paths of Ayr. As if reading my thoughts, Mati brushed my cheek with the back of her fingers.

"Things could change."

I looked out over the quiet beach, the shifting water, the shadowed islands. The sky was darkening to cobalt and stars were just starting to wink into sight. Nothing would change. Not in the seasons, not in the pearling, and not in me. But Mati smiled.

"You're always changing, Liise, my love."

I hugged my knees and shrugged.

"Not tonight."

"No," she agreed and rose to her feet. "Not tonight. Let's go home and get some sleep. I daresay you'll want to come back tomorrow."

I uncramped my body and stood up stiffly. I could barely make out the building now as it disappeared into the dark.

"Yes," I confessed without embarrassment. "I will."

*   *   *

On the second day, the refectory materialized between the bay and the dormitory. It only had a single room, filled with tables and benches, with a split-bamboo roof supported by fragrant cedar posts, all open on the east to the sea. On the third day, they assembled the fane, the pearling temple, just above the tide line. It was long and narrow, but small compared to the other two buildings, and closed and windowless. Its blue lacquered walls were ornately pierced to let in light and the cooling breeze, but no one would be allowed to see in, for the seeding was sacred and closely guarded. And all the while, Aedon chanted the prayers with Kes.

At dawn of the fourth day, the guards marched the slaves in front of the wagons and left.

The calling of Suna began after breakfast. Unlike the construction of the buildings, this was a full village festival. Everyone went. For a whole day, the merchant did no business, the boats lay on the sand, and the crops went untended. Walking down to the beach in our finest clothes, we carried baskets of food cooked the day before. Aside from the priests, only the village guard would work that day, patrolling our boundaries with redoubled vigilance, lest bandits or pirates think us vulnerable during the festival.

In previous years, Mati and I had hung back in the crowd, but this year I had to be in front. The benches in the refectory were reserved for women with babies, for the infirm and elderly, but chattering children sat on the floor with their legs dangling over the open edge. Talkative families spread woven mats on the sand in front of the refectory where the sun would shine in their eyes in the morning but the shade would shelter them after noon. Unmarried men and the slow to arrive could crouch at the edges with no shade at all, or retreat to the trees where the view was poor.

By the time we arrived with Sitta's family, excited voices drowned out the cries of the gulls overhead and all the best places were already filled. Although I hated to be seen, I tugged Mati to the front of the refectory, searching for a spot where I would be able to see and hear Aedon, and where there might be a scrap of shade for Mati in the worst of the heat. Some scowled as I passed in front of them, but Sitta took my other hand and stared them down while her husband and sons formed a protective arc behind us.

"Here," said an unexpected voice.

One of the village oyster tenders was scrambling to his feet. After the seeding, he would hang cypress branches under the rafts to catch the spat of the breeding oysters, and late in the fall, he would collect the babies and move them to cages where they would mature. His six braids showed his pearling rank. No one who lived in Ayr ranked higher than the tenders.

"Sit here," he offered, pulling his sputtering wife to her feet. She was the wife of a tender, and clearly felt it was her right to sit in the afternoon shade. Mati hesitated. I wanted to hide behind my hair, but the tender was looking directly at me.

"Please," the tender gestured again, quickly rolling their mat. "May Suna be with you."

Mati bowed her gratitude.

"May Suna reward your kindness," she spoke sincerely.

The wife bobbed her head with a sullen pout, but the tender bowed earnestly, first to Mati and then to me, and pushed the woman off to find another spot.

The vacated place was just big enough for two. Mati looked helplessly at Sitta, but dear Sitta just shoved her good-naturedly and strutted off with her husband and sons to settle contentedly in the sun. I sat beside Mati, feeling as if every eye were on me, but one advantage to sitting in front was that I didn't have to look back at them.

Moments later, a bright nasal note floated down to the beach from the village temple.

"O blessed Suna, come among us!"

In a rustling whoosh, the whole village stood. Our voices rose in one great voice.

"O blessed Suna, grant us your wisdom!"

Tallis led the little procession, followed by the stork-like Onald with the brazier. Then Kes in his ceremonial robe with the broad pearl collar, and Aedon behind him. They chanted the rest of the biddings together.

"O blessed Suna, be present among your devoted people."

"O blessed Suna, bless us with your radiant gifts," the village responded.

I forgot any sense of self-consciousness as the chanting continued, surrounding me in a sea of sound. The procession passed and made a full circuit around the fane. I could hear Aedon clearly above Kes and Tallis.

"O blessed Suna, cleanse this place for your habitation."

"O blessed Suna, make it worthy of your gifts."

When they reached the door, the chanting stopped. Onald set the brazier on the bottom step, and Tallis sprinkled spices and incense on the coals. A thread of fragrant smoke rose up, and we lifted our hearts and sang.

It is true that singing in voices was a special gift, and singing to the pearls was sacred, but it shouldn't be thought that no one else in the village sang, albeit in the ordinary manner. They sang planting songs while sowing the seeds and harvest songs while reaping the crops. They sang lullabies for their babies and threnodies for the dead. They sang lessons for their children and stories at their hearths. And most of all, they sang hymns on the prayer days and paeans at the festivals, weaving harmonies to the gods. I joined in this singing as heartily as anyone, and I could see Aedon adding his voice with enthusiasm.

After the first paean, Onald opened the door and moved the brazier to the threshold. More prayers were chanted. Then Tallis took the brazier inside with Kes behind him. Onald closed the door again, leaving himself and Aedon outside. We all sang energetic hymns while in the fane, Kes and Tallis droned their prayers to Suna, Skira, Tol, and Nazha, consecrating the birthplace of pearls. Wisps of smoke leaked out through the walls, showing their passage down one end and up the other.

This continued for an hour or so. Then Kes and Tallis emerged with more petitions and responses, and the procession returned up the slope to the temple. The fane was now cleansed and ready for the calling of the goddess in the afternoon. But first we would eat.

Once Kes and Tallis had disappeared through the temple gate with Aedon and Onald, the crowd dissolved into happy chatter and pulled out their dinners. People moved about freely, visited with friends and neighbors, and shared their food with everyone. Mati and I remained on our mat, but I heard the offers all around.

"Rice and egg?"

"Pork with leeks?"

"Chicken with walnuts, Sitta?"

Sitta grinned as she sat and offered Mati her dinner bowl. It was filled with bits and scraps from different people.

"Try some of this peppery fish," she offered, spooning some into Mati's bowl. Her husband and sons stood above us like guards. "And Amalisa, you'd like this—"

"Roasted rabbit, Aedon?" spoke the hunter sitting behind me.

"Cheese with chives, Aedon?" proffered the net maker's wife to my left.

He bounced down beside me, perching birdlike on his heels. He beamed as proudly as if he had consecrated the fane himself.

"An excellent day," he exclaimed and shoved his brimming bowl at me. It was overflowing with offerings from half of the village. "What's in yours?" he demanded without embarrassment, lifting it out of my hands. Then before I could answer, he leaned to my ear and whispered impishly, "Now isn't this better than hiding in the bushes?"

I must have turned the hue of mahogany as I pulled away, for Sitta's husband and sons took a warning step closer as if they thought Aedon were threatening me. Aedon laughed and sat back with a casual wave of his hand, and they moved away uneasily. I hid behind my hair.

"Where's Kes?"

He sampled Mati's honeyed duck with ramps and garlic and made appreciative noises.

"He's resting until the calling begins," he mumbled through a mouthful. "That gives me an hour."

Self-conscious, I stared at the bowl he had given me. Mati touched my hand.

"We're delighted you can join us," she welcomed Aedon. "More duck?"

He held out my bowl with a smile.

"It's as good as my mother's," he told her warmly.

She glowed at the compliment.

"I'm happy that it pleases you."

He leaned toward me confidentially.

"It's fancier than anything Kes ever makes."

I swayed back, startled.

"Kes cooks?"

"Of course he cooks," Aedon laughed. "I even help, a little. Mostly scrubbing vegetables. I'm not really much of a cook. My Mati and sisters did all that."

I tried to imagine Kes with a carving knife in his hand. I couldn't do it.

Aedon took another huge bite and openly regarded the colorful crowd. People milled and shared, and bits of food kept finding their way into our bowls. I lost track of all the different things I sampled while Aedon chatted amiably with Mati and Sitta. Sitta's sons and husband relaxed into laughter at his lighthearted jests. Even I began to enjoy myself and hardly noticed the sun making progress overhead. The shade of the refectory had just reached the edge of our mat when Aedon stood up.

"May Suna bless your open hands," he thanked Mati.

"May Suna be with you for the calling," Mati replied.

He looked down, forcing me to raise my face.

"May Suna be in your heart, Amalisa."

"And may Suna be in your calling, Aedon."

I lowered my face as soon as he left, yet I noticed that the crowd had made space for Sitta and her family beside us. I had to admit, though, I preferred to think they respected me for being Aedon's friend rather than for being the girl who earned Xander a beating.

*   *   *

The afternoon was much like the morning. Biddings, responses, prayers, and song. Except that it was hotter. Compared to the energetic morning, the hours felt long and drowsy. My mind seemed to wander while I watched the procession making the circuits around the fane. When Kes and Tallis lifted their arms and led the prayers to summon Suna, I rose to my feet with everyone else, but my eyes were fixed on the careful stitches around the neckline of Aedon's robes. My voice seemed to float through the top of my head, and the pearly cotton got whiter and whiter....

It didn't feel like passing out. The world just faded into light—light suffused with color, sweet flowery fragrances, and music. It was the music of the water, the wind, the forest—all the sounds I had listened to, echoed, and loved all my life—but marvelously blended in harmonies of such beauty that it crowded my heart with wonder. A gentle presence seemed to lift me, above our mat, above the crowd, above the beach. I felt as if I were looking down from a wondrous height, seeing into Aedon, into Kes, into the hearts that they offered so openly to the goddess—even into my own open heart. Then I felt myself descend like mist into the wind, into the fane, into the dark and secretive space where the pearls would be born.

"Liise?"

The music faded as Mati's voice filtered into my brain. Her tone was hushed, as if she thought I had fallen asleep.

"Liise?"

I blinked back into my own body and found myself slumped against Mati's side, supported by her maternal arm. I straightened with that absurd chagrin of having been caught dozing off when I shouldn't. But other than Mati, no one noticed. Everyone else was noticing Aedon, who seemed to have fainted in front of the fane.

The chanting had stopped and the crowd was silent. No one moved. Kes was kneeling at Aedon's side, touching his hand, while Tallis wiped a moistened cloth across Aedon's brow and Onald hovered anxiously. Before I could even consider movement, Aedon abruptly bolted upright, shaking his head and rubbing his eyes. He looked distinctly dazed.

"What—?" he started, then realized where he was. His eye caught mine—I couldn't help it—and in his glance was the same amazement as in my mind. Whatever it was that I had felt, he had felt it, too. He reddened and awkwardly tried to get up. Tallis helped him to his feet, and without a word, Kes rose beside him. Together they turned to face the fane and resumed the prayers where they had left off.

Mati looked from Aedon to me, and her voice was distracted throughout the final hymn of the day. Clearly aware of the stir he had caused, Aedon kept his eyes on the ground as the procession returned at last to the temple.

Immediately, bursts of excited speculation broke out among the villagers. Had the singer's apprentice merely fainted? Or had he been touched by the goddess herself when she entered the fane? The questions would richly spice their supper.

Mati exchanged a sharp glance with Sitta.

"We're leaving."

We never stayed for the music and dancing that would continue long into the night, but we usually ate before leaving. Sitta's sharp eyes grazed me before she nodded without further question.

"Suna grant you a peaceful night."

Mati rolled up our mat and tucked it firmly under her arm. She picked up our food basket, took my hand, and headed home. Briskly.

Halfway there, she stopped on the deserted path.

"What was that?" she demanded bluntly.

I cringed. She was angry. I wasn't sure why.

"I don't know."

But I knew what she thought. And I was pretty sure she was right. She heaved a sigh.

"Kes should be told," she challenged me.

I hung my head. From down on the beach came the babble of voices as our neighbors chewed over the day's events along with their supper. From the forest sighed the evening breeze, lifting my hair away from my cheek. No one knew I had the gift except Mati and Aedon. But if Suna had touched me, the gift was no longer mine to hide. I buried my face against Mati's skirts.

"Will you go with me?" I mumbled into her softness.

At once, her protective arm encircled me.

"Of course, my love. Of course I will."

I pulled in a breath filled with cedar and salt.

I could no longer see any reason to wait.

*   *   *

It was clear that Kes already knew. Before my foot even touched the ornamental flagstone in front of Kes's house, Aedon opened the door. He didn't look happy.

"May Suna guide you wisely," said Mati brusquely.

"May Suna's favor rest upon you," Aedon mumbled as he stood aside.

Mati marched me past him.

"I think Suna's favor has been lavishly bestowed already."

I had never been in the singer's house before. To my left, though a door in the cedar wall, was a whole separate room for the cooking hearth. Beyond the door, the wall was hung with scrolls, some simply painted, some bearing symbols that must have been words. Beneath them was a spruce-wood altar with a statue of Suna, Mother of Wisdom, with skin of polished walnut and robes of iridescent nacre. Flanking the altar were two chairs, with their backs to the wall, and in front of it lay a thick mat on the floor. To my right, shuttered windows extended from the wooden floor to the cedar beams. In front of me, a pair of doors stood open to a second room where I saw a lamp on a stand, a real bed covered with a woven white blanket, and Aedon's pallet rolled beside it. And off to my right, near the long shuttered windows, was a wide, low table with two carved chairs the proper size for the Curran resident.

And there he sat in his wave-patterned robe with his hands on his knees and his white eyes raised expectantly.

"Come here, child."

Mati gave me a little push. I stood before him.

"Amalisa."

I bowed my head.

"Yes, abuna."

"Amalisa, you have a gift."

I flushed with anger and whirled on Mati, but Kes forestalled me even before she could protest her innocence.

"No, Amalisa. Your mother has never betrayed your secret. You did that yourself, long before she even knew."

"But—" I sputtered.

His wrinkled face grew more creased with his smile.

"I may not be able to see, my child, but my hearing is excellent. And I still know my way around Ayr, and some of the paths in the forest around it."

I heard my heart pounding. He already knew I could sing in voices. He'd known it for years.

"But then why—?" I wasn't even sure what to ask.

"Why didn't I take you from your mother and make you study to be a singer?"

I swallowed unhappily.

"Yes."

"Child," he said kindly, shaking his head. "No one can force you to be a singer."

"Then why is Aedon here," I blurted, "instead of in his own village?"

Instead of answering, Kes inclined his face toward Aedon, who was standing next to Mati.

"Aedon. Come here."

Obedient, he stood beside me. His jaw was clenched at the hint that he might not have had to leave his family.

"Master," he managed.

"There are many answers to your question. One is that the singer in Cant is too young to train another singer. When he began to work with Aedon, he sent word to Darcy to ask the Master Singer to find him another teacher. And I was looking for just such a child."

"You were?" frowned Aedon.

Kes held out his palm, not to Aedon but to me. It was clear what he wanted. I gave him my hand and he pulled me closer, closing my hand between both of his. They were gnarled but gentle, the skin as soft as peony petals.

"I was seeking a student of Aedon's age. Of your age, Amalisa. Because you needed a friend your age, a friend with your gift, a friend like you."

Aedon's scowl deepened with confusion. Even Mati looked surprised. I pulled back my hand in disbelief.

"You brought Aedon here—because of me?"

Aedon recoiled with a wounded gasp, but Kes remained unruffled.

"Not just because of you, Amalisa. Aedon also has the gift, and the desire to serve the goddess. To become a singer, he would have had to leave his village anyway. But it was Suna who sent him here, to Ayr, to learn from me and to be your friend. And it was Suna who touched you today, who has chosen you to serve her, who is calling you to sing for her. Both of you. Together."

I felt slightly faint. My experience at the fane—I hadn't just dreamed it in a moment of drowsiness. The goddess had actually come to me, sung to me, lifted me up, and taken me into the fane with her. And the sensation of seeing into Aedon's heart...and Kes's.... It was a lot for my mind to grasp.

"You felt it, too?"

Kes sighed back into his chair and his blind eyes seemed to scan the past.

"There are no more than a few hundred Currans in all of Pini, and not all Currans have the gift. During my lifetime, I have worked with twenty or thirty who've had the gift, and not all of them have been called by Suna. Oh, yes, I have felt it, every time. But I've never felt two called at once before, nor quite so young."

I heard his words, but all I really grasped was that I was called to be a singer. I'd have to leave home. I'd have to leave Mati.

I just couldn't do it. I turned and fled into Mati's arms.

I heard Kes rise to his feet behind me. Afraid he would come for me then and there, I turned and saw the concern that creased his brow. Aedon gaped in disbelief, Mati stiffened protectively, and their words tumbled out on top of each other.

"Is she going to live here, too, now?" gasped Aedon, indignant.

"You'll never take her!" growled Mati with determination.

The anxiety cleared from Kes's brow as he understood our fears.

"No one is going to take her, Tirsa. And no, she is not going to live here, Aedon. She does not even have to study to be a singer. But if she does, she can still live at home, at least as long as I am her teacher."

His senses seemed to grope for me. I faced him but didn't leave Mati's arms.

"Amalisa," he told me, "I know what you felt at the fane. I have never known Suna to call one who could not serve her well. But only you can choose to serve her. Only you can decide if you truly want to become a singer."

Then all of them looked at me.

I wanted to hide behind my hair. I wanted to hide behind Mati. I wanted to run home and hide in my bed. But as I looked from Mati to Aedon to Kes, I knew I couldn't hide from Suna. I closed my eyes and remembered the feeling of being lifted, of being in the goddess's presence, of hearing the music the way she heard it. I suddenly realized I wanted all of that again. I wanted to be with Suna again. I wanted to please her. I wanted to serve her.

I wanted to sing.

"I do," I answered.

I just wasn't sure yet what that meant.

"Amalisa." Kes leaned forward in his chair and pinned me with his sightless eyes. "Do you want to become my apprentice?"

I looked at Aedon as I answered.

"Not unless you can have two apprentices."

With that, Aedon's tension escaped with a sigh and he finally smiled, even before Kes gave me his answer. Kes nodded approvingly.

"Yes, Amalisa. With the Master Singer's approval, I can have two apprentices."

"And I have to be able to stay with Mati," I added in a belligerent tone.

"Yes, Amalisa," Kes further assured me. "You can live with your mother and come to the temple for your training."

I breathed through my nose. If I chose to do this, my life would change. I would have to be seen, and I'd have to learn not to be afraid. I wasn't sure I could do it.

But then I looked at Mati. Her soft dark eyes were full of love and confidence. With Mati behind me, I could be brave.

I looked at Aedon. He looked dazed and exhausted and none too sure about any of this. But when his eyes met mine, they softened. Despite the confusion and disconcerting revelations, Aedon would still remain my friend. With Aedon's friendship, I could learn to let people see me as I was.

Kes's feathery eyebrows rose, as he patiently awaited my answer. Maybe his eyes were closed to the light, but I suddenly knew that he saw a different light altogether and he heard a more magnificent music. With Kes to teach me, I could learn to see that light and hear that music. With Kes's help, I could be a singer.

With a quaver of trepidation, I made my choice.

"Then yes. I will."

*   *   *

Nothing was said until after the seeding. Not even to Sitta. Kes said there were arrangements to make with the Master Singer in Darcy, which would take a fortnight at least. I was relieved by the delay. I needed time to absorb what had happened.

The day after the consecration of the fane, I slept all morning. I don't think I had ever been so tired. Mati couldn't even stir me. When I finally got up and washed, she looked at me as if I were someone unexpected at the door. She fed me silently and watched me drag myself out the door. She knew I was headed for my beach.

Aedon was lying on the sand, flat on his back, sound asleep. I touched his knee.

"Aedon?"

He woke with a start, jolted upright, shook his groggy head to clear it, and focused at last on my anxious face.

"Oh, Liise," he sighed, and threw his arms around my neck. "I thought you wouldn't come."

My arms wrapped around him.

"And I was afraid you'd be angry."

He pulled away.

"Angry? Why?"

"*You're* Kes's apprentice," I winced. "I don't want to make that less for you."

"Less?" he echoed. "Oh, Liise. How could you possibly make it less? You've made it more. Now we can learn to sing together, right out in the open. No more hiding."

No more hiding. My brows pinched together and he saw my fear. He placed his palm against my cheek, right over the mark, exactly as Mati so often did. I almost flinched.

"It'll be fine. You'll see. This won't matter anymore."

That was more than I could believe. But I had to try. I pulled in a breath and turned my thoughts to something else.

"Aedon," I said. "Yesterday, before you fell, what did you feel? What did you see? What did you hear?"

He sat back and laughed at my rush of questions.

"Oh, Liise," he grinned. "This is going to be amazing! We'll be the two youngest singers in Pini!"

Little did we know.

*　　*　　*

The seeders arrived that evening, and for the next five days, they seeded the pearls. I watched for a few hours from the laurels, content to observe while Aedon assisted. Mati sat with me all that morning, as if she were afraid the goddess would snatch me away while she wasn't looking.

"There," she pointed as the first ten women came out of the refectory after their breakfast. "Those are the seeders."

They were hardly any older than me, all wearing pearl-white shifts with creamy white girdles. Their hair was plaited in ten long braids to show their status, and they kept their heads down, not meeting the eyes of the curious villagers gathered at the edge of the beach, held off by the pearling guards in their blue-and-white armor. Even the guards were women. The only men on the beach were Aedon, holding the brazier for the offering spices, and Kes, singing the special seeding songs as the seeders proceeded into the fane. Someday Aedon would sing those songs. And so would I.

"And those are the trimmers," Mati continued as the next ten girls came out of the refectory. These were my age, more or less, with blue girdles and eight braids. I had no idea what trimmers did, but they followed the seeders into the fane.

Mati didn't have to point out the divers. They were close to twenty years old, I judged, with bright white girdles and six braids. They strode to the water and swam to a raft that had been towed close to shore the previous evening, swimming out to bring the oyster cages in to shore. They all swam to the same raft.

"They'll go to the same raft all day," observed Mati, "then a different raft tomorrow. Every day a different raft. Five days, five rafts. Next year, five different rafts."

I watched them disappear beneath the water and surface again, each towing an oyster cage to shore. At the water's edge, each cage was placed on a mat where four little girls, even younger than me, wearing four braids and girdles of gray, sat to clean the barnacles and seaweed from the oysters' shells. Clean oysters went into the buckets, beautiful blue enameled vessels with bright brass handles, which the divers passed through hinged panels into the fane. When the buckets came out, the oysters were returned to their cages and towed back to their raft. Back and forth, in and out, to the rhythm of the pearling songs, like wind and water over the women, the oysters, the fane....

"Liise," called Mati through the drifting sounds of Kes's song, of wet feet on sand, of scraping brushes on barnacled shells. I opened my eyes to the sparkle of sunlight slanting down through the spruce boughs overhead. "Come, my love," smiled Mati tenderly. "Let's go home and have some dinner. You can come back this afternoon."

Like a little child, I held her hand as we walked away. But just before the trees blocked my view, I looked back at the beach. Back and forth went the divers and cages. In and out of the fane went the oysters. I didn't know what happened in there, but someday, I would. I would learn the rituals, the spices, the songs—all the secrets of the seeding.

I smiled to myself.

Aedon and I would learn them together.

* * *

After the five days of seeding, the women left. In the progression up the coast, the next pearling village was Cant, and Aedon was allowed to send greetings to his family with the captain of the guard. Then workers came to dismantle the buildings and take them to another village.

A week after that, word came back from Darcy. Kes's request for a second apprentice had been granted.

The next morning, I rose with grasshoppers in my stomach. I dressed in the white shift and gown that Mati and I had made since the consecration of the fane. She walked with me down to the village temple. I tried to hold my head up high as people watched, but the habit of hiding was strong, and I couldn't help keeping my eyes down. Some people spoke respectful greetings, and some cast Suna's blessings like flowers in my path. At the temple gate, Mati kissed my brow and tried to keep her tears from showing. Aedon was standing on the flagstone in front of Kes's door with an enormous grin on his face. I took a deep breath.

Then I walked through the gate to become a singer.

Chapter 4: The Harvest

The months that followed were the best in my life. I had my singing, I had my Mati, and I had Aedon. I was openly learning to be a singer and no longer had to hide my gift. I no longer had to hide my face.

Every morning after breakfast, I went to the temple for lessons with Aedon. He was so far ahead of me in learning the prayers I thought I would never catch up. The prayers were in Pinian, so it wasn't that I couldn't understand them, but there were just so many of them, and they were so long.

In the voices, however, I wasn't behind at all.

"I know you can sing in voices," Kes told me the very first morning. He had taken us into the little fenced garden beside his house. It seemed a peculiar garden to me, a scattering of decorative plants, a path of irregular paving stones, some delicate trees. It wasn't a practical garden at all, not a thing to eat. It was simply beautiful, and I loved it.

We sat on a pair of white stone benches beneath a crimson maple tree no taller than the house. The lacy leaves spread above us in graceful planes, like dozens of hands that kindly sheltered us from the sun with their thousands of feathery fingers.

"I have heard you in the forest," smiled Kes. "You have head and throat and upper chest, and a decent range. We will begin by expanding your range with some exercises, one voice at a time."

He sang an exercise for the throat, going far deeper than I ever could, and nearly as high. It was one of the patterns Aedon had taught me.

"Let us begin with a part of that," he suggested, and sang the midmost half of the scale. Sitting beside me, completely silent, Aedon just grinned.

I repeated the notes, focusing on the round, clear tone, using the voice of a lark at dawn. Kes's feathery brows rose slightly.

"I see," he observed with the hint of a smile. "How far can you go?"

I thought Aedon would burst trying not to laugh. I closed my eyes so my notes wouldn't break into giggles, and sang the full exercise, middle to bottom and middle to top. I couldn't go nearly as low as Kes, but I almost made up for it at the high end. For the lower half, I used the voice of an autumn wind in the thatch of our roof, and for the upper, the voice of a fox.

"Of course," he nodded, turning his knowing white eyes on Aedon. "You have taught her well. And you," he added, returning to me, "have been teaching him, too. I noticed the change some time ago."

It pleased me that Kes could hear that difference in Aedon's voice, and in mine. He straightened briskly.

"Your range is good. But we can still expand it. And there is much you have yet to learn. Agility. Volume." He turned again to Aedon. "Now you. The same exercise, please. As exactly like Amalisa as possible."

Aedon composed himself and obeyed. It was very nearly the same as mine, but his wind was more playful and his fox was distinctly more male. I watched Kes tip his head to listen.

"Now together."

We did. It wasn't quite what I had done on my own, nor Aedon either, yet the sounds we made were completely indistinguishable from each other. A glimpse of surprise crossed Kes's face.

"Interesting," he mused to himself. "Yes. Very interesting indeed." But he said no more, and following Aedon's example, I remained silent and asked no questions.

"Well, then." He placed his hands on his knees. "Let us talk about chanting the prayers. Chanting is not singing. There are important differences."

I listened attentively, but in one corner of my mind, I wondered what Kes had found so unusual in our song.

It would be some time before I found out.

*   *   *

What I lost in those months was my mornings with Mati. I missed them. In the afternoons, I still helped with the sewing, did the weeding, collected ripe vegetables, gathered the eggs. Mati was fit to bursting with pride, but I knew she missed me. She asked with interest about my training, but at night when we made our devotions, I often caught her looking at me as if I would go up smoke with the spices we sprinkled on the hearth. And whenever she hugged me, she held me tighter than before.

I still met with Aedon at our beach. We practiced our voices, from shrilling cicadas to thundering waterfalls, simply to make each other laugh. We practiced the Morning Song and the Evening Song, which I had completely memorized. I started to go to the water each day, at sunrise and dusk, to listen to Kes. Soon it was part of my daily routine, part of my training, part of my life. I could hear the songs in the water, in the wind, in my sleep.

"I am pleased," Kes told me one morning at our lesson, "that you have been coming to hear the songs."

"Thank you, Master." I had grown used to calling him that.

"When you listen," he continued, "what do you hear?"

This surprised me. What did he expect me to hear? I tried to think of everything I heard in the songs.

"I hear you singing, Master. I hear your voices and where they come from. The Curran words and what they mean...."

"What else?"

All right. More than the songs. I inhaled the air of Kes's garden, growing sharp with an edge of autumn, fragrant with the creeping thyme that grew between the paving stones.

"I hear the water. The gulls. The forest birds. The wind on the sand and in the trees. I hear the fishermen at their boats and the women at their work. I hear children. A cat. An eagle. Rain."

He waited a moment. Above our heads, a warbler fluted in the scarlet maple.

"What else?"

I looked at Aedon. He raised his brows. He didn't know what Kes was looking for, either. Kes appraised our silence.

"Tell me, Amalisa, what do you listen for when I sing?"

"I listen for the way you sing it. For how you make the different voices. For the pitches and the tones. I listen for the way you pronounce the Curran words."

"And what do you listen for through the songs?"

Through the songs?

"The birds and wind and water, Master?"

"You hear a great many sounds, Amalisa, but those are all outside the songs. What do you listen for *through* the songs?"

Through the songs. If there was one thing I thought I knew how to do, it was listen. But listening *through* the songs? Aedon looked just as stumped as I was.

"I'm sorry, Master. I don't think I know how to listen through the songs."

"Aedon?"

He hung his head.

"No, Master."

Kes's expression softened.

"Then I will teach you."

"Master," dared Aedon, "what are we to listen *for*?"

Patient with Aedon's impertinence, Kes answered, "You will learn to listen for the oysters. And the pearls. And Suna."

My pulse quickened and the words just leaped out.

"Can you hear Suna when you sing?"

"Not always, Amalisa. But often."

A heat like longing rose in my breast and came out as passion in my voice.

"Like what happened at the fane?"

He stroked the woven lap of his robe.

"Like and unlike. But this you will have to discover for yourself. I cannot say how you will experience the goddess, or even if you will at all. I can only teach you how to listen."

"Now, Master?"

He smiled indulgently.

"Yes, Amalisa. If you can refrain from further questions?"

I straightened compliantly, as did Aedon beside me on our bench, and tried to quell my eagerness.

"Yes, Master," we answered in unison.

"Then close your eyes," he instructed, "and we will begin."

*   *   *

So I learned a whole new way to listen. Inside. During our lessons, we practiced the method of listening, and during the songs, we both went with Kes and tried to hear something, anything, through the singing, through the water, through our hearts. I experienced nothing, however, except a sense of strain and frustration. It was hard to be patient with the goddess.

Meanwhile, autumn was painting the willows gold in the forest, and the nights grew chilly enough to bring out the first set of winter blankets. A packet of cloth came to Kes from Darcy, and Mati and I spent a month making white quilted jackets for Aedon and me. Kes donned a second long-sleeved robe, overlapping in front, with long wide sleeves. When the fiery leaves of the maple fell, he moved our lessons inside from the garden to the table in his house and turned our studies to the prayers and rituals of the midwinter harvest of the pearls.

The harvest was the other annual pearling festival. Villagers brought their best winter clothing to Mati for repair. The rice merchant's daughter brought her eldest child, a boy of six with an arrogant pout, to be measured for a new-made jacket. And another length of cloth appeared for a white ceremonial robe—for me. It was to be exactly like Aedon's, and I worked on it just as carefully.

My days were full. Too full perhaps. I rose early for the singing at dawn. I had extra sewing and had to help Mati gather our crops. I had lessons with Kes, and I still met with Aedon two or three afternoons a week. And on top of all that, I was turning my attention inward to try to sense something through the songs.

Maybe that's why I wasn't paying enough attention when we walked back to Kes's house one autumn evening. It had started to rain, just enough to tame Kes's wispy silver hair and keep our heads down while we crossed the white gravel courtyard to his house. His hand was on Aedon's shoulder as usual, but Aedon was lagging as I dragged my feet.

"I just don't understand," I complained. "I haven't felt anything through the songs."

"Neither have I," Aedon echoed my discouragement. "I don't really know what I'm listening for."

Kes knew where he was—he had walked this route for dozens of years—but he was distracted by our complaints.

"Children," he started as he stepped on the flagstone outside his door. "You cannot hear the goddess with your ears." He released Aedon's shoulder to reach for the latch. "You must listen with your—"

I was so lost in my brooding mood that only a tiny part of my brain saw his foot rise short of the rain-slick step. Before I could realize what I was seeing, he stumbled sideways, away from Aedon, away from me, and fell on his side on the hard, wet stone.

"Master!" we cried, diving forward to raise him up.

"No!" he gasped, holding up a warning hand. It hadn't seemed like a heavy fall, yet he lay as tense as a startled cat and his face was clenched in a spasm of pain. "Don't lift me, children. Bring Tallis. And Onald."

Without a word, Aedon sprinted across the courtyard to Onald's house while I crouched beside Kes, bending over to shield his face from the rain.

"Master?" I whispered, afraid. In the twilight, every sound in the courtyard seemed amplified. I could hear Aedon knocking at Onald's door, his panting message, the crunch of Onald's feet on the gravel as he hurried to Tallis's house, which stood between Onald's and the temple. Kes lay breathing quietly, his hand still raised to ward us off.

Aedon returned and dropped beside me.

"They're coming, Master," he said as if saying so could help.

It was now raining steadily, pattering down on the rooftops, the gravel, the trees in the gardens. I heard Onald's knock, his urgent whisper, more crunching of feet. Tallis kneeled beside Kes across from me, with Onald hovering stork-like at his shoulder.

"Kes," he spoke calmly. His breath was scented with chicken, onion, and coriander. He had been in the middle of his supper. At the sound of his voice, Kes relaxed.

"Tallis."

"Are you injured?"

"I believe I broke something."

Tallis scanned Kes's body, his face, the way he was lying on the stone. His voice was quiet.

"We're going to take you inside."

"Yes," answered Kes.

Tallis nodded to Onald, who moved around Kes to crouch opposite Tallis, supplanting Aedon and me. We stumbled backward, suddenly superfluous, while they slid their hands under Kes and carefully lifted him. He looked absurdly small between them. I jumped up the step and opened the door.

Aedon ran ahead and drew back the bedding. They laid him down so gently only a crease between his brows betrayed the pain he must be in.

"Onald," said Tallis, removing Kes's sandals. "Go fetch Zenaida."

Onald bowed and flew out the door. I understood why Tallis didn't send Aedon or me—with his long legs, Onald could get there and back far faster than we could—but I needed to do something useful.

"Here," I offered, holding out my hands for the sandals. Silently, Tallis gave them to me. I carried them out to the mat by the door.

"Aedon," I heard him say behind me. "We must get him into something dry."

I went to the kitchen. Like ours, the hearth was raised in the center of the room, though not as high. Also, its stones were dressed and smooth, and there was a bellows with copper handles to fan the coals. Since I still ate my meals at home, I had never seen Kes make anything but tea. I set water to heat and looked for something to brew.

"It's here," said Aedon, fetching a box of dried anise and mint. "This is his favorite." He held the box against his chest, looking as if it were Kes's ashes.

"What were you going to eat tonight?"

He glanced up from spooning the herbs into a cup, and tears filled his eyes.

"I don't know."

"Oh, Aedon." I hugged him and he pressed his cheek into my shoulder. His sea aroma was sharp with fear. I thought how much worse this must be for him. In Ayr, Kes was his family. I collected myself.

"Well, what do you have?"

He dug through the baskets for carrots, a cabbage, some eggs, and rice. I sat him at the washtub to scrub the carrots, and put the rice on to boil.

When Zenaida arrived with her basket of remedies, Onald took her straight through to the bedroom. I was surprised to see Mati with them. She cast me a single worried glance before the door closed.

I cooked. I didn't know what else to do. The kitchen was filled with starchy steam and the pungent bite of onions, garlic, and spicy peppers when Mati emerged. We froze as she came into the kitchen. Her eyes smiled wearily.

"He'll be all right. His hip is broken, and that will take a long time to heal, but he's in no danger."

I rushed to her arms. A heartbeat later, so did Aedon. She held us both, kneeling on the kitchen floor, breathing relief into our bones.

"Is there tea?" she asked, rising.

Aedon poured. She took it to the bedroom, then returned to stir my shredded cabbage and thinly sliced carrots. She had to stoop a little at the hearth, and I suddenly noticed how well I fit in Kes's kitchen, a kitchen built for Currans.

The meal was cooked and ready to serve by the time Zenaida came out. I knew her solid figure, her beaky nose, her gull-gray braid, for she often visited our house to trade healing oils for herbs that wouldn't grow in her forest garden. She had the rich loamy smell of mulching leaves and shaded ferns. She came directly to Aedon and me. Her voice was rusty, as if she seldom used it.

"He wants to see you. Both of you."

Kes lay beneath the woven blanket, wearing a soft white cotton shift. His hair had dried and was fluffed rather wildly over the pillow. I could smell the cedary scent of valerian, the tincture Zenaida used for pain. I noticed an altar against one wall, with clothing chests on either side. On one of the chests were phials, a cup, and a flagon of Zenaida's sweet plum wine. Tallis closed the door behind us.

"Master. We're here."

Kes's sightless eyes were languid from the valerian.

"Aedon." His voice was so easy he might have been telling us what we were going to study next. "You must sing the songs for me."

Aedon jumped back in refusal.

"But, Master, I'm not allowed—"

A wave of Kes's hand cut him off.

"I know you have been practicing them ever since you came to Ayr. Probably when you were still in Cant. And I daresay Amalisa knows them as well as you do by now."

We hung our heads. Aedon's protests weakened.

"But we're not supposed to know them."

I listened to Kes's quiet breathing, scented sweet and spicy with the plum wine and valerian.

"The songs are sacred. Not to be taken lightly. Do you take them lightly, Aedon?"

"No, Master," Aedon answered gravely. "But—"

Another dismissive wave of the hand.

"You are my apprentice. My assistant. You will assist me. The Master Singer will understand."

"Yes, Master," Aedon agreed reluctantly.

"And Amalisa, too."

I jerked to attention.

"Me, Master?"

"Why not you, Amalisa? Do you know the songs any less than Aedon?"

I cringed, remembering how hard we had worked.

"Well, I—"

"And is your voice any less than his?"

This I was not embarrassed to claim.

"No, Master. But—"

"My children, your resistance wearies me." He closed his eyes and breathed, slowly, deliberately. "Consider my age. My voice is strong. But you are young, and your voices are young. Neither alone would reach through the water. But together I believe they will. You both must sing."

"Yes, Master," we replied as one. The corners of Kes's mouth gave a twitch.

"Exactly so. Now leave me, children. I wish to sleep."

Mati and Zenaida were talking quietly in the kitchen, but Tallis and Onald had returned to their suppers. We ate the meal I had prepared. I didn't taste a single bite. Zenaida took some in to Kes, but he was already asleep. She left the bowl covered with a cloth on the side of the hearth in case he woke hungry. Onald would bring her a pallet and she would sleep on the floor in Kes's room, on the other side of the bed from Aedon.

Aedon saw us to the door. It was raining hard now, straight and steady. In the temple courtyard, lights warmed the windows of Onald's and Tallis's houses, and a single lamp glowed in the depth of the temple. Mati waited on the flagstone while Aedon and I said goodnight. Except that we didn't say anything. We stood in the doorway, holding hands, excited and frightened. Tomorrow we would sing to the pearls. Alone. Together.

He closed the door. As Mati and I crossed the courtyard, I saw people gathered outside the gate in the heavy rain. They were bobbing their heads, muttering prayers, with Kes's name in every phrase. Word of his fall had already spread throughout the village.

They cleared a path as we emerged. The carpenter bowed. So did the rice merchant. All of them did. The rice merchant's son-in-law held up a lantern. Without a word, he lighted our path all the way home through the streaming rain.

*   *   *

I woke before dawn to the sound of birds in the purple plum and a brisk, cold wind in the rustling thatch. I lay for a while with crickets hopping in my stomach, worried that I would forget the words, mispronounce the Curran, misproduce the voices. I thought I would be sick.

It got worse when I left the house. There were people scattered along the path, not going about their usual business but waiting for me, to see me pass, to trail behind me, to hear me sing. I had barely been apprenticed for a single season, and I was going to sing to the pearls. I couldn't blame them for wanting to hear it, but I also couldn't help wishing they had all overslept.

Aedon was waiting at the gate, where a silent crowd had gathered. Like me, he was wearing his quilted white jacket. The morning was dawning crisp and bright, washed clean by the rain, with a sharp wind blowing cottony clouds across a sky of cerulean blue.

"How's Kes?"

"Better," grinned Aedon. "He said to stand up straight and tall."

It made me smile and eased my jitters.

"All right," I agreed. "We will."

Velvety cloud shadows chased each other across the strand as we walked to the water. The people trailed at a respectful distance, but still close enough to stretch my nerves. I inhaled deeply, as Kes had taught us, and tried to concentrate on the morning, on the water, on Aedon beside me. The sunrise glowed beyond the islands. Their black silhouettes were fringed with green against the brightening cobalt sky. I listened to the quiet bay, the haggling gulls, the impatient wind in the gold and crimson autumn leaves. My breathing grew calmer. So did Aedon's. We inhaled together and began.

Our voices flowed out like a single voice. We started with the throaty drone with just a hint of distant thunder, added the fluting upper voice, clear as a wren's, then the notes and words in the middle range, filled with the shimmer of sun on the water. The cloud shadows flickered across the bay, across the rafts, across my sight. Light and dark. Light and dark. Light and light and light and light....

Everything else seemed to fade away—the words from my brain, the sounds from my ears, the bay from my eyes. There was only the light, consuming my sight, filling my mind. And music, flowing out of the song, rising higher and sweeter, rumbling deeper, thrumming with oceans, typhoons, and whales. Then the vast, expansive presence of Suna, her patience, her wisdom, her swelling love. I heard nothing else, I felt nothing else, I wished for nothing more than this, than to be in the bliss of Suna's embrace.

Then something else. Something small and simple, dark and delicate, rocking in the gentle sea. Something responding to the song with a sense of well-being. Many of them. It was the oysters. And in their hearts, like shining secrets, the pearls. All bound in the swirl of Suna's song, in the blowing voices of wind and water, sun and sea. My heart expanded around them all, and I felt Aedon's heart flow into mine around the oysters, around the pearls. I could have been happy like that forever.

When the song ended, the oysters faded, the pearls slid away, and Aedon slipped back to the shape by my side. The light went kindly, like Mati's smile when the hearth-light vanishes into the night.

The world came back into my ears. I met Aedon's eyes. He had seen it, heard it, felt it, too. The light, the music, the oysters, the pearls. Suna. Everything. We looked back over the peaceful bay, where the islands now wore their emerald greens and the water sparkled blindingly beneath the rising sun. Time would restore Kes's broken hip, but Aedon and I had been changed forever. Suna had changed us, binding us to her and to each other. We turned and walked in unison between the people back up to the temple.

*   *   *

Zenaida stayed with Kes for a week, then visited daily for more than a month. Our lessons continued. There was still a lot to learn before the harvest. We brought a brazier to Kes's room and learned how to clean it, how to tell if the coals were ready, what spices were needed, and when to employ them in the rituals.

As autumn burned into the grays and browns of winter, we no longer went to our private beach. We didn't have time. We went instead to the farthest end of the pearling beach to practice our vocal exercises, and to cheer ourselves with the voices of Ayr. Over the water we sent the flutter of butterfly wings in the summer sun, the chitter of ground squirrels collecting nuts, the grumble of a winter bear disturbed in its sleep, and the joy of larks in the early spring. And our laughter.

For three whole months, Aedon and I sang every morning and every night. Suna didn't come every time. Only sometimes. I found that she came when Aedon and I were most attuned in our emotions. Sometimes Aedon was glowing with some success in our lessons that day, but I was tired from working late in the garden. Or I was excited because I had finished my new ceremonial robe, but Aedon was frustrated by a difficult part in the prayers to consecrate the fane for the harvest. On such occasions, she didn't come. Yet when we were equally joyful the day Kes took his first unaided steps again, or equally frightened when the harvest was suddenly only a fortnight away, the goddess came to us, lifting our spirits and binding us ever more closely to her, to each other, to the pearls. Yet goddess or no, every dawn and every dusk, we sang.

"I think I would like to come with you tonight," said Kes a week before the harvest.

Aedon jumped up in excitement, and I felt a blend of delight and dismay. Kes was ready to sing again! But I had grown used to the daily singing. No, not used to it. I had come to love it.

"Calmly, now, my boisterous child," he grinned as Aedon brought him his jacket. "I only want to hear you sing without the temple fence between us."

I was pleased and proud that he'd let us sing, and not at all nervous. The crowds no longer gathered to hear us—we'd lost our novelty within a fortnight—but it wouldn't have mattered to me anymore if half of Ayr had turned out to listen. Now I could lose myself in the song. I could sense the oysters in their cages even without the goddess's presence. And I could feel Aedon singing with me as if we had but one set of lungs, one throat, one mind. Nothing else mattered when we sang.

I washed my hands and fetched my jacket.

"I hope you'll be pleased by our singing, Master."

He smiled at us both as we opened the door.

"I have no doubt at all."

*   *   *

The army of slaves who came to assemble the pearling buildings was the same that had done it for the seeding six months earlier, though now they kept their shirts on to keep them warm against the raw midwinter wind. This time I wasn't hiding in the bushes to watch but walking with Kes for the Morning Song. Like Aedon, I wore the pearl-white ceremonial robe of a singer's apprentice, and proudly bore the weight of one of Kes's hands on my shoulder like a badge of honor. We must have looked quite the matched pair, with our freshly washed dark hair flowing down our backs to the waist, our crisp white robes, our hazelnut skin. Except for the mark on my face, of course, but I seldom thought of it anymore. Aedon was right—it no longer mattered.

After the song, we joined Tallis and Onald in the dance and sway of the growing foundation for the dormitory and blended our voices in the prayers. I hadn't quite learned them all, but no one noticed. Kes's step was slower now, but his powerful voice had not been diminished by the fall.

For three full days, we accompanied Kes in the building prayers. It was cold and damp on the pearling beach, but the sun shone clear, and the work went quickly. Up rose the sleeping hall, refectory, and fane, just as they had the previous summer. I watched each post, each plank, each beautiful panel being fitted into its proper place and was filled with a sense of its ritual rightness.

On the fourth day, the slaves departed and we blessed the fane. Without a qualm, I stood in front of all of Ayr through the morning of blessings, prayers, and songs. For the noontime meal, Aedon and I scampered back to Mati, who had been granted a place of honor, a full table in the refectory for herself and Sitta and Sitta's family. And late in the day, when Kes and Tallis chanted the prayer of bidding, summoning Suna into the fane, I was standing with Aedon, by Kes's side, when the goddess lifted us, filled us with song, and brought us with her into the fane. We had learned by now not to faint or fall when she came to us, and as our awareness of the world returned, both of us were smiling.

At dawn the next day, I dragged myself out of bed and down to the temple. Aedon could scarcely seem to haul himself out the door with Kes, and even Kes seemed asleep on his feet. I had never thought about how tiring it must have been for him to call the goddess into the fane. At the water, his voice seemed thin and weary. Aedon and I exchanged a glance behind Kes's back, and with one mind, joined our voices to his. Together, the three of us barely seemed equal to Kes on a normal day. But we struggled through the Morning Song, supporting each other to the end. After we stolidly marched back to the temple, Kes dismissed us to crawl back to bed. I strongly suspect he did the same.

I slept all day and certainly felt better rested when I returned to the temple that evening. Kes and Aedon both looked refreshed, and our steps had more spring as we walked to the water. On the fishing beach, the fishermen were hauling their boats up the sand, and the women were dragging out the nets, gutting the fish, spreading them on the racks to dry. Gulls screamed and squabbled over the scraps, and the guardian islands were dark as jade beyond the bay. Strong and clear, our voices reached across the water, over the rafts, down to the oysters. I felt the pearls, pure and secret, that soon would be harvested, sensed the cycle of birth and death in the ancient pearling, felt the blend of peace and sorrow in Suna's heart. With the ferocious joy of an eagle, the thrum of peace in a summer cricket, the mournful quaver of a dove, my voices soared out with Kes's and Aedon's, and in that moment, all was as it ought to be, and I was exactly where I belonged.

The final notes of the Evening Song floated over the water and faded into the winter twilight. We breathed as one and turned in step. The fishing beach was quieter now. Most of the fishermen and their families had finished their work and gone home to their suppers. I was only half startled to see a hundred women massed at the head of the pearling beach. The harvesters had just arrived, and instead of proceeding directly into the dormitory, it seemed they had stopped to hear our song.

I walked sedately up the beach with Aedon and Kes. The harvesting party was familiar, the very same women who had seeded the pearls in the heat of summer. Their robes were longer and warmer now, but the colored girdles and numbers of braids were all the same, as were the guards in their blue-and-white armor.

I also recognized other members of the group who came only for the harvest. There was an ox-drawn cart, heavily guarded by twenty men, that would carry the pearls back to Darcy. And behind the women, who traveled from village to village on foot, were five men on horseback. One of these was the pearl inspector, who came with the harvesters every year. His pearling rank of twelve braids was only seen in Ayr during the harvest. Another was the pearling scribe, a man of eight braids, who recorded the harvest in every village. They both wore garments of pearling white.

The other three men did not wear white. They wore knee-length coats of heavy raw silk, a dawn-sky blue, with collars and cuffs of a midnight hue trimmed with pearls and gems. Their hair was braided in tiny braids and threaded with pearls, creating hoods of shimmering nacre that hung to just above their shoulders. And above them on the evening breeze floated their banner, ocean blue with a single white circle, the pearl of Pini, in the center. They were Pinian princes.

As we walked toward them, I wasn't perturbed. At least one prince came to every harvest. I knew the eldest, for Prince Joron had been coming for the past ten years. In his middle thirties, he sat very tall and lean on his mount, with dark brown eyes that seemed to measure everything they rested on, and an olive complexion unblemished by labor or life in the elements. His features were refined but strong, and had long defined my mental standard of the princes' legendary beauty. He wore a pearl upon his brow, suspended from a silver band, for he was a priest dedicated to Suna, who had given the secrets of the pearls to the priest-prince Mannar hundreds of years ago.

Beside him, however, were two other princes I had never seen before. One of them was just past twenty, with quick dark eyes that didn't seem to rest at all. His features were broader than Prince Joron's, giving him a more boyish appearance. From his silver band hung a lump of amber, the size of a thumbprint, flat and irregular in shape. He kept leaning toward the youngest prince as if he wanted to tell him something, but our silent solemnity seemed to prevent him from speaking.

Yet it was the third I noticed most. Our passage released the women as if from a spell, and they filed in silence into the dormitory with their guards hovering around them. The wagon guards began to unload small white wooden chests and carry them up to the temple. But the men on horseback continued to watch us, especially the youngest. He alone of the three had no silver band, no colored stone upon his brow. He was fine-boned and delicate, surely no older than Aedon and me, with penetrating sea-colored eyes, now blue as an underwater cave, now green as the ocean before a storm, eyes that rested solely on me.

For a moment, the blood rushed hot to my face. I hadn't thought about the mark for months. Now, under the gaze of this beautiful youth, I felt as if it were burning my skin. I bent my head as I used to do, hiding behind my curtain of hair. Then a far worse thought occurred to me.

"Aedon," I whispered just as we entered the temple courtyard. In the failing light, I could hear the horsemen following us, the hooves of their horses making a sound seldom heard in Ayr. Aedon cast me a furtive glance behind Kes's back.

"What if they're angry?" I hissed.

"Who?"

"The pearl inspector. The scribe. The princes."

We turned together toward Kes's house and Aedon looked back at the five mounted men.

"Why would they be angry?" he asked, genuinely bewildered.

Kes's hands gripped our shoulders firmly as his feet touched the flagstone. Though the weather was dry, and Kes was wearing his winter clogs, he wasn't taking any chances.

"Don't you realize what we've done?" I whispered to Aedon.

Kes pushed the door open, stepped inside, and turned as if to bid me goodnight.

"We all sang," he said instead, swinging his face toward the horsemen coming through the gate. Few but Aedon and I could have heard the quiet note of concern beneath his words. "We all sang, my children."

And now we all stared as the riders passed us, approaching the temple. All of them watched us for a moment, then four looked ahead to where Tallis and Onald waited with a trio of boys to take the horses. Only the youngest continued to stare with his questioning eyes. Kes placed a reassuring hand on my head.

"Never fear. You are not to blame. If there is any fault to find, they will find it with me."

"No, Master, I—" But my words trailed off, forgotten, as I watched the royal party dismount. The youngest was smaller than I had expected, not even as tall as Prince Joron's shoulder. Tallis and Onald bowed profoundly, and Tallis made the greetings of welcome. I could see the riders reply with the blessings of guests, and could hear the musical tones of their voices, if not the words. The boys took the horses back out through the gate to stable them with the woodcutters' donkeys. No one in Ayr owned a beast as expensive as a horse, but at least the woodcutters knew how to feed them. Then Onald led the five of them to the guesthouse, which stood between Kes's house and the temple. It was the largest house in Ayr, even bigger than the rice merchant's. It had an upstairs.

They filed inside, following Onald, and Tallis returned into the temple. It was almost too dark to see them now, and nearly too dim for them to see us, yet the youngest prince lingered on the step, staring at me. I wanted to hide my face from him, but found I could not turn away. Finally, he followed his brothers into the house, and I breathed again.

"I guess princes don't need manners," snorted Aedon.

Kes suppressed a smile.

"Perhaps the prince has never seen such remarkable apprentices."

Aedon grinned.

"Just wait until they see us tomorrow!" Then he hastily added in a more suitably modest tone, "I mean, I hope we'll be a credit to your training, Master."

Kes laughed aloud.

"I suspect you would both be amazing even without me, my eager apprentice."

"Well, we won't be very amazing," I felt compelled to observe, "if we don't get some sleep."

"Quite so," agreed Kes. "But for the rest of the princes' visit, perhaps I had best sing the songs alone."

Aedon and I bowed obedient heads, but exchanged a silent grin between us. Singing with Kes had been divine. We could hardly wait to do it again when the harvest was over.

We had no idea how much things would change before then.

*   *   *

For the next five days, we were perfect apprentices. While Kes sang the special harvesting songs, I held the brazier and Aedon sprinkled the ritual spices. When the harvesters, princes, and pearling officials came down to the fane, I barely noticed the young prince's gaze, though he lingered the longest and entered last.

For five days the divers brought the cages from the rafts, the cleaners cleaned the oysters' shells, the buckets went in and out of the fane, and within the fane, the harvesters extracted the pearls. I now understood that these were the oysters that had been seeded three and a half years ago. This time, however, the oysters were not returned to their cages, but poured in lines at the end of the sand, line beside line, for a hundred feet along the water, and the screams of the gulls feasting on the expired oysters drowned out the songs Kes sang to bless them. And throughout the day, the pearls were taken on covered trays to the village temple for safekeeping.

By the end of it all, Aedon, Kes, and I were exhausted. When Kes sang the final pearling song to conclude the harvest, we barely had energy left for the Evening Song. Kes's hand on my shoulder was heavy that night, and yet I felt an intense satisfaction as we returned at last to Kes's house. We had done well. I had done well. I couldn't wait to go home to Mati, eat my supper, collapse on my pallet, and sleep like a rock.

But as we entered the temple courtyard, I could see it wouldn't be that simple.

In front of us in the temple porch stood Tallis, Onald, and all the visitors from Darcy.

"Oh," I breathed, abruptly alert.

Kes seemed to sense them. He didn't even turn toward his house, but continued straight to the temple steps. Supporting him on either side,

Aedon and I accompanied him. We must have looked very small to the Pinians standing in the porch.

"Suna's abundance be with you all," Kes greeted them calmly.

"And Suna's wisdom in your heart," returned Prince Joron, the one with Suna's pearl on his brow. His tone was stony, yet though he was clearly speaking to Kes, his measuring eyes were on Aedon and me.

"Your highness," Kes bowed. "Is there something amiss with the pearls?"

Tallis replied, his voice so gentle it frightened me.

"I think you should all come in and see."

We climbed the steps and entered the temple. Its vast pillared space and high wooden ceiling felt spacious and holy. At the far side was a wooden altar, ornately carved in swirling patterns of waves and dolphins, sails and pearls, all lacquered in polished blues and whites. The image of Suna that stood on the altar was robed in flowing greens and blues, with her bare brown arms upraised and a shining smile on her walnut face. At her feet lay an open scroll, a pot of ink, and a rack of pens with long white plumes. The scribe had been recording the harvest.

In front of the altar were two rows of lamps on tall brass stands, flanked by the guards who had come with the wagon. Between the lamps, on beautiful cross-legged trestles, sat twenty-one chests. The bands on twenty of them were silver, but the bands on the last were gleaming gold. More than half had sturdy locks, and I guessed that these had been filled at the previous pearling villages. The lids on the two nearest the altar were open, and as we approached in apprehension, I saw that the one with silver bands contained the pearls of Ayr, shimmering in the wavering light. Thousands of pearls. Thousands and thousands and thousands of pearls. I had never dreamed there would be so many.

Then I looked in the chest with the bands of gold, and even I could see what was different. Though the only pearls I had seen in my life were in Kes's ear and the princes' hair, I figured I knew how a pearl should look. These pearls were not the proper color. Within the chest were wooden trays, lined with silk. In one lay pearls of blushing pink. In another were pearls the color of blue morning mist. In another, the gray of a rainy day. There were yellow and gold and black and green.

Tallis picked up a green one and placed it in Kes's hand. My belly sank. The green were the fewest, most likely the worst. The one he had chosen was large as a pea, though thankfully not nearly as green. Kes rolled the pearl between his fingers. He touched it with the tip of his tongue. He scraped it lightly against his teeth.

"Green?" he queried.

"Green," said Tallis.

Kes put out his hands and felt the trays. He felt the pearls in all of them, running his fingers as lightly over them as a breeze on a hot, still day. He left the green one Tallis had given him in the tray with the other green ones. He seemed to count them. I cringed in horror. Had Aedon and I polluted the pearls with our untrained singing? How would they punish us? My pulse was jumping, and I could hear Aedon's panicked breathing.

The guests from Darcy were staring at us. The midnight gaze of the youngest prince seemed to bore through my skin in quest of my secrets.

"Amalisa," spoke Kes with great control. "How did you learn the pearling songs?"

I heard Aedon swallow, but I was forthright.

"I asked Aedon to teach them to me. But we didn't sing them here. Not until you asked us to."

Four of the faces across from me seemed to twitch in disapproval. The youngest merely became more intent. Kes's tone remained quietly curious.

"What else did he teach you?

"Just the exercises you taught him. The exercises for the voices."

His white eyes seemed to focus on me.

"And what did you teach him, Amalisa?"

"Just to listen. To sing the sounds of the wind, and the forest, and the bay. Just—" I halted as they stared at me. Blessed Suna, was that what had ruined the pearls? The childish games we played with our voices? I thought I would faint.

"Yes," he mused. "That must be it." He touched my hand. I must have felt as cold as winter. His words were insistently reassuring. "You have done nothing wrong, Amalisa. I should have understood before. But leave us now. Aedon, too. Wait in my house. We," he gestured around the circle of adults, "must talk."

Aedon's hand was as cold as mine as we left the temple. Before we reached the porch, I heard the muffled voices behind us, soothing, astonished, demanding, uncertain, completely dumbfounded. We pressed together, shoulder to shoulder. Whatever we'd done, it must have been dreadful.

Outside, the moon had risen. In the middle of the courtyard stood a figure, breathing mist in the chill night air, but solid, straight, and comfortable.

"Mati!" I gasped, and we ran to her arms. She held us wordlessly. "Oh, Mati," I sniffled. "We didn't mean any harm."

"I'm sure you didn't," she tried to console us, walking us into Kes's house.

We made hot tea and waited.

Onald came an hour later. Without a word, all three of us followed. Only the chest of colored pearls was open now, like an accusation. Kes looked weary. It had been a long harvest for him, and an especially tiring evening. He hadn't even had supper yet. All the other faces were grim. Even the brows of the youngest prince were drawn together above his searching lamp-lit eyes.

"My children," said Kes.

After all three of us bowed our respect, Mati held back while Aedon and I approached the chest.

"Master," we answered.

Subtle expressions I couldn't read flashed over the faces of our guests, but Kes was smiling.

"My children. These pearls....these colors..." His hand swept over the trays of iridescent colors, soft pinks and roses, blues and grays, and the muted green. "These are the precious gift of Suna."

Of course they were. The treasure of Pini. And we had spoiled them. We hung our heads.

"We're sorry, Master. We didn't mean to damage them."

"Damage—" The word jumped out of him, magnified by a collective gasp from the other men. Even the young prince's brows leaped upward. "Damage?" Kes repeated weakly. "You have damaged nothing, children." He lifted a pearl of sunset rose. "Why a single pearl of pink or yellow is worth a hundred normal pearls. A black, two hundred. A gold, four hundred. And a green...well, the green ones are exceedingly precious."

I squinted into the chest of colors. Surely I wasn't hearing right.

"How can that be?" I stammered, confused. "There are so many."

"Yes," said the pearl inspector sternly. His voice was lyrical and deep, but not as rich and complex as Kes's. "How can there possibly be so many? In any village, we might expect a hundred or so of the pinks or yellows, but rarely more than a score or two of the blues or golds. And the greens...." Words failed him. "Yet here in Ayr, in a single harvest, there are thirty-seven green, and ninety-one gold, and—and—"

Prince Joron placed a calming fingertip on the pearl inspector's wrist.

"Enough," he said to the sputtering man. Then he turned his measuring eyes on us. "Amalisa. Aedon. We believe your unusual singing has somehow...enriched the pearls."

Enriched the pearls? Our singing?

"We would like you to come to Darcy to finish your training as singers."

Darcy? As they silently they waited for a response, it dawned on me what the prince was saying. I was too astounded to be polite, even to a prince.

"You mean *now*?"

Every face remained serious. I suddenly thought I would be sick. I could hardly hear my own voice.

"Now?"

"Not instantly," conceded the prince, his voice still cool. "Tomorrow your priest will dedicate the pearls to Suna, then we leave for Cant. My brothers," he indicated the younger princes, "can take you ahead to Darcy from there."

Aedon's breath sucked in beside me, and Mati gasped outright. Leave Ayr tomorrow? My stomach heaved.

"We had heard," spoke Joron, "that two apprentices were singing to the pearls of Ayr. We never expected this result." His graceful hand waved above the pearls. "We wish to see what will happen when you complete your training."

Aedon found his voice.

"But we haven't finished our training with Kes."

Joron glanced at Kes.

"It is true," agreed Kes, "that there is still much I have yet to teach you. But I believe Suna has other plans for you, my children. You have contributed something remarkable, and I do not know how to teach you to use it. I think you will have to go to Darcy for that. And even there," he added with a nuance of caution, "your gift may be unfamiliar."

The pearl inspector bristled at this.

"The Master Singer will know what to do."

Prince Joron cast a stony eye at the pearl inspector.

"Perhaps," he conceded. "But that will be for the Master Singer to determine, and only," he added to Aedon and me, "if you choose to go."

Aedon looked uncertainly at Kes, but I spotted the glint of eagerness in his eyes.

"Master..." he faltered.

"Aedon," smiled Kes. "You are free to go. And if you choose, you are free to come back."

Overwhelmed, Aedon seized Kes's hand.

"Thank you, Master," he managed. Then he turned to the prince, recalling his manners. He bowed very deeply. "Thank you, your highness. It would be an immeasurable honor to serve the goddess as a singer. I offer myself for whatever training is judged to be fitting."

Then he whirled in excitement, oblivious to our audience.

"Liise!" he whispered, gripping my arms. "Darcy! Just think of it! Studying with the Master Singer! We'll be—"

He stopped abruptly, chilled into silence, no doubt, by my face. I was staring at him in open horror. Pain washed through his eyes.

"Oh, Liise," he breathed. "Won't you come?"

I winced away. Aedon would go. He would leave me behind. I suddenly realized how much I loved him.

Kes reached out and touched my shoulder. His quiet voice was filled with affection.

"Amalisa. You have an extraordinary gift. But no one can take it. You must give it freely."

I twisted in pain to look for Mati, still waiting anxiously in the shadows. Kes felt the movement.

"Go to her, child."

Without even bowing to the princes, I went. Mati kneeled to meet me. Her arms closed around me almost as fiercely as mine around her.

"Hush now," she murmured, feeling me shake. "You don't have to go."

Tears burned down my cheeks. The goddess had called me, away from my Mati, away from Ayr.

"Oh, Mati," I wept into her neck. "I do. I must. I belong to Suna."

I felt her wince against my hair, then she held me away and tried to smile.

"Then go with pride, my gifted girl. You are Amalisa of Ayr, and always will be. You have already been honored by this invitation. And if you come back, you will always carry that honor with you."

I forced my feet to return to the trestles. Aedon beamed in anticipation, and Kes was smiling with satisfaction. Tallis and Onald looked smug with pride, as if they were somehow responsible for this triumph in Ayr, while the pearl inspector and scribe remained reserved. The middle prince's dancing eyes were alight with unexpected delight, while the youngest still seemed to be probing for something hidden. He was the hardest to ignore as I faced Prince Joron across the pearls. I bowed profoundly.

"Your highness," I dared, trying to imitate Aedon's polished speech. "I cannot see how I am worthy of this honor, but I will come to Darcy as you request."

Aedon trembled with jubilation. Kes actually bowed to me.

"You honor your teacher, Amalisa. Go with Suna's blessing."

I wanted to cry. Prince Joron nodded.

"Good," he declared. "Then may I suggest we all retire. It has been a long day, and tomorrow we leave."

With bows and blessings, we left them to secure the pearls. Once safely outside in the silvery moonlight, Aedon seized me in a massive hug.

"Oh, Liise!" he cried. "We're going to Darcy!"

Kes calmly pried Aedon's arms away.

"You will both bring honor to Ayr, my children. But for now, I think we should eat and sleep. Come, Aedon. You will cook for us tonight. Let Amalisa go home with her mother."

Aedon leaped and crowed to Kes's house. I supported Kes after him.

"My dear Amalisa," he sighed in parting at his door. "Surely you are beloved of the goddess. If you offer your gifts to her willingly, you will bring everlasting honor to Ayr, to your teacher, to all of Pini."

"Master…" I fumbled. I wanted to throw my arm around him, to tell him I'd miss him, to tell him I loved him.

He smiled as if he knew all that.

"Sleep well, my child."

Then he kissed my brow and I went home to spend my last night with Mati.

Chapter 5: Darcy

At dawn, Mati rolled my clothes and pillow, with its hidden golden pheasant feather, in my pallet and tied it with cords. My new ceremonial robe she folded separately and wrapped in the leftover cloth from the quilted white jackets and then again in a length of muslin. Then she gave me a quilted drawstring purse that matched the jacket. In it were my boxwood comb, a flat square of soap in a little towel, and a fistful of coins knotted inside a square of cotton.

Aedon and I went with Kes to the water, but didn't sing. I couldn't have sung if I'd wanted to. I could only let his expanding song sink into my bones and seal in my heart the misty bay, the islands under the winter dawn, the gulls, the rafts, the oysters of Ayr.

When we returned to the temple courtyard, the riders were waiting beside their horses with their bedrolls behind their saddles.

"May Suna sing in your hearts," Kes blessed us, then stood with Tallis and Onald to see us off.

Mati hugged Aedon, then held me tightly.

"May Suna's wisdom always guide you," she whispered moistly against my neck.

Then she pushed me away with a tearful smile, and I turned to go.

To my surprise, Prince Joron stepped forward.

"If you will consent," he addressed us respectfully, and gestured toward his brothers' mounts.

I looked at the animals bobbing their heads and the two young princes holding their reins and had no idea what was being suggested. Aedon, however, caught on at once. His whole face lit up.

"Ride?" he gasped outright. "Really?"

Prince Joron smiled, the first time I had seen him do it.

"If it would please you."

Aedon quickly bowed.

"It would honor me far beyond my deserving," he answered with scarcely contained excitement.

"Prince Emryn will give you his horse," smiled Joron.

The boyish prince bowed with a grin and Aedon bounced toward him, raising his arms like a little child. Emryn hoisted him easily. Aedon's feet only reached halfway to the stirrups, but he didn't care. He snatched up the reins and flapped them gleefully. Fortunately, the horse ignored him.

My stomach sank as I risked a glance at the other horse. The young prince bowed. He didn't smile. I looked away from his questing gaze and bowed to Prince Joron.

"I am surely not worthy to take the horse from a prince," I dared.

Joron studied me, not unkindly. A tree could have sensed my fear of the beasts. His tone was solicitous.

"Prince Florian would be honored to lead you."

I wasn't so sure Prince Florian looked like he would be honored. A full foot shorter than his brothers, why would he walk when he could ride? His horse twitched his ears and stamped a hoof that could have squashed me as flat as a cabbage leaf.

"It's a long walk to Cant," Joron gently observed.

I was used to walking, but not that far, and not at the rate of Pinian legs. I bowed my consent.

"I would not like to hinder the princes' progress."

Although his was the smallest horse, Florian's mount looked huge close up. I couldn't have mounted alone if I'd tried, but I wasn't too happy about being lifted. Prince Florian's gaze was midnight blue and unabashed. He nodded politely.

"With your permission...." And without waiting for it, he bent his knees and placed his slender hands on my waist. His nearness took away my breath. I could see his lashes, long and dark, the straight clean line of his elegant nose, the arc and curve of his delicate mouth. He was older than I'd thought, shaving at least, almost twenty. I caught the incongruous fragrance of jasmine. In one sweeping motion, he lofted me gracefully into the air, and I scrambled to get my leg across the massive creature's back. My hands were shaking as I tried to figure out what to do with the tooled leather reins. Florian slapped the sturdy neck and something resembling amusement tugged at the corner of his mouth.

"Don't worry," he told me. "Titan won't bite."

Joron mounted, then the scribe and the pearl inspector. Florian held Titan's bridle and with Aedon and Emryn walking beside us, we followed the riders out the gate. I waved to Mati and thought she waved back; my eyes were too filled with tears to see.

76

Outside the fence, the pearling party was gathered and waiting. So was the entire village. A great cheer broke out as we came through the gate, for the princes, the pearlers, the wealth of Ayr's pearls. At least, that's what I thought it was for. Beside me on Prince Emryn's horse, Aedon waved like a conqueror. The cheers grew louder.

"Wave!" hissed Aedon. "They're cheering for us!"

"They're no such thing!" I hissed back, appalled.

But he was right. I could see the faces lifted to Aedon. Lifted to me. Sitta, the raft inspector, the woodcutters, the rice merchant. Even the fishermen had delayed launching their boats to see us off. They walked beside us while the pearling party fell in behind.

"Why us?" I asked Aedon.

"You ninny," he grinned. "Because of the pearls. The colored pearls."

I still didn't grasp how the colored pearls made us village heroes. Aedon rolled his eyes.

"Don't you know? In every village, the princes give a certain portion of the harvest to the goddess. They dedicate it in the temple after everything's recorded. That how the village maintains the singer, the priests, the temple...everything and everyone related to the pearls."

I saw the tender who had given his place to Mati at the seeding. Would the colored pearls increase his income? I raised a tentative hand in greeting and saw him cheer. I swallowed and put my hand back down. I wasn't so sure I wanted to be a village hero.

I saw Prince Florian watching me. His eyes were blue-green as the back of a teal. A question lurked between his brows, but he didn't speak. Instead, he turned his face ahead while the villagers dropped away at our sides and we struck out on the road for Darcy.

*   *   *

It took two days to get to Cant. I didn't enjoy it. I had never been out of Ayr before. Never supped on cold rations in the raw winter damp. Never unrolled my pallet to sleep on the ground. Never spent a night away from Mati. I thought my heart would burst with the pain. But with Aedon beside me, holding my hand and chattering brightly to cover my homesick silence, I survived, and we came into Cant on the second evening.

Aedon was elated with the joy of coming home. As soon as we spotted the village roofs through the forest twilight, he slid from the horse and ran ahead. Prince Emryn mounted and smiled at me, walking his horse by Titan's side.

"How long has he been away from home?"

"Nine months," I calculated.

He nodded, grinning.

"This is the first time we've gone with the harvest, Florian and me. It's only been about four months, but I can hardly wait to get back. And we don't even have wives, like Joron. I don't know how he stands it, traveling half of every year."

At Titan's head, Florian snorted.

"That's why Father sent us out. To see the pearling. To see some of Pini. And so far, it all looks like this."

He swept out a hand as we left the trees and I turned to see Cant spread out below us.

Cant looked like Ayr, but with everything scrambled. In the evening shadows, the cottages sprawled on a steeper slope, the temple fence had different trees reaching over the top, and the fishing beach was on the wrong side of the pearling beach. The islands, still touched by the last few rays of sunset, were in all the wrong places and shapes.

In front of a cottage not unlike my own we spotted Aedon, locked in a weeping woman's embrace. A Curran woman. Behind them hovered a Curran man, beaming with joy, and three little girls clinging to Aedon like barnacles with skirts.

"Liise!" he called me, half breaking free of his mother's arms. "Come meet my family!"

Florian guided Titan aside, letting the rest of the pearling party proceed to the buildings, which already stood on the pearling beach. Emryn pulled out to wait for his brother. Aedon's mother dried her face and the family bowed low to the princes.

"Your highnesses," Aedon's father spoke. "May the blessings of Suna light your way."

"And her kindness be upon you," responded Emryn, inclining his head.

Aedon's Mati bowed again.

"Your highness," she ventured, allowing her eyes to stray no higher than Emryn's leather shoe, "would it be permitted for the apprentice singers to reside with a temple gardener and his family during their stay in Cant?"

Would we otherwise stay with the singer of Cant? In the temple guest house with the princes? I tensed lest Emryn deny the request.

"It would," he assented with an amiable nod, and my muscles relaxed. "Their luggage will be sent directly."

It was scary getting down, but Florian's hands were strong and steady and set me solidly on my feet. His eyes had turned as blue as lapis and held me entranced while Emryn spoke.

"We'll come for you," he told me and Aedon, "an hour after the Morning Song." He nodded again to all of us. "May Suna protect you through the night."

I took a step backward, still caught in Florian's lapis gaze.

"Sleep well, Amalisa," he murmured softly, then swung himself up onto Titan's back and rode off with Emryn to join Prince Joron at the temple.

Immediately, I was clasped in the arms of Aedon's Mati, with the little girls wrapped around my legs. I couldn't help laughing, and Florian's seriousness slipped from my mind. Tonight I was going to enjoy myself—surrounded by Currans. They swept me inside on a tide of laughter, all of them trying to talk at once. The cottage was warm and smelled like chicken with lemony fennel.

"May Suna's kindness be with you forever!" I laughed on the threshold.

Aedon's Mati stopped with a jolt to stare at me. Even his father looked taken aback. Had I said something wrong? Neglected some custom I didn't know? The children fell silent in confusion. Aedon glanced between us then suddenly laughed.

"Her Mati did the same thing to me!" he exclaimed to his parents. "She sounds just like me, doesn't she!"

Aedon's Mati shook herself.

"Gracious Suna! With all that training, of course she must! Come in, dear child, and eat with us. We were just sitting down to our supper."

Aedon's father continued to stare at me a moment longer, until his wife smacked his arm with the back of her hand. He bent his head in apology.

"Forgive me, child. It was just a memory. Come in. Come in."

Then the children pulled me in, away from the princes, away from the pearls, and into the heart of their family.

*   *   *

It was hard for Aedon to leave so soon. His Mati and his sisters wept, and even his father had tears in his eyes. But they were proud, too, for their son had created magnificent pearls and been chosen for early training in Darcy, and the sacrifice became an honor.

We left the pearling of Cant behind and took the northern road toward Darcy. After traveling with a hundred women and three other riders, our party of four seemed small and silent. The forest, however, sang with birds and breezes, the bark of a fox, the chatter of squirrels, all crisp and clear in the winter morning.

"Aedon, listen," I whispered.

Beside me on Emryn's taller mount, Aedon dried his eyes and listened. "Deer?"

"Deer," I confirmed, and without really thinking, began to sing. I felt at home in the forest, even on top of a monstrous horse, with a prince who laughed and a prince who stared. I could forget all that in the forest. The honking bark of the deer came out in my middle range, from the back of my throat. I added a squirrel to make Aedon laugh, and he piped in with a wren, using his whistling upper voice. Titan snorted, and just for fun, I added that in my bottom range. The horse cast me a sideways glance around his shoulder. So did Florian. I balked, and the singing trickled away.

Florian released the bridle. His hand slid back along Titan's neck to rest on the massive, muscular shoulder while the horse walked ahead, keeping pace with Emryn. He regarded me with eyes as green as summer spruce.

"You're not like other singers I've met."

I stared at my hands on the leather reins. All sorts of responses flashed through my head. I looked for a safe one.

"Because I'm a girl?"

The mirth in his laugh was genuine.

"No, not because you're a girl. You're just...different."

My face grew hot. Of course. The mark. His eyes went dark as malachite and his snort was softly scornful.

"No, not because of that, either. It's your singing. In Ayr. And here."

"It isn't any different from Aedon's," I maintained.

He considered this.

"Maybe," he hedged. "I've heard a lot of singers in Darcy, and many others the past few months, and there's just something different when you do it. Something more."

"How can you tell it was me and not Aedon?"

"I guess I couldn't."

"Then why such an interest in me and not Aedon?" I hadn't meant to say it—it just came out. He laughed again, a wonderful laugh, and his eyes sparkled suddenly sapphire blue. He lifted his head to speak privately.

"He's pretty," he told me as if confessing, "but you're prettier."

Then before I could get my breath back, he quickened his steps to catch up with the bridle, leaving me gaping at his back. Aedon leaned toward me with a mischievous wink.

"Let's sing more. I think it rattles him."

With unspeakable insolence, excusable only by our childish ignorance, we let loose with a symphony of birdsong, thunderstorms, and barking seals. The horses threw up their heads and I clutched at the saddle in fear of falling off. The princes gripped the bridles and spoke in hasty calming tones, and I dared what I hoped was a soothing nicker for the horses. At once they settled. Emryn blinked up, as startled as I, but in the corner of Florian's mouth, there seemed to be a twitch of amusement. We all caught our breaths, the princes stroked the horses' necks, and with no more singing, we plodded on into the forest.

*　　　*　　　*

It took at least a week to reach Darcy. I lost track of all the pearling villages that we flustered by the unexpected arrival of princes, all the temple guest houses where the four of us unrolled our bedrolls together, all the nights in the open where we slept in a circle around a fire built by the princes.

"Just because I'm a prince doesn't mean I can't take care of myself," commented Florian one night when he caught me watching him nurse the fire under an iron tripod and pot of water. At the crown of his head, two or three inches of dark hair showed, as if the pearls had been added several months ago and the hair had grown out. It gave him a tonsure above the pearls, a vulnerable place, somehow endearing. Emryn and Joron had it, too, but it just didn't strike me in quite the same way.

"I'm sorry," I stammered, dropping to sit on my still-rolled bedroll. "I didn't mean—"

"Don't be wicked," Emryn scolded him with a laugh. He gave me my supper, cold spicy rice with scallions, wrapped in cabbage leaves, provided by the previous village. "We couldn't have done this a year ago. It wasn't until this trip that Joron made us learn. He says even a prince should be able to live on his own in the wild." He leaned forward in mock confidentiality. "Joron's a priest of Suna. Very wise."

I unwrapped my rice and pictured Joron.

"Is that why he wears the pearl on his brow?"

"Yes," nodded Emryn. "Just as my amber shows I'm a priest of Geiz'e, the god of healing. All my brothers are priests except Florian."

"The Pious Princes of Pini," contributed Aedon, sitting close to me on his bedroll. "All the princes are priests. It's traditional. The firstborn is a priest of Tol, responsible for the safety of Pini. He commands all the armies and guards. The second is a priest of Suna, responsible for the pearling. After that, they can choose for themselves."

I looked at Florian, with his hood of pearls partly hiding his face as he bent to feed the growing flame, and no stone hanging on his brow.

"Why not Florian?"

"He's the youngest," Emryn told us. "He just hasn't chosen yet."

The flames were caressing the pot by now. Florian sat back on his heels. His eyes were a serious cobalt blue.

"I haven't *been* chosen yet," he corrected his brother.

Chosen? Were the princes chosen by the gods they served? Aedon shrugged, as bemused as I. Emryn seemed used to this reaction.

"Florian wants to be called," he said indulgently, passing a packet of cabbage and rice to his younger brother. "None of our other brothers were called."

"Just you," noted Florian pointedly.

"Well, I'm the odd one," Emryn confessed without embarrassment.

"Emryn's a healer," Florian told us. "He has a gift."

I had a gift. So did Aedon. We had been called. I could understand Florian's desire. I absently rolled a ball of rice between my fingers.

"What gift would you like to have?" I dared ask.

Florian shrugged. His cobalt eyes gazed into the fire.

"I don't mind not having a gift. But I'd like to be called."

Emryn checked the water. It wasn't quite hot enough for tea. He set out four sturdy pottery cups.

"Take heart, little brother. You're only nineteen."

Florian pulled out a little box and spooned dried blossoms into the cups, revealing the source of his jasmine aroma. His eyes had turned a teasing turquoise.

"Maybe our newest singer can sing me into a choice."

I wondered how such a song would sound.

"I'll be sure to do that," I jested back, "if anyone can teach me how."

He leaned back his head in a lyrical laugh.

"Well, if anyone can teach you how, it would be Sirinta." His turquoise eyes smiled into crescents. "And if anyone can learn to do it," he added more softly, "I'm willing to wager it would be you."

*   *   *

I was totally unprepared for Darcy. The tumble of clay tile rooftops on the slopes surrounding the harbor. The forest of masts in the evening light. The sprawl of the palace on the hill. The endless streets, the houses, the shops. The sheer hugeness of it.

After the peaceful rhythms of Ayr, the city assaulted my senses. My darting eyes could hardly absorb the colors, the finery, the squalor, the goods. My nose was assailed by the smell of the sea tainted by tar, the odors of carrion, sweat, and waste. And my ears were overwhelmed by too many people, foreign tongues, clattering wagons, bawling beasts. By the time we reached the palace, my brain was numb and Aedon looked like someone had hit him with a rock.

The palace offered some relief, but even within the high white walls, the space was bigger than all of Ayr. There was the royal residence, terraced and white, with graceful roofs overhung by the winter branches of maples, oaks, and swaying willows. And there were the temples to various gods, together with their attendant buildings, each in a complex of gardens and painted wooden walls. Most prominent was the temple to Tol, the king of the gods. As we passed, I could see the golden god, as tall as a man, within the shadows. The other temples were blurs among the trees and gardens that partially shielded them from each other, until we reached the temple of Suna.

Suna's temple was blue and white, with a white gravel courtyard enclosed by a fence of lacquered blue. It felt like home except that there were so many buildings and so much space. The sun had set as the princes led us through the gate to the first house on the left. Aedon nearly fell from the saddle when we stopped, and I hardly felt Florian's hands as he lifted me down.

The woman who came to the door was taller than me by three or four inches and birdlike in her slenderness. In simple white garments of a fiber I wasn't familiar with, she must have been sixty. Her thick dark hair was streaked with silver. It wasn't braided. One of her ears was rimmed with pearls, and half of the other. I suddenly realized why Florian had laughed when I asked if my being a girl was what made me different from other singers.

"May Suna's favor be with you, Sirinta," bowed Emryn.

The Master Singer's dove-gray eyes were framed by wrinkles when she smiled.

"And Suna remember your highnesses' kindness forever!" she blessed him and Florian, waving us in. "We've been expecting you!"

Aedon and I stumbled over the threshold, murmuring blessings and trying to bow without falling over. Emryn and Florian placed our bedrolls inside the door but remained outside.

"We should go to our father," Emryn explained.

"Of course, of course," agreed Sirinta. "I've taken you from your first pearling excursion, and my gratitude is immeasurable. But I know the king and queen are both anxious to know of your safe return. Go with Suna's blessings."

Emryn bowed away to his horse, but Florian lingered. His eyes were a gentle smoky blue.

"I'll look in on you soon. To see how you're doing." He colored slightly and added, "Both of you."

I remembered to bow.

"Thank you, your highness. You have both been very kind. May Suna reward you."

He smiled, bowed to Sirinta, and mounted to ride away with Emryn. Only when they had passed through the gate did Sirinta close the door. She smelled sweet and fresh, like some kind of berry.

"Look at you," she said to us both. "You're exhausted. You must eat and sleep."

We picked up our bedrolls.

"This is the receiving room," Sirinta noted as we turned. It was as large as Kes's whole house. I noticed the altar, and the scrolls on the wall above it, exactly like the ones Kes had. Likewise the windows filling one wall, looking into the ornamental garden. I also saw two different sets of tables and chairs, one built to Pinian proportions and one for Currans, on opposite sides of the room. Beyond them, neutrally facing both, was a spruce-wood desk. On its polished surface stood a pot of ink and a rack of pens. "All business is conducted here, as will be your lessons in inclement weather."

Instead of doors at the back of the room as in Kes's house, there was a corridor off one corner. We followed her down it as if in a daze.

"This is my room," she said as we passed a closed door on our right. "This will be Aedon's," at the next. She opened the door and took his bedroll to place it inside. I scarcely glimpsed the empty space before the door was closed again. "This is Bina's," she told us, continuing past another. "And yours, Amalisa," she said at the last, repeating her efficient bedroll deposit. "There are no other apprentices now, so you'll both have your chambers to yourselves."

Aedon clutched my hand, but before the thought of sleeping alone could overwhelm us, we entered the kitchen. The central hearth was large enough for a dozen cooks to prepare a feast for twenty souls, and there was a table with eight chairs, all scaled for Currans. A woman was stirring a bubbling pot, and delicious aromas of lemony burnet, scallions, and fish filled the warm air.

"Bina," Sirinta addressed the woman, "these are the new apprentices."

No more than thirty and thin as a stick, Bina bowed. Her face was impassive.

"Welcome," she spoke in a grumbly voice.

I saw two bowls and spoons on the table. My manners kicked in.

"Forgive us," I bowed. "We've come just as you were about to eat."

"No, no," Sirinta reassured us. "We ate long since. As soon as you were seen approaching, word was sent of your arrival. We know you didn't stop to eat as you came through the city, so we were sure you would be hungry." A look of polite concern crossed her brow. "Would you rather just bathe and sleep?"

The smell of the food made my stomach growl.

"Not at all," I responded, bowing to both of them. "This is very kind of you."

Sirinta sat with us while Bina served us rice, fish stew, and oranges, then brought three cups of some kind of tea. It smelled like Sirinta. She cradled her cup and smiled.

"You've had a long journey. Tonight you must rest. You're free to explore the temple precinct, but please don't venture outside the wall without an escort. You are new and the palace is large, and it would not do to get lost right away."

She spared us questions while we ate, and I vaguely noticed Bina bustling in and out with buckets of water. When we finished our meal, Sirinta took us to our rooms.

"May Suna refresh you with peaceful rest. You'll begin your lessons tomorrow."

It was inexpressibly strange to close the door to a bedroom and be alone. Aside from my bedroll, it contained a washstand, a lacquered clothing chest, a desk and chair, and a wooden tub filled with steaming water.

Marveling, I approached the tub as if it were an altar. It was round and deep, decoratively carved, with a little shelf for the soap and cloth. Immediately, I stripped and climbed in. The water came up to my collarbone. I had never felt anything so luxurious. I sat, gazing out at the moonlit garden, until the water was cold enough to raise bumps on my skin. Then I unrolled my pallet, made my prayers, and curled up to sleep.

But sleep did not come easily. I was alone, without Mati snoring softly beside me, without the reassuring presence of Aedon and the princes. I was in Darcy, far from Mati, far from Kes, far from Ayr. I was in the home of the Master Singer, who had expectations of me and Aedon. What if the pearls had been a fluke? What if we couldn't do it again? What if it hadn't been Aedon and me at all? What would happen to us then? All I could do was close my eyes and pray to Suna to help us serve her without disgracing our families, our teacher, ourselves, and our villages. I must have prayed it a hundred times before I finally fell asleep.

*   *   *

"It seems," said Sirinta the following morning, "that both of you have a special gift."

Aedon and I looked at each other uncomfortably. Sirinta's garden was larger than Kes's, the trees far older, the plants more varied. But the white stone benches were much the same, beneath a similar bare-branched maple. I was wearing a fresh white outfit that I had found when I awoke, laid out on the floor where the tub had been the night before. Aedon, likewise, had new britches and shirt. They were made of the same unfamiliar fiber as Sirinta's, which Bina had told me at breakfast was linen. The new clothes were comfortable, but not very warm. In the cold morning air, I was glad of my quilted jacket.

"Master," I answered. "Prince Joron said we enriched the pearls."

Her quicksilver eyes inspected me.

"But you aren't sure," she surmised from my tone. "You don't know how."

"We don't know how," Aedon and I confirmed together.

She tipped her head at the sound of our voices.

"You sang the Morning and Evening Songs for several months. Please sing the Morning Song for me."

We glanced at each other.

"Here? Now?"

Her eyebrows rose at this challenge of her request. Immediately, we stood together, raised our arms, imagined a pearling bay before us, and sang. Both of us, in all three voices, infused with the bleating of orphaned fawns, the longing of winds on a winter night, the plaintive cry of the gulls of Ayr. She listened to the entire song.

"Remarkable," she murmured when we finally finished, but her tone returned promptly to business. "Amalisa, do you speak Curran?"

We remained standing.

"No, Master."

"Curious. Your inflection is very good."

"I listened to Aedon and Kes."

"Then you have a good ear. That will help you in learning Curran."

"Learning Curran?"

The eyebrows rose again.

"You don't suppose you can learn the pearling songs without learning Curran? It will help you understand the songs, their meaning, how we sing them, and how the goddess sings them through us. Indeed, as soon as possible, you'll be speaking only Curran here within the Curran precinct."

My belly dropped. My ear was good, but Curran was very different from Pinian.

"Yes, Master."

"And do you read?"

My belly sank further.

"Read?" I squeaked.

"Oh, dear," she sighed. "Aedon, do you read?"

"Yes, Master," he answered, standing straight. "At least," he amended, "I read fairly well in Curran, but only a little in Pinian."

"Good," she approved. "You will help Amalisa with her Curran."

He smiled in happy anticipation, as if learning to read in a language I didn't even speak would be fun.

"Yes, Master," he grinned.

"Do you know any other songs?" she inquired.

We shook our heads.

"Only the Morning and Evening Songs."

"Ah well," she sighed as if disappointed. Then she caught herself and looked more stern. "Of course it was wrong of you to learn even those."

We bent our heads to show contrition we didn't feel.

"Yes, Master. We know it was wrong."

A teasing smile wrinkled the corners of her eyes.

"But you did, and here you are. Now you only have to learn the others."

"The seeding songs," I dared to supply, "and the harvest songs."

"Yes," she agreed. "Can you name them?"

"No, Master," I had to confess.

"Aedon?"

I saw his fingers move as he counted.

"The Song of Opening. The Song of Comfort. The Song of Sleeping. These are all used both in seeding and harvesting. The Song of Healing is used in the seeding, and the Song of Honor and Gratitude is used in the harvest."

"Excellent, Aedon." She spread her hazelnut hands on her knees. "Now sing me the exercise Kes taught you for the upper chest."

So it went the rest of the morning, Sirinta determining what we knew and what we still had yet to learn. By dinnertime, I felt as if I had run uphill from Cant to Ayr. But she wasn't finished with us yet.

"Amalisa," she addressed me briskly. "Explain to me what you do with your voice."

Her eyes were a piercing silver-gray. I knew exactly what she meant.

"I sing what I hear. In the woods. In the wind. At the water. And I put those voices in the songs." I shuffled one foot. "I didn't know it would change the songs. Change the pearls."

She snorted sharply.

"That's why you're here. Both of you. Because you changed the pearls. I'm instructed to discover how you did it, and whether others can learn it, too."

"Yes, Master. We understand."

"Aedon. How did Amalisa teach you to use the voices of Ayr in your songs?"

He lifted his hands and gave a shrug.

"She just made me listen and sing what I heard." His face was almost apologetic. "It was hard at first, but it was fun."

"Can you do it for me now?"

We glanced at each other, then let our attention drift out through the garden.

"I hear doves," Aedon said. "Over there." He pointed to a naked beech where a pair of doves cooed at each other. His wrist tapped mine, and we cooed at each other exactly like the pair of doves. The wrinkles appeared at Sirinta's eyes as she listened intently.

"Wind," I said next. "In the eaves." And we breathed almost inaudibly with the shushing whispers of the wind.

"Gulls." Overhead. Scouting for scraps, even in the palace grounds. We used our upper voices to cry the catlike mew of the searching gulls. Sirinta winced ever so slightly. We hadn't meant to be quite so shrill.

"I see," she said, and stood up with more vigor than Aedon and I could have mustered together. "That will be enough for today. You have given me something to think about. Tomorrow we'll start your Curran lessons, Amalisa, and both of you will begin to learn the Song of Comfort."

We all ate together in the kitchen. Bina gave us some kind of meat, cooked in strips with purple onions and sweet fat peapods. I poked at it uncertainly. Bina stuck a fist on her hip.

"Never had beef?"

I questioned Aedon with startled eyes. He clearly relished this alien food.

"Beef," he whispered. "We used to have it in Cant sometimes. It's the meat of a cow."

"A cow," I repeated, as if he were speaking Curran already.

"You know. A cow. Gives milk like a goat."

"Oh," I nodded. "Like a goat." Sitta had given us goat a few times. I tasted the meat. It was vastly different from goat, but I had to admit to myself that I liked it.

Sirinta watched Aedon while he ate.

"I knew your mother, Aedon. She was a fine singer."

Aedon stopped chewing and swallowed. He stared at his bowl.

"You are kind to say so," he answered distantly.

She seemed to examine his face, his nose, the set of his eyes.

"You take after her," she smiled. "She was quite lovely."

He flushed, and I grinned. What boy wants to hear how lovely he is? But then I noticed Sirinta's examining eyes on me. Purely on reflex, I turned my head. Over the years, the mark had grown smoother, so all I could feel was puckered skin. But the color was there. Sirinta's voice became even gentler.

"People will notice the mark, Amalisa. And some will fail to see beyond it. But you have nothing to hide. You may not know your Curran parents, but there's no doubt that you are Curran and have a gift. Every Pinian will honor you."

I remembered Xander, the looks and remarks of my early youth. But that had been a long time ago. I lifted my head and let my hair swing away from my face.

"That's better," she smiled. Her eyebrows quirked. "It's funny," she mused. "You look like...." But her voice trailed off, and I dared not ask who she saw in me. The smile returned to her eyes. "No matter. You're in Darcy now. A singer's apprentice. And one day you will be a singer. That's all we need to know for now."

I savored the beef. Bina brought the tea. I stirred through the leaves and found a berry.

"Never had raspberries either?" scoffed Bina.

Sirinta laughed.

"I daresay there is much in Darcy you've never experienced before." She winked at us. "You'll get more of an education here than simply learning to be a singer."

Aedon and I almost laughed aloud. We had been in Darcy for less than a day, and already we knew we were going to get far more education than either of us had expected.

*   *   *

Florian found us in the garden that afternoon. We were watching the most remarkable bird. It was larger than my chickens at home, but its body was iridescent blue and its tail feathers trailed the ground behind it. It held its head proudly and issued a whiny, barky call. I was just about to imitate it when I heard his voice behind us.

"Beautiful, isn't it?"

I bowed at once. He was wearing a heavy silken coat of blue and green, no pearls or gems, but very princely. Aedon just laughed and casually slipped his hand into mine.

"Everything's beautiful here!"

And this was only Sirinta's garden. We hadn't even seen the rest of the temple precinct. Florian clasped his hands behind him.

"Would you like to see more?" he offered.

Aedon grimaced.

"We're not allowed out of the precinct without an escort."

Florian tipped his pearl-hooded head. His eyes matched the brilliant blue of the bird.

"Don't I count?"

Had we insulted him? I quickly tried to apologize.

"I— We—"

"It's all right," he laughed. "Sirinta knows. I wouldn't even dare address you without asking her permission first."

His eyes so enthralled me, I almost forgot to voice my question.

"Why not?"

He snorted softly. I already found the sound familiar.

"Now you're in Darcy, you're hers," he observed. "Both of you. Apprenticed to the Master Singer. I'd no more approach you without her permission than pick a flower from her garden. And if I escort you outside her garden," he added emphatically, "anyone else will have to ask permission from me."

I wasn't accustomed to feeling possessed. But I didn't think I'd mind being escorted. Evidently, neither did Aedon.

"Can you show us the temple?" he asked.

"Of course," smiled Florian without hesitation. "I can show you the whole temple precinct."

He gave us a very thorough tour. I was awed by the temple, much larger than the one in Ayr, with a dozen attendants busy with braziers and spices and lamps. They were all Curran. Florian introduced us to the temple priests, also Curran, with the pearl of Suna on their brows. With homesick tones, Aedon spoke to them in Curran, and I realized that his family had probably only spoken in Pinian during his visit out of courtesy to me.

There were other buildings, for the attendants, the priests, the stores. There was a guest house, a house for the gardeners, a shed for the tools. There was a stable for animals, where I first saw ponies the perfect size for Curran riders. And there were gardens, vast and ancient, with ponds and bridges, pavilions and waterfalls, paths and plantings so serene I thought I could rest in them forever. And birds I had never seen before. Florian pointed out peacocks, parrots, goldfinches, swans, and countless white doves sacred to Suna. He filled our entire afternoon.

"Next time," he suggested when he returned us to Sirinta's house, "you might like to see some other temples. Or maybe the royal residence."

Aedon and I didn't have to think. Our voices came out in unison.

"The royal residence, please."

Florian nodded seriously, but his peacock eyes were twinkling.

"That may take some time to arrange, but I will see what I can do."

Aedon went in to see what Bina was cooking for supper while I stayed behind to close the door. Before I did, I watched as Florian disappeared through the temple gate. I caught myself sighing. Sternly I pressed the door tightly closed. It was Aedon I loved. I belonged with him. More than for any other reason, I had come to Darcy to be with Aedon. Indeed, I could no longer think of being without him. And yet...and yet.... I leaned my brow against the door and let the rest of the sigh breathe out.

I had a crush on a Pinian prince.

Ah well. There it was. There was only one thing to do.

I pushed it aside, stiffened my back, and went in to supper.

*   *   *

In the morning, Sirinta began my lessons in Curran. Aedon attended so he would know what to reinforce in my reading lessons. I didn't actually mind learning Curran. It was pretty. Its sounds were the sighs of wind and waves, liquid and soughing. Not quite like the sounds of Pinian, with its ripple of water, its whisper of leaves, and its spicy accents. Sirinta used the Morning Song as a starting point, expanding on the meanings and changes of the words, how each noun adjusted to number and usage, how the verbs were formed according to number, tense, and person.

"So when you say 'you grow' to a single person of higher rank, it ends with *ouh*," she explained, "as opposed to the *uuh* ending if the person is of equal rank or the *oh* ending for a person of lower rank."

I tried to repeat the three words accurately. I could hear the difference, and make them correctly; I just wasn't sure I could remember them all.

"It isn't so different from Pinian," Aedon encouraged me. He spoke the three forms of "grow" in Pinian. I had used them so naturally all my life, I had never really thought about it. I nodded, enlightened.

"I see."

"Good," said Sirinta, rising from the garden bench. "Aedon, please teach her to write and read the first verse of the Morning Song by dinnertime. You'll find writing materials in your desks. You may study in the kitchen. I have business in the receiving room."

Writing was entirely different. While Bina scraped carrots and dredged white fish in herbs and flour, Aedon patiently showed me the characters for each word. I could copy them flawlessly, but I couldn't remember which meant which word. It didn't help that the grammar of Curran was different from Pinian, and there seemed to be too many words for the meaning.

"Here," Aedon tried to explain the "grow" word for the seventh time. "This curve represents a growing plant, and this hook shows the commanding voice."

I lowered my head onto my hands. It was warm in the kitchen, fragrant with pepper and lemon, and my empty belly distracted me.

"I'll never learn to read," I groaned. "Not in Curran."

Aedon leaned back.

"I could teach you what I know in Pinian, but that's not what Sirinta told us to do. And the characters are entirely different."

"Oh, wonderful," I moaned. "We've only been here for a couple of days, and I'm failing already."

He touched my shoulder.

"I don't think you're failing. You're just not learning it all in a day."

I raised my head to his teasing gold and umber eyes. How I loved his eyes.

"You're right," I conceded. "I'm just afraid...."

"I know," he nodded, leaning closer. His nearness was comforting and familiar. He still smelled like Ayr. "I'm afraid of that, too."

"Maybe you could explain this word again," I sighed, pointing to a character that made no sense to me.

"Sure," he grinned. "Let's try it again."

*   *   *

"Before we continue your Curran lessons," Sirinta began the following day, "I wonder if you can teach me a lesson."

Aedon and I passed a nervous glance back and forth between us.

"If we can," we promised together.

She folded her hands in her linen lap.

"Can you teach me the way you use your voice?"

I heard Aedon gulp and felt my own mouth twist with uncertainty.

"You only have to listen, Master. Then make the sounds you hear."

"Ah," said Sirinta with reserve. "All right, then. I will try."

She closed her eyes. We watched with curiosity and listened, too. I heard the usual breezy sounds in the leaves and eaves, a few hardy songbirds and the doves, a peacock, the gulls, and Bina grunting softly in the vegetable garden behind the house.

"The peacock," chose Sirinta.

She sat quite straight, composed her shoulders, and drew a breath. The sound that came out was in the proper middle range, and sounded vaguely like a peacock, but not as the bird himself would have made it. Rather it sounded like a person imitating a peacock's call. She opened her eyes.

I tried to make my smile look positive.

"Ah," she repeated, then tried again.

"Maybe you have to listen harder," ventured Aedon.

She sighed and abandoned the singer's posture.

"Maybe so. I will practice."

What a thought! We had given the Master Singer something to practice.

"Now back to your Curran, Amalisa. Today we will exchange proper greetings. Aedon. Would you please offer a suitable blessing for entering a relative's house."

Aedon spoke in wind and water, invoking assorted blessings of Suna. I heard the sounds and somehow managed to repeat them, but they washed through my brain and out like the tide. Could Aedon and I do something the Master Singer couldn't? Could we teach her? If we couldn't, would that be a failure meriting our return to Ayr?

"Amalisa," Sirinta spoke sharply. "I think you need to listen harder."

I barely managed not to smile. Both of us needed to listen harder.

*   *   *

A week passed before we saw Florian again. By then, we had learned about half of the Song of Comfort, I could bestow several blessings in Curran, and I could read the first verse of the Morning Song, although writing it was still a challenge. Sirinta had heard us make every voice we had ever used of wind and wood, of bird and beast, of sea and sky, and she still couldn't make a peacock's call. In the afternoons, we had riding lessons, after which we lingered in the stable and experimented with pony voices. Unafraid, Aedon liked to sit on the walls between the stalls, but I was still wary of the beasts and preferred to keep my feet on the floor. Some of our sounds made the ponies kick at the walls, some made them calm, and some made them lay back their ears and snap at us.

"That's what's different about you," said Florian, appearing suddenly just as a pony bit Aedon's sleeve. "You like to torment animals."

Aedon yelped as the pony on the other side latched onto his britches. I quickly nickered the softer sounds that settled them, and they let him go with haughty tosses of their heads.

"I think they're tormenting Aedon," I dared to tease the prince in turn. In the stable's dusky light, his eyes were deeply indigo.

"I hear you're learning to ride," he remarked, clearly pleased.

"Yes!" enthused Aedon. "I ride Fleck, here, and Liise rides Shale." He pointed out his shaggy bay, speckled with white, and my shaggier slate-colored gray.

"When Sirinta thinks you're good enough," Florian stroked Shale's velvet nose, "I can take you down into Darcy."

"Really?" pounced Aedon, leaping out of the stall so quickly he nearly knocked me over. The ponies shied and Florian caught my arm to steady me.

"Maybe I shouldn't," he laughed. "Not if you're going to make them bolt. Sirinta would never forgive me if I let anything happen to you."

I felt his gentle grip on my arm.

"What could happen to us in Darcy?"

"Oh, my," he laughed, sliding his hand down below my elbow. "You don't know much of the world, do you?"

Sapphire sparkles appeared in his eyes, brightening, lightening, drawing me in. I heard a flirtatious note in my voice and wondered who had put it there.

"Then I will find someone to teach me."

My arm floated up as Florian's touch glided down my wrist, until our fingers nearly met....

"To teach us both!" amended Aedon, bounding cheerfully to my side, casually clasping my other hand, pulling me back from the brink of Florian's eyes the way you right a toddling child before her feet have fully slipped. Florian's hand slid back to his side. His face lost none of its friendliness, but his eyes went abruptly dark as sloes, with only a memory of blue.

"That," he laughed as easily as before, "would be an adventure for all of us."

I held Aedon's hand in a grip that I hoped he mistook for excitement, but was actually the wash of fear that only comes after the almost fatal misstep at the edge of a cliff. I couldn't love a Pinian prince, and he certainly couldn't love me. If it weren't enough that he was a prince and I an apprentice, that he was Pinian and I was Curran, I had to remember that he was a youth of nearly twenty and I a mere girl still a week from fifteen. In Florian's eyes, in his beautiful ever-changing eyes, I could only be a child, a fascinating child perhaps, but still a child. I clung to the safety of

Aedon's love, and resolved not to let my childish fancy carry me away again.

"Can we go today?" begged Aedon eagerly.

"No," Florian laughed again. "I really only came to tell you I've made the arrangements for you to visit the royal residence. A fortnight from now, I'll present you to the king and queen."

Now *that* was as exciting to me as it was to Aedon! He and I embraced each other with giddy grins, then we bobbed in hasty, respectful bows.

"Thank you, your highness! You surely do us too much honor."

At our unison voices, his eyes transformed to a humorous teal and he shook his head with a marveling laugh.

"I want to see my parents' faces when you do that in court!"

*   *   *

Sirinta prepared us thoroughly, made us practice each move and word until we could do it with grace and dignity.

"Your manners are very fine for Ayr," she told us kindly, "but this is the royal court of Darcy. I'll not have anyone think you provincial."

She corrected my posture one more time as I stood in her receiving room, pretending Bina was the queen. She sat very stiff and dour in Sirinta's chair. I stumbled a little in my bow, which had to be far more elaborate than I was used to.

"You'll feel more comfortable," Sirinta assured me, "if you know exactly what to do, and what everyone else is likely to do."

Aedon modeled the bow for me again, then we tried it one more time together.

"Better," Sirinta encouraged us. "Besides," she added, whispering close to our lowered ears, "the queen isn't nearly as grim as Bina."

We stifled our giggles and started again.

On the day of the actual presentation, we wore our ceremonial robes. Sirinta, too. Only hers was silk, the yoke of pearls was wider than Kes's, and there was a broad stripe of pearls down the front and back, bordered with gold.

"Of course I'm going with you," she scoffed when a hint of surprise showed on Aedon's brow. "You are my apprentices. The prince and I will present you together."

Florian came to escort us in the beautiful jacket he had been wearing the first time I saw him. He was very solemn, his eyes pine green. He bowed to Sirinta and extended his hand, palm downward. She inclined her head and placed her hand on top of his. She was more than a foot shorter than he, yet her flawless posture and dignity made her stature somehow equal to his. Aedon and I fell in behind as we had been taught.

The gardens throughout the palace grounds were splashed with airy veils of color, the delicate, vibrant greens and yellows, rusts and golds, that heralded spring. As we walked to the royal residence, I heard the clear bright notes of finches, the mating calls of doves, the bark of peacocks, and the occasional careful whispers of courtiers in the gardens.

"...the youngest apprentices she's ever..."

"...nothing like them..."

"...and the greens..."

"...could sing the skin off a fox..."

I almost laughed, but the sight of the palace froze any laughter in my throat. Florian led us past guards at the gates, up marble steps, and into a vast entry glittering with ceramic tiles of lapis blue, pillars entwined with vines of jade and amethyst flowers, and sunlight sparkling through crystal windows. Waiting in this antechamber were knots of ambassadors, courtiers, petitioners, in linens and silks, in jewels and veils, in robes and gowns whose styles and forms I had never imagined in all my years of tailoring. Even more wondrous, the hues of their skin ranged from olive to copper, from walnut to bronze, from ochre to ivory. I tried unsuccessfully not to stare. Where did all these people come from?

With Florian and Sirinta in front, we passed them all, and they bowed as we passed. A pair of doors twice Joron's height opened before us, admitting us into the audience chamber.

Here the clusters of courtiers kneeled on either hand, facing the thrones at the end of the room. Long windows overlooked the gardens, the city, the harbor, but I scarcely noticed any of that. Between Florian's elbow and Sirinta's shoulder, all I could see was the king and queen.

A herald announced us and we started forward. Reached the dais, we kneeled on the gleaming cerulean tiles, and bowed our brows all the way to the floor. Even Florian.

"Prince Florian," spoke a velvety voice, richer than Tallis's, deeper than Kes's. "Master Sirinta. Come forward."

Leaving us sitting on our heels, they obeyed and made their bows before King Greve. When he became king, his hood of pearls had been shorn away to be replaced by the heavy crown of silver and pearls with its glassy blue enameled waves. Though only in his middle fifties, his hair fell silver to the upright, pearl-encrusted collar of his dawn and azure jacket. Tall and lean, his muscular frame was emphasized by the close-fitting silk, and the fine, long hands that emerged from the heavy cuffs were quietly strong, as if they could equally clasp the hand of a fallen comrade or flash out a sword to fell a foe. As he listened to Florian and Sirinta speak, the eyes he turned on Aedon and me were dark as polished ironwood, hard but observant, collecting and evaluating every detail of our carriage, attire, and motivations. The line of his mouth was stern and thoughtful as he nodded, but his was not the voice that spoke.

"Amalisa of Ayr. Aedon of Cant. You may come forward."

Queen Ilian's voice was cultured and lyrical. In a fitted gown of peacock blue embellished with pearls and bands of gold, she was tiny and delicate, even more petite than Florian. Even at fifty, her olive-brown skin had the velvety smoothness of youth, and her long, dark hair fell straight and unbraided down her back, silvering gracefully at the temples beneath a smaller version of her husband's crown. An enormous golden pearl nestled on a golden chain in the hollow of her throat. She gazed at us with surprising eyes the turquoise and sapphire of the sea and held out a slender, welcoming hand.

We rose together, mounted the dais, and kneeled again between Sirinta and Florian.

"Your majesties," we spoke as one. "May Suna's wisdom be with you forever."

Their majesties' eyebrows rose. The king's eyes darkened gravely, but Queen Ilian's mouth gave a twitch of amusement exactly as I had seen Florian's do.

"We have heard of your unusual gift," she said kindly. She smelled like lilacs, Greve like granite. "Suna has blessed you abundantly, and all of Pini through you."

"It is an honor to serve," we replied, bending our heads to show humility. Even Aedon was humble with royalty. The king gave a subtle nod of approval.

"Go in Suna's peace," the queen dismissed us.

We touched our brows to the ornate carpet at their feet, then backed from the dais, bowed again, and turned to leave. None of the courtiers positioned around the room made a single sound during our presentation, but I could feel every eye upon us as we left.

Heads turned more freely in the antechamber, and a figure stepped toward us from one of the whispering knots of petitioners. He bowed to Sirinta but not to the prince. As he laid a hand on Florian's arm, his smile was bright and optimistic.

"How did it go?" Emryn asked his brother. "Did Father approve?"

We continued out the door into the sunshine of early spring.

"Yes," beamed Florian. "He gave his permission."

Now that the presentation was over, our rigid formation dissolved. Walking behind us, Sirinta smiled as if she knew what permission the king had granted.

"Permission for what?" I dared to inquire.

Florian stopped to face Aedon and me. His eyes were bright as aquamarines.

"The pearling harvest is nearly finished. Joron will be home in a week. Then the princes will dance to honor the pearls."

I had often imagined the princes' dance. Mati used to say they danced beneath the equinox moon in the fall and spring, between the seeding and the harvest, between the harvest and the seeding. She said it was sacred, and no outsiders were allowed. Sitta said they danced like swaying lovers.... I wondered why Florian was telling us.

"Of course, he had to meet you first," continued Florian, "but once he did, he gave his approval."

"Approval for what?" I burst out again.

Florian's eye twinkled teal, and he stood up straight, then graciously bowed.

"For me to invite you to the dancing."

I was stunned, and Aedon's jaw dropped.

"Are you serious?" he demanded, overjoyed. "We're to be allowed to come to the dancing?"

"Yes!" blurted Emryn, who seemed to be even more excited than Florian was. "It's not as if no one else is allowed. There are musicians, after all. But it's been a long time since we had any guests." He looked at Sirinta. "You might have been the last one, in fact."

Sirinta's salted eyebrows twitched. She was clearly pleased. She started walking toward our precinct, forcing us all to walk with her. Aedon and I hopped sideways beside her, oblivious to the decorum expected in the company of princes.

"This is quite an honor," she informed us, attempting but failing to make her voice serious. "Very few are allowed to witness the princes' dance. You may be asked to sing."

"Sing what?" I gasped.

"The last time they invited me, six or seven years ago, I sang the Song of Honor and Gratitude. It's suitable for the end of the harvest." She paused with a look of real concern. "But you'll only have three weeks to learn it."

Aedon and I caught each other's glance with matching grins. In the past three weeks, we had mastered the Song of Comfort and most of the Song of Opening. Surely learning just one song in the same amount of time would be easy.

"But you can teach us," we begged in unison. "We're fast learners!"

She laughed her complex, musical laugh. I could see the confidence in her response on Emryn's glowing, boyish face, and in the clear azure of Florian's eyes.

"If we're going to do it, we'd better get started."

Chapter 6: The Equinox Moon

The princes danced under the full moon closest to the equinox, both fall and spring, in the month between one pearling season and the next. This year, the spring full moon fell a week after the equinox, which gave us time to learn and polish the Song of Honor and Gratitude.

"Well," sighed Sirinta the morning of the princes' dance, "I think you're ready. Except for one thing."

In the three weeks since our presentation, spring had come to Darcy. Sirinta's maple had put forth leaves of brilliant red that had already darkened into wine. Low clusters of yellow primula brightened the shade, and purple irises bloomed beside the shallow pond. Aedon and I could sing the new song in all three voices, and I could now converse in Curran. Both of us had turned fifteen. We were pleased with our accomplishments, and dismayed to think we were somehow lacking.

"It couldn't be our clothes," I observed. "We have our ceremonial robes."

"You can't wear those," Sirinta declared to our surprise. "They're far too stiff, and too devout. You need something elegant but comfortable."

Both of us slumped on the bench in dismay. We didn't have anything like that.

"Bina!" Sirinta called toward the house.

Bina appeared with her arms full of white. It was fresh new garments—britches and a knee-length tunic for Aedon, a shift and ankle-length gown for me. They were bright, bleached linen, embroidered subtly at the hems with ivory patterns of leaves and birds. The shift was as soft as the finest cotton against my skin, while the gown and tunic were sharp and crisp. Bina rolled her eyes at our slack-jawed surprise before returning to the kitchen, but Sirinta smiled.

"I can't send you among the princes in your everyday clothes. Think how that would reflect on me."

We clutched the clothes and bowed in gratitude.

"Thank you, Master."

Sirinta nodded approvingly.

"You've worked hard," she said, "and you've both done well. I know you will deport yourselves with dignity tonight, just as you would if I were there."

"Aren't you coming?" Aedon asked.

She shrugged her brows.

"I wasn't invited. You are the honored guests tonight."

Her gaze slid away, silver and gray, and shadows flitted through her eyes. I wondered if she were watching the princes dancing in her past or in our future. Then she shook herself and her eyes returned.

"You ought to go make sure those fit. There isn't much time if they need adjusting. The prince will be coming to fetch you at dusk."

Dutiful students, we hesitated.

"We still have our morning writing to do...."

A smile tugged her mouth.

"You can't write today. You'd get ink on your hands. It could get on your clothes." She teased us with silence while we held our breaths. "All right," she waved her hand in dismissal. "I'll see you at dinner."

*   *   *

I couldn't eat anything at dinner, though Aedon seemed to have no moths in his empty belly. He easily ate my portion of lamb as well as his own. That afternoon, instead of bouncing around the stable yard on Shale, I washed my hair. Then I spent an hour in the temple, praying to Suna to help me honor Sirinta, the princes, and the pearls.

Florian came an hour before the sun set. He wore a loose silk jacket and britches the clear, crisp blue of an autumn morning sky, embroidered with white and silver patterns of swirling winds. As he bowed to Sirinta and then to us, I noticed a change.

"Your hair," I blurted indelicately. "It's different."

"Yes," he nodded as if amused. "We have it done before the dancing, twice a year. I just spent the past three days with all my brothers, all my uncles, Father's uncles, and three of my nephews having the pearls removed from my hair, having my hair washed, getting it trimmed, and having the pearls put back again. It takes forever, but it does feel better."

I laughed. I couldn't imagine having pearls in my hair all the time.

"Doesn't it hurt? How do you sleep?"

He shrugged, undisturbed.

"At first it hurt. But I was seven. When you're a child, you could sleep on rocks. You get used to it." He gestured out the door. "We should go. We want to be there before sunset."

I held Aedon's hand all the way to the palace, more nervous than when we had been presented to Florian's parents.

Armed guards admitted us into the royal residence. We meandered through wide reception rooms, up broad marble staircases, down twisting corridors, under blue-tiled archways, through an empty, guarded audience chamber, and out onto a vast marble terrace that overlooked the gleaming bay. The sun had sunk into the hills behind the palace, and silky tissues of lavender, peach, and rose were draped across the sky. Torches burned on the tessellated walls, illuminating the lacey leaves of feathery maples and gilding hundreds of pale white lilies that clumped around a whispering fountain. There was a linen-covered table burdened with bowls of fruit, platters of cold meats, dishes of crisp, raw vegetables, and round cups of wine. I had never seen so much food for so few people.

Musicians sat at one edge of the terrace, tuning harps, viols, a theorbo, testing the notes against flutes and oboes, lutes and drums. They wore dark clothes that blended into the trees behind them, rendering them nearly invisible. Threads and strands of musical notes fell randomly throughout the garden into the quiet conversations of the princes.

But I marveled most at the princes themselves, scattered in groups around the terrace. I had never imagined there'd be so many! There must have been twenty, ranging in age from seven to seventy, all dressed in shades of blue and teal, turquoise and mist, silver and white, sapphire and cream. Most of them had some sort of stone suspended from silver on their brows, and all wore the shimmering hood of pearls.

"Who are they all?" I whispered to Florian. He and Aedon were waiting for me as I hung in the doorway, reluctant to step out into the torchlight. He laughed and started by pointing out a muscular man in his middle thirties, sitting on a fanciful throne that faced the sea. He was speaking to a serious lad no more than twelve while a boy of seven squirmed on his knee.

"That's my oldest brother, Gavin, and two of his sons. There's another around here somewhere." He craned to spot the other son, a boy of ten, examining with some restraint an array of tarts and finger cakes. "Gavin's youngest two aren't old enough yet to come to the dancing." He gestured vaguely around the terrace, the guarded room behind me, the nearby windows and terraces. "This is all Gavin's apartments."

"He's the crown prince," breathed Aedon ardently. "See the topaz? He's a priest of Tol and the leader of all of Pini's armies."

"So you've mentioned," I smiled, amused.

Florian pointed next to a cluster of men in their forties and fifties, casually clustered around the food, although not eating. They talked and laughed among themselves, waving wine cups in their hands.

"Those are my uncles. Father's brothers. And those," of a group in their sixties and seventies, sitting on benches at another edge of the terrace, "are Father's uncles, the brothers of my grandfather, King Nysus. There would be even more, but only the eldest sons and their sons are considered princes."

Aedon gawked at the numerous princes, but I must have looked completely stumped. Florian laughed and took my elbow. There was still one group he hadn't named.

"But come," he coaxed. "I'll introduce you to my brothers."

They stood near Gavin, heckling Joron, who looked a great deal more relaxed than he had in Ayr.

"He's been back for almost three weeks," confided Florian in a whisper. "Tonight's the first time he's been out his chambers since he got home. His wife's had a child every winter for years."

Aedon had to stifle his laugh as we approached and the princes turned to greet the Master Singer's apprentices. Even Gavin rose to his feet, sending his little son off with the eldest. Each of them bowed and wished us the various blessings of Suna. We bowed to the crown prince, then to each of the other five. But after these formalities, Gavin casually sat back down while the rest of them chortled and jostled each other like boys no older than Gavin's sons.

All of them towered over Florian. Even Emryn, the shortest among them, topped Florian by a full foot. With the boyish grin I had come to know, and the pearl of Suna on his brow, he hung an arm over Florian's shoulder.

"He's the runt of the litter," he laughed to me. "The only one of us strapping lads to inherit our mother's diminutive size."

"And her eyes," remarked a brother, with a sparkle in the dark brown eyes that their father had given the rest of them. He was almost thirty, taller and slimmer than the others.

"Prince Andren," bowed Aedon.

"Very good," he beamed with a courteous flourish in return.

"How do you know?" I hissed sideways at Aedon.

"I know them all," he gushed with delight. "Look. Prince Andren wears the moonstone of Nazha. He knows all the turnings of the moon and organizes the equinox dances." He nodded to the next eldest prince, with a spiraling slice of shell on his brow. "Prince Rion wears the shell to show he's a priest of Skira. He sails a ship called *The Destiny*." Prince Rion bent his head in acknowledgement. His skin was more weathered than that of his brothers, no doubt from spending more time at sea. "And Prince Kyan's a priest of the forest god, Yra, who can breathe on wood and turn it to stone. He's a master huntsman, and no one else has ever been able to draw his bow."

The last prince gave a hearty laugh, wrinkling his brow beneath a disk of polished stone with the brown concentric rings of wood. His voice was rich and growly, like a bear's.

"You seem to know a lot about us for one so young and so recently arrived in Darcy. Surely Sirinta hasn't been teaching you how to tell one prince from another?"

Aedon flushed proudly.

"My father came to Darcy once when I was small."

"Aradus," Joron supplied unexpectedly. His measuring eyes seemed to read Aedon's face as if his lineage were written there. "And your mother was Coraya."

The flush drained out of Aedon's face.

"Did you meet my mother?"

Joron gave a solemn nod.

"Only once. But I know Sirinta felt her loss."

Moisture gathered in Aedon's eyes, and I pressed his hand.

"Every singer is precious to Sirinta," Andren observed with due respect.

Emryn abruptly turned to Joron with a question between his brows.

"And what did Sirinta want with you that couldn't wait until you'd had time to remember your wife?"

That got everyone's attention, even Aedon's. But Joron only measured his brother, quirked a brow, and answered wryly.

"That's between Sirinta and me. At least for now." He pointed eastward with his chin. "I think it's time."

All of us turned, and every voice in the garden hushed. The sky had darkened overhead and the last shreds of purple had disappeared. Stars were pricking through the canopy, and at the edge of sea and sky, the rim of the moon had just appeared, sharp and bright as a slash of ice. Suddenly cold, I shivered.

Gavin rose and lifted his arms. Every prince stood and faced the moon as the crown prince chanted in a clear, rich baritone.

"Blessed Nazha, eye of night, pearl of the gods, behold our dance. We give ourselves in worship to you, to Suna, to Tol, to all the gods who give us wisdom and give us life. We praise the gods for the gift of the pearls that make the line of Mannar strong. Pour your light into our hearts that we may be worthy to do you honor."

At the end of his words, a single note grew out of the air in the torchlit garden, the round nasal tone of an oboe, moaning like wind into the night. The haunting whine of a psaltery followed, swelling from nothing then fading away. The viol came next, twining into the oboe's voice, lilting into a melody that seemed to coax the moon's white edge to shimmer upward out of the sea.

A flute soared over the viol and oboe, weaving a love song to the moon, and Gavin stepped forward. I watched, entranced, as his slippered feet trod silently into the midst of the terrace. Graceful and languid, his body swayed in time with the music. His silken robes of blues and silvers undulated like the sea. With his arms upraised, he closed his eyes, tipped back his head, and turned in a dreamy pirouette.

All of the princes were on their feet, drawn by the moon as it swelled from the sea, pulled by the music that grew and flowed, moved by the prince who bent and swayed like sea grass in a rising tide. Joron slid past us, then Andren like a bending reed. Greve's brothers stepped out, one at a time, as the moon spilled brilliance across the black sea and the voices of harps added rolling waves below the melody. Emryn hooked an arm over Aedon's shoulders and merrily pointed out an uncle, a skipping leap, the pinch of ecstasy on a brow.

The moon heaved up, almost free of the sea. The music quickened. So did the princes. Rion and Kyan moved to join them, then all of Greve's uncles, their aging backs easing into the rhythm. The theorbo spoke in a thrumming drone, then the lutes came in with bright, quick notes. The princes swirled, and the open skirts of their blue silk jackets swirled like water above the terrace. Only Emryn and Florian held back, and the little boys lingering by the food.

With a final shimmer of sea and air, the moon broke free. At once, the drum picked up the beat and quickened the tempo little by little, like the heart of a girl as her lover approaches. Gavin's sons leaped in like colts, jumping and frolicking, sometimes spinning like their elders, sometimes tumbling onto the ground then laughing and jumping up again. Faster and faster danced the princes, possessed by some spell of ice-white fire that burned from the moon into their souls. Emryn yielded at last, slid away from Aedon, and lunged in with an audible sigh of release.

Only Florian remained. I felt him tremble by my side, saw his eyes pearl green in the silver light. The music pulsed and pulled at him. I wasn't sure he could even hear me.

"Go," I said, and touched his back.

His eyes flicked to mine, and he was gone, irresistibly drawn by something powerful in his blood. Edging closer to Aedon's side, I watched my prince fling back his head and whirl in the spell of Nazha's flame.

The music pounded, wailed, and soared. Time lost all meaning in the dance. The moon climbed, dwindling, over the bay, and the silver sank into the waves. Then one of the elderly uncles spun to the edge of the terrace, swayed to a stop, and staggered dizzily to a bench. His smile was blissful, his gaze still lost in the thrall of the dance. As he dropped down, panting, another elderly uncle joined him. The music slowed, just a little. One by one, the old uncles dropped out, then Gavin's sons, exhausted by their extravagance. The instruments began falling away, the music thinned. Florian stumbled to my side and Emryn to Aedon's. Slower and quieter crooned the music while the few remaining princes spun ever more slowly, swayed ever more gently, and wove to the margins little by little. In the end, only Gavin remained, drowsily drifting to the plaintive sound of a single flute. When the last breathy note finally faded away, Gavin gave a heaving sigh, and the dance was over.

For just a few heartbeats, there was silence. No one moved. Then Gavin opened his weary eyes like one awakening from sleep, and his brothers surged to his side with a cheer. His children jumped and leaped around him, and some of his uncles mustered the strength to step up and clap him on the shoulders. Aedon shook himself from the spell and I felt as if I had just returned from an alien land to familiar ground that no longer looked quite the same.

"Now we eat," Emryn announced with a breathless laugh. "Then we'll dance again when the moon is directly overhead. Some of us, anyway. After they've eaten, Gavin will send his sons to bed, and Father's uncles are usually gone well before midnight. But anyone else who's still on his feet will dance again. By then we're mostly pretty drunk, and it starts off fast." He grinned in avid anticipation. "It gets pretty wild."

Florian panted at my side, sweating in the cool night air.

"She comes to you, doesn't she?" I asked. "Nazha. To all of you."

He lifted his head and regarded his kin.

"Someone comes." He flattened a hand against his breast. "Here. It's as if we are all one body, dancing with moonbeams." Silver glints shone in his eyes as they drifted back for a moment to Nazha. Then they cleared and turned to me. "You know what it's like," he asserted gently. "To have a goddess touch you...."

"Yes." I remembered Suna's presence, wondrous, compelling, though she hadn't touched us since we left Ayr. I looked for Aedon, already filling a plate at the table. As if he could feel me, he turned with a reassuring smile. Emryn gave him a cup of wine. I watched him taste it and grin.

"I'll bring you something to eat," offered Florian, but I wasn't sure he could carry two plates plus the cup of wine I was sure he'd want.

"I'll come," I demurred.

He proffered an elbow. With only the slightest hesitation, I slipped my hand through it and wove with him into the tide of princes.

They ate and drank, talking loudly, laughing, circulating freely. Aedon attached himself to Emryn while Florian dutifully watched over me. There were foul and fish I couldn't name, plus venison, boar, beef, and lamb. There were fruits and berries I didn't think could be ripe in that season, and Florian gave me an almond tart that had more sugar in it than I had ever consumed in a year. I resisted the wine and ate as sparingly as I could, knowing what was coming next.

Sure enough, when Gavin was rested and amply fed, he stood and spoke for all to hear. Aedon and Emryn sidled our way.

"Brothers and uncles, the apprentices of our Master Singer are here tonight as honored guests. Because of them, this year's pearling harvest was the richest in a hundred years."

Our eyes flew wide. We hadn't known. Gavin turned his gaze on us.

"Would our worthy guests grant us the blessing of a song in tribute to the pearls and in thanks to the gods for so rich a harvest?"

I was glad Sirinta had prepared us, and that Aedon, too, had refrained from wine. He moved to my side and we bowed our consent.

"You do us too much honor," we said. "We offer this song in respect for the pearls and the princes of Pini."

There were general murmurs of approval, and we sang.

The Song of Honor and Gratitude is long. Even longer than the Morning Song. But though most of the princes were drinking, and all had eaten generously, only two of the elder uncles nodded off about halfway through. The rest remained attentive and courteous, even Gavin's youngest son. When we finished, there was a silent moment for appreciation, then all of them rose and bowed to us. Gavin spoke.

"Amalisa of Ayr and Aedon of Cant, we thank you for your heartfelt service. May Suna forever bless your song."

We bowed profoundly in return.

"May Suna bless the princes of Pini."

The company then dissolved again into voices and laughter, with claps on the shoulder for Aedon and kindly bows for me. Florian disappeared for a moment then pressed a wine cup into my hand. His eyes were sapphire as he smiled.

"Here. You've earned it."

I tasted it. It wasn't sweet and heavy like Zenaida's plum wine, but its sharpness was somehow clean and light. It burned going down.

"It's good," I smiled.

He laughed to realize I'd never had grape wine before. It went down quickly. So did the second. I watched the princes laugh and drink, watched Aedon flit like a bird among them with Emryn always at his side. Florian's brothers came and went, chatting with Florian, chatting with me, airy nothings quickly forgotten. I heard Aedon laugh from across the terrace. He was drunk. So was I. I suddenly held out my cup to Florian. I wanted more. He laughed and took it, then wove through the princes toward the table.

I heard an owl somewhere in the garden. The moon had mounted high overhead but was still an hour from the zenith. I closed my eyes, just a little drowsy, and smiled in anticipation of seeing the princes dance again, of seeing Florian yield to the spell. I wondered how wild Emryn meant by "wild...."

Suddenly sober, Florian appeared with my cup in his hand. The wine was trembling in ragged rings, and his eyes were an angry undergrowth green. I had never seen him angry before.

"What?" I demanded. My eyes darted quickly around the terrace, but there was Aedon, safe and sound, laughing with Kyan, whose bow could be pulled by no one else. "Where's Emryn?"

Florian offered me my cup then promptly took it back again.

"He was with me. They're sending you out to go with the seeding. Sirinta's going to tell you tomorrow. You leave in a week."

His words made no sense to my tipsy brain.

"What?"

He paced back and forth in front of me.

"They want you to go. Both of you. With the seeding. Five months. You won't come back for five months."

I could only grasp one little part. Five months. A different village every week. It sounded exhausting. I didn't actually believe him.

"Whose idea was that?"

"My father's," he answered bitterly. "Sirinta fought it and tried to get Joron to fight it for her. He even tried. But Father is adamant. You're going."

My brain was muddling the facts.

"Did Joron tell you all of this?"

"Of course not," he scoffed, waving my cup and sloshing the wine. "You couldn't get blood out of Joron with an ax if he didn't want you to have it. No, he asked Andren to speak to Father, and Andren told Emryn so Emryn would stop asking Joron why Sirinta invaded his first night home, and Emryn told me just now when I went to get you more wine."

This was too much for me to absorb. My brain slipped back to the five months part. Five months away from Florian. Not that it mattered, except that I might grow out of my childish crush on him. And it couldn't matter to Florian. Could it? I suddenly looked at him keenly, my brain growing soberer by the second.

"Florian," I ventured cautiously, "why are you so angry?"

In scarcely the time it took to draw breath, I saw the anger flare in his eyes, anger at his father's decree, then a shift to green in surprise at my question, then all at once, a clear and naked forget-me-not blue, and the emotion I had felt in my heart but had never seen in his eyes before was completely exposed.

"Oh, Florian," I breathed.

Instantly, he turned away. His voice was hard.

"I'll take you back to Sirinta now."

And he walked away.

"Wait!" I called, reaching after him. But he disappeared among the princes and couldn't hear me through their laughter. I reeled back against a bench and sat down, hard. Florian loved me. I had seen it in his eyes.

He came back talking, face averted, eyes hidden. I jumped to my feet.

"Emryn will take Aedon back later. No need for him to leave so early."

"Florian." My tone was pleading. "No need for me to go early, either."

He swung away to go.

"I— I— I can't stay," he stammered gruffly. "And I'll not have someone else take you home. I brought you here; I'll take you back."

I followed after him, dizzy with emotion. It wasn't just a childish crush. Florian loved me and I loved him.

Once we passed through the archways and into the empty corridor, the music and voices faded into a muffled wash like waves on rocks in the distance behind us.

"Florian, wait."

He stopped with his back to me, ten feet ahead.

"I'm sorry," he mumbled, only half looking back over his shoulder. "I meant no discourtesy. Come take my arm. I will escort you properly."

He crooked his elbow. I slipped my hand through it, but when he tried to walk ahead, I didn't move. Tenderness crept into my voice.

"Florian," I said again. "Why are you so angry?"

He turned his head, but not before I saw the pain between his brows, at the corners of his mouth.

"Let me take you home," he begged.

"Not before you answer me."

He pulled in a breath, deep and shaky. Then he looked at me with eyes that naked crystal blue.

"You belong with Aedon, Amalisa. Can't we leave it at that?"

Of course I couldn't.

"Why?" I insisted. "Why do I belong with Aedon?"

His sigh was exasperated. Shadows of green flitted through his eyes and vanished again.

"You share a gift that no one else seems to have. Even Sirinta, who can sing in six voices at once, can't do what you and Aedon do. You're both apprenticed to be singers. You're the same age. You're both Currans. And Currans only marry Currans. Any one of those reasons would be enough."

My hand pressed his arm.

"All of those reasons together wouldn't be enough if you love me."

His eyes turned a wild, storm-warning blue. He shook off my hold and backed away.

"I can never love you, Amalisa."

"Why?" I pressed blindly. "Are you betrothed?"

"No," he admitted, "but that doesn't matter. I'm a Pinian prince. We only marry in certain bloodlines. Pinian bloodlines. Prince Mannar's bloodlines."

I moved closer, close enough for our hems to touch, close enough to smell the jasmine on his skin.

"But that hasn't stopped you from loving me."

He winced away.

"Why torment me when you love Aedon?"

I jerked back as if he had thrown cold seawater in my face. He was right. I did love Aedon, and Aedon loved me. Aedon was comfortable and familiar. Aedon was safe. What I felt for Florian was awkward, disquieting, dangerous.

"Yes, I love Aedon. If I hadn't met you, I'd spend the rest of my life with Aedon and be happy. But I don't love Aedon the way I love you."

His eyes half opened as if the dim torchlight were too bright for him. I could barely hear his voice.

"Do you love me, Amalisa?"

"Oh, Florian," I sighed. "Yes, I love you."

With wonder swimming in his eyes, he eased to his knees, reached out his hand, and placed his palm against my cheek. His thumb caressed the mark the same way Mati's used to do, but his eyes caressed my face in a totally different way. I leaned into his touch and let his voice caress my heart.

"Do you know you're beautiful?"

And hearing him say it, I was. He lifted his hand to stroke my hair, and I linked my arms around his neck. The pearls brushed coolly against my skin. He kissed my brow, my cheek, my chin, sweet leisurely kisses finding their way in no great hurry. My lips touched his brow, his perfect nose. Then his mouth covered mine, and for a long time, there was nothing but our kiss, heady and sweet, stronger than the clear red wine. I felt his heartbeat in my veins, heard the pulse of his passion in my ears.

I heard voices coming from the terrace, footsteps shuffling into the corridor. We sprang apart and ran like children, holding hands, racing the elderly uncles behind us. I doubt they even noticed us, but our hearts raced wildly as we ran, and we ran for the racing wildness of it. After a couple of twisting corridors and two or three stairways, we pelted out a guarded door and dashed into the open night. Running blind, I had no idea where we were until he pulled me off the path and ducked behind a sycamore tree. He lifted me onto a white stone bench, pressed me against the palace wall, and kissed me again as wildly and blindly as we had been running.

A long time later, we leaned apart. Florian stifled incredulous laughter.

"Tell me again," he panted against the notch at my throat.

"I love you," I sighed, giddy and drunk, but not with wine. Suddenly reckless, I lifted his chin. "Take me to Darcy."

My words were entirely unexpected, to both of us.

"Darcy?" he choked with a gasping laugh. "It's the middle of the night! Look at the moon!"

I wouldn't look. I knew the moon was overhead. From high above us, I heard the first whirling sound of the viol accompanied straightaway by the drum. The princes were beginning to dance.

"I want to see Darcy," I insisted.

He nestled his face into my neck.

"There's nothing in Darcy better than this."

But I clasped his face between my hands. I was determined to see the city.

"You said you would take me. Tomorrow I'll learn that I'm leaving Darcy in a week, and we still have three of the songs to learn. I won't have a minute alone with you until I come back, and I won't come back for five whole months. I want to see Darcy before I go. Just for an hour. We can be back before anyone misses us."

His eyes were dark in the black moon shadow, but I could feel their impishness.

"There isn't much open this time of night. Taverns, mostly. And brothels."

"Well," I confessed, "I don't much want to see a brothel. But I want to see a tavern. I want to taste ale."

Plum wine was the drink of choice in Ayr, and grape wine among the wealthy of Pini. But I had also heard of ale. It came from Kennis, the land to the east. My beloved shook his head, setting the hood of pearls shimmering in the moonlight.

"Ale," he informed me, "is awful stuff after Pinian wine."

I gripped a handful of pearls.

"I want to taste ale."

He laughed and pulled me into a kiss, but a brief and teasing one.

"All right. Ale it is. But I can't get Shale at this time of night. You'll have to ride on Titan with me."

I grinned into his shadowed eyes.

"That sounds like fun."

He tried to look stern.

"And you'll have to behave yourself. Not wander off for some other fellow to steal you from me."

"I'll be good. I promise."

"You'd better," he chuckled. "But first...."

And he pulled me into one more kiss.

*   *   *

Sharing a saddle was actually very uncomfortable, but I hardly noticed. I was in Florian's arms.

I didn't think much about anything else as we rode down through Darcy to the harbor. I didn't think about Aedon, about how he'd feel that we went down to Darcy without him, about how he'd feel that we loved each other. I didn't think about how my behavior would shame Sirinta, or Kes, or even Mati. I only thought about Florian and that he loved me. I was selfish, dishonorable, and shamelessly happy.

The houses and shops we had passed coming into the city just six weeks ago loomed large and impassive by moonlight and torchlight. Further downhill in the poorer sections, the torches were scarcer, and the buildings were hunched so close together less moonlight could reach the cobbled streets. People roamed on foot or on horseback in twos or threes. They passed without speaking. Florian had saddled Titan with nondescript harness and found us a pair of old cloaks in the stable. His had a hood to hide the pearls. Mine was too long, but it hid my white clothes. He had dug out a pair of stiff leather boots to replace the slippers he'd worn for dancing. It all seemed a frivolous game to me then, like children who dressed in their parents' clothes. I had no idea of the peril for princes, the danger for singers, in the harbor late at night, and I pressed my head beneath his chin in the blissful joy of ignorance.

We descended into the smell of tar and the creaking of masts. The harbor streets were far from quiet that time of night. I openly stared at the languid women with pallid skin and open necklines, the shadowy men in shadowy cloaks, the scuttling children in tattered rags. There had been nothing like this in Ayr.

The tavern stood in a narrow street that stank of ale, burnt fish stew, and open latrines. The swinging sign sported a pair of ropes intertwined in a complex knot. Florian tethered Titan outside and reached up his arms to lift me down.

"Oh," he paused.

"What?" I whispered, delighted with the risks we were taking.

"Your feet. They're bare. And the street..." He gave a little grunt, surveying the depth of muck below. "Let's just say you don't want to stand in it."

I giggled as he traced a finger up the top of one bare foot.

"Then you'll have to put me on the step."

I slid into his upraised arms and stole a kiss before he set me in the door. Looking into his clear blue eyes, I was enchanted, lost in a dream. I could have stood there, with my arms around his neck, kissing him ardently forever.

The door abruptly opened behind us and someone snarled a guttural oath regarding Skira. Stinking of something sharp and yeasty, he pushed us aside with a muscular arm and skidded onto the mucky cobbles. Course curses spattered behind him as he clomped away.

"Engarese sailor," apologized Florian. He pressed his hands to the wall behind me, closing me in the cage of his arms. My heart was pounding. Every figure in the street suddenly looked more frightening.

"We don't have to go in," he said.

But I had come this far. My hands made fists in the front of his cloak.

"Yes, we do," I dared him.

He shook his head, resigned to my madness.

"Stay covered," he warned me and opened the door.

I don't know what I had expected, but not the crowded, noisy, murky cave we entered. It was crammed with a wild assortment of men of all complexions, with women in sundry degrees of dress, with boisterous music of strings and song, with the stench of sweat and sour ale. The ceiling was low and the lighting bad.

"So you can't see the food," whispered Florian, sliding onto a bench near the wall. I slid in beside him.

"Why don't you want to see the food?" I whispered back.

Before he could answer, a pair of wooden cups thumped down on the table. Ale jumped out and flung itself into the cracks and scars in the uneven wood.

"Stew, lads?" asked a burly man with a bearded chin and skin the color of walnut meats. He peered at us, then repeated the question in something windy that sounded like Curran.

"No," said Florian in Curran, slapping a coin onto the table. He kept his head low and wrapped a hand around one of the cups. "Just ale."

The man swiped the table with a grimy cloth that hung at his waist and stalked away to look for customers willing to part with more of their money. Florian pressed his arm to mine.

"That's Teck. From Kennis. He runs this place for the foreign sailors. Owns a couple of other taverns along the docks. Makes a fortune, I daresay. He thinks we're Curran cabin boys."

What a lark! I imagined being a cabin boy on a Curran ship. A cabin boy with Florian. Pulling off some sea captain's boots. I smiled to myself and decided I'd rather pull Florian's boots off instead.

I tasted the ale. He was right. After the wine, it tasted awful. I drank some more and surveyed the crowd.

"Where do they come from?"

"Those are from Trent, to the north of Pini." He pointed at men with weathered skin the simple brown of fresh-cut maple. "Honest traders. Good musicians." Another group was pale as birchwood. "Those are from Marnak, north of Trent. Trappers and traders. Decent sailors. Brutish men." Others were sallow as bad fish, with yellow hair plaited in four braids, like people of rank in the pearling. I raised my brows. "No," smiled Florian. "All the Axian men I've ever seen wear their hair that way. It doesn't mean they have any importance. Those are just sailors, like most of the men you see in here."

I drank more ale. It tasted better now that I'd had some time to get used to it.

"What about him?"

Florian followed my furtive glance. A squat, round man sat alone with a cup of ale, an empty bowl that might have held stew, and half a loaf of course, brown bread. His dark, curly hair sat on his head like the pelt of a bear, and his broad, flat face was nearly as pale as Nanny's milk, as if he seldom saw the sun. He watched us with eyes as black as frog eggs.

"Looks Marnaki," Florian guessed. "Not a sailor. A merchant, maybe."

The man looked away, speaking to Teck in some language I didn't recognize, finding some other drinkers to stare at.

114

"How do you even know this place?" I questioned Florian. He settled back against the wall, caressing his cup without drinking the ale.

"Emryn brings me. Twice a year, right before the dancing, there's just one night when we have no pearls." A glimmer of Emryn's mischievous smile crossed Florian's face. "It's the only time we can go about and pretend we're not princes."

I stared at him, trying to picture his hair without the pearls. I couldn't do it. I finished my ale and propped my chin. My voice became teasingly indolent.

"And what do you do here when you come?"

He leaned his face close to mine. I could hardly see his sparkling eyes in the shadow of his hood. His answer was distinct and slow, spoken with a languorous smile.

"I just drink ale."

I touched his chin with the tip of my finger.

"Isn't there anything else we could do?"

"Not you," he teased back, then added ruefully, "and not me."

I sighed with a smile. It was the answer I had expected.

"Then maybe it's time to go back."

He dropped another coin on the table and stood to go. Glancing past him, I saw that the staring Marnaki merchant was gone. He vanished as easily from my thoughts. I slid off the bench and followed Florian out the door.

The air outside seemed fresh and clean after the smells in the Sailor's Knot. I inhaled deeply. The moon had moved beyond the zenith, leaving the rooftops gilt with silver, the street below as dark as a pit save for the light of the torch by the door. The princes would have finished dancing, and Emryn would be walking Aedon back to Sirinta's house. Florian and I would soon be missed. As I stood on the step and he in the street, Florian drew me into his arms.

"Ama...."

He still tasted like wine. He sighed away, closing his eyes, his brow to mine.

"I'll take you back now."

"I know," I sighed. I didn't want our jaunt to end, but knew it must.

"Amalisa," he breathed on my lips. "I'm going to speak to my father."

Something melted behind my knees. I searched his eyes, that perfect blue.

"So he won't send me with the seeding?"

His breathing quickened beneath my ribs.

"So he'll let me marry you." I held his eyes, sealing their color in my heart, sealing the moment within my bones. "If he lets us, will you?"

I didn't need words to answer him. The kiss was better. I felt his heart leap when he drew away, a giddy grin across his face.

"I love you," he whispered.

"I love you," I breathed.

Still holding my eyes, with one hand lingering in mine, he stepped away to untie his horse. Titan raised his massive head with a piercing whinny. But the sound I heard, the sound that blasted all other sound and thought from my brain, was the crack of a fist against Florian's jaw. His head flew back, his body lifted clear off the ground, and he fell in the street with a sickening thud.

"Florian!" I screamed as his hand pulled from mine. "Flor—"

The rest of his name never left my lips. The dark, squat figure that punched him swerved, and a cloud of cloth swooped out of the air, closing around me, pinning my arms, smothering my frantic screams. I kicked and thrashed, but someone wrestled the sacking down until I was completely encased. It reeked of dead animals. I panicked, and a wave of fear sent me flailing wildly with incoherent pleas for freedom.

They were denied.

Something hit the side of my head.

There was a burst of brilliant stars.

After that, I knew nothing more.

Chapter 7: Marnak

The first thing I did when I woke was be sick.
The second was to pass out again.

*   *   *

The next time I woke, I understood why I had been sick, and immediately did it again. This time I found a chamber pot beside the bed.

The bed was moving, making me nauseous. Everything heaved, inside and out. The wine, the ale, the almond tart—none of it seemed like a good idea now.

At last, my stomach was totally empty. I didn't feel especially better. My belly hurt, my head hurt, and my brain was incapable of thought.

I drifted back into unconsciousness.

*   *   *

The next time, things weren't heaving so much. I opened my eyes and looked around.

I was in the littlest room I had ever seen. A faint glow of light seeped in through a small square window with a cover bolted over it. I could barely make out the bed I was on and the door. There was no more space on the floor than there was on the bed. The air was close and thick with the smells of seawater and tar, but someone had cleaned the chamber pot.

"Florian?"

My voice was small, dry and cracked. There was no answer.

I tried to sit up, with little success. The room was still moving, but less erratically. The bed creaked. The walls creaked. Masts creaked. Water lapped wood. I was on a ship.

117

"Florian?" I called again. I sounded pitiful. Unless he was stowed in one of the cabinets under the bed, he couldn't have heard me.

"Florian…."

I started to cry. What had I done? If I hadn't asked Florian to take me to Darcy, I would be safe with Sirinta now. And where was Florian? Was he somewhere on the ship? Had he been left outside the Sailor's Knot? Was he hurt? Was he dead?

The door opened. My heart nearly stopped as a squat, round figure filled the door. In the dusky light, I recognized the pelt of hair, the tallow skin, the froggy eyes. Panicked with fear, I scrabbled backward, dragging half of the bedclothes with me, and pressed myself into the farthest corner of the bed.

"So," he croaked in heavily accented Pinian. "You're awake."

He stepped inside and closed the door. I saw that he carried a bowl in his hand, and I smelled fish stew. My stomach wasn't ready for it, even if it wasn't burnt. I heaved over the side of the bed, but there was nothing in me.

"Pity," he sniffed through a nose squashed flat against his face as if he had been in too many fights. "After more than a day at sea, I thought you might be ready for food." He extracted something from his wallet. "Maybe this would suit you better." He placed a flattened chunk of bread near my toes then hoisted himself onto the bed. His booted feet dangled over the side.

"Symus," he bluntly announced his name while investigating the stew with his spoon. "You don't know me, but I know you." He found some interesting bit of fish and lifted it into his wide mouth. "You're one of those Curran apprentices they talk about up there on the hill. I was up there a few weeks ago. Doing business with someone who works for the Marnaki ambassador. Saw you walking, the four of you. On your way to meet the king."

My voice came out plaintive and frightened.

"What do you want?"

"Mm," he approved, closing his eyes and chewing something rubbery. "Octopus." It seemed a long time before he swallowed. He searched for another rubbery bite. "Silly of you to go out with that little prince alone. In the middle of the night. Down to the harbor. It's hard to hide those princely pearls, but not as hard as hiding that mark."

I choked with alarm.

"What did you do with Florian?"

He ate another bite and shrugged.

"Just left him there. Too risky to take him. They'd track me down and hack me to bits. But a scrap of a girl," he turned his glossy eyes on me, "a scrap of a girl with a mark on her face, well, who'd even miss her?"

Florian would, I wanted to say. Aedon would. They'd look for me. But my certainty was squelched by dread as I looked around the tiny room. The room on a ship. They'd look for me, but how would they find me?

"Where are you taking me?"

He finished the last of the chunks in his stew.

"Marnak," he belched with great satisfaction. "You're going to make me a rich man."

"How?" I gasped.

"Not by ransom," he grinned with his wide, ugly mouth, revealing horrible ochrous teeth. "And not by selling you as a slave." I shuddered, chilled. That thought hadn't even occurred to me. He scraped the bowl. "No, little girl. You're going to make me rich by singing."

I clutched the bedclothes to my chest.

"I'll do no such thing."

He jumped off the bed.

"Oh, you'll do whatever you're told to do. All of them have. But none of the others were any good." He shook the empty bowl at me. "You're the one that's going to work. You have the gift. They say you could sing the skin off a fox. That's pretty much what you'll be doing." He jutted what passed for a chin at the bread. "Don't let it go to waste," he advised. "I've only booked passage for one, so you'll only get what I choose to share. And be sparing with the water." He nudged a rough wooden bucket with his toe. "Drink what you want, but none of your Pinian washing. There's precious little fresh water at sea."

He opened the door. I tried to scramble off the bed, but the bedclothes and my own weakness just tumbled me headlong onto the floor. He croaked a laugh.

"And don't imagine you'll escape. I keep it locked, and there's no one here who'll help you. You're a stowaway. Stowaways get thrown overboard. The sharks would get you before you'd even have time to drown."

The latch clicked solidly closed behind him, and I heard him turn the key in the lock. Bruised and weak, I retrieved the bedclothes and the bread and pulled myself back onto the bed.

"They'll find me," I tried to assure myself. But I wasn't convinced.

Gripping the bread but unable to eat, I cried until I fell asleep.

*   *   *

The voyage was miserable. Symus brought me just enough food to keep me alive and never let me out of the cabin. He slept every night in the berth with me. Fortunately, it was built to accommodate Pinian height, and he only used two thirds of it. I huddled at the other end, wishing for Florian, Aedon, and home, while Symus snored and belched foul fumes like a stagnant pond. I slept in the daytime while he was out doing whatever normal passengers did on a ship at sea. We never spoke.

Despite being locked below in the dark, I learned the sounds of the open sea. There were weeks of calm when the water whispered against the wood and the wind sang sweetly in the sails. There were violent storms of crashing waves and smashing cargo, howling winds and hurling meals. There were visits in ports with shouting voices, running rope, and thumping feet, with cargo loading on and off, with drunken sailors, wheedling gulls, and snapping sails. But I never dared sing the sounds I heard, even if I'd had the heart to sing, lest I be discovered and thrown to the sharks.

In my fear and misery, I had but a single comfort. When my dread of discovery and revulsion for Symus threatened to overwhelm my brain, I returned to Florian in my mind, reliving our last hour together. Curled on my bunk, I could drift out of time and back to the flavor of clear red wine on his lips, the brush of his thumb against my cheek, the sweetness and warmth of his breath in my hair. I could feel his muscular frame in my arms and the coolness of pearls against my palms. His jasmine fragrance filled my nose, his trembling voice sang in my ears, and I swam in the naked blue of his eyes. Clasped in the memory of his embrace, my soul survived even as my flesh was withering.

Months went by, and it seemed I might grow old and die on that stinking ship if I didn't just waste into dry bones first. When we came into another port, it was just another port. I lay on the bunk in the sleepy stupor that had become my normal state.

"Up with you now," croaked Symus, coming through the door. "Knar at last."

He pulled his baggage out of the cabinets under the bed. The sack looked sickeningly familiar. I huddled in the corner, but he grimaced with determination.

"If you don't get in on your own, I'll have to knock your head again."

The sack still reeked of animal bodies.

"Don't struggle," he growled, tying the sack. "One got on and one gets off. You'll be out again soon enough."

It wasn't soon enough at all. After bouncing me up to the deck on his back, he thumped me down while the plank was lowered. Voices shouted all around me. I didn't understand the words. Quick and clicky, they certainly weren't Pinian. Nothing sounded Pinian. The water slapped the posts of docks with a high hollow sound underneath. The call of the gulls was deeper and more resonant, as if the gulls were bigger than ours. Even the wind seemed to blow through trees with denser foliage, massive oaks and heavy pines.

Symus hoisted me up again and clomped down a plank that swayed up and down with his leaden tread. He and some other men spoke in that quick, clicky tongue, then he strode away with the sack on his back.

The sounds of the waterfront were soon muffled as buildings closed in around us. Women called, children laughed, Symus bellowed as slops hit the cobbles. The smells of rotting vegetable peelings, chamber pots, and horse manure. A quieter street, a heavy door, a hard drop onto a wooden floor. Some kind of stew and something like ale. Staccato voices, undoubtedly negotiating a room. Loud footsteps ascending a creaky stair and the click of a latch.

I gasped for air as he let me out. The room was so bright it hurt my eyes. It didn't smell too bad. Not as bad as I did.

"I'll be back," Symus said and left, locking the door.

After months of inactivity, my legs barely held me long enough to stumble to the nearest bed. There were two. Gradually, my eyes adjusted. There were also two crudely made chairs and a chamber pot. The view from the window, when my eyes could bear to squint outside, showed wood-shingle rooftops, a thicket of masts, and the sea beyond. It was the deep blue-green of spruce, but duller.

I pulled a chair over and stuck out my head. I was three stories high, at least. I pulled back quickly, dizzy at the outrageous height. Another cautious peek showed no way to climb down, and the eaves were too far for me to reach. Symus must have asked for the highest room to prevent my escape.

He returned about an hour later with a bundle of clothes and a fir-wood comb. Behind him came a boy with a large basin and a water bucket. The water was hot.

"Wash," Symus said when the boy was gone, "and change your clothes." And out he went.

It felt wonderful to be clean again.

The clothes were rough and coarsely woven. An undergown that came to my feet, a shapeless brown overgown, a leather girdle, scratchy hose, and leather boots. My feet rebelled, but I put on the rest. My poor white clothes, so new and fresh a lifetime ago in Darcy, were soiled and gray. I rolled them for washing.

The sky was brushed with iris and rose by the time he came back. He scanned me briefly.

"Your hair. Braid it."

I took a step backward. My hair, unbraided, showed my status. I'd wear the itchy, ugly clothes, but I wouldn't braid my hair.

"No."

Symus's eyes grew blacker.

"Braid it."

"No."

For someone so squat and round, he could move remarkably fast. His clammy hand was clamped on my wrist before I even saw the movement. His lips drew back from yellow teeth.

"You're not in Pini now, little girl. No one in Marnak cares if a Curran lives or dies. You're nothing but a fingerling here. You're mine, and you'll do what I tell you to do. I can break this like a chicken bone, and you'll still be able to sing."

He bent the arm backward, forcing me down on my knees. A whimper of pain escaped from my throat.

"Braid it," he growled.

Wincing, I managed a ragged nod. When he let go, I gasped and tried to rub the pain away. With trembling fingers, I braided my hair in a single plait. Still damp from washing, it wasn't neat, but it was braided.

"Boots," growled Symus.

He waited while I skinned the hose up over my legs and shoved my feet into the boots.

"Now we eat."

Tears welled in my eyes. Whatever delusions I had clung to in the dark evaporated in that room. I was no longer a Curran apprentice to the Master Singer of Pini. I was a slave. Symus opened the door, and when he said, "Come," I went, leaving my former life behind with the ruined white garments on the bed.

*   *   *

The stairs were dark and narrow, hemmed in by beam and plaster walls. Everything in the tavern below felt lightless, airless, hopeless. The nasal music assaulted my ears, the smelly men offended my nose, and the coarse remarks needed no translation. The food was heavy with barley and boar, salt and sage. I ate to feed my wasted body but nothing nourished my wasting soul.

"Time for you to start learning Marnaki," Symus announced over his cup of the dark beer that smelled like concentrated ale. "Tenrek doesn't speak Pinian." He clapped the cup in front of me and told me the words for "cup" and "beer." I repeated them flawlessly, and his black eyes glinted with eager greed.

"Oh, yes. You're the one. You're most definitely the one."

With fresh delight, he told me the words for "bowl" and "stew."

Symus left me locked in the room for several days, though we took all our meals in the tavern. He taught me Marnaki words and phrases, but I still had no idea how he meant for me to make him rich until the morning he packed up his baggage and took me outside for the first time since our arrival in Knar. Beneath the sign of a green-and-brown toad with yellow spots, there were three mules loaded with massive packs and a saddled horse.

"Where are we going?" I dared to ask as he hoisted me up onto one of the mules.

He settled me on a folded blanket, knotted a rope around my waist, and tied me securely to the load.

"Kragknoll. That's where you'll sing. My brother's a trapper. I trade the furs."

"You want me to sing for your brother?"

He climbed a mounting block to clamber up onto the horse and tossed a sneer over his shoulder.

"Not for Tenrek. For the animals. To bring them into the traps."

"What?" I yelped, yanking at the unyielding rope. "You don't really think I'll do that, do you?"

The mules flicked their ears at his croaking laugh and we started away from the Spotted Toad.

"Believe me, little fingerling. When Tenrek gets hold of you, that's exactly what you'll do."

He was still laughing as he turned us away from the swaying masts that poked above the rooftops and led the mules uphill through the city. Threading through streets overhung with the upper stories of houses, diving through markets filled with foreign wares, pushing through people as if they were no more to be noticed than sea grass at low tide, we were generally ignored. No one noticed a blotch-faced girl with hazelnut skin tied up like a sack of grain with all the other supplies and chattels.

Late in the day, we came to a river that lay in a steep-walled bed of stone at the eastern edge of the city. Dull as lead, it scarcely moved.

"The Riy," said Symus as we crossed a broad stone bridge.

From the peak of the arch, I glimpsed a red stone castle in the distance, hunkering watchfully over Knar. Did the King of Marnak live in that castle? Would a Marnaki king give audience to an abducted Curran? Would a Marnaki queen take pity on a girl enslaved by a Marnaki trader? Would a Marnaki prince have compassion for a foolish child who imperiled a fellow prince with her folly? I'd never have a chance to find out. We lurched down the other side of the bridge, left Knar behind, and struck out into the countryside.

*   *   *

Central Marnak was nothing like the graceful forests and wandering coastline of Pini. I had never seen open farmland before, with its russet browns, sprouting greens, and ripening golds laid out in tessellated patterns. I had never seen cattle with great horned heads and shaggy red coats, nor heard the bellow of bulls, the lowing of cows, and the plaints of their calves. I had never seen hills of scrubby pasture sprinkled with sheep, nor heard the ridiculous bleat of parted ewes and lambs calling back and forth across a stream.

For that matter, I had never seen sheep, and Symus had to explain what they were, how their hair became the clothes I wore, how their meat became mutton stew or roast lamb. He had to explain the villages, clusters of cottages huddled together, surrounded by fields and clumpy stands of firewood. He named the crops, the trees, the livestock and birds, and he did it in Marnaki. At the taverns where we slept each night, I asked for the names of furnishings, foods, and musical instruments, even if I already knew the Pinian words for them. I also listened to other people, arguing, bargaining, singing, and wooing over their beer and mutton stew. By the time we reached the mountains, I could have been fairly conversational if anyone had conversed with me. But I had learned not to bow, not to offer the blessings of Suna, not to show or expect respect. I was less than a dog in a land of barbarians.

The mountains took me by surprise. The Riy was young here, racing and laughing over rocks in its narrow course, and the road ran under pines and spruce that stretched as high as a gull would fly. For several days, we climbed through mists as thick as sea foam sprayed through the forest, for even though it was high summer, the days were as wet as a Pinian spring and the nights were colder than winter in Ayr. Then late one afternoon, a month out of Knar, the sun came out and we broke from the trees at the crest of a hill. In front of us, the land reared up, bristling with evergreens, clothed in sunset rose and gold. I had never imagined such heights. Beyond their flowing robes of green, their bald heads were crowned by the painted clouds. Symus laughed.

"The Teresendran Mountains," he said. "And those are just the beginning."

If the mountains' appearance was surprising, their extent was astonishing. Day after day, week after week, the road grew steeper, the inns less frequent. Summer fell away behind us, and Tol, god of the sun, walked at night beneath the trees, burning the leaves of birch and ash. Symus pulled out woolen cloaks and leather gloves to keep us warm. After a fortnight, the Riy was little more than a rill that wandered off into realms of its own. Symus walked to ease the horse, though he still kept me tied with the baggage in order to prevent my escape. I had quickly discovered that, awkward as he looked, he was quite adept with knots.

After a month, we ran out of inns and slept on the ground. I could hear unfamiliar owls calling each other through the wood. On windy nights, I listened to the creak of tree boles rubbing together and the scuttle of leaves across the ground. Once a scream came curdling out of the dark, and I practically jumped into Symus's arms. His teeth were sulfurous in the firelight.

"Mountain lion," he leered.

A few nights later, there were wolves. I didn't know what wolves were, but even Symus feared them. He tied the mules close together, built up the fire, and sat up all night keeping watch.

The following morning, we reached the top of the pass and began our descent down the other side. A week later, we had our first sight of the land beyond. In swaths of evergreen, slashes of granite, and patches of gold, it plunged and plummeted away in far more haste to descend than it had been to rise.

"There," pointed Symus into the distance. "Right on the border. Almost in Undria. Kragknoll."

I peered into the glaring light that seemed to burn the forests below, but all I could see was more mountains, more trees, and two more weeks before our destination.

At least I didn't have to walk.

*   *   *

Kragknoll was nothing but a house built of rough-hewn logs and cedar shingles. And not an especially large house at that. Symus tied the horse and mules and left me secured with the supplies.

"Tenrek!" he shouted, bursting in through the oaken door.

No one was home.

Symus stomped out onto the porch. He glowered around the picketed yard. It smelled strongly of dog. He strode to a shed against the fence and threw the door open. It hung lopsidedly on one hinge. I glimpsed a vast number of animal pelts, most of them bundled and tied with ropes, many still stretched and pegged to cure. Symus came out. He marched past a well to a stable with a sagging roof. No Tenrek there, either.

While he untied my rope with impatient hands, I glanced at the fence. Although it was easily eight feet high, some of the pales were pocked with rot. I wondered if it would keep out the wolves. I wondered if wolves were as big as bears. Then I wondered if Marnak had bears.

Inside, the house was one big room. A broad hearth, with a wide stone chimney and swiveling iron arms for pots, dominated one wall. Huge kettles, dirty pots, and long forks littered the space that passed for a kitchen. A heavy bed stood in a corner, randomly strewn with hairy skins. There was a thick oaken table with two massive chairs, covered with knives, chains, leather straps, and dishes of half-eaten food in various stages of furry growth. Chains, ropes, wires, and traps crowded the edges of the room. I heard scrabbling in the rafters, and a rat fled into the haphazard pile of firewood.

The house was as cold inside as out. Symus stirred the coals, but the fire was dead.

"Good," he grumbled. "He's out with the traps." He stared at the hearth. Then he stared at me. "Can you cook?"

I regarded the wood where the rat had gone, and quailed. Symus had built all the fires in the mountains but he didn't look inclined to do so now. Then I remembered watching Florian nurture his flames on the way to Darcy. If he, a prince, could build a fire, so could I. I clenched my teeth and nodded.

The rat did not reappear while I swept the hearth, gathered kindling, picked out tinder, and laid the fire. And I can't deny the sense of satisfaction it gave me to see the spark catch hold and grow. I listened to the expanding crackle and wished Florian could see it, too.

While I dug around for salted meat, Symus brought in the provisions, giving me access to oat flour and barley groats. I soaked the meat, boiled the groats, and baked flat oatcakes on the hearth.

Two hours later, Symus took one bite of the food and grunted.

"It'll do," he grimaced, then ate in silence.

After supper, while I scrubbed pots, Symus watered and fed the beasts. He dragged in the blankets from the mules, kicked dirty pots and dirtier clothes out of a corner beside the hearth, and threw down the blankets. That was my bed.

That night, as I lay with my back against the warm stones of the hearth, a full moon hung above the trees and sent splinters of silver through the crooked shutters to prick at my skin. It was the autumn equinox moon. Six months had passed since I was abducted. My heart swelled painfully in my throat. The princes would be dancing now. Florian would be dancing now. Florian, who loved me.

I buried my face to hide my tears from Nazha's eye. In my memory, I could hear Gavin begin the chant. The oboe, psaltery, viol, and flute urged the moon upward, the pearl of the gods. I felt the princes sway and spin, felt Florian dancing, whirling with Nazha's ecstasy, felt Aedon beside me, his hand in mine, both of us caught in the spell and passion of the dance.

The moonlight must have touched my face. I felt its light seep into my brain, heard the goddess's silvery music cover the sound of Symus's snores. The song came out of me, soft and longing, a song for Florian, my heart to his. The gentle presence lifted me up and I floated into light and love. Florian's love. Aedon's love. Suna's love. I felt her sorrow reflecting mine, heard her music in my heart, felt her comfort fill my soul. In Suna's embrace, I drifted through time, expanded through space, and heard a voice call my name.

I opened my eyes. The moonlight had crept across the floor. Who had spoken? Suna? Aedon? Florian? I followed the moonlight with my gaze. The goddess had not abandoned me. But what about Aedon and Florian? Had they looked for me? Of course they had. But they hadn't found me. They'd never find me. I'd spend the rest of my life out here on the backside of the world, singing and cooking and who knew what else for trapper barbarians. The silver light shimmered across the floor and touched a trap with rusting teeth.

The rest of my life didn't look very promising.

*   *   *

Days passed. The weather got colder. Colder than Ayr had ever been. Symus gave me woolen britches for under my skirts and a sheepskin jacket to wear outside for fetching water from the well. They were bulky and made me feel like I was back in the sack coming off the ship, but it was better than feeling the gnawing cold.

I had just about finished cleaning the kitchen when Tenrek showed up. The door slammed open against the wall, admitting a blast of cold, raw evening and a terrible din of barking dogs.

"Whut's this?" bellowed Tenrek in a voice as deep as a bullfrog's croak. He dropped his gear and slammed the door, only partially shutting out the din.

He was rounder and squatter than Symus, with leathery skin the color of wax and a thatch of curly, uncombed hair. Neckless and chinless, his head thrust toward me, and he made a bowlegged rush across the clean-swept floor.

"Aeh!" he yelped and leaped a foot into the air. When he landed, his black eyes glared at me fiercely. "Whutta yuh dun tuh muh hous?"

He lunged again, but jerked to a halt in the midst of his stride with his eyes bulging out. I flattened myself into a corner.

"She's mine," croaked Symus, gripping the back of his brother's jacket. "At least until I leave again."

Tenrek twisted, wildly flailing his fists in the air. His yellow face was splotched with purple like a turnip. Symus just laughed. He dropped his brother on the floor in an ungainly sprawl.

"I'm glad to see you, too!" he guffawed.

Tenrek hopped to his feet and threw his arms around his brother. Both were roaring with laughter now, clapping each other on the back. I tried to shrink further into the corner, glad they were ignoring me. It didn't last.

Symus threw out an arm in my direction.

"Look what I brought you!"

Tenrek whirled, crouching low as if I might attack him.

"Anuther un? Nun uh thuh uthurs worked. Whuy wud this un?"

I barely understood his words. His speech was loutish from being too much alone, I supposed. Symus shook his brother's arm.

"But this one works!" he claimed excitedly. "This one changed the colors of pearls. This one sings to birds and beasts. They say she could sing the skin off a fox."

I wished I knew who had slandered me so that day as we walked to meet King Greve.

Tenrek sidled closer with skeptically narrowed eyes. He smelled of leather, wool, and blood.

"Ha yuh seen er dun it?"

"She can make any sound she hears," boasted Symus. "She can call the beasts. I know she can."

Tenrek crouched so low, his head was scarcely higher than mine. His nose was broad and flat, turned up at the end to offer an unappealing view as if into the dark recesses of his brain. His eyes were meaner than his brother's.

"W'ull see," he muttered.

Tenrek had brought back twenty pelts and eight dead animals. It seemed he ate most of them out in the mountains while skinning and drying the hides. One of the beasts was our dinner that night; another he threw out the door to the dogs. I stewed the hare with onions from Knar and dried mushrooms from Tenrek's stores. While I scrubbed the pot, Symus produced a leather bottle.

"Yra's heart," belched Tenrek, invoking the goddess of forest creatures and swiping the table clean with his reach. "Gie ut ere!"

Symus dangled it for a moment, then yielded it with the genial laugh that comes from a warm hearth and a full stomach.

"Yra knows," he conceded, "you've earned it."

Tenrek pulled a long swig from the bottle.

"Yra's knees," he sighed, passing the bottle back to Symus. "Uh miss yuh when yuh're gon. Whuy mun it allus be suh long?"

Side by side at the table, Symus wrapped an arm around Tenrek's shoulder.

"It's taken a long time to find a good one. A lot of journeys to Curra and Pini, making connections, finding out where the gift could lie. But this is the one they talk about. This is the one that's going to work."

Symus conversed so little with me, he seemed downright garrulous with his brother. He drank and passed the bottle back.

"Listen," he coaxed as if he were selling a swaybacked horse. "With this one, we'll have so many furs, I'll be able to make all the money we need without going further than Marnak and Undria. And now that we've got her, I won't have to go back to Curra or Pini to look for another."

I hung up the dishcloth and settled on my pile of blankets. Tenrek drank, splayed his elbows on the table, and squinted at me with greedy eyes.

"I wannuh hous. Uh real un. Nodda stinkin heap uh sticks luyk this un. A real hous wih suvvants an fuyn husses an uh big hearth fur the dogs. An no rats."

His leer was so intent, I thought he was talking to me until Symus swigged and chuckled back.

"We'll get all that. A house as big as Father's."

Tenrek scowled. I could smell the wine on their breath all the way from my corner, sharp and acidic.

"Kelaart's got Fahder's hous. We cud jus kill Kelaart an taek back Fahder's hous. It yussed to be ar hous, too, yuh know."

Symus propped his chin on his hands and stared at me languidly.

"You can't kill Kelaart," he snorted with scorn. "Not our own brother. No, we'll get a house all our own. Anywhere you want."

Tenrek brightened at this promise.

"Uh wanna hous in Undria."

Symus's eyelids were drooping now.

"Undria it is. Up on a hill, where you can look right out across the plain."

"Uh wanna hors."

Symus's head bobbed with wine.

"A stable full of Undrian mares. All the best bloodlines money can buy."

Tenrek's eyes glinted as if I had spit a gold coin on the floor.

"Uh wanna wuhman."

Symus chortled against the table and pointed a spatulate finger in my direction.

"You can use the fingerling."

Before I could recoil in horror, Tenrek made a retching sound.

"Dusgustin! Uh'd soonur yuse wunna muh hounds! Uh wanna real wuhman. Uh wanna wuyf."

Symus popped up and the back of his hand smacked his brother's arm.

"A wife!" he guffawed. "What woman would want to live with you?"

Tenrek heaved himself to his feet. His face turned into a turnip again.

"By Yra's mound, uh'll buy a wuyf if uh haftuh!" he swaggered, and gave his brother a mighty shove. The chair toppled backward with Symus in it. Paralyzed, I winced at the crack of Symus's head against the floor, but in a flash, he scrambled up and dealt a blow to Tenrek's jaw.

"You lout!" he snarled. "You'd have to tie her to the bed!"

Tenrek bounced back on his bandy legs.

"Uh got plenty uh rope!" he shouted, landing a clout on Symus's chin. "An mebbe uh'll tie yew up, too!"

"I'd like to see you try!" roared Symus, flinging himself at Tenrek's chest. They crashed to the floor and rolled about, punching and shouting, knocking against the table legs. The leather bottle flew over the edge and arced toward their heads, splashing out garnet drops of wine. A hand shot up from the floor and caught it around the neck as neatly as a frog snags flies.

"Got it!" snapped Symus.

Just for an instant, the brawl was suspended and nothing moved. Then both of the men broke out in a laugh that made me jump. They howled with hilarity, sprawled on the floor, their great bellies jiggling like half-set custard.

"Great Tol," croaked Symus, rolling drunkenly to his knees. "Let's get some sleep."

Still flat on his back, Tenrek snatched the bottle and drained it. His arm flopped limply back to the floor.

"Sleep," he mumbled. "Uh get thuh bed...."

Before he could move, his jaw dropped open and he was asleep. Symus crawled to the bed, lurched over the side, and sagged in a lump on top of the bedding. In seconds, the house was shaking with snores.

With a trembling breath, I loosened my grip around my knees and uncramped my legs. The firelight flickered on Tenrek's face. This was the man Symus said I would sing for, luring the beasts to die in his traps.

I turned away and curled up under my mule-scented blankets.

I would sooner die myself.

*   *   *

For most of a week, they slept until noon, ate what I cooked, drank and fought and slept again. They labored in the tanning shed, worked up a sweat as they bundled the pelts, talked about where to sell the furs. They wrestled wildly with Tenrek's dogs, all of them—men and dogs alike—growling and biting and rolling around in the smelly yard. There were only two dogs, but they sounded like ten.

During this time, the brothers paid little attention to me. I know I could have escaped had I tried. Although the gates were locked at night, I could have kicked out the rotten pales and fled through the forest. But this was not the forest of Ayr, full of squirrels and birds and the occasional fox, where I knew the trails and was never really far from home. This was a wild and ancient wood, where wolves howled in the moonlight, mountain lions screamed before killing, and bears snuffled through the midden outside the palings late at night. In short, I was scared. I preferred my chances with Symus and Tenrek to my chances with the wolves.

Then one cloudy morning, the mules were loaded and Symus led out his saddled horse.

"I'm off to Undria," he told Tenrek. "Too late to cross back through Marnak now. The pass will already be filled with snow." He pointed at me. "Take care not to lose her. She's worth all the others put together."

Tenrek looked to the door where I was sweeping, ostensibly cleaning the house, but really more interested in their farewells. He grinned with teeth even darker than Symus's.

"Don wurry. Uh won let thuh wulves git er."

At that, Symus threw back his head and laughed. Somehow that frightened me more than anything else he had done.

"See you next year, brother!"

He was still laughing as he left.

Tenrek wasted no time. He turned to me with a lipless grin.

"No," he said. "Uh won let thuh wulves git yuh. Yuh's gunna hep me git thuh wulves. An yuh'll start by singin tuh thuh dawgs."

The broom went motionless in my hands and the chill on my skin wasn't caused by the wind. My words came out in a startled squeak.

"Sing to the dogs?"

He swaggered toward me, and when I shrank back, pushed through the door and snatched up a chain off the cluttered floor. Before his intention dawned on me, he had seized the back of my jacket and hauled me out into the yard. I kicked and screamed and tried to bite, but he just picked me up, hoisted me over to a post, and clapped the shackle around my ankle. I yanked and shrieked, half blind with terror. Aroused by the clamor, the dogs were straining at their chains, jumping and lunging, barking and snuffling. Tenrek snickered and walked to the house.

"When yuh can sing tuh thuh dawgs, yuh can come in an eat."

Then he closed the door, leaving me chained on one side of the yard and the dogs on the other.

Stubbornly, I resolved to resist. If I did as he asked, he would use me to help him kill in the forest. I had decided I'd rather die. I could sit there until I starved to death. I stifled my tears, buried my face in my folded arms, and ignored the dogs.

Then something truly awful happened. Something tiny stung my hand. My head jerked up and I saw another tiny white flake fall on my wrist. It burned like a cinder but vanished instantly, leaving a droplet of icy water. More flakes appeared to land on my skin, my head, my clothes. I scrabbled back against the fence, frantically trying to brush them away, but they filled the air like morning mist. I tried to hide inside my jacket, but they struck my neck and clung to my hair. The air grew thicker with swirling flakes. They were sticking together on the ground, slowly whitening the yard. Each infinitesimal touch of cold chilled deeper and deeper into my bones until I was shuddering uncontrollably. I could bear the thought of starving to death, but not freezing to death in a blanket of snow. With tears in my eyes, I lifted my head and looked at the dogs.

They were hideous. Their brindled coats were too short for warmth, their faces were lost in a mass of wrinkles, and they surely saw more with their noses than with their invisible eyes. How could I sing to such frightening creatures?

I closed my eyes and tried to think. I remembered the pleading whines they made when Tenrek threw their food to them. I tried it, high in my upper voice. There was instant silence across the yard. I looked. The beasts had rocked back on their haunches as if in surprise. Then they started to lunge even more insanely, barking madly with every breath.

So I tried the bark, making the explosive sound in my middle voice. Again the silent moment of shock, again the renewed attempts to attack.

Then I saw that their tails were waving from side to side, and their floppy ears were pushing forward, not laid back against their heads. Maybe they weren't really trying to kill me.

I tried a growl in my lower voice. This caused them to lay back their ears and growl in turn. More barking made them lift their ears and bark again. I tried a variety of whines and found one that made them bounce up and down with high-pitched whimpers, then turn on each other with snapping nips and roll on the ground in obvious play. Altogether, we had quite an educational conversation.

It was mid-afternoon when Tenrek came out. Without a word, he sauntered over to the dogs and undid their chains. They lunged at me but he held them back.

"Show me," he commanded simply, then let them go.

I sang. With my upper voice, I whimpered their greetings, bringing them bounding to my side. With my middle voice, I barked in play, and they bounced around me, tugging my sleeves with their terrible teeth and licking my face with their slobbery tongues. They were huge close up, and terrifying, but somehow I managed to control them.

Duly impressed, Tenrek leered with greed.

"Guhd. Yuh can come in nouw. An next yuh'll lern tuh call thuh beasts."

I didn't fight as he unlocked the chain. There was no fight left in me. He had made me sing against my will. Whatever else he asked me to do, I no longer had any strength to refuse. Defeated and miserable, I followed him into the house.

But if I had thought the snow was bad, the cage was even worse.

*   *   *

The horrid stuff was up to my knees when Tenrek took me into the woods a few days later. I hated the snow. It was worse than merely being cold. It chilled my flesh, my bones, my soul.

Tenrek had a pair of mules for hauling out his gear and food, and for hauling back the corpses and pelts. As with Symus, he tied me up with the provisions. The dogs came, too, but he let them run. They bounced along, snuffing and digging and rolling in the detestable snow. They were young.

He was well armed, too. In addition to various knives, he had a bow and a quiver filled with streaked brown fletchings. The first day out, the dogs flushed a pheasant. Almost before I could recognize the blur of wings, he had lifted the bow, knocked an arrow, and released the string. A dull *thwick*, a burst of feathers, a truncated cry, and the bird tumbled down for the dogs to find. That night we had spitted pheasant for dinner.

For three days, we slogged up the mountain slopes and I learned the sounds of snow—its special silence, the hiss it made falling in the night, the crunch it made under boots and hooves. Tenrek checked his traps and snares along the way, resetting them after collecting the victims. He could skin a rabbit in less than a minute, and every night we ate fresh meat.

On the fourth afternoon, we reached the cage.

It was solidly built of trimmed oak saplings thicker than my wrist, and big enough for Tenrek to take three strides in any direction inside. Each corner was lashed to a sturdy tree, so nothing could move it or knock it down. I imagined a bear could dance on top and not cave it in. Into the middle, Tenrek dumped a sack of food and all the skins he had gathered so far. Then he untied my rope, dragged me down, and deposited me beside the sack. The door was chained shut before I could reach it. Inanely, I shook it.

"What are you doing?" I wailed.

He stepped a few paces from the cage, thrust his hand into the snow, and pulled up a chain with a trap at the end.

"Ther's a whuyt wulf in these parts. Uh've been tryin tuh ketch im fur years. Three uther fingerlins tried tuh sing im intuh muh traps. But nunna them cud sing luyk yew."

Ignoring my pleas and reaching hands, he cleared the snow from around the cage. At the edge of this perimeter, he dug out twenty traps or more, reset them, and covered them thinly with snow.

"Uh'll be back in three days."

And off he went with the dogs and the mules, leaving me screaming after him.

I threw myself down on my knees and wept.

Then, just to make matters even worse, it started to snow.

The wind wasn't bad. The cage was sheltered on one side by towering rocks and on the others by thick spruce and fir. But the snow lay in mounds inside and out. I was kneeling on freezing piles of the stuff. In a rage of frustration, I scooped up a patch to throw it out, and it stuck together in my glove. Marveling, I picked up more. I could shape it any way I pleased. I looked at the branches that formed the roof, then jammed a fistful of snow in the space between two of them. It stayed.

It took me a couple of hours to plaster the entire roof. Now the snow fell around the cage, but not on me, and helpfully thickened the roof from above. I scraped the residue off my gloves.

Next I investigated the sack. I found dried meat, hard oatcakes, three leather bottles of water, and more dried meat. I wouldn't starve.

Then I sat down to wait. I thought I was waiting for Tenrek's return. I didn't know I was waiting for the wolves.

They didn't come until after dark. With my heart in my mouth, I could barely see the shadows take shape through the falling snow and circle the cage on silent feet. They stayed in the tracks of Tenrek's boots, as if they knew where the traps were hidden. Shadows flowed in and out of shadows as I crouched in the center of the cage. A long, slim darkness reached in through the bars, and I understood why the cage was so large. Once in a while I heard a sniff, but otherwise they made no sound. I tried to count them. Seven, nine, perhaps a dozen. Enough to petrify me with fear.

Then something gleamed among the shadows. Snowlight formed a flowing shape that circled with the darker shapes like a lone white fish weaving in and out among dark-backed trout in a murky pond. In all the dark and colorless world, his eyes alone burned amber gold.

After briefly examining me, he paced the edge of the beaten perimeter, sniffing where Tenrek had covered the traps. I couldn't see them from inside the cage, but the white wolf's nose was keen. He paused at one, turned his back, and made a few quick digs with his back feet. Clods of snow flew into the air and landed directly on the trap.

Snap!

They bolted, melting up the slope as if there were no more light to shape them. Last among them, the gleam of white surged up through the rocks, paused for an instant, then disappeared.

Later, toward midnight, I heard them howl. They were far away, high on the mountain. The low voice first, dipping and rising, mournful, melodic, joined by others to double the notes, quadruple the notes, then the chorus in haunting harmonies. Their eerie song thrilled through my blood. For the first time since I was taken from Darcy, my heart sang back.

During the day, I slept, buried under the pile of skins. When night came, so did the wolves. This time I waited eagerly, a little closer to the bars. The snow had stopped and a half-moon frosted the night with crystals. The silvery light revealed low heads, bristled backs, cautious ears. Again he came last, shoulder to shoulder with one of the females. They circled and sniffed. I heard soft whines, a querulous whimper, a snarl and the snap of polished teeth. He rounded the cage, sniffing the ground. One by one, he triggered a dozen of the traps. His comrades ran, whispering into the rocks like wind.

Satisfied with his work of the night, he turned to look at me, unafraid.

I whimpered experimentally. His eyes caught the light and his ears perked forward. Then his hackles rose, his head went down, and he growled in his chest. I tested the whine, high and submissive. His body sprang taut, head up, ears high. Slowly as moonlight gliding over the snowy ground, he eased toward the cage.

A cloud crossed the moon, dissolving the light into darkness. When the cloud passed, the wolf was gone.

Later, when they sang in the mountains, I sang, too.

Another day passed partly in sleep, partly in listening to the forest. I lay in my cocoon of skins and sang back.

That night, they came before it was dark. Materializing one by one, they milled less warily near me now and moonlight gleamed in their curious eyes. When I whimpered their greeting, they pricked their ears and moved away, perhaps confused by this unwolf creature that spoke their tongue. The moon-white wolf glittered out of the shadows, shadowed by his darker mate. He sniffed out the traps and set them off, sending his pack into leaps of alarm with every retort of metal teeth. But they didn't run. Some of them went to him, waving their tails, crouching and whining until he nipped at their noses or throats. They bounded up, cavorting and playing, his mate among them.

He came to the cage. I whimpered. He sniffed. I pressed my shoulder to the ground as the wolves had done. He regarded me with his amber eyes. I reached out my hand. Slowly, his nose approached the cage.

SNAMPH!! and a cry that shot through my heart. It was his mate!

"No!" I screamed as he leaped to her side and the rest of the pack yelped and bolted into the night. She jumped and pulled, dragging the trap out from under the snow. The chain rattled dully with Tenrek's scorn. She pleaded, she begged, she thrashed and whined while her mate dug frantically, trying to free her. Drops of darkness spattered the snow.

"No!" I wept. My arms reached helplessly through the bars. "No!"

I couldn't help them. All I could do was weep and rage while they struggled futilely for her life. Some time in the night, she lay down, exhausted, and he lay beside her, licking her shoulder, licking her leg, licking her face.

Dawn found us that way, my head on the arm that reached out through the bars and the white wolf stretched beside his mate as she whimpered with pain and fretted at the steel-trapped leg. And hours later, as dawn had found us, so did Tenrek and the dogs. I had slipped into a doze, but was startled awake by the sound of the arrow striking the ground where the white wolf had been not a moment before. His mate lurched up with a single plea.

"Yra's bloody feet," he swore, and before I could beg for her release, his vengeful arrow had pierced her heart. Stunned and speechless, I felt as if it had pierced my own.

It took four days to get back to Kragknoll, our progress slowed by the crusted snow as deep as the knees of the burdened mules. I shivered but no longer felt the cold atop the mountain of fresh pelts. When we stopped at night, I scarcely tasted the roasted rabbit, the roasted squirrel, the roasted hare. But in the night, I heard the wolves, distant, plaintive, mourning their loss. Tenrek only cursed at the sound, chilling my heart more deeply than snow.

"He gits muh traps evry tuym," he growled, tearing a hare with his yellow teeth, "but by Yra's blood, next tuym he'll be thuh wun in thuh trap." He fixed me with his furious eyes. "Yuh'll not fayl me twice."

I listened to the white wolf howl, his voice much nearer than the pack's, and made a promise into the night. I'd never go into the cage again.

*   *   *

Tenrek dropped me in the house with his other gear. I crawled to the hearth and went to sleep.

That night I sat awake while he drank a whole bottle of wine by himself. He ranted at the elusive wolf and fell asleep across the table. The second day and night were the same. And while he slept, I made my plan.

The third night, I waited. When he had been snoring for more than an hour, I took enough food to last a few days and walked out the door. The dogs heaved to their feet and wagged their tails. Ignoring them, I went to a rotten patch of fence and kicked my way through. I was free. I had no weapons, no protection of any kind, but the night was bright with a round, full moon, and I wasn't afraid of the wolves anymore.

I headed east.

I walked all night, pushing through the chest-deep snow with blind determination. At dawn I rested, ate some food, and broke the ice on a stream to drink. Then I walked all day.

By nightfall, I was sore and tired. But it wasn't the pain or exhaustion that stopped me. It was the sound of Tenrek's dogs.

When they hunted, they didn't bark but bayed. It was a horrible howling sound that twined unstoppably through the trees. It chilled me more than the mournful howling of the wolves, for the wolves were talking to each other, but the dogs were speaking to their prey, saying there was no escape.

There wasn't any point in running. I went up a tree.

It didn't take long for the dogs to find me. I hadn't been trying to hide my trail. They bounded and barked at the base of the tree, and from high in the branches, I heard Tenrek's voice.

"Git down here!"

I pushed my way higher into the branches, startling a roosting raven, hoping Tenrek couldn't climb.

"Git down here!" he yelled, "or uh'll shoot yuh down!"

It would have been easy to sing to the dogs, but I couldn't sing to Tenrek's bow. The first arrow zinged right past my elbow. The second struck me like a hammer, square in the thigh, with so much force the head broke through the other side. My cry of pain came out like the startled shriek of the raven as Tenrek's next arrow impaled its breast.

Blinded with pain, I clung to the tree and fumbled for the murdered bird. It had flung out its wings in an impulse to fly in the moment before the arrow killed it, so it caught on the branches before it could fall. As another arrow blew past my hip, I squawked like the raven and dropped its body to the ground.

The dogs jumped back as the black-feathered object fell from above. Whipped to a frenzy, they nearly tore the poor thing to shreds before Tenrek snatched it from their teeth.

"Yra's bones, whut trick is this?"

I held my breath and hoped the dogs would find the raven more compelling than the prey in the tree. Young and foolish, they did.

Tenrek dropped the raven as if it had burned him. The dogs crouched to play, which seemed to convince him even more.

"Blood of thuh gods!" he swore to himself. "She turned to uh burd!" Then he backed away, stunned by what he thought he had done. "An uh killed it."

I clung to my branch, dizzy with pain, trying for all I was worth not to breathe. I could barely glimpse his moon-blanched face gaping upward into the tree. Maybe he didn't believe after all. To my dismay, he tied the dogs, poked at the bird, and squatted down to wait for dawn. I couldn't pull the arrow out. I couldn't take a drink of water. I couldn't move or make a sound. I could do nothing but sit and wait.

Praise Suna I was small. When the sun came up, Tenrek marched around the tree, trying to peer into the dense branches, but the evergreen foliage hid me completely. At last, with the raven hanging head-down at his hip, he untied the dogs and followed them home.

As soon as the dogs were out of earshot, I tried to move. It wasn't easy. The cold had stiffened me overnight. I could barely sit up and lean my back against the trunk. The effort caused excruciating pain where the arrow was still stuck in my leg. I had to get it out.

Desperately thirsty, I drank some water, but my stomach rebelled at the smell of food. I could eat once I got the arrow out. If I could get the arrow out.

I knew I should break the fletching off and pull the arrow through the leg. I touched the shaft and had to stifle a cry of pain. I tried again, and it was worse. How did the heroes in stories manage it? I'd try again later.

Just to be safe, I stayed in the tree for the rest of the day. Once in a while, I considered pulling the arrow out, but I never managed to touch it again. Toward evening, the moon rose through the wood. I had to get down. But first I had to turn around to face the trunk.

I shifted my weight. A wave of nausea washed up my throat, the moon went dark, and the tree let go. Just for an instant, the ground rushed up.

I never felt my body hit it.

Chapter 8: Nanomi

I fell into light that shimmered with opalescent colors like nacre inside the oyster shells. It was bright with music. Suna's music, iridescent like the light. Singing in the voices of water, wind, and wood, of open ocean, ships, and sails, of northern forests, snow, and wolves. For time unmeasured, I drifted in the light and music, gently upheld in Suna's arms.

Slowly, slowly, the singing shifted, from Suna's infinite harmonies to a single voice, a single song, a simple childlike melody. I slipped away from Suna's embrace into a place of warmth and wool and someone singing in wind and water. The words washed over me, soft and comfortable. Curran words.

Bit by bit, my senses came back into the world. Singing. Heat. Woolen blankets and linen sheets. And pain. Dull and aching, the pain came last but most forcefully. Someone had succeeded where I had failed, in breaking the arrow and pulling it through. I heard a whimper and knew it was mine. The voice that answered was pure and high, like that of a child.

"Gracious Geiz'e," it squeaked, "you're awake!" A cool, wet cloth caressed my brow, soothing the fever that warmed my flesh. "I'll get you some tea."

But the pain and fever didn't let me wait for tea. They pulled me down, like an undertow, into a dark where the tea and the singing couldn't reach me.

*   *   *

The next thing I knew was the smell of soup. It was rich with onions, garlic, lemon, sage, and something resembling chicken. The high, clear voice was singing a healer's litany to the scraping rhythm of a spoon in the soup pot.

> With betony I'll heal your hurts,
> and rosy althea,
> with melilot and arnica
> and sweet calendula.
>
> I'll soothe the ache with feverfew
> and pale blue rosemary,
> with purple flax and lavender
> and reddest centaury,
> with bergamot, angelica,
> and fragrant savory,
>
> My blue vervain will cool the flame,
> my borage and milfoil;
> I'll give you sage and sanicle
> and boneset in oil.
>
> I'll crush the leaves of marjoram
> with violet and balm,
> and give you thyme to make you sleep
> and aniseed for calm.

I didn't recognize most of the names, but the tune was cheerful and caught in the mind. For a while, I just listened. The pain was quiet, the fever just a distant hum, but the sounds of cooking were homely and comforting.

> With dittany for sickening
> and mandragora's—

I must have made some noise or movement, for the song broke off and the voice approached in solicitous inquiry.

"Does it hurt? I can brew some primrose tea."

My eyes were reluctant to open, although the lamp and hearth were dim. Through gummy lashes, I made out a dainty, pointed face with a long, narrow nose, a miniscule chin, and enormous eyes the color of rich brown pine bark streaked with golden sap. It was most distinctly a Curran face. She clasped her hazelnut hands together and smiled an earnest smile.

"Geiz'e's tears, my dear, but you've been sleeping ever so long." She scurried back to her hearth, a crude construction of stone against an earthen wall, and swung out a pot from over the flames. "When I heard those dogs out hunting in the middle of the night, I thought to myself, Nanomi, that awful Symus must have snatched some other poor Curran and tried to make her sing the beasts into his traps." She pinched dried primrose and mullein flowers into a cup, and the boiling water released their perfume into the air. "Suna knows, my dear, what a horrible pair those monsters are. The men, I mean. I didn't know the dogs, myself." She added honey to the brew, rambling cheerfully as she stirred. "They've only had the dogs for a year. I ran away the winter before. I couldn't sing to save my life. Not the way he wanted me to." She brought me the cup in her tiny hands. "I don't know why that stupid Symus thinks every Curran has the gift. Isn't that ridiculous?"

She sat by the bed on a three-legged stool. Her face was still young, her skin still smooth. She couldn't have been more than twenty-five. Her dark Curran hair was finer than mine, pulled back in a braid that hung to her waist, framing pretty ears that stuck out just a bit too far. She peered at me over the fine glazed cup.

"He took me from Curra three years ago. He found out my husband had died that winter and neither of us had any kin. No one would look for me." She shook her head ruefully, blowing the tea before spooning it between my lips. "I daresay he took you in much the same way. Thought you could sing like those Currans in Pini. If he had the brain he thinks he has, he wouldn't waste his time on Curra. Almost all the ones with the gift end up in Pini. I hear it's a pretty nice life for them there, but no one in my family had the gift. My father and mother worked in the lemon groves. To spare me, they sold me in my childhood to an innkeeper in Eyth, who raised me in the kitchen, scrubbing pots. Turned out I had a way with food, so I chopped and diced, then mixed and stirred, then he let me try my hand at soup, and there I was, just seventeen, cooking for all the merchants and sailors who came to Curra for lemons and spices and, as it turned out, girls they thought had the gift of voices." Her words spilled out almost faster than she could feed me the tea. The spoon clinked into the empty cup, and Nanomi sat back as if startled by her impassioned outburst.

"Geiz'e's living breath," she panted. Her hand brushed the front of her gray woolen tunic, which fit her badly. "I'll wear you out, going on like that. And you just awake after four days burning up with fever. It's a good thing I found you out there in the snow. You'd have frozen to death for sure. That leg got nasty after I pulled the arrow out, and then the fever set in. Lucky I learned so much from my husband."

With a wink of her eye, she returned to her soup. "I didn't get snatched at seventeen. Not by Symus, anyway." She added seasonings to the soup from a table covered with roots and jars and birch-bark boxes. Wax-covered cheeses stood on a shelf with pots of honey and jars of oil. Drying onions, garlic, and herbs hung from the ceiling. Clothes spilled from a chest in a shadowy corner. The walls and ceiling were stone and dirt, like a hole in the ground. I saw no windows and only one door, with iron wings reaching out from the hinges to reinforce the heavy oak. I wondered what lay on the other side.

"No," she continued amiably, "it was Musk who carried me off, back in Eyth, when I was twenty. He was a healer and I had a garden behind the tavern, for vegetables and kitchen herbs. He used to say he came looking for herbs and picked a daisy." Ladling soup into a bowl, she shook her head at her distant past.

"Silly man," she remarked as she brought me the soup and fed it to me. It was rich with fowl, thick with peas, complex with the flavors of shallots and herbs. "Plain as an ox," she prattled on. "But he liked to talk. And he liked to sing. He taught me dozens of healing songs. Not *healing* songs like the ones he would sing to heal the sick or mend a bone, but songs about what he used for healing. He sang them while we picked the herbs or hunted for plants in the countryside. I helped him mix his salves and potions. He used to say I was almost as good at it as he was." She paused with the spoon above the bowl, gazing a moment into memory. "Maybe that singing was what made Symus think I had the gift he wanted." Her eyes came back and she shrugged. "No matter. I didn't. And when Tenrek tried to beat me into having it, I ran away." Her eyebrows rose in little arches above her eyes. "Just like you, I'd venture. Only he didn't have the dogs back then. So I got away. You almost didn't."

She seemed to be waiting for some response, but I didn't have one. I was just glad Sirinta had made me learn Curran, or I couldn't have understood a word Nanomi was saying. As it was, I understood most of it, but in a vague and pondering way, and I couldn't have framed a Curran sentence in reply. At least, not yet. She didn't wait long.

"Poor dear," she crooned, cleaning my chin and adjusting the blankets. "I've worn you out. I haven't seen another Curran since Symus took me away from Eyth, so you must forgive me for rattling on. You rest now. I'm sure you'll feel stronger tomorrow. And then you can tell me all your adventures."

She trimmed the lamp and went back to the hearth. I could hear her singing again while she puttered and cleaned, and I drifted to sleep on the tide of her voice.

*   *   *

For most of a week, I floated in and out of sleep. Nanomi fed me tea and soup, tended my leg, sang her songs, and slept beside me in her bed. In troubled dreams, I pushed through the snow as high as my chest. Sometimes I heard the dogs behind me. Sometimes the wolves. Sometimes I heard a voice call my name. Sometimes it was Mati's voice. Sometimes Aedon's. Sometimes Florian's. I tried to reach them through the snow, but it hindered my legs, pulled at my arms, and filled my mouth so I couldn't even call out to them. At the end of every dream, the snow let go, I fell from the tree, and jolted awake in Nanomi's bed, with Nanomi singing beside the hearth or sleeping beside me in the dark. And every time, as I listened to my racing heart, I wondered remotely where I was and how I would ever get home again.

*   *   *

Nanomi loved to talk, even more than she loved to cook. And it didn't take much to get her going.

"Where are we?" I ventured about a week later. The fever had yielded to Nanomi's teas, and the arrow wound was now clean of corruption. Her potions of willow bark and valerian kept the pain at bay, and her nourishing broths were renewing my strength. I still couldn't stand, but I could sit up in bed and sew. Nanomi had produced a needle and thread and a pair of shears so I could mend the clothes that were torn when Tenrek shot me. Nanomi had already soaked out the blood.

"Geiz'e's feet," she exclaimed. "Don't you know? Why we're just over the border from Marnak into Undria." She was slicing onions and parsnips for stew. "You know about Undria, of course? Where they breed the best horses in the world? Most of Undria's flat and grassy. Endless grazing. Good for horses. The pride of Undria. There's a herd nearby at Gelderscarth. A man named Galemis breeds them there." She threw the onions into the pot. "He's decent enough. I trade with him for flour and such. For things that weren't already here. For things I can't grow in my little garden up above." While she stirred, she gazed wistfully into the future. "Someday I'll trade with him for a horse and ride down the Denig to the sea. I want to go home. To Curra. To Eyth."

I also wanted to go home. To Pini. To Darcy. I wondered what I could trade for a horse. Just a little horse. Maybe my services as a tailor. I shook out the mended gown, and Nanomi shook off her reverie.

144

"Did Symus give you that?" she scoffed. "It's just as bad as the one he gave me." She held out the skirt of her shapeless gray tunic and twirled around like a little girl. I had to smile.

"I could fix it for you."

She clapped her hands in sudden delight.

"Could you?"

"Of course. You've been so good to me I'd like to do something for you in return."

"That would be wonderful!" she bounced. "I haven't had clothes that fit me right since Symus stuck me in that sack."

I couldn't help laughing.

"I bet he used the same one on me."

She screwed up her nose as if she could still smell the stench in the sack, and we shuddered together. It was not a memory I wanted to dwell on.

"Do you have some string? Something I could use for measuring?"

Nanomi winked.

"I'll find you some string."

Nanomi had string. In her overflowing clothing chest, she also had a length of linen, several enormous woolen gowns, some bedraggled shifts, a sheepskin jacket with splitting seams, and a fur-lined cloak that actually fit her. She spread it all across the bed.

"I traded for that," she said of the cloak. "It was made for an Undrian child just about my size. It's very warm. I hate the snow."

I stroked the fur, glad it was only common rabbit.

"So do I." I pulled the string straight. "Come stand where I can measure you."

She stood by the bed while I measured her back from neck to waist, from waist to knee, making knots to mark the lengths.

"Who taught you to sew?"

It was the first time she asked anything about me, aside from my name.

"My mother was a tailor."

I took the distance from shoulder to shoulder. She cast me a curious glance over one.

"Did you live in Eyth?"

She still assumed I was from Curra. From what she had said, I had gathered that Eyth was the capital city.

"No."

"In the countryside, then?"

I wrapped the string around her waist.

"I grew up in a fishing village."

"Oh." She turned to let me measure her hips and raised her arms for the girth of her chest. "What took you to the city?"

I smiled.

"A horse."

It made her laugh.

"And was there a man with you on the horse?"

I bent my head to make a knot, and I suddenly couldn't see the string. She saw a tear fall onto my hand.

"Oh." Her touch was gentle on my cheek. "Then Symus found you."

I could only nod. She patted my hand and spoke with kindly determination.

"And then I found you."

"And saved me from Tenrek," I managed to sniffle.

"And the dogs," she added.

"And the snow," I concluded, mocking horror.

She collected the clothes to put them away. I held onto one of the linen shifts. Dumping the rest in the open chest, she gestured around her cluttered room.

"And you're certainly safe from the snow in here!"

I heaved a sigh. The room was cozy, but small and cluttered. Even when Nanomi went out, which she did for hours at a time, it felt crowded and close. I longed to see the sun again, even if it shone on snow.

"Does it last long?"

Nanomi threw her hands in the air.

"The snow? Blessed Suna! Months and months! The woods will be deep long after the equinox. Spring comes late and cold in the north. You'll have plenty of time to heal, my dear, before we go venturing out again."

"And plenty of time to sew," I rejoined, forcing a grimace of cheer.

Nanomi pulled a bulb of garlic from a hook in the ceiling. A dusting of dirt shook loose with it. I was buried somewhere beneath the ground. But winter wouldn't last forever. Someday I'd see the sky again. Spring would come. I would go to Gelderscarth and offer my services as a tailor. I'd trade for a horse. And I'd find my way home.

I picked up the shears and began to pick the shift apart. Plenty of time.

If Aedon and Florian couldn't find me, I'd have to find them.

*   *   *

While Nanomi talked and cooked and sang, I spent the winter sewing. Before the solstice, Nanomi had a linen shift, a woolen gown, and a sheepskin jacket that fit. Within another month, so did I. Not tightly, though. I had grown thin with Symus and Tenrek, and thinner with the wound and fever. I had to be careful in shaping my clothes, for the flesh was returning, and differently. My figure had changed since I made my ceremonial gown, a lifetime ago. I wasn't budding anymore. Despite the leanness, I now shaped the seams to a woman's form.

As conclusive evidence of my maturation, my monthly flow began that winter. I knew what it was and what to do, for Mati had taught me. After all, I was almost sixteen, and all the other girls in Ayr had started much younger. Nanomi gave me what I needed and said I was the right age for a Curran. I was just grateful to Suna that it hadn't happened while I was with Symus or Tenrek.

With all Nanomi's care and attention, my leg healed quickly. The underground room felt smaller and smaller as I began to walk again. The day she asked if I'd like to go with her for water, I nearly jumped out the door on her heels.

"Guiz'e's cup," she laughed at my eagerness. "You've really been closed in too long!"

Outside the door was a passage roofed with rotting beams through which light sprayed in broken shafts. Our booted footsteps echoed in the resulting twilight.

"I fell on this place when I ran away from Tenrek," she told me. "I landed right about here." She swung her bucket over a spot beneath a gaping hole. The air was cold and smelled of snow as if winter had also fallen in and couldn't get out. I was grateful for my sheepskin jacket. "It didn't take long to find the root cellar. That's the room I live in now. It was one of the few that still had a roof and a solid door. I built the fireplace myself. It took me months."

I squinted up into morning sunlight, the first I had seen since leaving Kragknoll.

"Didn't he ever look for you here?"

She kicked aside debris so I could follow with my limping step.

"Suna never favored Tenrek," she snorted with open scorn. "When he got the dogs, I dug the escape hole. They're good Ponnish hounds and could have tracked me in half a day, but my scent was cold long before he got them. And I don't think they'd go up the chimney to find me," she concluded with a laugh.

The passage was lined with oaken doors, some intact, some hanging uselessly on their hinges, some fallen completely into the gaping darks beyond. The dark I peered into held nothing but tumbled timbers, rocks, and dirt.

"What are all these rooms?"

"This one's a granary." She opened one of the working doors. The dim space was filled with barrels and sacks. Most of the sacks sagged with loss, and I heard the scuttle of furtive rats. Nanomi shrugged. "I don't use the grain, but some of the barrels still hold good meal. It takes some digging to find what doesn't have mold or worms, but I don't need much. These provisions were meant for a household of dozens, and I eat no more than a mouse next to them."

The next door revealed a buttery crammed with small casks that even a Curran might manage to lift. The air was dusty but sharply sweet.

"Wine," she remarked with a note of pride. "Not Undrian, either. Good Pinian wine. Galemis loves it."

As she latched the door, I had to drag my heart back from Pini.

"That's why you stay here. Because of the wine you can trade to Galemis."

"Yes," she admitted without embarrassment. "And not just wine."

She led me up a steep stone stair at the end of the passage. With some satisfaction, I noted the rhythmic sweep and sway of her hems, of the tunic and shift I had reconstructed, of the clothes that fit her perfectly. Distracted by my handiwork, I was taken completely by surprise by the space that suddenly opened above us.

"This is Terskwold," announced Nanomi.

It must have been magnificent once. Now it was a blackened cage of charred oak beams, ruined walls, and shattered glass. The outer shell of sooty stumps outlined the shapes of a hall, a temple, and the gutted kitchen where we had emerged. Adjoining rooms I couldn't name were carpeted now with drifted snow. Fireplaces hung in the air above the stubs of ceiling beams that no longer held up bedroom floors. A staircase spiraled halfway up a crumbling tower, the only stone structure in the sprawling complex. Surrounding an enormous yard were the black remains of timber stables, a stockade fence, a wooden gatehouse and corner towers. Beyond were cottages, cold and empty, and a vast snowy plain reaching toward the horizon.

"This is where I search for treasure." She pointed from one heap of ash to another. "Some things I've kept. Some of the kitchen knives. Some of the pots. The hooks in my hearth." Her chin waved vaguely beyond the kitchen. "Most of the rest I've traded to Galemis. The rest of the knives. A silver comb. A garnet ring. But there's nothing of any significant value. Nothing worth a horse. Not yet, anyway."

So this was where she came alone, to search for something to trade for a horse.

She stepped across a fallen beam. The empty bucket knocked against it and shot an echo through the ruins. Several score of startled birds flew up in a whistling cloud of wings.

"Pigeons," smiled Nanomi. She picked her way to a blackened hearth. Its hood had fallen, leaving a scar, a shelf cut into the face of the stone. Twigs and sticks stuck out of the scar. Nanomi reached in and lifted out a gray and white bird nearly ready to fledge. Its wings spread out to cover her hand, but otherwise it lay quiet and docile.

"They nest all year. Very convenient."

With a sudden twist, she wrung its neck and tucked its feet into her girdle.

"Dinner."

The killing startled but didn't disturb me. It was meat. The soups and stews that had nursed me to health were full of squab, and the mattress we slept on was stuffed with feathers. Convenient and practical.

"Who lived here before the pigeons?"

Nanomi made her way to the tower. The hook and winch above the well had survived the disaster that razed the House.

"Galemis says they were breeders like him." She hung the bucket on the hook and lowered the chain into the well. "Five or six years ago, there was a drought." The bucket splashed into water below. "Everything dried up, crops and forest, land and wood. A summer storm. A bolt of lightning. Piles of ash."

She raised the bucket. I thought of the great House, dry as tinder, pictured the lightning, the flash of fire, the rage of flames. I could hear the roaring in my mind, see the polished wood, woolen tapestries, silken draperies, linen bedding, clothes and furniture, buildings and beasts, all lost in the blaze. A splash of water across my feet brought me back as Nanomi hoisted the bucket onto the wall and unhooked the handle.

"Where did they go?"

She calmly regarded her domain, painted in strokes of charcoal and snow.

"They moved away and rebuilt elsewhere. Galemis says if they rebuilt here, the horses would remember the fire and never get over the fear. The stallions would be too wild to breed and the mares would be flighty and throw their foals. Tol has cursed the ground with fire, and Teisik can't reverse the curse."

"Teisik?" I questioned.

"Oh, yes," she grinned, resting her arm on the bucket. "To you and me, he's the god of virility, just as we honor him in Curra, but the Undrians style him the god of horses. If Teisik doesn't bless the herd, there are no foals. If Teisik doesn't bless the land, there can be no herd. It grows my vegetables and herbs, but it won't grow horses. Not anymore." She gestured grandly at all around us. "So here I am, living the life of an Undrian lord. Except," she laughed, "for not having a horse."

A mournful wind moaned through the beams. The sunlight was fading. I closed my jacket. I couldn't imagine living in this ghost of a House. Not forever. But neither would the resourceful Nanomi.

"You'll find something good. Something of value. Something you can trade for a horse."

We lifted the heavy bucket between us and hauled it back down to Nanomi's burrow. We both felt sure she would get a horse.

We didn't know it would be so soon.

*　　*　　*

When I could walk well enough, I went for water alone.

Without any windows, we couldn't tell the time of day. We lived by the rhythms of sleep and hunger, which didn't always match the sun. Sometimes when I went for water, it was noon in the world above, sometimes sunset, sometimes dawn. If it was dark, I didn't go, and we waited for daylight. At those times, when it was dark, I just stood on the stair and listened until the cold drove me back. I often heard owls. I heard no wolves.

One freezing, windless night it snowed, draping the ruins in clothes of white. I stood alone at the top of the stair and listened to the whisper of flakes as they sank through the air and congregated on rotting wood. When I closed my eyes, I could almost hear the whisper of water against the sand, or the hiss of rain into the thatch of Mati's roof. I swayed with longing. I longed to stand on the beach at dawn and mingle my voices with Aedon's and Kes's, to sing to the pearls, to feel the wonder of Suna's love. I could hear the deep notes of waterfalls in the jade-green forest, the middling tones of a summer breeze as it teased my hair, the clear, high call of seagulls coasting on the wind.

Something moved in the ruins, jarring me back into Undrian winter. Startled, I turned, but I didn't know where the sound had come from, and nothing moved against the snow. Maybe some beast was prowling for prey that hid in the wreckage. If it was a wolf, I had nothing to fear. But if it was Tenrek… Frightened, I edged back into the stair, pattered down, and fled to the safety of Nanomi's lair.

"Ah," she sighed as I closed the door to shut out the fear. "So we have a snowy night."

My face must have registered blank bewilderment. How did she know?

Her smile was smug as she took the bucket.

"You never draw water in the dark," she observed, "and there's snow on your shoulders."

I shrugged off my jacket. She was right. I shook off the snow and hung the jacket on its hook. Nanomi returned to the hearth and started to sing.

> With betony I'll heal your hurts,
> and rosy althea....

Without really thinking, I sang, too. I had heard her songs a hundred times and knew them all. She sang like ordinary people, not the way a singer sang, but single notes in a single voice. I liked the cheerful melodies, and couldn't help harmonizing with her high, clear voice.

"That was pretty," she remarked at the end, dishing our supper into bowls. "You can make more notes for the song. And you have an interesting voice." A pucker appeared between her brows. "As if it were more...complicated."

I took my bowl and sat at the table. Things were simple in this room. Nanomi cooked and slept and sang. She grew a garden in the summer, collected fledglings for her stews, and scrounged for treasures to trade for a horse. Her life was a simple melody of cheerful survival. I shouldn't have sung the harmony. I didn't want things to be complicated. Nanomi smiled as if they weren't.

"You like to sing," she noted simply.

"Just like you," I tried to smile back.

"Ah," she said. "Not like me. I just sing. You sing...more." Her smile persisted, but shifted somehow. Now it was more...complicated. She picked up her spoon. "No," she smiled into her soup. "Not like me at all."

*   *   *

"I'm going to Gelderscarth tomorrow," said Nanomi a few days later. "We're almost out of lard."

Mending the sleeve of a linen shift, my needle paused in the midst of a stitch. Her announcement was both expected and welcome. We were nearly out of several provisions, but I didn't care about the supplies. She looked at me over the squab she was plucking.

"Do you want to come? You don't have to. I'm sure you'd be fine alone for a while. You certainly know your way around by now. I'll probably be gone for a week. It takes a day just to get there, and a while to negotiate my trades. But you might find Gelderscarth interesting."

Of course I would. I wanted to meet this man Galemis and find out if I could trade for a horse. Or maybe a pony, if he had one. But Nanomi had been kind to me, and I didn't want to seem eager to leave her.

"I don't think I want to stay here alone. It's so close to Kragknoll. What if Tenrek's dogs caught my scent? Do you mind if I come?"

Nanomi smiled down at the squab being systematically denuded.

"Of course not, my dear. Your company will brighten the journey. Bring whatever you think you'll need. Galemis is a hospitable fellow. He'll probably want to take you around. The first time I went, he spent three days just showing off his herd."

She laughed at the memory, but if she said more, I hardly noticed. I was too busy praying Galemis needed a tailor.

I had been with Nanomi for four months, all of them snowy and bitterly cold. But the cold didn't seem to reach my skin as we set out for Gelderscarth in the morning. My leg had healed, so walking no longer gave me pain. I was wearing my newly tailored clothes, as was Nanomi. I hoped they would impress Galemis.

Nanomi seemed cheerfully optimistic, too. We pulled a small sledge with several casks of the Pinian wine. Beyond the ribs of house and stables, fingers of forest reached from the west, but mostly the land was broad and open. Rolling hillocks, meandering streams, abandoned orchards, and empty cottages sprawled in front of us under a hardened coat of snow.

"Lard," she reminded herself what she needed. "Nuts. Dried apples. A cheese for sure. Maybe some beef. I haven't had salted beef in months. And eggs. Just a few. It's hard to get them home, of course, but it would be nice to have some eggs. Chicken eggs. Or maybe duck. The pigeon eggs are just so small, and I'd rather let them hatch for meat. But wouldn't a fresh egg be divine?"

It would, I thought. I hadn't had an egg since before reaching Kragknoll. But a horse was of far more interest to me. With luck, I wouldn't be returning to Terskwold with Nanomi. With luck, I would stay at Gelderscarth to trade my talent for a horse.

"Oats, if Galemis will let me have some. Otherwise, barley. Peas, of course. And beans."

She rattled on. I didn't mind. It kept me from thinking too much about Ayr, the ride to Darcy, Florian's eyes, their changing colors. I tried instead to admire the crystal winter sky, the brisk, clear air, the crisp, clean lie of the pristine snow.

For it truly was beautiful. The shapes it formed in sweeping drifts, the mounds it made on the branches of trees, its glitter in the morning sun.

Too light to break through, our feet crunched over the crusted snow. The sled scraped stolidly behind. A scarlet bird sang in a pine. I stored the winter sounds away, hoarding them like private treasures, someday to be recalled as part of my grand escape from Undria. Nanomi smiled as if she shared my secret hope.

Some time before noon, we reached a bridge arching over a river. Through a layer of ice in marvelous shapes, we could see water rushing past. Nanomi pulled the sledge up the bridge.

"This is the border of Terskwold," she said. "You'll see no horses cross this bridge. No breeder will take a horse onto cursed land."

I glanced behind us. Even under its sparkling blanket, the land of Terskwold seemed forlorn. Empty. Forsaken. Even the mill further up the river was vacant and still.

"Is there any way to break the curse?"

Nanomi looked back with a thoughtful look on her pointed face.

"Galemis said something about Tol's sister, Nazha. A white foal born of a white mare under a full moon. But I don't remember how it works."

Then she shrugged and turned away from Terskwold, and I followed her down the arch of the bridge into the sweeping grasslands of Gelderscarth.

*   *   *

We arrived at the House by sunset. Walking had warmed me throughout the day, but as the full moon edged over the rim of the plain and the sun retreated into the ridge of mountains behind us, the air grew colder, and I could scarcely feel my feet by the time we reached the outer stockade. The guards who called down from the wooden gatehouse were clearly acquainted with Nanomi. She answered their hail in words that echoed the wind singing across an ocean of grass and the thudding rhythm of horses' hooves. I pulled in a breath.

"Nanomi," I whispered. "I don't speak any Undrian."

She watched the enormous wooden gate swing open before us.

"Don't worry. Galemis speaks Marnaki. You speak Marnaki, don't you?"

We had only spoken Curran together.

"Yes," I answered. "Symus taught me."

She smiled again as we walked through the gate.

"Then you'll be fine."

Gelderscarth was much like Terskwold, only bigger and not burned down. Within the stockade was a village of cottages, dominated by a House on a rise with a sturdy wooden wall of its own. As we trudged up the central street, Undrian women with skin pale as cream were calling their children to supper, shepherding them with woolen skirts of brightly dyed wool. Undrian men with flaxen hair pulled sledges of firewood home to their hearths before the sky could darken from its sunset mood of lavender and goldenrod to one of violet and silver.

The guards who patrolled the wall of the House were lighting torches as we approached. The gate was opened by more guards. Guards with swords. Guards who stared. For the first time in months, I felt small.

In the inner ward, I felt even smaller. The yard was huge, hemmed on both sides by wooden stables with decorative eaves and carved maple doors that were split at the middle so the top half could open while the bottom was closed. There must have been twenty on either side. Most of the doors were closed already, some were being latched as we passed, but a few were still open and hooked in place, allowing the residents to look out. And this they did. The six or eight horses who watched us had delicate heads with well-defined lines, attentive ears, and large dark eyes that seemed to view us as new and interesting strangers. They were shades of white with manes and forelocks in shades of gray. Only one had a mane of white. She bobbed her silvery head and nickered. I almost nickered back, but caught myself just as a groom closed her door.

Nanomi nodded, noticing where my eye had strayed.

"You'll see that one again," she promised. "She's Galemis's hope for the future."

I might have inquired what hope that was, but we had nearly reached the House.

The House was larger than at Terskwold. It was three stories high, with the ends of the beams sticking out from the walls, carved like the heads of racing horses, their necks stretched out, their ears laid back, their teeth and eyes wild. Icicles hung from the horses' chins and fringed the eaves of the roof above. Instead of approaching the House, however, Nanomi turned aside to a storehouse.

A man was waiting in the door. He was trim of form in a close-fitting tunic of silver and black, and his manner was crisp and efficient. Nanomi dragged the sledge inside. The building was filled with sacks and barrels, chests and boxes, and irregular objects tied up in cloth, but it smelled of beeswax, herbs and spices, wood and leather, summer hay. A staging point for goods coming in and going out. He spoke with Nanomi, trotting words back and forth between them. Tally sticks flashed between his hands and they reached an agreement. With a wooden stylus, he made neat marks on a shallow tray of black wax. His eyes surveyed me up and down in open curiosity. Nanomi explained; I heard my name. Without reciprocal introductions, he made more marks, tucked the tablet under his arm, waited while we collected our packs, then led us across the yard to the House.

"He's the steward," she told me in Curran, mounting the steps. "His name is Scaur. He handles all of Galemis's business." Her smile was prim as we entered through the huge, carved door. "But I always speak to Galemis myself."

While Scaur disappeared through a private door, I gaped at the hall. A shadowy ceiling rose high overhead, supported by beams of sturdy beech. Tall windows reflected the light of torches, of masses of candles on long trestle tables, of birch logs burning in a pit as big as Tenrok's entire house. Everything was heavily carved. The space was noisy with dogs and dishes as servants, or slaves, laid the tables for a feast.

Scaur ushered us through the private door. The room was warm with wood and wool and a blazing hearth under a marble hood. Behind a polished cherry desk sat a corpulent man, not much beyond fifty, with milky skin and fine black hair cut very short, like the velvety coat of a well-fed cat. A close black beard framed his paunchy face, emphasizing a turned-up nose and squinty eyes as dark as night.

"Ah, Nanomi," he purred, rising to leave the waxen tablet and circumnavigate the desk. The elegant robes that draped his girth were of heavy black brocaded silk with tiny brilliants sewn into the pattern like midnight stars. His collar and cuffs were of silver fur. He spoke to Scaur, giving instructions and sending him out. The steward bowed and closed the door. I hadn't seen anyone bow since Darcy. Then Nanomi bowed and I followed suit. Her voice was as smooth as oiled glass.

"Milord Galemis."

He stretched out his nose as if he were scenting me rather than seeing me. From him I caught the dusty odors of parchment, ink, and ancient leather.

"You've brought a friend," he observed in Marnaki. "How delightful."

"Milord, this is Amalisa...." My name trailed off on her lips, and I realized she was looking for an appellation and couldn't find one.

"Amalisa of Ayr," I provided reflexively, hoping Nanomi wouldn't recognize the name as Pinian. I wouldn't lie, but it was more convenient to let her believe I hailed from some obscure fishing village in outer Curra. Something flickered through her eyes, but she accepted the name and repeated it gracefully.

"Amalisa of Ayr." Then she gave me his name. "Baron Galemis of Gelderscarth."

He inclined his head, letting his nearsighted eyes wander down and up. I hoped he was noting my tailoring skills.

"A pleasure."

I bowed again and hoped my response wouldn't give me away. I hadn't needed to demonstrate public courtesy in nearly three seasons, and I knew nothing of Curran or Undrian etiquette.

"You honor me with your welcome, milord."

His eyebrows twitched.

"Yes. Well. You must stay with us a while. A room has been prepared for you. Scaur will take you. You'll want to refresh yourselves before dinner. Tonight you must eat and enjoy yourselves."

We bowed again.

"Thank you, milord. You have always extended an open hand."

At the door, we turned to bow again, but he was no longer watching us. He had returned to his desk and lifted the wax accounting tablet close to his face. His eyebrows rose with far more interest than I thought a few casks of wine would merit. Then just before Scaur closed the door, I saw Galemis press the tablet to his breast, lean back his head, close his nearsighted eyes, and smile.

*   *   *

Our room smelled of pinesap, soap, and fur. A steaming bath in a copper tub stood near the hearth, and the windows were shuttered against the cold. The bed was huge, with massive posts that supported a frame from which hung heavy brocaded drapes. When these were closed, the bed would be like a little room inside the room. I saw at least seven kinds of furs strewn across the bed—deer, bear, lion, elk, and, sadly, wolf among them. Nanomi and I would be warm that night.

Before the door was completely closed, Nanomi dropped her pack on the floor and crossed to a desk with a straight-backed chair. A bright brass tray held two stemless cups of snow-white pottery, two pewter spoons, a bowl of sugar, a ewer of water, and a dish arrayed with lemon slices. With patent delight, she pressed some lemon into a cup, added sugar, and poured water over the resulting syrup. One sip produced an exalted expression on her face.

"Ah," she sighed happily. "Galemis knows how much I love it. Here." She fixed some for me. "It tastes like home."

Gingerly, I tasted it. Tart and sweet. It didn't taste like home at all, but it certainly was delicious. I smiled at Nanomi. Her smile was supremely satisfied.

An hour later, clean and refreshed, I sat with Nanomi in the hall, feeling distinctly out of place. I had eaten with all of Ayr at the seeding and harvest festivals. I had eaten with the Pinian princes when they danced at the equinox moon. But I had never eaten at high table in a baronial hall. The household was noisy, high-spirited, lusty. They argued, laughed, and sang. They didn't sing as we did in Ayr, but raucously, loudly, and out of tune, like drunken tavern patrons in Marnak. Few gave Nanomi any notice, but I felt many inquisitive glances. For the first time since Darcy, I wished I could hide behind my hair, but I had grown used to wearing it braided, and it no longer hid me from curious eyes.

Nanomi sat on Galemis's left, in the place of honor, with me beyond her. On my other hand was one of his sons, a muscular man of about thirty years, big as an oak and pale as almonds. If he spoke Marnaki, he never let on, sparing us both the onus of pleasantries. Galemis and Nanomi, however, enjoyed a spirited conversation, entirely in Undrian. Thus isolated, I sampled scarlet beets sprinkled with blazing yellow saffron, roasted pheasant stuffed with chestnuts, and pink-fleshed salmon in apricot sauce.

"Do try the wine," Galemis suggested across Nanomi while someone served me mussels stewed in savory cream. "Nanomi says she never drinks it, but maybe you will appreciate its fresh, fruity crispness, its subtle overtones of oak."

I had no idea what he meant by that, but to be polite, I sipped the portion he poured in my cup. The memories nearly overpowered me.

"It's excellent, I'm sure."

Galemis waved his cup in approval.

"Tomorrow we'll tour the stables," he said. "Perhaps you have an interest in horses?"

I leaped at the opening.

"I can ride," I dared to boast. I chose not to mention the size of my mount. My claim earned a startled glance from Nanomi. Genial with wine, Galemis just smiled.

"I'll introduce you to my mares. During your stay, you must spend as much time as you please with them. Maybe you'll take a liking to one."

Was he inviting me to choose?

"Your horses must be of great value," I probed.

Galemis squinted cannily while Nanomi's eyes turned to thoughtful slits.

"Here in the north," Galemis remarked, "almost anything can be bought in trade. For the proper price."

A bard appeared, a harp in one hand, a stool in the other. She bowed and addressed him, presumably saying what she would play. While she sat and tuned, I wondered how many hours of tailoring would amount to the proper price of a mount to carry me back to Florian. From the placid smile on Nanomi's lips, I suspected she was considering her assets, too, and I wondered what treasure she had recently found that could be worth the price of a horse.

It wouldn't be long before I found out.

*   *   *

The next morning, bundled in my sheepskin jacket, I followed Galemis and Nanomi out to the stables. As we crossed the yard, at least thirty pairs of equine eyes considered our approach with interest. I spotted the silver-locked mare at once. Her ears flicked forward, and she gave us a welcoming whicker. At least, it seemed welcoming to me.

Galemis squinted and kept his head low, as if the sunlight hurt his eyes, until we reached the stable's gloom. A probing wind poked through every door and blew wisps of straw around the floor, but the air inside was warm with horses and sweet with hay. As soon as we entered, scores of hooves shuffled and clomped as the animals turned from their outside doors to examine us over their inside gates. They reached their necks into the aisle, extending their velvety noses toward us. All appeared to be curious, gentle, intelligent. All except one, who laid back his ears and bared his teeth as Galemis stopped just out of reach.

"The jewel of the Gelderscarth line," said the baron. "Gelderscarth Mehadimar, out of Mesara, by Gelderscarth Tavalian, both of the bloodline of Gelderscarth Elsevier."

The owner of this wordy lineage had the largest box in the stable, but his elegant head was securely tied. He jerked at the rope, shaking ripples down his ebony mane. His polished coat shone like nacre. A young man nearly as pale as the horse stood in the stall with his arms hanging easily over the top until he saw us and straightened as tall and upright as a birch.

"Hyg," Galemis acknowledged him.

"Master," the youth responded crisply.

I promptly heard other feet, human feet, in almost all the other stalls, as other boys scrambled up and dusted off to present themselves.

"They sleep with the horses," Galemis remarked as if the boys were mere furnishings, like hay racks or water buckets. "It gentles the mares

158

and keeps the stallion manageable. Most of the herd is out all year, which gives the line its hardiness. But we bring the brood mares in for the winter to keep them safe and to shelter the foals if they come before spring. After their summer wild on the plain, they can be pretty flighty. And Mehadimar can be downright testy." He waved a possessive hand, and the stallion violently kicked the wall behind him. I jumped in alarm at the wood-splitting crash, but Galemis smiled with satisfaction. "He'd rather be out with the herd," he snorted. "But that's his father's job. His job," he returned the stallion's glare, "is to father a pure white foal for me. Something his father has never managed."

"To break the curse on Terskwold?" I dared.

Galemis raised his sleek black brows.

"So Nanomi told you something of that?"

I glanced at Nanomi.

"I only remember something about a white foal born of a white mare under a full moon," she told him.

"Not merely white," he elaborated, "but purely white. As white as moonlight, both mare and foal. And the foal must be born in the full moon's light. That's the foal that can break the curse." He clasped his hands behind his back and led us further down the aisle.

"But how?" I couldn't help but ask.

"Simply by stepping on Terskwold soil. The touch of Nazha to counteract the touch of Tol. And by Undrian law, whoever can break the curse on the land can claim the land."

The mares we passed were milk white, cream white, alabaster, white as birch, with manes of dove gray, gull gray, ash gray, and beech gray. Only the one I had noticed yesterday was white as snow with a mane like silver. She was five stalls down the aisle. Her ears perked forward as we approached and she greeted me with a welcoming nicker.

"Ah," smiled Galemis. "I see you've met my fair Gwenarian."

She reached for me with her velvety nose. I wanted to touch her but wasn't sure if it was allowed.

"Not really," I forced myself to say. "She only saw us walk in yesterday."

"Then allow me to introduce you properly."

He unlatched the gate and swung it wide. Untethered, the mare took one step toward me and lowered her head to the level of mine. She didn't need to come any closer. She pulled me with her intelligent eyes, dark as night, yet bright and inquisitive. Whiter than pearls, she seemed to be shaped out of milk and moonlight. There were stars in her gaze. I didn't even feel my feet move into the stall. I put out my hand, and she nuzzled it with lips as soft as a summer breeze.

"She likes you already," he purred behind me.

I didn't answer. I'd never felt so drawn to a beast. Not even the wolf. There I was, not much more than half the height of the white mare's withers, yet I felt as if we belonged to each other. My hand looked tiny against her brow as I scratched beneath her silver forelock. I scanned the length of her beautiful body. I didn't know much about horses, but even I could see the enormity of her belly.

"Is she carrying a white foal?"

Galemis gave a wishful snort.

"I pray to Nazha that she is. But there's no way to know until it's born."

"And will that be under a full moon?" How little I knew about horses. If Galemis felt any contempt for my ignorance, though, he hid it well.

"The gods may know, but I do not. I would give a great deal to have any knowledge or say in the matter."

I scarcely heard his concluding words. Gwenarian was pressing her face to my chest. She could have easily knocked me over, but there was a gentleness in the movement, a genuine sweetness, a curiosity. I turned to Nanomi, a silly grin across my face.

"Did she do this to you?"

Nanomi's brows rose in evident surprise.

"Not to me. She paid me no mind."

I heard a sound in the straw behind me, became aware of the boy in the stall. He was taller than me, pale as butter, with gossamer hair as fine as spider webs. He was scrawny and scared-looking. He couldn't have been much more than nine.

"Bohrn," Galemis addressed the boy. He continued in Undrian, giving some casual command. A flicker of terror crossed Bohrn's pale eyes, but I took it for fear of his master's displeasure, and since Galemis was so delighted, I thought Bohrn's fears were groundless. But if I knew little about horses, I knew even less about their breeders. At least, this one.

Bohrn answered crisply, as if Galemis had told him simply to bring the mare her daily oats. Then he left the stall without looking back.

It took me some time to realize I was alone with the mare. Galemis had taken Nanomi on, I supposed, to see the others. I no longer heard the other boys, or even noticed the other horses. I was too entranced by Gwenarian.

She nibbled my shoulder, tickling my neck, and I laughed. Her breath was sweet as summer grass. Impetuously, I wrapped my arms around her muzzle, pressing my cheek to her bony nose. She bobbed her head as if in laughter, nearly lifting me off my feet. I closed my eyes in happiness, the first real joy I had felt since Darcy. It swelled in my breast like a song of spring, some Undrian spring I could only imagine, as if it flowed out of Gwenarian's heart and into mine. It rumbled with swollen mountain streams, rang with a bursting explosion of green, soared on the wings of golden eagles.

I lost all awareness of the stable, of any other horse but this and her unborn foal. My senses pooled in Gwenarian's eyes until I seemed to float in their depths, in the starry night of her knowing gaze. I felt my heart sink into hers, felt the heartbeat of her foal, small and rapid compared with the mother's. Their light enveloped me, shining and clear, and I felt the comforting hand of Suna cradle us all.

I don't think I even knew I was singing. I thought it was only my heart that sang, to the beautiful mare, to her beautiful foal, to my beautiful goddess. Only when the light receded, leaving me warm in an Undrian stall with my arms clasped around Gwenarian's head, did I actually hear the sounds coming out of me. Instantly, they trailed away into echoes among the stable rafters.

"Excellent," breathed Galemis's voice.

My head went light, and I nearly fainted. I could barely turn around without falling.

There they were, in the stable aisle, as smug as cats with a wounded bird. My pack hung from Nanomi's hand.

"She's everything you said she is," he said to Nanomi.

My heart nearly stopped. My voice choked out in a pleading whisper.

"Did you always know?"

She looked immensely pleased with herself.

"That you were a Pinian singer? No. Not until a week ago. The snowy night you went for water and didn't come back for so long I went to check on you. I heard the voices, and all of them were coming from you."

It all came clear. Her calculated announcement of a trip to Gelderscarth. The haggling with Scaur. The tour of the stable. Leaving me alone with the mare. As neatly and dispassionately as she had wrung the pigeon's neck, Nanomi had sold me to Galemis.

"So now you have a horse," I concluded.

She shrugged complacently.

"Not exactly. But a mule is better. More my size. More my speed. And far less likely to be stolen out from under me before I reach the sea."

"And you're leaving me here."

She showed no remorse as she pushed my pack into my arms.

"You won't be harmed. You're too valuable. But only as long as you do as he asks. You can give him the foal he needs. You can call it out in the full of the moon." She shrugged again. "Once you've done that, he might let you go with a mule of your own."

Galemis smiled with his squinty eyes, crossed his arms over his corpulent belly, and laughed. Nanomi bowed, first to him, then to me.

"Goodbye, Amalisa of Ayr."

Then she turned away and walked out of the stable, leaving me once again a slave.

Chapter 9: Undria

I clutched my pack and watched her go.

"You can put that in here," Galemis smirked, waving toward an open door across the aisle from Gwenarian's stall. "This room is yours, and yours alone, for washing and dressing. The boys share a room of their own for all that." He cast a significant glance down the aisle, and the faces poking out of the stalls briefly disappeared. Galemis returned his attention to me. "You'll also find more appropriate clothes."

I could see them through the door, a pair of unbleached linen britches, a linen shirt, and a woolen tunic almost as white as Gwenarian, all laid out on a wooden chest that stood a couple of feet from the wall as if it had recently been dragged in. My tailoring skills would be of no use to me here after all. I also saw a wooden bath. Evidently, Galemis prized cleanliness. His voice took on an imperative tone.

"You'll sing to the mare every day," he commanded. "Every morning and every night, and any time the mood should strike you."

He squinted at me meaningfully. It was clear the mood should strike me often.

"Bohrn tends the mare," Galemis added. I saw Bohrn then. He had already slipped back into the stall, where he stood with his arms stiff at his sides in a mixture of fear of his master and defiance toward me. "All you have to do is sing."

All I had to do, I already knew, was make Gwenarian's foal as white as she was, and make Gwenarian give birth in the light of the full moon. From the look of her, I guessed it would be the next full moon. That gave me a month. I had no idea how I could accomplish any of this, either by singing or otherwise, but neither did Galemis. For all I knew, my singing could make the foal green, like the pearls.

"I understand," I told him coldly.

"Good," he snapped and strode away.

The instant his shadow was gone from the door, twenty boys leaped the walls and pressed around me. Hyg pushed to the front, grabbed Bohrn by the shoulder, and made the others back off into a jostling circle surrounding the three of us. Even the youngest was taller than me.

"Gwenarian belongs to Bohrn," he challenged, speaking accented Marnaki. He was tall and slender, straight and pale, like a white-barked birch. I judged him to be about eighteen, the eldest by at least two years. Their eyes darted back and forth between us. I guessed he was the only one who knew Marnaki.

"Yes," I agreed, trying to pack a tone of belligerence into my voice.

"I'm Hyg," he announced, "and I'm in charge around here. I been doin' this for thirteen years. It's honest work. But you," he pronounced the word scornfully, "aren't nothin' but a slave and a freak."

Even now, it stung. I held my head high, refusing to hide. I couldn't, however, ignore the threat.

"I may be a slave, but Galemis will know if anything happens to me."

"Don't worry," Hyg snorted his contempt. "Not one of us would stoop to touch you."

His eyes scanned me up and down, however, and I could see my shape reflected in them. To Symus and Tenrek, I had been little more than a dog, a creature too low to contemplate. But to Hyg, only two or three years older than me, I was most decidedly female, the only girl in a stable of boys.

"Good," I retorted. I could make threats, too. "Because if anything happened to me, it would affect the way I sing. And that would have an effect on the mare. And the foal might come out wrong."

I saw the uncertainty flick through his eyes. As I suspected, he understood what the foal meant to Galemis. I dared to push my advantage.

"You sleep with the horses," I stated clearly, staring each boy in the eye in turn, "not with me. That goes for Bohrn, too."

Every boy tore his eyes away from me and turned to Hyg. Glowering, he repeated my declaration in Undrian. When they looked back at me, their gazes were wider with grudging awe. Briskly, I hefted my pack.

"Now, if you'll excuse me, I think I should change."

I slipped through the circle and ducked into the room Galemis had designated for my use. At the door, something caught my eye. It was, after all, right at the level of my eye. A key. In the lock. As I swung the door closed, I nipped out the key. If none of my threats protected me, I could lock myself in and be safe.

I just hoped I wouldn't need to.

*　　*　　*

The rest of that day swept by in a blur, though soon enough, the routine would be as familiar to me as the pearling songs. Shortly after my installation, the horses were taken out for exercise. Then they were groomed. Some time after noon, the boys were fed in their common room and food was brought to mine. There was more than I needed of venison stew, dried sliced apples, syrupy cider, and dense black bread. Then two more hours of exercise. More grooming, food for all. Mucking out and washing up. All the while, I hung in the corners, uncertain what I was supposed to do. Except at sunset. Then I knew exactly what I was supposed to do.

I sang to the mare. I didn't consider what to sing; I just fell back on habit. I placed my palms against her flank and sang the Evening Song. In the song, I could leave it all behind—Nanomi's selling me back into slavery, the ludicrous task assigned to me, the twenty boys listening, entranced, to the multiple voices of my song. When it ended, nineteen faces turned away, pretending they hadn't been spellbound. Only Hyg continued to stare, with wonder and suspicion.

Then suddenly the sun was gone and the stalls were closed. The boys wrapped themselves in heavy blankets and lay in the straw, right under the beasts that could crush their bones like sparrow eggs. I stood with my back against the gate, hugging one of the blankets I had found in my changing room.

"You can lie down," came a voice through the dark. "She'll never step on you. None of them ever step on us."

He couldn't possibly have seen me. Not from his stall. There were no torches, no lanterns, no lamps. Just a glimmer of moonlight seeped through the outer doors, just enough to make Gwenarian glow like a wraith in the night. But even in the brilliance of noon, Hyg couldn't have seen me. I simply wasn't tall enough. So how did he know I was still standing up? He answered as if he could read my thoughts.

"Everyone's scared to lie down the first time."

I wrapped the blanket around myself but I didn't lie down.

"How d'you do that? Sing that way? Like more than one person when you ain't."

That would be difficult to explain.

"I just do. It's a gift from Suna."

A thoughtful pause, then a defensive note crept into his voice.

"I'm not lookin' after myself, you know."

I could feel the other boys listening, even though none of them spoke Marnaki.

"My father's the miller," Hyg continued. "He's important. Galemis can't just throw me out. But Bohrn's only been here a couple of winters, and his father died last summer, and Bohrn's the only boy his mother's got. It's a good job, this. A good job for the winter. Half a year, while the mill stream's froze and the fields are empty. You're warm and you're fed and your family gets your wages. It's Bohrn who'll get hurt if the foal comes out wrong. Not me."

I wondered.

"Then why is Bohrn with Gwenarian? If she's so important, and her foal's so important, why didn't Galemis put an older boy with her? A boy with more experience? Someone more like you?"

I confess I threw in the compliment to flatter him, but it kept him talking.

"I'm the only one strong enough for Mehadimar," bragged Hyg. "I was with his father, Tavalian, for three winters. But Tav never sired no pure white foals, and this year Galemis brought in Mehadimar instead. But Bohrn, well, he's quiet, you know. Doesn't fight or misbehave. He's wonderful calming with Gwenarian, and this is her first time with foal. Galemis says Bohrn'll be good for the foal, help it come out right. Galemis doesn't like disappointment."

The stable door opened, admitting a draft of icy air and a guard on patrol. I slid down the wall and sat hunched in a corner, listening to the guard walk by. I would try not to disappoint Galemis, but not for Bohrn's sake. If the foal came out white in the full of the moon, maybe Galemis would give me a mule and let me go home.

Then again, maybe he wouldn't.

It was the only hope I had.

*   *   *

As it turned out, living at Gelderscarth wasn't so bad. It was Bohrn who still fed and groomed the mare, Bohrn who did the mucking out, and Bohrn who took her for exercise. The younger mares were led on leads by younger boys, while older mares were ridden by their older boys. Round and round the yard they went, an hour or two every morning, an hour or two every afternoon, no matter what the weather.

The spirited Mehadimar was exercised alone. Hyg took him out, but only Galemis rode the stallion. Despite his bulk, Galemis had a steady hand, an upright posture, a decisive heel, and a calming voice. The stallion might flinch and toss his head, or bare his teeth and roll his eyes, but he did precisely what he was told. Just like the mares. Just like the boys. And just like me.

At night, the stable rustled softly with boys and horses. Bohrn and the other young boys slept, worn out with work. The older boys whispered. The Undrian I picked up through the days was all about feeding and grooming and exercising, so I understood very little at night, but sometimes words weren't necessary. Sometimes a boy would sneak in with another and the rustling sounds were low and muffled, carefully timed between the guards that walked through twice an hour. Sometimes boys jumped over the walls and fought in the aisle until Hyg pulled them apart, shoving them back into their stalls before the next guard. But usually they merely gossiped, groused, or dreamed of a better life than this. Those voices didn't need translation.

None of them tried to come in with me. Even Hyg kept his distance. I knew my threats didn't keep them out, but the fear of Galemis's reprisal if anything went wrong with the foal.

And that was my job. To sing to Gwenarian and her foal. Every morning and every night, and whenever the mood might strike me.

Happily for all of us, the mood struck me often. I loved Gwenarian, and she loved me. I don't know why. Perhaps something in me called to her. Maybe she was beloved of Nazha, as I was. Whatever the reason, she drew from me the sounds of spring, the sounds of the forest, the sounds of the plains. To my song she added the sounds of horses, their stamping and breathing, their whinnies and snorts, their habitual movements and comfortable warmth. And singing to her, I could forget that I was a slave with only a month to produce a pure white foal in the full moon's light.

Signs of spring began to appear as the month crept by. The snow that fell in my first few days at Gelderscarth was wet and heavy. It lay in dirty piles around the yard and clotted in the horses' fetlocks, making daily grooming a messy ordeal. The following week, the snow came down in soggy clumps that melted as soon as they hit the ground. The horses churned the yard into mud, and the boys had to dip their hooves into buckets of water to get them clean. The following week was bright and sunny, and the breeze was soft with grass and mud and sprouting leaves. At the end of my third week at Gelderscarth, on the day of the equinox, it rained.

That evening, when I sang to the mare, Suna came to me. Winds filled my song, the harsh winds of winter, the soft winds of spring, the warm, wet winds of Ayr, and light flowed into my open soul. Suna's love raised me up as it had so long ago in Ayr, and my spirit expanded into the mare, into the foal, filling us with joy and light. Then, unexpectedly, far beyond, I felt Aedon and Florian. Their loved blended into the love of the goddess, filled with aching, filled with resolve, and suddenly, horribly, filled with pain.

It shocked me back into my body with a cry, but the pain wasn't gone. It struck me as hard as Tenrek's arrow, stunning my flesh, piercing my heart. I dropped to the straw, clutching my arms around my ribs, blinded by the pain.

"What is it?" cried Hyg, running into the stall. I felt the others press in around me. Their fear and alarm were palpable. Even Gwenarian pushed at my shoulder, nickering worriedly. Hyg fell to his knees and gripped my arm.

"What?" he demanded. "Is it the foal? Is something wrong?"

I tried to scrub the tears away, but they wouldn't stop. I couldn't understand what had happened. I had never felt pain through Suna before. Sorrow, grieving, tender loss, but never physical agony. Had something happened to Aedon? To Florian? They felt so near, yet they couldn't be. What had Suna been telling me?

"What happened?" yelled Hyg, beginning to panic.

I blinked up, finding his frightened face and all the terrified eyes beyond.

"No," I stammered. "Not the foal. The foal's all right."

The panic drained out of all their faces and Hyg sank back on his heels.

"What then?" he pressed, remembering there was still some reason for my distress.

I shook my head. The pain was fading like a dream. I unclenched my arms and took a breath. It didn't hurt now.

"I don't know," I answered feebly. "The foal's all right. The mare's all right. It's something...else." How to explain without explaining? "A memory, maybe. From when I was shot," though the pain hadn't been where Tenrek shot me.

Surprise lifted twenty pairs of brows. They didn't know I had been shot. I pushed myself up and managed to stand, holding Gwenarian's mane for support.

"I'm sorry," I told them. "I'm all right. I think I'd like to wash my face."

Hyg barked a command in Undrian, clearing a path for me out of the stall. I moved my foot and staggered. His hand cupped my elbow to steady my steps across the aisle. His brow was still furrowed with concern as I shut the door and closed them out.

With trembling hands, I lighted the lantern that let me see in my windowless room. Then I sagged down onto the wooden chest and dropped my head in my hands. Something had happened. Something terrible. To Aedon. Or Florian. Or both. The tears came back unchecked. I had been lost for so long, I had hardened my heart, had resigned myself to not being found. But I still believed they were out there somewhere, looking for me in their separate ways, loving me still.

And I loved them, in separate ways. My heart and flesh craved Florian, his wine-flavored kiss, his sudden embrace, yet my soul and song needed Aedon, his certainty, his laughter. I couldn't choose one, and I couldn't lose either. I needed them both. I needed them both unharmed and alive.

Something had happened. I had to find them. As soon as I could.

The full moon was only a week away. By Suna's grace, my job would be done. I would leave Gelderscarth one way or another.

I only needed to figure out how.

*   *   *

The day before the full moon, Galemis came to Gwenarian's stall. He ran his hands over her bulging belly and pressed his ear to her silver flank.

"The foal is ready. Tomorrow you will sing it forth."

I had expected that.

"Yes," I conceded, "but only if you will set me free as soon as it's born."

His small eyes narrowed to greedy slits.

"No. The curse must be broken first."

As if she could sense that I wanted to leave her, Gwenarian pushed her face to my chest. I scratched her brow while I contemplated this counteroffer.

"When?"

"A fortnight after the foal is born. In the dark of the moon."

I eyed him with doubt. I was a slave. What could make him keep his word?

"All right. But if you try to hold me after breaking the curse, I will call down the wolves from the mountains to kill any horse that ever steps foot on Terskwold soil again. And no one will know how to break that curse."

His eyes flared under his scowling brow. He didn't know if I could do it. Neither did I. But I knew he couldn't take the chance.

"The curse must be broken first," he snarled.

I wondered how we'd know.

"Agreed."

Furious, he stalked down the aisle to Mehadimar's stall. The stallion would get a stiff riding that day. I pressed my brow to Gwenarian's face.

"I'm sorry," I whispered in Pinian. "There are people I love more than you."

She nudged me as if she understood.

To comfort us both, I wrapped my arms around her head, closed my eyes, and sang.

*   *   *

The following evening, Galemis himself led Gwenarian out into the yard. The cobalt sky was splashed with buttercup, rose, and plum, and the gates were open to show where the full moon would shortly rise above the village. The breeze was soft with fresh-tilled soil, sprouting oats, streams in spate, and violets.

All the stable doors were open; all the boys and horses watched. Only Bohrn and I went with the mare, he at her halter, I at her side. Bohrn had scrubbed her until she shone, Bohrn and I sported new black tunics, and Galemis wore his baronial finery. His coal-black cloak was lined with sable, his fingers were heavy with rings of onyx and dark brown sard, and on his brow gleamed a golden baronial coronet set with onyx cabochons.

In the center of the yard was a woven carpet twice the size of Gwenarian's stall. It was patterned with scarlet, black, and gold, with a fringe of white at either end. I had never seen anything like it, not even in Crown Prince Gavin's apartments. Galemis positioned the mare at the center of this magnificent rug, clearly to cushion the birth of the foal and to keep it from falling on the dirt. That's how precious this foal was to him, that he would soil a valuable carpet rather than soil the foal.

Galemis had also invited guests. They stood with Scaur and a brown-robed priest at the edge of the rug, presumably to verify that the pure white foal was Gwenarian's. Warmly wrapped in a woolen cloak, one man searched the stable doors, found Hyg, and nodded. The miller, no doubt. Others had come from a greater distance; their mounts were clustered near the gate. One guest had a cloak with a collar of fox, another a silver chain on his breast. One wore a golden band on his brow, set with lapis. He must be a baron like Galemis. He peered at me with greedy eyes, and I guessed Galemis was planning to sell me if the foal truly broke the curse.

The mood was solemn, though slaves served wine and trays of food. All the guests drank, a few of them ate. Gwenarian twitched with nervousness, and I rather wished for some wine, myself, as the moon appeared, dark as a garnet, above the rooftops of Gelderscarth.

The yard grew dark. No torches were lighted on the walls, no lamps or lanterns were brought outside. The windows of the House were dark.

Only Nazha's light must fall on the foal. The visitors' horses faded in shadow, the witnesses blurred in the failing light, but I could still see Galemis's eyes, holding me in their expectant gaze.

"Begin," he commanded.

I pressed my brow to Gwenarian's shoulder. She was trembling. I closed my eyes and prayed to Suna. How could I call forth a foal from a mare? And Suna came into my mind and told me.

It was a harvest, like that of the pearls, but without sorrow, only joy. Without death, only life.

With joy and thanksgiving, I began the Song of Comfort.

At the first deep note from my lower chest, the yard fell silent, as if every breath was caught in surprise. Then the flutelike tones from my upper range floated out like the voice of a wistful gull. Then the watery, windy syllables flowed out between them, echoed around the quiet yard, and found Gwenarian's flicking ear. Her trembling stopped.

The moon edged upward, round and full, brightening to tangerine. The song continued, the mare relaxed, suspended breaths eased out again. From tangerine to striated lemon, the moon crept higher through the gate, leaving the cottage roofs behind. The Song of Comfort rocked and swayed, and Gwenarian languidly sank to her knees.

The moon climbed over the open gate and heaved into the velvet sky, burning colder into white. I washed the mare with my watery words while the moon washed her brighter with its light. She rolled to her side and I kneeled by her shoulder, stroking her neck. She snorted softly and closed her eyes.

Shadows shifted around the yard as I shifted into the Song of Opening. Galemis stood behind the mare, surrounded by the witnesses. Gwenarian moaned and her belly clenched with the first contraction.

Tenderly, gently, I poured my song into her ear. Only her tightening belly tensed; her heart and breathing were calm and relaxed. The moon rose higher, brighter, whiter, flooding the yard with silver light. At the edge of my brain, I heard hushed voices exclaim at the emergence of a nose, an ear, a cloud-shrouded head. And as the moon reached its highest point, Gwenarian gave a mighty push, and the foal flowed out in a rush of fluid.

I moved from the Song of Opening back to the Song of Comfort. The mare rolled upright, lurched to her feet, and reached for the foal. Still singing, I saw the cloudy covering. Without hesitation, Gwenarian cleaned the shroud away, revealing a creature of ice and light.

He was so white it almost hurt to look at him. His coat was moonlight, his mane and tail were spun by the gods from fallen snow, and his tiny hooves were carved from silver. Under his mother's ministrations, he raised his head and opened eyes that seemed to have no color at all. Even the lashes were white as ice. Only when he blinked up at me did I see some darkness at the center, pink as a rose.

The witnesses behind Galemis eased back with a stifled gasp of wonder. Galemis crossed his arms on his chest with complete satisfaction. I had kept my part of the bargain. A fortnight must pass before I would know if he'd keep his.

The moon slid down and the Song of Comfort came to an end. As if released from a spell, the witnesses crowded around the colt. Galemis took Gwenarian's halter and stood as proud as if he had birthed the colt himself. Bohrn stood at her head, entranced by the foal.

"Lunarian!" Galemis announced in a booming voice. A tremendous cheer rose in reply.

I edged from the circle. Even the mare had forgotten me.

I was exhausted. I wanted to sleep. Not even the stall boys at their doors paid me any mind as I stepped from the carpet and walked to the stable. In the dark, I felt my way to my private room, thinking only of blankets and sleep.

The door was ajar.

I quickly glanced back up the aisle. Where was Hyg? I heard a sound from inside the room. A rasping breath. I listened harder. I seemed to hear a skipping heart, a heated pulse. I pushed the door open. Moonlight from the open stalls seeped dimly into the windowless room. Something moved in the space behind the chest. Someone moaned. It wasn't Hyg.

In a flash, I slipped inside, closed the door, and locked it behind me. I lighted the lantern and held it high. It looked like someone had dropped a blanket between the chest and the wall, but I knew better. Someone was hiding under the blanket. Someone even smaller than Bohrn.

I hung up the lantern and dragged the chest away from the wall. The blanket sagged, exposing a tangle of long dark hair. I turned back the blanket and gazed on the face, the fine, straight nose, the hazelnut skin, the unexpected straggle of beard.

"Aedon! Oh, Aedon!"

Tears blurred my sight as I fell at his side. He licked his lips. His eyes barely opened.

"Liise?" he mumbled. His voice was husky, scarcely the voice I remembered at all. I touched his face and felt sweat on his brow. He burned with fever.

"Oh, Aedon," I choked. "What are you doing here?"

His eyes drooped closed.

"Dying," he rasped in wry reply.

I lifted the blanket and understood.

172

He lay on his side with the shot arm uppermost. The arrow had gone clear through the limb, just like one that had pierced my leg. The streaked brown fletching stuck out in front and the arrowhead stuck out at the back. Aedon couldn't pull his out, either.

Suddenly ill, I sat down hard. Aedon was shot. Shot by Tenrek. And I must pull the arrow out.

"Aedon," I whispered.

He didn't answer. I swallowed fear.

"Aedon, my dear. I have to pull the arrow out."

Quickly, I thought, while he was unconscious.

I fetched my washbasin, soap, and a towel. Then I gripped the knock end with both hands, clenched my teeth, and broke the shaft. Aedon moaned but didn't wake. I wrapped my fist around the shaft above the barb, closed my eyes, and, with a sickening tearing of wood against flesh, pulled it through. He stiffened, and his cry of pain must have been heard clear down to the mill.

My head went light and my stomach rebelled. I barely reached the chamber pot before being sick.

I heard the latch and raised my head. Someone pounded on the door.

"Hey!" called Hyg. "Are you all right?"

I wiped my mouth, blew out the lantern, and went to the door. I only opened it a crack.

"It's bringing out the foal," I claimed. "That kind of singing. I feel rather sick. I think I should sleep alone tonight."

He stared at me, but I knew I must look as bad as I felt.

"Well," he hesitated. "They're all still out there, makin' a fuss over that new colt. I guess it took a deal out of you. Go on to sleep. I'll tell Bohrn where you are. If he even makes it back tonight. They could be there til dawn." One side of his mouth turned up in a smile.

"Thank you, Hyg."

I locked the door and relighted the lantern.

Breathing with care so I wouldn't faint, I freed Aedon's arm from his sheepskin jacket and linen shirt. It was swollen and red from elbow to shoulder. I washed the wounds and wrapped the arm in some of the linens provided for my monthly flow. Then I bathed his face and sang to him. I sang the light on shifting water, the tang of pines, the sweet hot wind in the southern forest, the sounds of Ayr, the sounds of home. I sang my longing and loneliness, my love for Aedon, whose voice matched mine, my yearning for Florian....

I didn't sing long. It was well after midnight, and I was exhausted. After a while, I blew out the lantern, lay down beside him, pressed my ear to his fluttering breast, and fell deeply asleep.

*　　　*　　　*

Someone was knocking on the door. I blinked in confusion, felt Aedon's heart beneath my ear, and abruptly remembered everything. I scrambled up, covered Aedon, and pushed the chest back to its normal place. No one would see my hidden fugitive from the door.

I turned the key and opened the door.

A boy from the house held my usual breakfast of oatmeal, cider, dried apples, and bread. I could hear the stall boys already tearing into their food in their common room, and saw Gwenarian pulling at hay in her stall. Hyg stood at her gate, leaning against it, arms crossed, watching me.

"Have they gone?" I asked. Hyg knew who I meant. He shook his head.

"They've all gone up to the House to eat. Galemis is mighty pleased with that colt. He's puttin' on a regular feast."

Waiting for me to take the tray, the boy scarcely dared to look in my face. I had created the pure white colt. I guessed that, except for Galemis, every soul in Gelderscarth would now regard me with awe. It could work to my advantage.

"Hyg," I said, "I don't feel well." I knew I looked awful. My hair was coming out of its braid, my face must be gaunt, and my rumpled black tunic was spattered with what I had spewed last night. "I wonder if Cook could send me some tea." My brain raced through Nanomi's songs. "Borage, maybe. Milfoil. Sanicle. Anything for fever."

Hyg spoke to the boy, but stumbled over the names of the herbs. Maybe their names were different in Undrian. I pressed the back of my hand to my brow. The boy might not remember the herbs, but he'd remember fever.

"He'll ask," Hyg told me.

I finally took the tray, and the boy turned and ran.

"Hyg," I said before he could follow. "I...I hurt myself in the dark last night." He'd believe that. He'd heard the cry when I pulled out the arrow. "Are there salves for the horses when they get hurt?"

He squinted at me uncertainly.

"Where are you hurt?"

I felt the blood rush to my face at his challenge, but I'd give him a good excuse for the flush.

"I can't. It's.... Well...it wouldn't be proper."

With his birch-white skin, his flush was more dramatic than mine.

"Sure," he mumbled. "We got salves. I'll get you somethin'."

I waited while he ducked into the common room and came back with a stoppered pot. Some of the other boys poked out their heads, but returned to their meal under Hyg's dark scowl. He put the crock on the tray with my food.

"Here. If this don't work, I'll get you another. But this is the first one we use on the horses."

"Thank you, Hyg." And I locked the door.

I put down the tray, lighted the lantern, and moved the chest.

"Aedon?"

He moaned. I unwrapped the arm. It didn't look better. I washed it again, applied the salve, wrapped it in fresh linens, and bundled the bloody ones for washing. I covered him warmly and spooned some cider between his lips. It made him cough and turn away. I made myself eat. I had to stay strong. When the boy returned with a steaming cup, I gave him the cloths. Cook would send replacements. She always did. I just hoped she wasn't counting the weeks since my previous flow.

The tea went down better than the cider. While he slept, I sang of cool autumn breezes over the sea, of the deep green forest, of our private beach to cool his brow and push back the fire in his arm. Toward noon, he woke. He squinted from under a scowl of pain, and the golden flecks in his umber eyes seemed to glitter with fever.

"Where's Liise?" His voice was thick and mumbly, as if his tongue were swollen from thirst. I quickly bent over him.

"I'm here, my dear." I tried to smile, but his eyes frowned shut and he shook his head.

"No," he groaned. "I can hear her voice. I have to find her...."

"Aedon," I attempted again. "It's me. It's Liise."

His unhurt hand found mine and gripped it.

"I hear you," he whispered, his eyes clenched shut. "I'll find you, Liise...."

He didn't know me. It must be the fever. But then, I reflected, I hardly looked like the Liise he knew. I waited until his grip relaxed, then bathed my body, washed my hair, and dressed in a fresh white tunic.

He didn't wake until late that night. By then, I had given him three cups of tea, washed and salved his wound twice more, and combed his tangled hair. It was still as long as mine. He looked somewhat better. I hoped I looked more familiar, too.

"Liise?" he called out abruptly.

I rushed to his bed behind the chest.

"I'm here, my dear."

I held his hand and he stared at me, his dark eyes wide, still bright with fever.

"Liise?"

"Yes, dear Aedon," I smiled. "It's me."

He pulled back his hand and lifted it to touch the puckered skin of my cheek. I closed my eyes and leaned into his palm. How long it had been since I had felt a loving touch. His hand fell away.

"You can't be Liise."

The shock jolted through me like icy water.

"But, Aedon..."

He frowned in confusion.

"You sound like Liise," he whimpered. "You look like Liise.... But the mark..."

My heart was jumping as I covered my cheek. This made no sense.

"Aedon, you know me." I tried to stay calm. "You know my voice."

Still frowning, he pulled my hand from my face. His fingers traced my cheek again.

"But the mark," he repeated. "It's gone."

I leaped to my feet and backed away, grasping for an explanation.

"It's the light. The fever. Of course, it's there."

His hand fell back across his breast and his eyes tried to follow me.

"No," he rasped. "It's gone."

I paced in alarm. How long had it been since I'd seen a mirror? There hadn't been any at Kragknoll or Terskwold.... Suddenly I understood. Nazha had done it. She ruled a woman's monthly flow. When mine began, she must have taken the mark away. At once, my fright became excitement.

"Oh, Aedon, is it really gone?"

"Are you really Liise?"

I could only think of one way to convince him. I blew out the lantern.

"Aedon," I spoke. "You taught me the Morning Song and I taught you to listen. Our hearts were joined when Kes called Suna into the fane. We sang the songs after Kes broke his hip, and we made the pearls turn green."

I heard him struggle to sit up.

"Liise? It is really you?"

I dropped to his side and slid my arms around him.

"Oh, Aedon," I breathed into his neck. "It's really me, my dear."

"Well," he coughed in my tight embrace, "I guess it's only fair that you've changed, too."

I heard it then. The depth of his voice. It wasn't just the fever or thirst.

"Your voice has changed!" I pulled away and heard him fall back with a gasp of pain. "Oh, Aedon, I'm sorry...!"

Then I heard a sound I hadn't heard in nearly a year. Aedon laughed.

"Maybe you'd better light that lantern. I think I'm safer when you can see."

I did. He tried to give me a grin of relief, but it looked more like a grimace of pain. I fetched the tea.

"How did you get here?" I asked, supporting him to help him sip.

"On Fleck," he told me. "The past few days, we heard you singing. I thought I was dreaming, but he heard it, too, and he followed your song."

"You came to Gelderscarth on Fleck? After Tenrek shot you?"

He nodded in the crook of my arm. It made sense. Anything could have wandered in while I was singing under the moon. I remembered how the shadows had shifted. I wondered what had become of the pony.

"But how did you get into the stable?"

"I think I crawled. It's such a blur. I only wanted a place to hide."

I brought him my stew, but he pushed it away. I dipped some bread in the sauce and fed it to him.

"Aedon," I faltered. "What happened when they learned I was gone?"

"Ah," he sighed, lying back. "It seems so long ago." It did. It seemed like someone else's life to me now. He closed his eyes and took a weary breath. "I'll tell you tomorrow...."

Tenderly, I covered him and blew out the lamp. It was late. The story would wait until tomorrow. For now it was enough to have him here. I curled beside him, wrapped my arms around his waist, and went to sleep.

*   *   *

In the morning, Galemis was outside my door behind my breakfast. Scowling.

"What's this I hear about fever?"

I held the door almost all the way open. He could see most of the room from there. I didn't want to look like I was hiding something. I hoped Aedon wouldn't wake up while Galemis was there.

"Singing the foal out for you was harder than I expected. And I'm not used to being outside all night in the cold. I got sick. But I'm better today." All this was true, if not quite the way it would sound to Galemis. "A day or so more of that fever tea should be enough."

"And you've been singing. In there." He jerked his chin at my room. "Alone."

"I sing of my home," I explained in defense. "I'm...homesick."

He looked me severely up and down, unimpressed by my confession.

"And what about my mare?" he demanded.

I was genuinely surprised.

"She has her foal. She doesn't need me anymore."

That was true, too. I could see that the mare was happier with her beautiful colt than she had been with me. Bohrn was happy, too. I had seen him coming and going to meals with a blissful smile on his butter-pale face.

"Then what about the colt?" persisted Galemis.

I answered patiently.

"What does Lunarian need from me? I can hardly make him whiter. You'll take us to Terskwold and break the curse and I'll go free. Until then, I'd like to sleep in my room. Get back my strength. I couldn't make that journey now."

I saw his fists close at his sides, but I knew he wouldn't hurt me. All he needed from me now was for me to stay at Gelderscarth until the trip to Terskwold. A sudden thought glinted in his eyes.

"You're right, of course. You're coming to Terskwold. But there's no need for you to walk. I've found the perfect mount for you." He took my shoulder and steered me further down the aisle, away from Mehadimar, away from Gwenarian, to the stall at the end. I felt the boys watching. He opened the gate. Whatever mare was normally there had been moved out, presumably in with another mare. The new occupant was a stocky bay, speckled with white, not even as tall as the new foal. I knew him at once. He was twice as shaggy as the last time I saw him. It was Fleck.

"Suna's tears!" I exclaimed to cover the fact that I recognized him. "Where did he come from?"

"No one knows," Galemis replied in a tone of mystery. "He appeared among the mounts of my guests the night Lunarian was born. No one even noticed him until the following morning."

Fleck was far more interested in his rack of hay than in me, and I was glad the ponies had never shown me any affection as Gwenarian had. And good thing for him he was gelded; I doubted Galemis would ever have let him into the stable otherwise.

"You mean he just wandered in here out of the wild?"

"Oh, no," Galemis contradicted, watching me keenly. "He had tack. Pinian tack. Nothing fancy, no owner's marks, but I know a Pinian saddle and bridle when I see them."

I turned to confront his scrutiny.

"You don't think he's mine?" I asked, incredulous. "I was taken from Pini against my will, and I certainly didn't have a pony."

"So you say," Galemis squinted.

"Nazha's eye. Do you think Nanomi would have sold me for a mule if I'd had a pony she could have taken?"

Doubt flitted across his face at that, and I rather regretted convincing him. I didn't want him searching out the pony's true owner. I made my face eager.

"But you'll let me ride him to Terskwold?"

"Most likely," he hedged. Then his manner turned brisk. "But until then, you may as well care for the beast. I'm sure you've learned how to feed and groom and muck by now."

I could feel a disconcerted frown creep over my face. I had certainly learned what the stall boys did, but that was quite different from doing it. Nevertheless...

"That seems fair," I heard myself say.

"Good," he pronounced, though his eyes were still filled with mistrust. The boys all vanished back into their stalls as he strode down the aisle, but I watched his back until he was gone. Did he guess I was hiding someone in my room? Did he think I would try to run away? I had to make sure he didn't find out before the Terskwold expedition.

*   *   *

I quickly learned to balance caring for the pony with tending Aedon. During the day, I fell into the boys' routine of feeding, grooming, and mucking out. Hyg showed me how to saddle Fleck and slip the bit between his teeth without being bitten. I sang to the pony to call him out when he was reluctant to leave his hay, and to calm him among the bigger horses. And with all the hours of exercise, my riding skills rapidly improved.

I no longer ate my meals alone, but no one knew that except Aedon. Somehow Cook had never caught on that I didn't eat as much as the boys. She sent me the fever teas I requested, the extra linens, some extra clothes, extra lamp oil, and extra water. We were pretty well supplied, in fact. I even purloined a hoof knife so Aedon could shave.

For most of a week, Aedon slept almost all the time, while the fever abated and the arrow wound healed. At night, I curled beside him and sang. He didn't dare add his voice to mine; we knew the boys could hear my song, and they'd certainly notice if I suddenly sprouted a tenor range or two. And bit by bit, in the snatches of time when we could talk, he whispered his tale of the whole past year.

"I'd never been drunk before," he confessed as I handed him my bowl of stew about a week after his arrival. "When I went back to Sirinta's house, I thought you were already there, asleep." His eyes slid away. I could almost feel the soft spring air in Sirinta's garden in his memory. He returned to stew in a windowless room.

"Sirinta woke me in the morning. She seemed so calm. I didn't know anything was wrong. She asked where you were." His mouth twitched wryly. "I didn't want to tell her at first. I saw you and Florian leave together." He shifted his arm. It was better now, no longer swollen or corrupt. I wanted to jump ahead in the story, to find out what happened to Florian, but I had to let Aedon set his own pace.

"So I told her you had gone with Florian." He met my gaze with his gold-flecked eyes. "I'll never forget the look on her face. Her expression didn't change, but it was as if she turned to stone. I thought it was anger, but I was wrong. It was fear."

I saw the brimming in his eyes as his own fear resurfaced, sharp and clear. I touched his knee.

"You've found me now."

He covered my hand with his, and told me no more that afternoon, but that night he went on when I lay down beside him.

"Two guards took us to the palace, not to the king, but to Crown Prince Gavin."

That surprised me.

"Gavin? Why Gavin?"

Under my head, his unhurt shoulder gave a shrug.

"Gavin took charge of the whole affair. All the brothers were there. All seven of them."

"Florian, too?" Praise Suna, he was still alive!

"He looked awful," snorted Aedon. "His clothes were a mess, there was muck in his hair, and he had a huge bruise on the side of his face." Aedon moved his jaw as if he had felt the blow himself. "And his eyes.... His eyes...." He struggled to speak past some sudden obstruction. His voice came out rough. "I thought you were dead."

We held each other in the dark, and that was all he could tell that night.

While I dressed his wound in the morning, he continued.

"There wasn't any shouting. They seemed to see it like a battle. Who would do what." His fingers curled as he counted the princes.

"Gavin's the crown prince, so he had to stay in Darcy. Any news would go straight to him, and he'd tell the others. Florian was to stay with Gavin, sort of under house arrest, as punishment for putting your life in danger to begin with."

I cringed at the thought of Florian punished for my idiotic whim.

"It wasn't his fault," I confessed in a whisper.

"I know," Aedon whispered back. "He told me later. But he didn't tell his brothers that." He resumed his tally of Florian's brothers, from second youngest to second eldest.

"Emryn would stay in Darcy, too, in case you were found and needed healing. Kyan would hunt for you in the mountains. Rion would take *The Destiny* and search up and down the Pinian coast. Andren would search for signs of you in the face of Nazha and in the stars. Joron would search the pearling coast. He was the one who would tell your mother you were lost. And I guess he ended up telling my family that I disappeared with Florian."

I jolted upright and found the lantern, barely able to light it in my agitation.

"But you said Florian was staying in Darcy!"

Aedon squinted against the light as he lifted himself on his unhurt elbow.

"He was supposed to. But as soon as the princes finished their council, he came to me at Sirinta's house. And he told me what he hadn't told his brothers. That he thought the man who took you was the one from inside the Sailor's Knot. The man who spoke Marnaki."

I pushed my back against the wall and hugged my knees.

"Then he found out it was Symus."

Aedon shook his head.

"No. Not then. We didn't know his name until later. The tavern keeper didn't know it. But Florian went to the harbormaster and asked about ships bound for Marnak."

"Then Rion brought you both to Marnak?"

"Florian didn't tell Rion. He didn't tell anyone. He wasn't supposed to be looking for you. As if they could stop him," he snorted. He met my eyes then. "He asked me to help."

I buried my face, unwilling to see what he was saying. For a year, I had been torn between them. Now Aedon was here and Florian wasn't. I didn't know what to do.

"Liise," he said, reaching out with his voice, the voice that had changed from a boy's to a youth's in the year I was gone.

"What?" I sniffled.

I heard him sit up and edge toward me until his shoulder was touching mine.

"It's all right, Liise."

"No," I stammered, still hiding my face. "It isn't all right."

"Liise." He leaned his head beside mine. "I love you. But not like that. I used to think I would, but I don't. You're my closest friend in all the world. I'll always love you as my friend. But I just can't look at you that way. Like a lover. Like Florian does."

"Oh, Aedon," I sobbed and turned to wrap my arms around him. "I didn't mean to love him...."

He pressed his cheek against my hair.

"He didn't mean to love you, either. But he does. We've had a lot of time to talk."

I pushed away and swiped at the tears.

"But how did you find me?"

He leaned back and sighed.

"He booked us onto a ship for Knar. No one knew. They wouldn't have let us go if they had. I can tell you, I'm not looking forward to going back to Sirinta's wrath."

I punched his leg.

"Tell me!"

He held up his hand to ward me off, but his eyes were twinkling, just as they used to do in Ayr.

"We looked for you in every port, asking about a Curran girl with a mark on her face, but no one had seen you until we reached Knar. It took us a week to find out where you stayed, at the Spotted Toad. That's where we found out Symus's name and where he lived. Florian went to the King of Marnak, but he wouldn't help us. He didn't think a Curran girl was of any importance."

"Symus told me no one would care," I recalled to Aedon. "He said I was just a fingerling and no one would care if I lived or died."

He pulled me toward him and kissed my brow.

"I got that, too, a couple of times." With another weary sigh, he forged on. "By the time we left Knar, we could barely make it halfway up the mountains before we were snowed in for the winter. Three months freezing in some mountain tavern, listening to the most awful music. We couldn't cross until a couple of months ago, and we didn't reach Symus's house until the equinox."

I lurched up again.

"That's when you were shot! I felt it!"

His brows flew up.

"You did?"

"I was singing to the mare—I had to sing to her every day, morning and night—and Suna came to me—"

"I felt her, too! And you—"

"And I knew something awful had happened to you!"

"Well, it certainly wasn't pleasant," he sniffed.

"And Florian—" I bit my hand. "Was he shot, too?"

He hung his head.

"I don't know," he winced. "Florian thought Symus wouldn't hurt him because he was a prince, but almost as soon as we got there, the dogs came out and I got shot...." His eyes seemed to fill with the pain I felt. "I'm sorry, Liise. I don't know what happened to Florian."

I trembled with fear.

"It wasn't Symus."

That confused him.

"What? You mean we weren't even in the right place?"

"No, no," I assured him. "You were in the right place. But that wasn't Symus. Symus left soon after we got there. That was Tenrek, his brother. He shot me, too."

Aedon's eyes flared and he gripped my arm.

"What do you mean, he shot you, too?"

"When I escaped," I answered simply. I'd have to tell him my own story later. "It's all healed now. But that was Tenrek with the dogs. He's meaner than they are. There's no telling what he'll do to Florian. He put me in a cage...."

I choked on tears and Aedon's arm went around me quickly.

"Liise," he whispered. "He's still alive. If he weren't, you'd know."

He was right. Suna had told me when Aedon was shot; surely she'd tell me if anything terrible happened to Florian.

"Yes," I sniffled. "He must be alive...."

"We'll get him out. Now we're together, we'll get him out."

I reached for the lamp; he blew it out. We lay down together behind the chest. Worn by the telling, he soon fell asleep, but I lay awake for a long, long time.

*   *   *

Suddenly, twelve days had passed. The expedition would leave tomorrow. The following day, the foal would cross the Terskwold bridge. And that night would be the dark of the moon.

"You're going to have to look like me," I insisted to Aedon.

Stubbornly, he crossed his arms. The wound was closed and no longer needed a dressing.

"I'm not so sure this plan will work."

"Of course it will work. There are so many people here, no one will notice where I am or how many times I come and go."

"They'll notice if you're with the pony and then you're not. And Galemis will have a sharp eye on you. You said it yourself. He wants to keep you until he's sure that curse is broken."

I shook my head.

"Galemis will see me with the pony. That's all he'll notice. Aside from that, he'll be so wrapped up in Gwenarian's colt and all these people who've come to see him break the curse, he won't be looking anywhere else."

"But—"

"Aedon," I said, holding his eyes. "It's going to work."

"But..." he pouted, "I've never braided my hair in my life."

I shoved his knee.

"You never had to pretend you were a girl before."

"Suna's ears," he groused. "I'll never forgive you if you tell."

"All right," I promised, trying to suppress my smile. "I won't tell a soul."

The following morning, the yard was crammed. I had seen the arrival of the baron with the gold and lapis coronet, two other men with coronets, the official with the silver chain, and numerous others, all with respectable entourages. Every mare was dancing with excitement, and I could hear Mehadimar's nervous whinnies. For the first time since the birth of the foal, I sang to Gwenarian to calm her. Bohrn anxiously brushed Lunarian, though his silvery coat already glistened as bright as ice.

"You think you're not coming back," spoke a voice at the gate.

It was Hyg. Like Bohrn and me, he was crisp and clean in a fresh black tunic. None of the other boys were going.

"Once Lunarian breaks the curse," I answered calmly, "Galemis has to set me free."

"Right," snorted Hyg. "But Galemis doesn't like to give up what he thinks is his. And you're still his slave."

He walked away. But I already knew not to trust Galemis. I only needed him not to catch me.

The chaos helped.

Galemis was mounted on Mehadimar in the middle of the yard. Beside him was Bohrn with Gwenarian on a short lead. The colt would naturally follow his mother, but Galemis held him on a lead to ensure his safety. I could barely lead Fleck out through the mob. Hyg held the stallion's bridle while his master surveyed the crowd. As if without thinking, he translated for me.

"Friends!" called Galemis. "We have seen the birth of a pure white foal, born of a white mare in the light of the full moon. Today we walk to the cursed land of Terskwold, where tomorrow, at noon, under the blazing eye of Tol, by the grace of Nazha, the curse will be broken!"

Resounding cheers rose up from the crowd. From my low vantage, not even mounted, I couldn't see past the household members nearest me. Galemis was bringing a staff of servants, cooks, and slaves, with cartloads of furniture, bedding, pavilions, and food, for a feast tonight and a massive celebration tomorrow. The guests were similarly encumbered, and none of the households knew everyone in all of the others. Abruptly, I passed Fleck's reins to Hyg.

"I forgot my pack. I'll be right back."

"Wait!" he tried to call after me, but I darted away, leaving him holding the stallion by one hand and Fleck by the other.

I didn't head straight for the stable, but wove erratically through every household between Galemis and the stable, excusing myself as I bumped into horses and jostled knees, making sure as many people as possible noticed me. I could hear Galemis still talking. When I reached the stable, I dashed down the aisle, ducked into my room, and locked the door.

"It's time," I panted, facing my double.

"Ready," snapped Aedon, and tossed me my pack. His hair was braided exactly like mine, he carried a pack as much like mine as we could manage, and he wore the black tunic I had worn at Lunarian's birth. It fit him oddly, but at least it fit.

"All right, then. You go out through Gwenarian's stall and I'll go out from the end of the aisle in a minute or two. There are plenty of carts you can walk behind. I think almost everyone saw me come in here. Just don't talk. And—"

"Liise," he stopped me. "I know the plan. It's going to work."

I scanned him fretfully.

"It's so far to walk. And your arm—"

Both of his arms embraced me equally.

"My arm's all right. And it's not that far. Hardly a day."

"But when you get there—"

He kissed me lightly and gave me the confident grin I remembered.

"I know what to look for. I know where to hide. I've got plenty of food. And I'll see you tomorrow at midnight."

"As soon after midnight as I can get there," I corrected him.

"I'll wait," he assured me with that smile. "And if you don't come, I'll find you. I did it before, I can do it again."

I turned the key, kissed him quickly, and opened the door.

With all the stall boys watching the yard, no one saw him cross the aisle and disappear through Gwenarian's stall. And no one saw me a moment later slip down the aisle and out the door. Galemis was just concluding his speech when I reached for Fleck's rein.

"I wasn't sure you were coming back," Hyg growled as Galemis spurred Mehadimar toward the gate.

"Not coming back?" I scrambled to mount. "Why, Hyg. I wouldn't miss this for all the pearls in Pini."

Chapter 10: Florian

I rode beside Galemis with Hyg between us on foot. Galemis led Gwenarian, with Bohrn and the colt beside her. Beyond them rode the priest in brown, a hawk-faced man with lanky limbs.

"He's the one says it's gotta be done in the dark of the moon," Hyg informed me, nodding his chin toward the stringy priest.

"That makes sense," I snorted with irony. For sixteen years, I had lived with what Nazha could do in the dark of the moon.

Although most of the party was mounted, some weren't, including Hyg and Bohrn, so we went no faster than Nanomi and I six weeks ago. This time, however, the air was mild and full of green and the sun shone warmly on our backs. It would have been a delightful jaunt if I hadn't been worried lest somebody notice a dark-skinned Curran trailing along behind the baggage, a dark-skinned Curran who wasn't me. But no one seemed to care if one of Galemis's household was relegated to the rear, and the day wore on with no alarms.

In the mid-afternoon, we reached the bridge arching over the river. The water was free of its coat of ice, and tumbled wildly, swift and wide. Upriver, the mill wheel rattled loosely, sped by the rush of a channeled stream. There was no deep rumble inside the mill; the grinding stone was not engaged. I guessed that the mill had been deserted as long as the land had been cursed.

They pitched their camp at the Gelderscarth end of the bridge. Bright pavilions such as I had never seen before sprang up on the plain like colorful toadstools scattered by Nazha's whimsical hand. There was even a tent for the mare and foal, where I would sleep along with Bohrn. He beamed with importance while Galemis proudly trotted visitors in and out, showing off the miraculous colt and me beside him. I could see them appraising me, judging my value, and guessed he was planning to auction me off once the curse was broken. I didn't care. I had no intention of being there when they finished bidding.

They feasted in an enormous pavilion. Galemis displayed me for a while, serving me roasted quails stuffed with grapes, pasties filled with trout and mushrooms, tender fiddleheads, and rich custards. I avoided the wine and was glad when I could slip away to the horse tent to sleep. I knew I would need my rest for tomorrow.

Curled in my blanket, I let my anxieties keep me awake while Bohrn snored softly beyond the mare. Was Aedon safe? Had he been able to cross the river? Had he found the hiding place? Could he sleep? Then, casting past Aedon, was Florian still in Tenrek's clutches? Had Tenrek hurt him? How could Aedon and I get him out? But exhaustion eventually overruled worry, and before I knew it, the sun was shining through the canvas, and the camp was astir with anticipation of breaking the curse.

Late in the morning, Galemis assembled his witnesses at the bridge. In addition to Bohrn and me with the mare and colt, the priest was there, together with all the officials and barons. Hyg watched from the end of the bridge.

When the sun was directly overhead, Galemis took Lunarian's lead and set one foot on the bridge. But before the colt's hoof touched the stone, something shifted in the light. Some color or intensity. Some subtle difference like wavering candlelight, changing nothing but looking different.

Expecting something but not knowing what, people looked around, at the bridge, at the water, at the land. Then the priest looked up, and all eyes followed. Like everyone else, I gasped.

The dark face of Nazha was edging across the face of Tol.

Entranced, we watched as the goddess overpowered her brother. Slowly, slowly the sunlight dimmed. The sky grew dark. An eerie twilight settled over the land of Terskwold. If it also touched Gelderscarth, no one cared. Birds hid in the trees, the horses nickered in confusion. People dropped to their knees in awe. As Nazha completely covered Tol, the priest cried a prayer, speaking over the heads of the crowd, and they bowed in worship. Moved by the goddess's frightening power, I lowered myself in full prostration and prayed.

I prayed to Nazha, I prayed to Tol, I prayed to Suna. I prayed for my life, for Aedon's life, for Florian's life. In that supernatural starlit noon, nothing else mattered.

At that precise moment, Lunarian stepped onto the bridge. The sound of his tiny, silver hooves rang brightly in the unnatural light, and he nickered on the crest of the arch. Perhaps he was only calling his mother, but it was Nazha who replied.

She moved her face away from Tol. As slowly as the light had faded, it returned. It shifted through colors of gray and green, from cold to warm, and at last revealed the land of Terskwold in golden glory. Not a single soul could harbor doubt.

The curse was broken.

In a voice that carried above the crowd, the priest proclaimed a benediction. Galemis raised his arms overhead and rejoiced aloud. The people rose with shouts and cheers, and Galemis led Lunarian down the far side of the bridge in blazing triumph.

My legs were shaky as I stood. Nazha had delivered Terskwold from its curse. I prayed again, with utter conviction, that Nazha and Suna would continue to grant their divine protection, would deliver Aedon, Florian, and me, and would see us safely home together.

I wouldn't wait long for the answer.

*   *   *

The entire encampment crossed the bridge and reassembled on Terskwold soil. I suppose it showed a strength of faith on the part of Undrians in general that all of the horses were moved as well. I certainly had no doubt of their safety. Nazha's display had been very convincing.

The feast that night was massive, just as Galemis had promised. Cartloads of food had been brought from Gelderscarth, and the preparations went on for the rest of the afternoon. Galemis didn't wait that long to bring out the wine, though, and all of the principal guests were as drunk as he was before the sun set. Once again, he displayed me at dinner, and everyone made a great fuss over me. I nibbled at the hearty roasts, the savory tarts, the sweet stewed fruits, and bided my time.

Midnight approached, and still they caroused, with music and jugglers and men who danced like stomping horses. Galemis received congratulations with toasts and cheers. One by one, the other barons bent their heads to Galemis's ear, and I guessed that the bidding had begun. Seated on Galemis's left, with a stack of cushions on my chair to raise me to a convenient height, I made a show of draining my cup as another greedy-eyed baron approached.

"Your pardon, milord. I have to go out." I tipped my cup; my need was clear. With an unconcerned sniff, he waved me away, far more eager to hear the next offer.

Even outside, the music was loud. I staggered and yawned as I passed the guards at the horses' tent. They barely blinked; they expected me. Bohrn and Lunarian were asleep. Only Gwenarian lifted her head as I snagged my pack, lifted the cloth at the back of the tent, and rolled out under it.

"Going somewhere?"

Still flat on the ground, I clutched at my breast. A dark figure stood against the stars, barely visible in the torchlight that filtered through the tents.

"Suna's eyebrows," I swore up at Hyg. "What are you doing here?"

He planted his foot on the strap of my pack.

"I was going to ask you that."

I tried to calm my racing heart as I clambered to my feet.

"Sometimes," I informed him flatly, "a girl needs a little privacy." I yanked my pack from under his foot and tugged out a corner of linen cloth. Even in the feeble light, it showed against the darker pack.

The night hid his blush, but I could hear it in his voice.

"Oh…well," he stammered. "But didn't you…I mean…when the colt was born…just a couple of weeks ago…?"

I wondered how much he knew about girls. I pushed the cloth back into the pack.

"Nazha chooses the time, not me."

Repulsed, he stepped back. I turned on my heel and walked away, heading for the sound of water. I went several paces before he spoke.

"You're not free yet," he sniped at my back.

I didn't reply and I didn't slow down. During my time at Gelderscarth, Hyg had been decent, but leaving him behind was easy. Leaving Fleck was hard.

Putting the light of the camp behind me, I ducked behind a few pavilions and reached the river. It was bordered with brush, but I could follow it by the sound. I stumbled and tripped a time or two, but the noise of my progress was surely obscured by the noisier revelry behind me.

The mill was a ragged hulk in the night. It took a few minutes to find the door. It hung at an angle, leaving an ample gap at the bottom. Good thing I wasn't afraid of the dark.

"Aedon?" I whispered, slipping inside.

"I'm here," he breathed back and found my arm. We hugged each other fiercely.

"Hurry," I urged. "It won't take them long to discover I'm gone."

Carefully, quietly, holding hands, we ran. The road was overgrown with grass but still hard enough to distinguish from the adjacent turf when we strayed aside. It had taken a couple of hours to reach the bridge from the House, and in the dark, it would take longer to reach the House from the bridge. I was certain Galemis would look for me there, for he surely knew where Nanomi had lived, but I didn't know anywhere else to hide.

And our only hope of escape was in hiding; we'd never be able to outrun pursuit. By Nazha's grace, they wouldn't come after us in the dark.

Nazha was with us. We ran for a while, then walked as briskly as we could. Aedon's grip was tight on my hand. I didn't ask if he were afraid; I could feel it in his pulse. But although I feared pursuit, I didn't fear the night. The rustle of leaves was comforting, and the hooting of owls reassuring. No pounding of hooves came behind us.

By the time we found the House, Aedon's strength was flagging. He hesitated at the bleak skeleton of the complex, but to me it felt like a welcoming refuge, even without its shroud of white.

"Careful," I warned him, pulling him cautiously into the ruins. "No one has walked here since there was snow. I don't want them to see our footprints."

He peered at the ground that had once been the floor of the Hall, near where Nanomi had killed the pigeon.

"Looks like plenty of footprints to me."

I quickly bent and scanned the area. Even by starlight, I could see the booted footprints all through the ash. Little footprints, Nanomi's size. I had no idea they would last so long.

The door to Nanomi's den was locked, but I knew where she kept the key and soon had it open. I lighted the lamp and saw with relief that little had changed in the past six weeks. The roots on the table were green with mold, the water in the bucket was scummy, and a fine layer of dust coated everything, but nothing had been disturbed or taken. The room was still safe.

"You lived here?" asked Aedon, looking around. I had told him my story; he knew all about my time with Nanomi.

"Four months," I reminded him.

He looked at the onions overhead, at the cheeses and honey on the shelves, at the birch-bark boxes on the table.

"Is there anything we can eat?"

I didn't want to disturb the dust. It was bad enough we were walking in it.

"Later," I decided. "After they've searched. For now, I think we'd better hide."

I took the lamp into the hearth and stood up in the chimney. There it was—Nanomi's escape hole, hollowed out of the side of the chimney. Aedon held the lamp. I could barely scramble into it without knocking the burned-out logs to pieces. Aedon passed me the lamp, the flint and steel for lighting it, and a jug of oil. Then I pulled him up with me. With both of us and both of our packs, it was a bit crowded, but not too bad. Nanomi had made it big enough to lie down in and sleep. It even had a pillow and blankets, and Aedon found a wax-covered cheese. He grinned in the lamplight just before I blew out the lamp.

* * *

The searchers woke me. In our narrow tunnel, Aedon and I lay tangled together. He jerked awake just after I did. Neither of us moved or breathed. It was totally dark.

I heard the voices from up the chimney. Male voices. Heavy steps in the burned-out ruins. The words were garbled by ash and distance; I couldn't have understood them even if I knew Undrian.

They moved away. We dared to breathe, but we didn't move. Presently, I thought I heard footsteps outside the chamber.

The door burst open with a crash. A glimmer of light filtered up the chimney, flickering on the crooked stones across from the tunnel entrance. They clearly had torches. Was it still night? The voices were clear but not loud. Three or four of them. I jumped at the sounds of crockery breaking, pots being dumped, water sloshing, bedding and clothes being thrown about. They were searching thoroughly. The noises subsided to wreckage being kicked about and short remarks in derisive tones. They slammed the door against the wall as they left.

Gradually, our hearts stopped racing and our breathing slowed, but we still didn't dare to move or speak. At length, I drifted back to sleep.

* * *

The next time I woke, it was quiet. I thought I heard birds, high-pitched and cheery, somewhere above. I lighted the lamp. Aedon lifted himself on his elbow and looked at me with soulful eyes.

"Can we eat something now?"

I smothered my laughter with my hands.

We both had leather water bottles in our packs, so we ate and drank and slept again.

By the time we woke again, I had no idea how much time had passed. But it was quiet, and birds were singing somewhere above. We left the chimney.

The room was a mess, and it snagged at my heart. It was idiotic, I suppose, but even though Nanomi had sold me back into slavery, my four months with her had been pleasant. I was sorry to see her hidden home so wantonly wrecked.

My sorrow was brief, though. Aedon was already rummaging through the mess for any kind of salvageable food. In the end, we each took a blanket, a cheese, and a sturdy knife. We left the door open as we departed in case they came back for another look.

It was late morning when we emerged. I would have preferred to leave at night, just to be less visible, but I couldn't bear waiting any longer. I had to find Florian.

We went due west. Neither of us had any idea where Kragknoll was with respect to Terskwold. Both of us had been shot on departure and carried away unconscious. But I knew how to get us there.

The land rolled upward all afternoon, and by evening, we had reached the forest. That night, we didn't build a fire, though the meager sliver of Nazha's eye shed no useful light through the heavy foliage.

"I know we don't need it for cooking," groused Aedon, hacking off a hunk of cheese, "but I'd rather like it for the light. And a bit of warmth," he shivered.

"No," I insisted. I picked at bits of the crumbly cheese. I regretted leaving our jackets behind, but warmth wasn't uppermost on my mind.

High up the slopes, a wolf howled. Both of us jumped, holding our blankets around our shoulders.

"Now can we have a fire?" begged Aedon, holding his knife out as if the wolves were already surrounding us.

"No," I cautioned. "It might scare them off."

Aedon's gaze darted around the clearing.

"Exactly," he urged.

But I didn't answer him. I answered them. I lifted my voice in a howl like theirs.

"Are you out of your mind?" he squawked in alarm.

I shook my head and listened intently.

The wolf called back. His deep voice shimmered through the trees, then we heard the harmonies of his pack. Aedon grabbed my arm.

"What in Suna's name are you doing?" he hissed.

"Calling them," I answered placidly. My voice floated back to them up the mountains. Aedon shivered.

For most of an hour, we didn't hear them. Hooting owls, rustling feet, whispering foliage, but no more howling. We huddled against a cluster of trees, wrapped in our blankets. We were both too tense to sleep, though for different reasons. Aedon's was fear; mine was hope.

Then we heard it again, quite close. Aedon jerked like a rabbit in a snare. He whispered in panic.

"Suna's heart, Liise!"

I touched his arm.

"Hush. Just be still and they won't hurt you."

"Who—"

But his words broke off as the first shape materialized from the darkness. Others followed, shifting from shadow into form, circling silently, heads held low, watching us with starlit eyes. They kept their distance, wary, uncertain. Aedon trembled. I waited, motionless, crouched on my heels.

He came last, emerging like fog from between the trees. White and powerful he came, pacing through his cautious pack to stop directly in front of me. He lowered his head and growled.

At once, I bowed and placed my elbows on the ground. I lowered my eyes and whined in submission. He edged toward me, sniffing. I could feel Aedon holding his breath. The wolf growled softly. I touched Aedon's knee. Very slowly, he copied my posture. His eyes were closed. I knew he was sure we were going to die.

The wolf backed away and lifted his head. I dared to look up. He gazed at me boldly. I gazed back. Carefully, softly, I started to sing. At the first sound, he flinched, but he didn't run, though his pack darted back into the night. In my voices, I sang of the cage, the traps, the arrows, the wrenching pain. He listened with twitching, attentive ears. When I stopped, he sniffed as if considering. Then he turned away, walked a few paces, and looked back over his shoulder at us.

"Come on," I breathed.

"Where?" quivered Aedon.

"To Kragknoll," I answered as the wolf loped away.

I grabbed Aedon's hand, yanked him up, and hastily struck out after the wolf.

*   *   *

It felt as if we ran for hours. The wolf was sure and seemed to lead where we wouldn't stumble, wouldn't trip on rocks or roots, wouldn't fall into swamps or streams. When I thought we couldn't go any further, he stopped and gave me a sidelong look, then bolted away like a trick of the light. Aedon leaned his hands on his knees.

"Are we there yet?" he panted. I panted back.

"I think he knows we need to rest."

We staggered to a stand of pines, pulled our blankets out of our packs, fell on a spongy bed of moss, and were almost instantly asleep.

The sun was shining on our faces when Aedon woke me. The wolf was lying fifty paces up the slope, looking perfectly relaxed. He waited while we ate some cheese, drank from a stream, splashed our faces. Then he stood up, glanced over his shoulder, and set off again.

We went more slowly during the day. Maybe he sensed that we couldn't keep up with his easy lope. Maybe he sensed that the steeper hills and thicker woods were more of a challenge. Whatever the reason, he led us upward with adequate rests for catching our breath and for eating a meal in the afternoon. We never saw his pack all day.

An hour or two before sunset, he stopped on a ridge and let us catch up. I crouched to look over the rocky outcrop and saw the house in the meadow below.

It was Kragknoll. From our elevated vantage, we could see the fence, the house, the stable, most of the yard. But all my heart saw was Florian, a dark, limp figure chained to the post where I had been chained. With a strangled cry, I lurched to my feet.

"No!" hissed Aedon, dragging me back. I struggled, enraged, but he threw himself on top of me and pinned my limbs with his hands and shins. "The dogs!" he grated. "You can't just run down there! You'll get us all shot! Starting with Florian!"

I thrashed again in desperation, but Aedon was right. It took a few minutes to calm myself.

"All right," I panted. "Let me take another look."

Aedon rolled off me and let me crawl back to the edge of the ridge.

It hurt to look, to see Florian chained, to see him motionless, possibly wounded or sick or— I forced myself to examine the yard. The dogs were chained in their usual spot, and smoke lazed upward from the chimney to wander eastward above the trees. Tenrek was home.

For a long time, the three of us lay on the ridge, side by side.

"So how do we get him out?" whispered Aedon, glancing past me at the wolf. The wolf only watched the house below. I struggled to think.

"I think it's just Tenrek. If Symus were there, it would be a lot noisier this time of day."

"We could wait until night, when he's asleep."

I pondered this option.

"That won't work. The dogs are always outside. If they scent us or hear us, they'll go berserk, and Tenrek will come out shooting."

Aedon cast me a skeptical glance.

"You seem to have learned how to talk to beasts. Can you sing to the dogs?"

I recalled my enlightening day with the dogs.

"I could try, but once they know I'm here, they're going to make noise, one way or another. I think it's too risky. Tenrek's a mighty good shot."

Aedon grimaced. He knew that as well as I did.

"Then when should we go?"

"Well," I mused, "Tenrek throws food out to the dogs a couple of times a day. They make such a racket when he feeds them, he wouldn't notice if they notice us, and we want to catch him off guard, outside, without his bow. The problem is he's not very regular about it. There's no way to tell when he'll do it."

Aedon nodded toward the wolf.

"I bet he could tell us if we could get close enough. He'd smell the food. He'd hear the latch. He'd know when Tenrek's about to come out."

"Yes. That's perfect. We'll just have to get as close as we can without being noticed by the dogs. We'll stay downwind and be as quiet as the wolf."

The wolf seemed to understand our goal. Or perhaps he simply shared it. We went very carefully. Very quietly. Very slowly. And not too close. Just close enough for a clear view of the gate, with the merest glimpse of the door through a rotten patch in the fence. The wolf's ears twitched. He could hear the dogs and other sounds that Aedon and I couldn't hear. We didn't dare go any closer.

We waited there for a long time. The sun went down. The air turned cold. We ate some cheese. Beneath the winking eye of Nazha, I felt the twilight shadows move. Glancing around, I saw the shifting shapes of the wolves. Silently, in a crescent behind us, they settled to wait.

It was almost dark when the white wolf rose. His ears stood up, his hackles lifted, and a low growl issued from his throat. The whole pack flowed to their feet. I didn't question what he knew. As one, we moved forward.

Then I heard the dogs. They barked and whined, and I heard the rattle of snapping chains. Tenrek had come to the door with food. As we reached the fence, I heard his voice.

"Ere yuh go," he cackled. "This rabbit's gone a bit rank for me tuh—"

Before he could finish, before the rank rabbit had thudded down in front of the dogs, a gleam of white arced over our heads, sailed over the fence, and landed silently in the yard. The dogs went wild. Abandoning caution, Aedon and I sprang up to spy through the rotting pickets. Tenrek was only a pace or two outside the door. I saw his greedy eyes go wide at the sight of his long-hunted prey.

"Yra's blood!" he crowed. "After all this time, yuh come tuh me."

He moved very gingerly one step backward. He wanted his bow. The wolf eased forward, stalking his quarry. As Tenrek's foot began to shift for another step, the rest of the pack launched from behind us, soared over the fence, and appeared in the yard like the sudden shadows of a storm. Tenrek's face went utterly white, and the white wolf sprang.

What I saw then was horrible, even in the split second before I turned and pressed my back to the fence. I closed my eyes, but I couldn't close out the sickening sounds, the screams and snarls, the tearing of cloth, and the rending of flesh. Aedon pulled me into his arms, and we sank to our heels. It was all I could manage not to be sick.

The screams didn't last long. The feeding did. I could hear the dogs whimpering, but the wolves ignored them. I dropped my face into my folded arms and wept. Aedon made no attempt to stop me, but sat with his arm around my shoulders, shaking.

At last it ended. The first dark shape came over the fence, scrabbling a bit at the top, and landed heavily outside the gate. The others followed, less fleet than when they had gone in. They raced each other across the meadow, snarling and laughing amongst themselves, and melted into the forest night. Last of all, the white wolf dropped to the ground at our feet. He turned, and I gasped at the blood that covered his muzzle and legs. He lowered his head. I dropped to my elbows and whimpered submissively. Aedon quickly copied my action, though not the whimper. The wolf stepped toward me and sniffed my ear. I could smell his fur, his breath, the blood. He pushed his nose against my cheek with a little whine. Then he backed a step, turned away, and flowed like a muscular streak of moonlight off through the trees.

The night seemed very quiet then. I heard Aedon breathing hard beside me. I pushed myself up on my wobbly feet and started feeling along the fence.

"There are rotten spots," I explained to Aedon as he watched. "That's how I got out, and that's how we'll get in."

Aedon promptly probed with me. A few minutes later, we smashed an opening through the pickets. Before I could push my way inside, Aedon held me back.

"Wait," he said. "Let me go first. I'll get a blanket and...."

I nodded numbly, grateful not to have to look. I heard him run across the yard, slam through the door, rummage inside, and come back out.

"I did what I could," he muttered when he returned. He had found a lamp and held it high.

I ignored the dogs, lunging and barking, eager to reach me. I barely even saw the carnage, only partially hidden by the bearskin Aedon had dragged outside, no doubt from the bed. My only thought was for Florian.

We ran to his side and together straightened his crumpled form. He was bony, bruised, and patchily bearded. He had no jacket, his clothes were torn, he was crusted in filth. I folded my blanket beneath his head and stroked his brow while Aedon checked him all over for wounds.

"Nothing," he told me with patent relief.

"The key." I pointed at the shackle. "We need to unlock it. I think he keeps the key—"

Florian moaned. His face clenched with effort. His eyes barely opened, dark as the depths of a forest well. His hand rose, groping, and found Aedon's shoulder.

"Aedon," he croaked. "Did you find her?"

Aedon just looked at me, eyes brimming, leading Florian's gaze to my face. His fingers uncurled from Aedon's shoulder and rose to my cheek. His touch was light and tentative, but his eyes held mine, and I knew he knew me.

"Ama," he breathed, and his eyes bloomed clear, forget-me-not blue. With sudden, unexpected strength, his hand reached up behind my head and pulled me down to a swift, consuming, passionate kiss, a kiss full of hunger, the kiss of a man who had searched the world for more than a year for the woman he loved. And mine was the kiss of the woman he found, filled with equal longing. When we came up for air, Aedon was unlocking the chain.

"I found the key," he informed us smugly.

Florian tensed in sudden panic and lurched to one elbow. His bony hands tried to push us away.

"Tenrek! He'll shoot you! Go now! Hurry!"

"No, my love," I soothed him quickly. "Tenrek's gone. He's not coming back."

His frantic gaze flew around the yard, found the bearskin blanket, saw the puddles of blood and clots of flesh. His skin drew tight.

"He's dead?" he gagged. "But how—"

Aedon's voice was firm and steady.

"Wolves," he stated.

"Wolves?" echoed Florian, searching the shadows.

"A special wolf," I amended distantly. "Tenrek killed his mate."

Both of them stared at me. I blinked. This was not the time for that tale. My fingers returned to Florian's face, the sharp lines of his cheek.

"How long have you been here?"

"Weeks," he rasped, plunging into my eyes. "Since we found the place."

I stroked his hair without seeing it.

"I mean how long have you been chained outside?"

"Weeks," he repeated. "Since the day we arrived." He reached out his hand, and Aedon took it. He pulled Aedon close and tore his eyes away from mine.

"He shot you," he recalled with pain. "I heard you cry out. But the dogs pulled me down, and he... I'm sorry I couldn't help you...."

Aedon flushed at his prince's apology.

"Did he hurt you?" he asked in an apology of his own.

Florian moved, trying to sit. We gripped his arms and helped him lean against the fence. He rubbed his ankle with one hand. Above his low boot, his britches were crusted with old, dried blood.

"Not directly. He just left me out here. He threw me food, just like the dogs." He winced with this humiliation, and I squeezed his hand. I knew what it meant. Rabbits and squirrels fresh out of the traps. Or not so fresh. Certainly neither cooked nor skinned. "I didn't eat much the first couple of weeks."

The lamplight guttered in a wind, and Florian shivered.

"We've got to get you into the house," I said decisively.

We pulled him up. He could hardly stand. Taking his arms across our shoulders, we helped him stagger toward the house. Although he was small for a Pinian, he was still taller than both of us, which made for somewhat awkward going. As we moved away, the dogs barked madly, still wanting to reach me. But they had been fed, and although their master had been devoured in front of them, it seemed they had already fully recovered. The dogs would wait until tomorrow. We skirted the bearskin that hid the remains, and the ground that was spattered and black with blood. When we reached the door, Aedon went back to get the lamp. Florian leaned against the frame, and I wrapped my arms around his waist. The wavering hearth light cast deep shadows across his face.

"Didn't he know who you were?" I mourned.

"I think he believed me," he sighed. "I think he was going to sell me to someone. He certainly planned to sell my horse. At least he was taking good care of my horse."

"Titan? He's here?"

"In the stable," he nodded. "With the mules."

Aedon brought the lamp. Florian looked at the messy room, the dirty dishes, the chains and traps. His eyes came to rest of the skin-strewn bed. He looked at me with a flash of alarm.

"Did he—"

"No!" I rushed to forestall his fears. "I slept over there!"

Pulling him in so Aedon could close and bolt the door, I pointed at the pile of blankets still heaped by the chimney. This didn't seem much better to him. He fell back against the edge of the table.

"Oh, Ama...." He drew me close in a tight embrace, full of pain for both of us.

Aedon snorted, surveying the room.

"He doesn't seem to need any convincing," he quipped ironically.

With his brow to mine, Florian swiveled his glance toward Aedon.

"Convincing of what?"

"That she's really Liise," Aedon chuckled. He walked to the bed and made a face. I could smell the stink from the door. "Poor girl had to put out the lamp to prove it to me."

Florian's eyes came back to mine, clear and bright in the wavering light.

"I can't imagine why," he murmured.

Aedon piled more wood on the hearth and checked the pot hanging over the fire.

"Didn't you notice? The mark is gone."

Florian smiled. Without leaving mine, his eyes turned a tender sea-mist green.

"What mark?"

A foolish grin spread over my face. I twined my fingers in his hair and kissed him again.

Then, with a jolt, I saw his hair. It was dark and dirty and hung in tangled hanks to his shoulders.

"Your pearls!" I gasped, and outrage flooded through my blood. "Did Tenrek—"

"Oh, that," Aedon mumbled as if he had overlooked something important. I whirled to see him pulling a wooden spoon from the pot, looking distinctly embarrassed. "I forgot to tell you," he confessed. "Back in Knar, when Florian realized the Marnaki king wasn't going to help us find you, he took the pearls out of his hair. He's been using them to pay the expenses of looking for you. We still had almost half of them when we got here."

Florian straightened with a frown and looked around distractedly.

"Tenrek took them."

It didn't take long to find the pearls. Tenrek had tossed the leather pouch on the table among the dirty dishes. Tenrek was a lousy housekeeper. I pressed the pouch into Florian's hand and he sagged into the nearest chair. His elbow pushed a bowl of something moldy onto the floor. We both stared stupidly at the mess.

"I know," he suggested. "We could go find a nice clean tavern for the night."

I couldn't help a feeble laugh. Then I buried my face in Florian's shoulder and burst into tears.

"He could have killed you," I sobbed.

His arms closed around me.

"He could have killed you, too," he breathed.

I lifted my face, no doubt tear-streaked and dirty.

"He could have killed both of you."

"But he didn't," chimed Aedon, touching my arm. "He tried, but you saved us. You called my pony and sang the fever out of me. Then you called the wolves, who led us here and devoured Tenrek. He could have killed all of us, but he failed. Because of you, Liise."

He raised his brows at me, and a look of wonder filled Florian's face. Aedon turned away to clean up the moldy mess on the floor. Florian held my hands in his.

"Did you really call Aedon's pony?"

I looked at our hands and shook my head.

"I was singing to a horse at the time," I told him. "I didn't know Aedon was even out there until he showed up in my room in the stable."

"And you cured his fever by singing?"

"I guess so," I shrugged. "I thought I was singing to comfort him. But I guess it did more."

"And you called the wolves? The wolves that killed Tenrek?"

That one was hard. I hadn't intended to murder the man. I hung my head.

"We had met before. When I was here. Tenrek wanted to trap the white wolf and he wanted me to help him. The white wolf's mate was killed instead."

His arms enfolded me once more.

"Then it was the wolf's revenge."

I nodded mutely against his breast. He smelled awful. I didn't care. He was safe. And we were together. All three of us. That was all that mattered.

"Dinner," piped Aedon with a grin.

We turned to look. He had cleared the mess, cleaned the table, and set out bowls of steaming stew. Boar, I guessed.

We ate and washed. I pulled the animal skins off the bed while Aedon helped Florian bathe and change into cleaner clothes. They fit as badly as the garments Symus had given me. We settled him in the tidied bed. Clean and combed, his dark hair shone against the pillow. His hollow eyes held me more forcefully than his hand.

"Ama," he sighed. "So many times, I dreamed you were with me. I could hear your voice. Feel your arms. Taste your kiss. Will you still be here when I wake up, or is this all just another dream?"

Tears filled my eyes as I smiled at him.

"No dream, my love. I'll still be here when you wake up, tomorrow and every other day."

He tugged on my hand ever so gently. I bent to kiss him. I was still by his side when he fell asleep.

The fire burned low.

"What are you going to do?" Aedon stood at my shoulder. His voice was quiet with compassion. I was still holding Florian's hand.

"I don't know," I admitted. He didn't have to tell me the problem. I knew it too well. Ever since Florian had said he loved me, I had pretended it didn't exist. But it was still there. I was a Curran, and Florian was a Pinian prince. We still couldn't marry. When we got home, we wouldn't be able to be together. But until that time, nothing would part us.

I slept on the floor beside the bed, with Aedon curled up by my side. The blankets still smelled like mules. It was oddly familiar, somehow safe. But Aedon slept with a knife at his hand. We didn't want Symus to surprise us.

We spent a week nursing Florian back to health. When I woke that first morning, Aedon had cleaned out the spoiled food and washed all the dishes. He had fed the dogs, and a pot of porridge was simmering over the fire. But he hadn't touched Tenrek's remains.

"We have to burn them." He sat with his elbows on his knees, uncharacteristically subdued. "We have to send his soul to Tol."

I didn't especially want to send his soul to Tol, but I didn't want it bound to the earth, where I was, either. I nodded my somber agreement.

Aedon bravely gathered what he could, the bones and flesh that could be collected, and placed them together on the bearskin. We built the pyre where he had died and laid the bearskin on it. Leaning heavily on my shoulder, Florian spoke some funeral prayers. All three of us lighted the pyre together. Although he had given us reason to hate him, we had caused his death, and it only seemed fair to free his soul.

Florian rested for several days. Gradually, he began to move about the house, gathering strength. Aedon cleaned, I washed laundry, and we shared the cooking. I found my neglected apprentice garments, still rolled for washing since the Spotted Toad; I washed them and bleached them in the sun. While I soaked the blood out of Florian's clothes, I picked apart some garments I found and restitched them to fit him. I tended the dogs, the mules, and Titan, happy to see the big horse again. Unlike Florian, Titan was in superb condition. Tenrek knew better than to mistreat an animal Symus could sell for a profit. I cleaned the stable and exercised him every day, walking him around the yard. I couldn't saddle him, of course, but I could mount from a stall rail, and with some strategic singing, he was docile enough for me to ride bareback.

"You're not afraid of him anymore," Florian said one afternoon. It was darkly cloudy, promising rain, but mild enough for my stable clothes from Gelderscarth.

Startled by his appearance in the door, I nearly slipped off Titan's back. The stallion tossed his massive head at my loss of composure, and I quickly sang a soothing whinny. The horse then continued around the yard, so I had to twist and turn back and forth to keep Florian in sight. He leaned in the doorway, arms crossed on his chest, wearing the shirt and britches I'd remade for him. Without the pearls, his dark, silky hair caressed his shoulders.

"And you don't look much like a prince anymore," I quipped in return.

He snorted a laugh.

"I don't feel much like a prince anymore."

He stepped from the doorway. Aedon had long since buried the ashes and rain had washed away the blood. No sign of Tenrek remained in the yard.

"Where are the dogs?" Florian asked, noticing the empty chains.

Titan circled back and forth.

"Aedon took them out hunting. They've really taken to each other, Aedon and the dogs. They don't catch much, but the exercise is good for them. Mostly Aedon's been bringing back mushrooms and garlic scapes."

Florian watched Titan's muscles bunch and stretch under glossy skin.

"He looks good. Ready to travel."

I halted Titan at the stump where Aedon spilt firewood.

"Soon you'll be ready, too," I encouraged. "You're getting stronger every day."

He took the bridle and I slid off Titan's back. It was a long way down, but Florian caught me and eased my feet onto the stump. He released the bridle. Wrapped in the circle of his arms, I looked up into his eyes. They were a serious malachite green, and his voice was thick, as if there were something in his throat. Titan wandered away.

"We have to leave here, Ama. Soon."

I placed my palms against his chest. His ribs still made ridges beneath my hands, but behind them his heart was strong and steady. Mine, however, quavered.

"Not yet," I pleaded. "A few more days. You're not strong enough to go."

He shook his head. The jagged lines of jaw and cheek, made sharp by starvation, had softened a bit with returning flesh, but the shadows still lay deep in his eyes. They shifted from green to a tormented teal.

"Ama...."

He lifted his hands to touch my face, and his fingers wandered over my brows, my cheeks, my nose. His eyes seemed to linger on every feature, as if I might vanish and leave him bereft for another year. I could feel the hunger in his breathing, in his belly, in his heart. The same hunger ached in my heart, too. When his eyes and fingers reached my lips, at the first light touch, at his tender caress, the hunger in my heart ignited and poured through my blood. My arms twined up around his neck and my mouth found his in a giddy rush.

Instantly, his arms closed around me and held me more tightly than Tenrek's chains. Our kiss was feverish, searching, starving. Our bodies pressed against each other, moving urgently, seeking the heat of each other's passion. His hands roved my back, slid over my ribs, slipped up inside the front of my shirt....

It jolted us both, and he pulled back his hands as if he had touched the wick of a lamp. Our eyes met, and we gasped at our peril. With a stifled sob, he gripped my waist and pressed his face to the curve of my throat. Our bodies clenched in sudden stillness.

"Ama," he mourned, and I felt his tears slide down my neck. "You say I'm not strong enough to go. But I'm not strong enough to stay."

Weeping, I buried my face in his shoulder. I hadn't wanted his hands to stop. I wasn't strong enough, either.

"All right," I choked. I lifted my face and laid my palm alongside his cheek. "We'll go tomorrow."

His eyes winced closed, and he placed a trembling kiss on my brow. I felt his words against my skin.

"I love you, Ama."

"I love you, Florian," I breathed back.

But we couldn't do more. Despite our desires, we were who we were. Our blood stood between us.

With a wrenching effort, I pulled away, to stable Titan, to feed the mules, to plan what to take for the journey home. He wrapped his arms around himself, then turned and walked back to the house. The door closed quietly behind him just as Aedon came in with the dogs and it began to rain.

*   *   *

It stormed all night, but cleared by dawn. We took the mules for Aedon and me, and all the provisions we could pack. We took the dogs, too. They would have died if we left them behind, and Aedon had grown very fond of them. Maybe they'd actually catch some game for us to eat along the way. We left the bow. Neither Aedon nor I could shoot, and Florian wouldn't touch it. Knives would have to suffice for us all. Grim and silent, we left Kragknoll without looking back.

I was afraid to go through Undria, so we traveled over the mountains to Knar. This time it was lovely. Spring bloomed in the undergrowth, pink and white, purple and blue, flowers I didn't know by name. Streams gushed and hurried beside the trail, hastening into the valleys behind us. Birds sang in the trees and I learned their songs, though they all sounded sad when I sang them. We slept in our blankets around a fire and never saw or heard the wolves.

Spring seemed to halt for the month it took us to reach the pass, then it rushed headlong down the other side. High near the pass, wild strawberries bloomed, and a few days later we found ripe fruits. In less than a week, we reached the first inn, where we shared a room at the cost of a pearl. We ate the stew and endured the music, but none of us would drink the beer. Aedon couldn't bear the taste; Florian and I couldn't bear the memories. Even the smell was too much like ale, and after that, we avoided inns whenever the weather was dry enough to sleep outside.

Ten days later, we found the Riy, an infant trickle that grew to a freshet, a rill, a brook with each day we descended, rocking and swaying on our mounts. Within a fortnight, it had blossomed into a river that raced over rocks and sang all night in more voices than Aedon and I could mimic together.

One evening we came to an inn in a sheltered grotto. The sign showed a bronze-colored stag jumping over a brook. Florian didn't even turn his head, but clucked his tongue to urge Titan past the smell of a stable with hay and oats. Lagging behind, Aedon sidled his mule next to mine.

"That's where we spent the winter," he told me. "The Leaping Stag. Believe me, neither of us wants to sleep there again."

We slept in the woods that night instead. Florian sat very close to me while we ate chicken pasties and barley bread from the inn where we'd spent the previous night. He stared at the flames, silent, wishful, and dejected. His eyes were pensive, green as jade. Even Aedon was subdued, watching me from across the fire, with the dogs stretched out asleep behind him.

"The night we arrived," he commented vaguely, "something odd happened."

His voice pulled me out of my distraction.

"At the Leaping Stag? What sort of thing?"

He picked up a stick and poked at the fire, raising a shower of sparks that cast glittering lights across his face.

"The snow had started early that day. By the time we got here, the winds were howling and we could barely find the inn. It was so hard to see, we had to get down and lead our mounts. Fleck balked, so I started to sing to him. You know, the way we used to in Darcy."

"Yes," I sniffed with half a laugh. "I've done a lot of that."

A glimmer of humor flicked through his eyes. He knew what I had done in Gelderscarth. But amusement changed to a frown of confusion as his gaze returned to the fire.

"Suna came. I didn't expect her. It wasn't like when we sang in Ayr. I was just singing to calm the pony. But her light came into me, and it was as if you were there with me. I could feel you, the way it was at the fane, but then there was this horrible pain." His troubled eyes rose to mine. "It knocked me right onto my knees," he marveled. "It was just as bad as when I got shot."

That startled me.

"What night was that?"

He shrugged.

"I don't know. Six or seven months ago. It would have been a full moon, I think, if it hadn't been snowing so blessed hard."

I counted the months.

"That must be when I was shot," I gaped. "The same thing happened to me in Gelderscarth, about a week before you showed up in the stable—"

"—when I got shot," Aedon finished, amazed.

We stared at the fire, stunned into silence. I had known since the fane that we were connected, but hadn't realized it went so far.

"You see?" said Florian quietly. "You ought to marry Aedon."

Aedon gave me a knowing smile before responding.

"Thanks all the same, my honored prince, but I don't actually want to marry her."

Florian crossed his arms on his knees and laid his head sideways on his arms, regarding me wearily. I mirrored his pose.

"I feel you, too," I told him gently. "I felt you dancing. My first night at Kragknoll. That would have been at the equinox moon. Last fall."

Aedon bounced upright.

"He *did* dance that night!" He gestured excitedly with the stick. "He didn't want to go to an inn, so we slept in the woods. It was just like in Darcy, in Gavin's apartments. He couldn't resist. It was just as if he heard the music."

I drifted back to the memories, of watching the princes dance in Darcy, of feeling Florian dancing alone, swaying, spinning, caught in the spell.

"It was you I heard," said Florian softly. "That night in the woods. I heard you singing. It was sad but beautiful. Lonely. It called me. You called me." The color shifted in his eyes. My heart sang out to that clear, bright blue. "You're calling me still."

I touched his cheek.

"I will always call you," I told him.

In the golden light, his eyes shone bright as aquamarines. He melted toward me, and then we were kissing, softly this time, tenderly, languidly, oblivious to Aedon, who discreetly decided to bank the fire and roll himself into his blanket for sleep. I barely noticed his satisfied smirk as he turned his back and laid down his head on a dog for a pillow. I wrapped my arms around Florian's neck. We hadn't kissed since Kragknoll, but like the embers that glowed at our feet, our fires were banked, and I wasn't afraid.

"We'll find a way," he murmured once while nuzzling my neck. "We'll find a way to be together. For now," he sighed, eyes swimming in mine, "this is enough."

I smiled. It was. Not because it had to be, but because we could now choose it to be. Now we knew that Suna had bound us, heart and mind. Someday, somehow, there would be more. We could wait.

In the soft, dark night, I kissed him again.

*   *   *

I woke with my head cradled on his arm and his other arm around my waist. I felt his breath on the back of my neck. One blanket covered both of us, and both of us were still fully dressed. My sigh was full of happiness. Aedon beamed from across the fire, where the dogs were contentedly chewing the bones of something they'd caught.

"You'd better get up," he suggested affably. "It's almost noon, and we still have a long way to go."

After that, the heavy mood lifted from our hearts and we went with good cheer. Aedon jested, Florian laughed, and I sang with every bird and breeze.

A week or so after the Leaping Stag, the road turned sharply, lifted itself over an outcrop of rock, and swooped down out of the evergreens into the foothills of western Marnak. The Riy matured in width and depth, and we paid for passage downriver to Knar on a flat-bottomed barge. We sandwiched the mules between kegs of Marnaki beer from the foothills and bales of furs from the mountain forests. I kept my distance from the furs, preferring instead to stand at the rail with Florian's arms around my shoulders, leaning my head against his breast. We floated past orchards of tiny green pears and fields of hops that lifted their blooms to the warming sun, and arrived in Knar a few weeks after the summer solstice. I filled my lungs with the smell of salt. I hadn't realized how much I missed it.

"We're not going to stay at the Spotted Toad," I voiced my reticence as we led the animals off the barge at a river wharf.

"No, by Suna," spat Florian, gripping my hand so hard it hurt.

Aedon took the question more lightly.

"I think we can do better than that. We only sampled half the taverns within a mile of the waterfront. A few of them actually weren't too bad."

The Seven Sails was up the hill from the noisy docks in a quiet section near elegant homes. A room cost Florian three of his pearls, but the bedding was clean and the air was fresh. We dined that night on haddock pie, spinach with cheese, and raspberry tarts. We drank crisp cider and listened to a southern bard who played a lute and sang in at least five languages. We all had baths and slept like babes in a room with a lock.

The following morning, we rode to the docks, where Florian spoke to the harbormaster to find the fastest ship to Darcy. *The Osprey* was an Arulian bark, sleek and high, with a glossy black hull trimmed with white and gold. The master was brisk but not unpleasant, busy unloading Arulian silk and spices from Curra and taking on Marnaki furs and gems. Although he was Arulian, his Curran was good, and Florian booked our passage, with meals, including for Titan and the dogs, for half of his remaining pearls. We'd keep the mules until our departure, then sell them to the innkeeper at the Seven Sails, who'd sell them to someone else in turn.

As we turned to go, the captain looked very pleased with the bargain.

"We've paid him well," remarked Florian simply, "and he'll treat us well. He'll make sure we reach Darcy alive and in good health. He hopes to see some additional payment on our arrival."

As we rode away along the quay, I cast him an admiring glance. I would have had no idea at all how to purchase passage on a ship. He laughed at my ignorance.

"Darcy is an important port, and my brother Rion has his own ship with a crew of forty. I've learned a little along the way."

"Did you tell him you were a Pinian prince?"

"Of course not," he answered. "We didn't tell anyone coming here, and I'm not telling anyone going back. All they need to know is that I can pay."

Aedon snorted and guided his mule out of the path of a cartload of lumber.

"And all you need to do is not get robbed. Or knocked out and left in an alley."

Florian gave a rueful shrug.

"Good thing I have a friend to watch my back." He smiled at Aedon significantly. I didn't think I wanted to know how he and Aedon had warded off trouble before they reached Kragknoll.

We headed our mounts uphill and caught a glimpse of the red stone castle above the city. Aedon looked sideways at Florian. His voice was edged with sarcasm.

"Planning to pay your respects to the king?"

"Respects?" scoffed Florian. "Look how well that went the first time. I can imagine the look on his face if I walked in there with *two* fingerlings." He sniffed with scorn. "He didn't have any interest then, so why would he have any interest now?"

"Maybe you'd rather show me the city," I proposed in an effort to lighten his mood. "Surely you found *something* pleasant in Knar."

A smile twitched the corners of Florian's mouth.

"Oh, here and there. Aedon, how about that brothel—"

I smacked his leg and tried not to grin.

"Oh, all right," he laughed. "No brothels."

"And no ale," I added. "This time, I want to board the ship on my own two feet."

His eyes sparkled sapphire in the sun.

"You and me both," he agreed. "No ale."

Chapter 11: Homecoming

I dreaded the sea voyage back to Pini, but it turned out to be completely different from my first. The Axian ship was neat and trim, and our cabin was elegantly appointed, not like the berth I had shared with Symus. Standing on deck as we left the port, I experienced only a hint of nausea that passed when we reached open sea. The salt spray washed my upturned face and the scream of gulls called to my heart like music from home. I took off my boots and hurled them away into the sea.

My time was leisurely on the ship. I sat in the sun with Florian's arm draped over my shoulder and sang with Aedon. We hadn't practiced the pearling songs in over a year, and our voices were no longer identical. We spent hours learning to match and coordinate our pitches, blending my three ranges with his three new ones, each deeper and more resonant than before. Florian's eyes shone crystal blue whenever we sang, as if the sound were drawing his heart straight into mine. Each time we finished, he pulled me into his eager arms for blissful kisses while Aedon just laughed and called us silly, sotted fools. Which, of course, we were. Happy ones, too, until our last few nights at sea.

Even with fair summer weather, the voyage took more than ten weeks. We tacked down the western coast of Marnak, Trent, and Pini, skimmed before a following wind through the Axian strait and around the southern tip of Pini, and slipped up into the Gulf of Yar. As the only three passengers on a merchant ship, we kept pretty much to ourselves. Aedon fetched our meals from the cook each day, we avoided the crew when we went on deck, and we had no occasion to bother the master. Yet as we drew closer to Darcy, Florian's mood quietly shifted from sunny to somber. One afternoon, when Aedon and I completed our first perfect practice of the Song of Honor and Gratitude, I grinned and reached for Florian's hand, but he didn't take it. He didn't smile. Instead, he turned away and leaned his elbows on the rail.

"Suna's ears," Aedon exclaimed as the sun sank into scarlet clouds. "I didn't realize how late it was." He stretched his back. We stood to sing, as we always had, but shifting our weight to move with the ship was sometimes tiring, however natural it had become. "I think I'll just go fetch our supper."

I stepped up onto a coil of rope to grip the rail beside Florian. His brow was pinched, and his eyes, staring westward, were dark as the jade-colored water flowing swiftly by below. I just waited. The sun had vanished before he spoke.

"Can you see the land?" He pointed his chin toward the crimson clouds.

I followed the gesture. On the horizon, a slash of brilliance parted the clouds from their reflection. Squinting into the glare, I detected a dark, irregular line.

"That's the islands between the pearling villages and the sea." His voice was calm, as if he were telling me how much grain to feed Titan at sea. "Beyond those islands are Ayr and Cant. And tomorrow *The Osprey* will come into Darcy."

In the warm, moist air that felt like home, my fingers slid down the rail to his.

"It's going to be all right," I said, trying to sound like I believed it.

"No," he said flatly, turning to face me. "It won't be all right. They're going to take you away from me. I can't let them do that." His jaw muscles clenched. "But I don't know how to stop them."

I reached my arms around his neck. On the coil of rope, I was tall enough to look down at his face. My gaze caressed his silken hair, his curving brows, the ridge of his cheeks. He was leaner now than back in Darcy. His travels had hardened him. Kragknoll had hardened him.

"You'll find a way," I told him with confidence. "Maybe Suna will tell you how."

He lifted his eyes, shining and moist.

"I try to hear her. Every day. When I wake. When you're singing. When you're sleeping in my arms."

I searched his eyes.

"Shall we listen together?"

He tipped his head.

"Yes."

His hands clasped my waist and our foreheads touched. I opened my mind, my heart, my soul, and the song simply rose from within my being. I don't even think I knew what I sang. It was Suna's song, her harmonies of wind and water, of forest and gull, of oyster and pearl. It was her music of love and sorrow, of joy and tenderness, passion and peace. I felt her love flow into me and into Florian, and I felt his sudden ecstasy in the shining presence of the goddess.

The light seeped away, within and without. When I opened my eyes, Florian smiled. His eyes were aquamarine with love.

"Yes," he spoke boldly. "Yes."

"Yes, what?" demanded Aedon, juggling bowls of mussel stew and short brown rice.

Florian beamed.

"Yes, I will," he replied enigmatically, taking his meal.

Aedon questioned me with a look, but I couldn't answer. I only shrugged. Florian spooned out a plump, fleshy mussel and ate it with relish.

"I don't think he's going to tell us," I speculated brashly to Aedon.

"I'm not," mumbled Florian around the mussel. "Not until I'm sure it will work."

I watched him eat, unable to touch my food myself.

"But when will that be?" I demanded at last.

He set down his bowl and seized my hands. His eyes were eager, his tone restrained.

"If all goes well," he promised, "tomorrow."

*   *   *

We sailed into Darcy the following noon, the day before the princes' dance. I dressed in my apprentice garments, then unbraided and combed out my hair. We had been gone for eighteen months.

Since the master of *The Osprey* never knew who we were, no word was rowed ahead, no runners were sent to the palace, and no official greeting party awaited us on the dock. We disembarked without any fanfare and waited for the dogs and Titan to be unloaded. The master delivered the horse in person, and Florian slipped him a few more pearls. He pocketed the pearls with a smile, bade us farewell, and returned to the ship while the dogs leaped at Aedon in tongue-lolling joy. Florian grinned above Aedon's laughter and hoisted our packs over Titan's saddle.

"I think that's everything we—"

Suddenly, Emryn rushed from between the bales of furs and a pile of chests containing gems and threw his arms around his brother.

"Em!" cried Florian in astonishment.

They clasped each other vigorously. Emryn's shimmering hood of pearls trembled with emotion.

"Florian," he choked again and again. "Oh, Florian."

212

Florian finally struggled free to gaze at his brother.

"Suna's eyes, Em, how did you ever find out we were here?"

The princely pearls were attracting attention. Emryn clapped his brother's shoulder and pulled us away from the waterfront. We crowded between his mount and Titan.

"Geiz'e's teeth! You think you can saunter into Darcy with two young Currans and not be noticed? Sirinta has her own way of keeping an eye on things, and believe me, she's been looking for you since the day you both vanished."

Leading Titan, Florian balked.

"And Sirinta sent word to you?"

Emryn's devotion welled in his eyes.

"She didn't send word to anyone. I've been going to her house every day for a year and a half, hoping she'd have some sign of you. And I can tell you, it hasn't been dull!"

"What do you mean?" I dared to ask. He turned his warm, dark eyes on us and raised his brows with a snort of warning.

"You can't hide much from Sirinta once she claims you as her own. She has always enjoyed the favor of Suna, and Suna watches Sirinta's own."

"So what does that mean?" I persisted. "What could she know?"

He steered us up a quiet street and pointed a meaningful finger at me.

"That you were taken against your will—"

"—which I knew from the start," contributed Florian. Emryn glared him into silence, then turned back to me.

"She knows you were hurt one night last winter, and you," he added, pointing at Aedon, "were hurt in the spring."

Aedon and I exchanged reverent glances.

"Suna told her," I stated with certainty.

"Right," confirmed Emryn. "And she knows a thing or two about you," he told Florian, raising his brows with significance. "And last night, Suna told her you were coming home today."

Florian cringed as we climbed through streets of narrow, overhanging houses.

"Did Sirinta tell Father?"

Emryn twisted his mouth in apology.

"I did that myself. It seemed only fair. Sirinta and Father have barely spoken since Amalisa disappeared. She's mad at him, and he's mad at you. So I asked him to let me come down alone. If he had come, it wouldn't be pretty."

We walked in a knot between the horses. Their hooves clattered loudly, masking our voices. Florian looked as if he'd been caught stealing peaches from a neighbor's tree.

"Is Father furious?"

"Oh, he's furious, all right," Emryn confirmed, plodding upward. "Mother's in tears. Gavin's ready to wring your neck. Joron's planning to burn you alive on the altar of Tol. Andren says we ought to throw you to the sharks. Kyan would probably shoot you if I hadn't taken his bow away. And only the fact that you found Amalisa stopped Rion from sinking your ship before you even reached the harbor." His sparkling eyes glanced quickly among us, scanning for wounds. "Anyone need a healer? No? Well," he confided to Aedon and me, "you might by the time Sirinta gets through with you." He swung back to Florian, suddenly noticing his hair. "Geiz'e's tears! What have you done? Where are your pearls?"

Florian gave him a wry snort as we reached the outer palace gate.

"I had to pay the expenses somehow."

"Well, you'll barely have time to replace them before the dancing tomorrow. The rest of us just finished with our pearls yesterday."

As we passed through the gate, Florian scanned the saluting guards, the lush summer gardens that lined the road, the temples beyond, and the glistening palace that sprawled ahead. A distant trumpet announced our approach. Florian slipped his hand into mine.

"I think the pearls will have to wait," he told his brother. "Father will want to see me first." He turned to me with midnight eyes. "And I don't think he'll like what I'm going to say."

*   *   *

The antechamber was jammed. People had to press together to make enough room for us to walk through. Their eyes were eager, their voices excited. The prince had returned with the lost apprentice.

The audience chamber was even more crowded. Here the courtiers kneeled in silence, facing the thrones, but their eyes slipped sideways in expectation. Emryn left us at the door to slip around and join his brothers from behind. The herald's voice proclaimed our names. I kept my eyes trained ahead as Florian strode the length of the hall with Aedon and me on either side.

The king and queen were still and solemn. Behind their parents, whispering hotly amongst themselves, the princes fell silent at our approach. Gavin stepped forward beside his father. Sirinta stood beside the queen in her opulent ceremonial robe. Framed by her flowing silvered hair, the lines of her face were tight and grim. Meeting her eyes, I wanted to cry.

The queen's composure was tenuous. Her face was anxious, and tears streamed unchecked down her cheeks. Her hand fluttered up to her trembling lips at the sight of her son without pearls in his hair.

The cerulean tiles were cool on my skin as we knelt and pressed our brows to the floor. This time, there was no velvet in King Greve's voice. It was hard as granite.

"Prince Florian. Come forward."

Aedon and I rocked back on our heels as Florian rose, stepped onto the dais, and to the gasping astonishment of all, presented himself in full prostration.

"My lord king," he spoke to the carpet at their feet. "I have brought Amalisa of Ayr back to Pini. It was by my fault that she was lost, and it was my desire to bring her home that led me to go in secret to Marnak with Aedon of Cant, without asking leave of my lord and king. But not by my valor was she delivered from slavery in Marnak and Undria. Rather it was she who escaped and saved her fellow apprentice and me from likely death. Thus have I sinned against my king, both by putting her life at risk, and by risking my own life and Aedon's. Your anger against me is justified."

I understood this ritual. On a smaller scale, it was practiced in Ayr when someone transgressed and was brought before Tallis and Kes for justice. They could protest, as Xander had done, and earn a beating or other due penalty, or they could throw themselves on the mercy of the priests to gain forgiveness and a lighter punishment. A furrow appeared between the king's brows. Florian had not asked for mercy. The king displayed no softening, not in his face and not in his voice.

"Florian of Pini. Your conduct has been rash and reckless. You endangered yourself and two apprentices of the Master Singer. You have caused much grief to the Master Singer and great suffering to the crown." I knew from the gravity of his sons and the queen's distress that the crown was Florian's entire family. The king continued without pause. "You confess your wrongdoing, but show no remorse, and you do not submit your fate to our will. Explain yourself."

At this command, Florian sat back on his heels but kept his head bowed.

"My lord king. I acted selfishly, without regard for the good of Pini. But I would do the same again if Amalisa were in danger. I have returned, but I cannot return as a prince of Pini. I wish to be released."

Every prince exhibited shock. The king's face flushed mahogany, while the queen gave a little cry of pain. Sirinta's eyes narrowed and shot intently from Florian to me. I was stunned by sudden comprehension.

The king rose up like a tidal wave, and every courtier threw his forehead to the floor.

"It has not been done in a hundred years," grated the king in his granite voice. "You are a prince. So you shall remain."

Florian dared to lift his head and meet his father's steely eyes. Courtiers twisted their necks to see.

"My lord king. As a Pinian prince, I am constrained to wed within the line of Mannar. I wish to wed Amalisa of Ayr. I cannot do that as a Pinian prince. Therefore I humbly beg for release."

An audible gasp flew around the chamber. The queen's hand touched the pearl at her throat. Only Sirinta showed no surprise. My heart was racing. I had never imagined Florian's intention. The king breathed deeply several times.

"I must consider your request. Six seasons ago, I commanded that two young apprentices leave their master and go with the seeding of the pearls. The Master Singer opposed my choice. I tried to defy the Master Singer, not to serve the gods, but for worldly profit. It was my decree that precipitated these rash events, and the crown has been punished for my arrogance. I would not wish to be so obdurate twice. Therefore, I will seek the guidance of the gods. My six elder sons are pledged as priests, and I reverently ask that they lay your petition before the gods in meditation through the night. You, as well, will spend the night in prayerful contemplation, in the temple of whichever god you choose. I will do the same. And on the morrow, I will obey the will of the gods."

At his tone of conclusion, the courtiers resumed their kneeling posture, filling the hall with the rustle of silks. Then the king elevated his ironwood gaze and rested his glare on Aedon and me. His voice remained stern.

"Amalisa of Ayr and Aedon of Cant, we give thanks to the gods for your safe return. But as for the marriage of any apprentice, that remains at the discretion of the master."

The air left my lungs in a startled rush. I hadn't known....

"Master Sirinta," spoke Greve's hard voice. "Your lost apprentices are returned. You may take them and do with them as you will."

Sirinta took only one step forward, intending no doubt to bow to the king before taking her leave and reclaiming us, but Florian's hand shot out and seized the hem of her robe. Another gasp hissed around the room.

"Honored Sirinta," Florian begged, "beloved of Suna, do not take Amalisa from me."

Small as she was, Sirinta seemed to tower over him. Her dove-grey eyes were grave.

"Your highness," she spoke in her complex voice. "She is not yours."

Florian bowed his brow to the floor at Sirinta's feet.

"But I am hers."

Sirinta remained dispassionate.

"Perhaps, your highness. But tonight she is still mine."

Gently but firmly, she pulled her robe from Florian's grasp. Moving forward, she turned and bowed to the king and queen.

"Your majesties. I give thanks to Suna for restoring my lost apprentices. Praise Suna, they are safe and well. I will take them now. By your wise example, I, too, shall spend the night in prayer, beseeching Suna for her guidance. By Suna's grace, may we find agreement on the morrow."

She came to where Aedon and I still sat. Without a word, we rose to bow to the king and queen, then trailed our master from the room.

Like a chastised child, I held Aedon's hand as we followed Sirinta to her house. She was silent all the way. Silent enough for us to hear the hushed exclamations of those we passed.

"Look! They're back!"

"...wants to marry..."

"Surely the king..."

"...never allow it..."

We escaped to the solace of the Master Singer's house. As she stood in the doorway to let us pass, I could see her draw breath to speak, but a scornful grunt preempted her.

"So you're back," huffed Bina. She stood in the passage beyond the receiving room, arms crossed over her bony chest. "Your packs were delivered an hour ago. They're in your rooms. I've set up the baths. They should still be hot. There's whiting and sorrel when you're ready." With her characteristic brusqueness, she turned and retreated to the kitchen, but not before I saw her dab at her eyes. She'd never admit she was glad we were safe.

Sirinta closed the door. At once, Aedon dropped to his knees before her and bowed his head in sincere contrition.

"Master, forgive me. I shouldn't have gone without telling you. I was wrong."

Compassion broke over her hazelnut face, and she took his hands between her own.

"Oh, Aedon," she sighed as she lifted him up. "You weren't wrong. You followed your heart and Suna's wisdom. If you had come to me, I wouldn't have let you go, and Amalisa might not have been found. Of course," she turned to glare at me, "she might well have found her own way home, but I do not fault you for seeking her." She folded him in a tight embrace, then held him away at arm's length. "You were hurt," she stated, looking for scars. "And sick. But I see you've recovered."

Aedon gave her a lopsided grin.

"I was shot," he confessed. "And the fever almost did me in. But Amalisa healed me. By singing."

Her eyes went wide and regarded me with renewed surprise.

"Indeed. By singing."

"You wouldn't believe what she did by singing," Aedon expounded excitedly. "She called my pony, and made a foal white, and made the mare deliver it, and called the wolves—" He paused for breath, and Sirinta edged into the gap.

"It seems I still have much to learn about your abilities, Amalisa. More, perhaps, than you still need to learn from me."

I kneeled and bowed.

"Please, Master. I still wish to serve the goddess. I still want to sing to the pearls. I beg you to let me complete my training."

She lifted my chin.

"I fear, my child, that what I can teach you will seem too tame after all your adventures."

My eyes filled with tears.

"Believe me, Master. I've had more adventures than I could want. Tame would be more than welcome to me."

She took my hands and raised me up.

"Then welcome back, my dear."

She held me close, and I dared to embrace her birdlike frame.

"I'm sorry," I whispered against her shoulder. "This was all my fault."

"My dear," she scolded, holding me off, "that may be true. But if Suna forgives you, which clearly she has long since done, we need no longer dwell on it. You were a child, and have, I suspect, gained much of wisdom in your travels. Now we must focus on what comes next. The issue of marriage. Marriage to Florian." She peered at me keenly. "Do you love him?"

My heart clogged my throat.

"Yes," I managed.

"Yes," she nodded. "I felt it was so. Suna showed me. But I still had to hear you say it." She straightened briskly. "Tonight, then, we pray. We open ourselves to Suna's wisdom and offer obedience to her will. But first," she declared, including Aedon with her glance, "you must wash and eat. Aedon may sleep, but for you, Amalisa, it's going to be a long night."

I glanced at the altar where we would pray, at the Curran words on the scrolls above it, words Aedon had taught me how to read. "Wisdom." "Grace." "Compassion." "Peace." Suna had granted me all of these on far longer nights than this would be. Confident in the goddess's love, I went to my room to prepare.

*   *   *

At dawn, Sirinta rose to her feet, bowed to the goddess, and let me go. My muscles were stiff as I walked to my room, but I wasn't tired. Suna had sustained my hope. Soon I would be reunited with Florian. Even Aedon beamed with confidence over our breakfast.

My heart was light as Sirinta and I were escorted to the palace later that morning. As before, whispers accompanied us all the way, through the entry, and into the audience chamber. The king, the queen, and all the princes were as we had left them. Even Florian was the same, on his knees before the king. His dark hair shone, freshly washed, still without pearls. If anything, the king looked grimmer.

"Master Sirinta." At least his voice had regained the velvet.

She touched my arm. I approached beside her and pressed my brow against the floor.

"My lord king," Sirinta spoke.

His hands were clamped on the arms of his throne, and the queen's eyes were red.

"The gods have spoken," the king said simply. "Tol has moved within my heart, and each of my sons has been touched by his god. Master Sirinta, how were you answered in your prayer?"

She stood at my side.

"It is Suna's wisdom," she replied, "that these two hearts are bound in love. Song united them. Time divided them. Pain has strengthened them. We no longer have the right to part them."

The king's eyes glistened. I wasn't expecting the sudden grief that tightened his jaw, or the tears that tracked down the queen's taut face. But there was no quaver in his voice as he stood to pronounce his judgment.

"We cannot rejoice in the loss of a son, but we must obey the will of the gods. Prince Florian will be released. The pearls will no longer grace his hair. He will not dance at the equinox moon. To ensure that this is truly his wish, he will remain alone in his chambers for the space of a month. If, after that time, he still desires to be released, it will be done."

My mouth fell open and I almost spoke, but Sirinta's cautioning touch on my arm stilled my protest before I made it. A month? A month? Hadn't Suna said we were not to be parted? My heart cried out, but Florian only bowed his head before the king. He made no sound. He did not turn. I could not see the color of his eyes.

"Your majesty," Sirinta bowed. "May Suna's wisdom uphold you forever."

She gripped my elbow, guided my bow, then towed me silently from the chamber. Tears of anger obscured my vision all the way back to her house.

"A month?" I spluttered as soon as the door was closed behind us.

"What?" cried Aedon, waiting in the receiving chamber.

Before Sirinta could explain, someone knocked.

"Master Sirinta," said Emryn quietly. "Could I please speak to—"

"A month?" I exclaimed, throwing up my hands. "Emryn, a month? Can I see him?"

He sighed and placed his hands on my shoulders. His hood of pearls swung gently as he shook his head.

"No, Amalisa. I'm sorry. You can't. He can't come out, and no one but family can go in. I never knew there was such a law until last night. But he asked me to tell you the month won't matter. It won't change his mind. It won't change his heart."

I tried to calm my angry heart.

"It won't change my heart either, Emryn. Tell him that. I am his now, and I'll be his then."

He smiled, though wanly.

"I will."

"But why a month? Why so long? Why can't he be released today?"

Emryn glanced at Sirinta.

"I think you should tell her." She sounded like she was consoling the dead.

"Tell me what?"

Emryn sat down in one of the chairs for Pinian guests.

"Being released—it's more than the pearls. More than the dancing. It's more than renouncing his claim to the crown, however miniscule that might be. If Florian does this, he won't be our father's son anymore. Our mother will no longer be his mother. He won't be our—" Something caught in his throat, and his voice was rough when he tried again. "He won't be my brother anymore."

I backed away, stunned.

"Oh, Emryn," I breathed. "I didn't know...." I found myself in a Curran chair that Aedon had quickly placed behind me. With my whole heart, I leaned toward Florian's brother. "I can't let him do that, Emryn. Tell him he doesn't have to do it. You're close to him. He'll listen to you."

He shook his head.

"No, Amalisa. All he can hear in his heart is you. He isn't afraid, and he isn't sad. But you should know what it will mean to the rest of us."

For a while, I just sat, imagining Florian's family without him. Imagining Florian without them. Imagining Florian not a prince.

"I think I understand, Emryn. But I still love him. I can't help loving him."

"Good." He smiled a small, sad smile. "Because that's how Florian feels about you. And I needed to know you'll be waiting for him at the end of the month."

I met his eyes, the eyes of the brother who loved him so well.

"We were parted for a year. A month will be nothing after that."

He stood to go.

"Suna be with you, Amalisa. And with my brother."

"Emryn," I said, and quickly rose. "Thank you for coming."

He hesitated for just a moment, then gave me a quick, impulsive hug.

"I'll come again," he promised sincerely. "He told me to ask you to sing for him."

That brightened my heart.

"I will," I assured him with a smile. "For the rest of my life."

*   *   *

The month flew by. Aedon and I resumed our training. Sirinta continued to study the way we sang together. With all the sounds I had learned abroad, and with Aedon's deepened registers, we could sing with increased variety, leaving Sirinta more baffled than ever. Emryn visited often, telling me Florian remained steadfast in his resolve, and I knew he heard every song I sang. On the last afternoon, Sirinta set us free from our lessons and Aedon walked with me in the garden.

"Tomorrow's the day," he commented idly. The garden was quiet, sweetened by birdsong. The day after the princes danced, Aedon had given the dogs to Kyan. They would make excellent hunting dogs. They hadn't done much for the garden. The quiet was peaceful and calmed my heart.

"Yes," I smiled. I was wearing my quilted jacket. There had been frost on the leaves of the scarlet maple at dawn that morning. "Tomorrow Florian will be released."

"It won't be so bad," Aedon reflected. "When we're ordained and Sirinta sends us to a village, he can come with us. That wouldn't be easy if he were a prince."

I laughed at the thought of Florian with his hood of pearls, living in a pearling village.

"You're right," I laughed. "Though I can't imagine him hauling in a fishing net."

"No," snorted Aedon, clearly amused. "But he could be a gardener. Like my Tadde."

I liked that idea. I could see him tenderly planting lilies and pulling the weeds around burgeoning peonies.

"I bet he could." A chill breeze stirred my unbraided hair. I took Aedon's hand and we walked to the house. There was plenty of time for a bath before supper. In the kitchen, Bina was cooking fish. A lot of fish. More fish than I had ever seen her cook before.

"What's going on?" I asked in jest. "Are we expecting company?"

All at once, Aedon stiffened.

"Who's here?" he asked Bina. But he didn't wait to hear her answer, not that she answered. Frowning, he headed down the passage as if in a dream. Close on his heels, I heard the voices in the receiving room and saw the two guests as soon as he did. They were talking respectfully to Sirinta, looking awkward in the Curran chairs, even though they were Curran themselves.

"Tadde!" yelped Aedon, rushing toward them. "Mati!"

"Aedon!" they cried and jumped up to seize him with tears of joy.

Then I saw the third guest, perched on one of the Pinian chairs.

"Mati?" I breathed. She turned. "Mati!" I gasped and ran to her arms.

We hugged and kissed and wept and laughed.

"Oh, my Liise. My Liise," she said a hundred times. She touched my face, marveling at the puckered skin where the mark had been. "Zenaida said it would go away. But I couldn't be sure, so I never told you."

"It's all right, Mati. I'm glad you never told me that. I would have spent all those years waiting, and what if it didn't go away?"

"Now you're a woman," she yearned through her tears, "and I wasn't there to see it happen."

"I didn't see it either," I laughed, and we fell on each other's necks again.

At last I looked up. Aedon's parents still beamed at their son, each of them holding one of his hands. I hadn't seen him look so happy since stopping in Cant on the way to Darcy. Sirinta, sitting against her desk, looked decidedly pleased with herself.

"Amalisa, I'm sure you remember Socorra and Aradus, Aedon's parents."

"Oh, Master!" I cried in abrupt understanding. "You brought them here for the—" I bit off the word. No one had spoken of a wedding. But Sirinta smiled.

"I brought them to discuss it," she said. "I am your master, and I must agree. But you also should have your parents' consent."

I gripped Mati's hands.

"Oh, Mati," I gushed. "You saw him in Ayr. The small one. The one who let me ride his horse. Florian."

"I know," Mati laughed. "Sirinta has told me all about him. All about everything. Yes, my love. Of course, I consent."

"Oh, Mati," I thanked her, and threw my arms around her neck.

"But Liise," she spoke into my hair. "There's something else."

My heart gave a thud. Her voice was strained. What else could there be? I didn't think I could bear bad news. Not today. Not when the month was so nearly gone. Not when my Mati was holding me close. I pulled away and examined her face. There was certainly something, but whether it was good or bad, I couldn't tell. I took a deep breath.

"What is it, then?"

Mati inhaled. She opened her mouth. She closed it again.

"I think Sirinta can explain it best."

I turned, afraid. Aedon's parents were staring at me. Aedon looked worried. Whatever it was, he didn't know, either. But I must be strong. I had been through so much already. How bad could it be?

"Sit down, Amalisa," Sirinta said.

Mati and I both sat down.

"When you came here, Amalisa, no one knew your parentage. But when I saw you, I saw a resemblance to someone I knew, and I began to look for answers."

"The very next day!" I deduced, remembering having to work in the kitchen while she had business in the receiving room.

"Yes," she confirmed. "I sent people to ask questions, to find people, and ultimately to bring them here. And this is what I learned."

She folded her hands and told the tale.

"Some years ago, a midwife attended a Curran woman in childbirth. It was not an easy birth, and a servant assisted the midwife. When the child was born, the mother began to bleed, so the midwife sent the servant out to take the baby to the father. While the midwife was alone with the mother, something unexpected happened. Another baby was born. No one expected another child, for everyone knows Currans never bear twins. I had never heard of Curran twins before, myself."

I listened raptly, quite unaware of anyone else in the room.

"Then," she continued, "the mother died. Now alone with the second child, the midwife did something terrible. She wrapped the baby in a sheet, hid the child in her bag, made her condolences to the father, and took the child with her when she went."

From the corner of my eye, I saw Aedon's father cover his mouth with the back of his hand. I knew he had lost Aedon's mother in childbirth, and felt for his loss more keenly now. But my attention was still on Sirinta.

"The midwife intended to sell the child. Of course," she observed to Aedon and me, "as your parents well know, this is a sin, a crime that merits execution, but there are indeed people who'll buy a Curran child, just as there are people who'll steal one."

I certainly knew that, all too well. Sirinta went on.

"But the infant was only one month old when a blemish appeared, an unsightly birthmark, blighting her face. The midwife knew she couldn't sell a blemished child, so she took the baby to a witch to remove the birthmark. Maybe the woman wasn't a witch, or maybe she simply refused to help, but she told the midwife there was nothing she could do. Disgusted, the midwife left the child and disappeared." Sirinta paused, and a ripple of passion tightened her lips before she controlled it and resumed. "It took a year to find that midwife, and she has paid for what she did."

I didn't think I wanted to know how the midwife had paid, but I could guess.

"So what became of the child?" she posed, though by now we had all figured out the answer. "The witch, a simple village healer, was visited by a childless woman. She gave the woman a magic seed and told her how to get a child from the goddess Nazha. The woman obeyed, and a few nights later, under the light of a full moon, the infant appeared in the woman's garden."

"Zenaida," sighed Mati and looked at me in apology. "I'm sorry, Liise. I knew you didn't come from the seed, but I didn't know where you really came from, before Zenaida. I didn't want to know. And I didn't want anyone else to find out. I didn't want them to take you away." Tears spilled out. "I'm sorry, my love." Then she turned to Sirinta and bowed her head. "I beg forgiveness. I meant no wrong. I thought she was an unwanted child."

"In a way," sighed Sirinta, "she was. The midwife didn't want her. Zenaida couldn't keep her. And her father didn't know she existed. But now," she stated, looking at me, "I know who he is."

She let me decide if I wanted to know. I had been kidnapped, discarded, and marked, but I had been loved. Mati had loved me. If I found out who my father was, could Mati love me less? Would I have to learn to love someone new? Someone I'd never known before? And what about the other baby? Did I have a sibling? I took a deep breath.

"I want to know."

Sirinta smiled, but she didn't speak. I looked at Mati. Her eyes were bright with tears of amazement, but she wasn't looking at me. She was looking across the room. I followed her gaze, and saw the same look on Aedon's face, and on the face of Aedon's father. I lurched to my feet.

"Aedon?" I choked, though my eyes were on his father, Aradus. It all came together in my brain. The way Mati reacted to Aedon's voice and Kes to mine. The memories my visit brought back to Aradus. The way Sirinta looked at me that first day in Darcy. How alike we had looked in our matching clothes at Gelderscarth. I took a tentative step toward Aradus. "You're my father, aren't you?"

He stumbled toward me, holding his hands in front of him as if he were afraid to touch me.

"My child," he wept. "I didn't know. I didn't know."

I let him embrace me. Suddenly I had a father. I wasn't sure what to make of it. But over his shoulder, I saw Aedon, yearning toward me.

"Aedon," I breathed, leaving his father and reaching for him.

He rushed to my arms and nearly squeezed all the air from my lungs.

"Sister," he whispered through his tears. Then he burst out laughing. "Suna's eyes! It's a good thing you're not in love with me!"

I laughed right back.

"And a good thing you don't want to marry me!"

"Which brings us back to marriage," Sirinta reminded us with a smile. "Tirsa. Aradus. Why don't you sit down, and I'll have Bina bring us some tea."

*   *   *

The following morning, Florian was released. The audience chamber was so full the courtiers had to sit totally upright on their heels. Aedon, his parents, Mati, and I kneeled with Sirinta near the front. There was only a narrow aisle down the middle for Florian to approach the thrones. His fine, dark hair reached his collarbone now, and his robes were simple white and blue, devoid of silver, gold, or pearls.

It didn't take long. Florian prostrated himself on the floor. His mother sat very straight on her throne, weeping silently, and his father's voice was thick as he spoke.

"Prince Florian of Pini, you have asked for release from your claim to the blood of Prince Mannar. In the name of Tol, in the name of Suna, in the names of all the gods, I, King Greve, release you from the royal house of Pini. You are no longer an heir to the throne, no longer a prince, no longer our son. Go with Suna's peace, Florian of Darcy."

Without a word, Florian stood and bowed profoundly to the king and queen who were no longer his parents. But as he turned and our glances met, his entire being radiated joy, and his eyes were a perfect forget-me-not blue.

When court was over and we finally escaped, he was waiting outside. In the chattering crowd streaming out the doors, all I saw was Florian. When we embraced, when we kissed for the first time in a month, the rest of the world simply disappeared.

"Ama," he breathed, pulling away to adore my face. "Will you have me as I am, without any family, without any property?"

I sank into his clear blue eyes.

"Of course, I will."

"Then you'll marry me?"

As if he had to ask.

"Everything is ready, my love. I even have a father now."

Aedon and I explained it all on the way back to Sirinta's house. After meeting Aradus, Florian laughed.

"Will you always be so full of surprises?"

"Not always," I promised. "Just once in a while."

We were married that very afternoon by the Curran high priest in the temple of Suna. Sirinta herself made the ritual cut across our palms for the mingling of blood, even though Florian was no longer technically a prince. All of Florian's former brothers were there. His former parents stood quietly through the ceremony, kissed our cheeks when it was over, and slipped away before the celebration in Sirinta's garden.

It was a joyous celebration, with a sumptuous feast of three kinds of fish, copious fruits, abundant sweets. The princes contributed fine grape wine, and Florian and I shared more than one cup. After the meal, as the full moon rose, Aedon and Emryn cornered us.

"You know you can't sleep here," Aedon teased with his back to the house.

It hadn't occurred to me, where we would sleep. Mati had shared my room last night. It would be odd to spend my first night of marriage on a pallet beside my mother. Emryn nodded knowingly.

"Come with us," he commanded, grinning.

Everyone followed us out of the garden, past the temple, across the courtyard. They all seemed to know where we were going. Aedon opened the guesthouse door.

What I saw took my breath away. The paneled walls were hung with sprays of feathery maple leaves in gold and crimson autumn hues. The tiled floor was thickly strewn with white rose petals. Instead of common sleeping pallets, a broad frame bed had been placed in the center of the room, surrounded by a dozen lamps. The blue silken coverlet was turned back, and the embroidered sheets were sprinkled with fragrant dried jasmine blossoms. A tray of fruit and wine stood on a table beside the bed. Aedon beamed.

"We did it together. All of us."

Their smiles were blurred by the tears in my eyes.

Sirinta kissed me before departing.

"May Suna bless you abundantly."

Aradus lightly kissed my cheek. Mati hugged me and cried, and Aradus escorted her out. The princes kissed both of us, clapped Florian soundly on the back, and left with a chorus of chortled blessings.

"I could stay as the witness," Aedon jested, the last to go. I hugged him fiercely, pecked his cheek, and shoved him firmly out the door.

"Neither of us has a thing to inherit. We don't need a witness."

"I could—"

He was still laughing as I closed the door. Florian's arms wrapped tightly around me from behind.

"Ama," he breathed in the curve of my neck.

A song of joy swelled in my heart.

"I hear that," he whispered, kissing the place behind my ear.

After that, no words were needed as our hearts and bodies joined in song.

*   *   *

Mati and my newfound father stayed through the winter. Aradus and Florian spent a lot of time together in the garden. Aedon and I completed our training, and in the spring, we were ordained. At seventeen, we were the youngest singers in Pini. Each of us received the singer's first piercing and pearl in the left ear, and Sirinta got two for training us.

"Kes will need two new pearls, too," I realized afterward to Mati. Then I wistfully added, "I wish he could have been here to see it."

To my surprise, her shoulders stiffened and sorrow pulled at the edge of her mouth.

"Liise, my love, he would have come, but he isn't well."

"Isn't well?" I repeated, alarmed. "How long has Kes not been well?"

"Almost a year. He's eighty-seven now, my love. Not even a singer can live forever."

Aedon was as stunned as I was. Sirinta, of course, had known.

"Why didn't you tell us?" we demanded, sitting with her on the white stone benches.

"Your parents and I didn't want you to worry. You had quite enough to deal with already."

"Well," I snorted, "we've dealt with all that. And now we can go home and take care of Kes."

She touched my hand.

"He won't recover this time."

"Why? What's wrong?"

"He's old, Amalisa. Just old."

I understood. And with that understanding came another. Sirinta saw it in my eyes.

"You won't be coming back," she realized.

"No," confirmed Aedon.

Her sigh was resigned.

"As I expected. I wish I could keep you here, but I can't. You must go to Ayr, and not just for Kes. Your training is finished. It's time for you to return to the pearls. I will make the arrangements."

Leaving Sirinta behind was hard. Leaving Darcy wasn't. We were in Ayr by the equinox, leaving Aedon's parents in Cant on the way.

The sun was setting when we arrived. Mati left us at the temple. She hadn't been home in nearly five months. Florian, Aedon, and I dismounted at the temple gate.

Down on the beach, Kes was singing the Evening Song.

"I'll take the horses in," Florian offered, graciously lumping the ponies with Titan, whom Emryn had given him as a gift. Aedon and I hardly heard his words. With one accord, we started down the slope toward Kes.

He looked old and frail. His thin white hair was barely a mist around his head. His shoulders were stooped, and he leaned on a polished staff for support. But his voice was strong, in all its ranges. The watery syllables soared out over the lapping waves to the pearling rafts, washed rose and gold by the setting sun. I sensed the oysters beneath the water, small and simple, holding in their hearts the pearls. My hand clasped Aedon's. We opened our souls and twined our voices into Kes's. Nine separate voices rang over the water, and Suna rejoiced.

When we finished, he turned with a beautiful smile.

"Welcome home, my children. Welcome home."

*　　　*　　　*

Three months later, when he died, Aedon and I were by his side, each holding one of his mottled hands, singing him into the arms of Suna. His gentle face simply relaxed and his breath melted into the afternoon breeze.

We sang for him at the funeral. The flames freed his soul into brilliant light, and we scattered his ashes over the bay on a westerly wind. After caring for Kes, Aedon simply remained in the house. Florian and I stayed in the guesthouse until a new house was built for us beside the singer's. Florian gardened. Aedon and I sang together, every dawn and every dusk. At the next harvest, the pearls were amazing—pink and blue, black and gray, gold and green, and rainbow pearls of remarkable depth—and we visited with Joron and Emryn, laughing and hearing the family news long into the night.

Ayr changed little when Aedon and I became the singers. It was now the most carefully guarded village in all of Pini, and when I walked by, people bowed and spoke my name. But Tallis remained the village priest with Onald as his attendant, and Mati was still the village tailor. Sitta's husband and sons had taken Xander under their wing and made a fine fisherman of him. He and his mother lived comfortably now in Zenaida's house. I met him one morning on the beach. It was spring, a full year after Aedon and I had returned to Ayr. We had just finished singing the Morning Song, and Xander was heading for the boat. He could barely meet my eye.

"I'm sorry for what was done to you," I told him with genuine regret.

He shrugged.

"We were children," he said in the voice of a man. "I thank Suna for the kindness that gave me a chance to make something better of myself. I might not have had that if I hadn't thrown that stupid stone."

A smile tugged his mouth, and I smiled back. Both of our lives had changed since then.

Florian met me at the gate. His hair was now long enough for a short single braid. There was dirt beneath his fingernails, and soil on the hems of his cotton clothes. He still smelled like jasmine.

"I just found something curious," he said. His eyes were indigo with interest. "Back in the garden. Behind our house."

I wrapped my arms around his waist. Beneath his ribs, I could feel the contentment in his heart.

"What is it?" I smiled, completely at peace.

He took my hand and led me in.

"I didn't plant it, so I'm not sure, but I do believe it's a moonflower."

Made in the USA
Charleston, SC
26 October 2013